ALIEN INVASION, STEVE WALKER-STYLE!

Then on St George's Day, April 23, 2076, they landed, outside the town hall in Middlesborough 622 in former Scotland. Aliens, pleasy-do. Venusians from the Venus of a remote galaxy. 14 of them. In a spaceship like a sunnyside-up fried egg. It seemed that they had been in suspended animation for a little over 100 years. It had taken them that long to get here from that distant Venus of theirs. Before inducing sleep they had picked up one of our 20th Century television broadcasts on their equipment, and watched enthralled a production known as *Dr Finlay's Casebook*, which depicted the dull life of an irascible Scottish doctor in the 1930s in a Highland village called Tanochbrae. Thinking that what they had seen depicted the full truth of the nature of the planet they were off to, they spent their sleep in a soupy metamorphosis intended to transform them into characters from the playlet, pleasy-do. Thus they intended to emerge in the village of Tanochbrae – itself, sadly, as fictional as Brigadoon – and blend in with the natives.

As it was, the metamorphosis didn't come out quite right and one morning in the place where Tanochbrae might have been but never was, 13 shapeless green Scottish doctors and a shapeless green Scotswoman emerged, lost on the streets of Middlesborough . . .

About the author

Steve Walker, playwright, poet, artist, novelist, teller-of-tales and historian of the future, was born in Gateshead in 1956. He travelled extensively throughout the 1970s. Returning to Britain in the 1980s, he held 64 one-man shows of his paintings and embarked on a stupendously successful radio drama career – he has written some 30 plays for radio and is the only playwright to have won two consecutive Giles Cooper Awards for Year's Best Radioplay.

21st Century Blues

Steve Walker

The Book of the Century, Being the Life
and Times of Chaff Chaffinch, the Famous
Stylite, Sometime Archbishop of Canterbury,
Leader of the Revolution of '24, Saviour of
the World, Etcetera, Spoken by Himself,
Mostly in the Year 2099, Up a Pole in
Ethiopia, Written Down by his Long-
Suffering Disciple and Lost Soul, Tadese
Mblook.

CORONET BOOKS
Hodder and Stoughton

First published in 1995 by Hodder and Stoughton
A division of Hodder Headline PLC

A Coronet paperback

10 9 8 7 6 5 4 3 2 1

British Library Cataloguing in Publication Data

Walker, Steve
Twenty-first Century Blues
I. Title
823.914 [F]

ISBN 0-340-61841-8

Typeset by Hewer Text Composition Services, Edinburgh
Printed and bound in Great Britain by
Cox & Wyman, Reading, Berks.

Hodder and Stoughton Ltd,
A division of Hodder Headline PLC
338 Euston Road
London NW1 3BH

CONTENTS

Early Days
The Revolting Chaffinches

The Pnong Age
The Golfing Chaffinch

Quiet Years Under the Despots
The Exploding Mrs Chaffinch

Americana
Severiano's Spiritual Exercises

Theocracy for Beginners
The Venusian Sex Survey

Archie Bishop's Wartime Memoirs
The Sleepless Chaffinch

THE EPILOGUE

Final Days
Hans Feet and Bumpsidaisy

Postscript to the Edition of 2039

Appendices

EARLY DAYS

The Revolting Chaffinches

Quotes of the Century:

'Revolution? What revolution?'
Conrad Smithers, British Prime Minister, 2024

'Nudism is as important in my life as Catholicism.'
Lassie II, Pope, 2020

'Piggn marvellous what yer can do if no bugger can
stop yer.'
*Whelk Blint, British Agriculture Minister on the
reintroduction of the Corn Laws, 2025*

1

An Old Bird Says Hello

I have forgotten the year again, have I not? The 21st Century must be nearly over. And as I was born on the stroke of midnight just as the revellers were saying vaya con dios to 1999, that makes this old bird 100 years old, does it not? 100, glory be!

I am Chaff Chaffinch, am I not? I am, and have been these 17 years, a stylite. Do you know what that is? It is a religious nut who lives on a platform at the top of a pole. This is, I urinate in shame to admit, only the latest in a variety of religious nutteries I have pursued in my long life. But be of cheer! I shall be dead soon! 100 and not out! – what was that game again, they played it before pnong was all the rage? Tadese! Tadese!

Tadese doesn't know. He is my disciple. He puts the food in my bucket and hauls it up, and also, poor soul, hauls down the bucket full of my slops and excretions. It is, further shame, the same bucket. But I am free of disease, am I not? Tadese is also writing down these words for you, whoever you are, already in an entirely different century. Though he complains, it was his idea.

'Why don't you write a booky-do?' he said.

And as I've been sitting here thinking over and over about the members of my family, the Chaffinches, a crazy wonky sillymost beloved flock of birds, who have lived sad lives with joyous moments in this century of ours, as I have sat here in peaceful, sobbing reveries of memory, visions of them before my eyes, it seemed to me, did it not – it did! – that I should like to do that, to chant ecstatic sermons from the top of my pole, for Tadese to write down for a future congregation. And here we all are, no fooly-doos, doing just that.

I shall not be speaking about myself. But of the other

Chaffinches. My brothers Robin and Cod. My string of nieces and nephews – Rainbow and Haha, poor cousin Seve, Bug and Rhino and September the war hero. Their faces fashioned by the times they lived in are appearing to me now, masks of laughter through pain. Yes, I see them all, as in a vision! Perhaps, this old featherless fraud is a holy man after all! I think not. Just a gooseberry fool perched ontop a stick of rhubarb. Chehheee!!!

What's that you say, Tadese? Tell them where I am. Oh! This is Ethiopia, is it not? In the vast empty continent of Africa. To the east is the serious depression of the Ogaden desert. But here, with Lake Stephanie visible from my pole, all is green, an oasis of calm and delight, with, in the middle of it all, a Chaffinch up a pole.

I am not breaking my rule about speaking about myself if I tell you about my pole. How I love it! I do, do I not? But it is not the first pole I have loved, no, no. My first pole, in 2079, was eighteen feet tall. I had sat peacefully upon it for some weeks when the truism drifted into my thinkings that the tallest giraffes are about that same height, eighteen footers, and if they came by in the middle of the night, and for a wheeze, if they go in for wheezes, which from the look of them I would say out of all God's creatures they certainly do, they might wheeze me right off my pole. I'd crash through the roof of Tadese's little hut, one broken flightless chaffinch. Or I'd wake from this 21st Century nightmare to find myself in an unbelievable reality, clinging to the neck of a chortling giraffe as it gallops to Somaliland!

This giraffe story is merely to tell you how urgent it was to build me a higher pole. This one is 23 feet tall, its platform just long enough for me to stretch out my little body any way I care to arrange it. I still get visitors, ants mostly, who make the long climb to see what I look like, steal a crumb, and hurry back to their hill with it. They are always welcome, my little friends. In moments of weakness, I have been known to eat them. Yes, Tadese, I do – as the Baptist ate locusts, so do I eat of the anthill. The bigger juicier ones look as if they might taste of blackcurrant. And although one hassent yet, one might one day, mightn't it?

One insect, however, which is never welcome is the Goliath Bee. These were bred in Spain, were they not, back in the 60s to make swimming pools full of honey. Bigger bees, more honey – a sensible enough idea in a commercial world. But the bees kept on getting bigger, and the apiarists were so fascinated they just let them grow until they were the size of elephants. Of course, they escaped, and for one ludicrous summer they swarmed up and down the Mediterranean, bombing the olives from their gnarly trees. This was before the Mufti's War, and people weren't so nervous then. Out they came, fascinated, to see the bees. Thousands of people in beachwear, cheering a lost bee as it bumbled smack into a resort hotel. Pleasy-do, but they were rotten fliers. Look, Tadese! There's one, summoned by my thoughts – it's coming our way!

Cheheee! Tadese is hiding in his hut. Fooley-doos, Tadese! You custard! Boo-hoos, but crew-cut Davids chased the Goliaths pell-mell with their helicopters and they shot them all down in flames, to the final bee, buzzing its last in an Alpine meadow. People were sorry. What about the workers? they said, meaning that the bees should be accorded some rights. Pah, in a world where people were losing theirs, what chance a freaklymost bee. But a few made it into Africa and we do indeed, do we not, see the odd drone from time to time, crossing the pink horizon, making a sound like a boy dreaming of his first shave. Cheeehoo!

I think I'm right in this, Tadese, if I assume my readers know utterly fluff about the 21st Century. Yes, you see, when I was a very young religious nut my favourite reading was Saint Augustine – but who, these days, knows fluff about the sixth century when he ate his custard? Yes, I'm right. But, of course, having spent a life in seclusion, in caves, up poles, in ashrams and monastic cells, I've seen little of the 21st Century myself! I'm like a bespectacled man at an all-nude opera with a seat right behind a pillar! Yes, they went in for nudism a lot in the 30s, when it was hot and the icebergs all melted. But I was never any good at nudism due to my unexpected stiffenings. Never could control them. Even here, up my pole, 100 years old, sometimes – oh yes, Tadese. Not that my mind's wells have been much clogged with impure jellies – rarely-so have I been porned through with sexual thoughts, if the Virgin birth isn't a sexual thought, or the ontological argument, or whatever poshly grit I wasted my life doddling over. No, my unexpected stiffenings would come when least expected, and a naked monk with an stiffening is a subject of ridicule – indeed without an stiffening he is fool enough. But, like everyone else, I went nude for years, and the best that can be said of the situation is, that in a room full of bishops I was rarely the only one with a stiffening. I suppose my stiffenings came from a lascivious chaffinch caged within me, who railed at being a virgin at 30, 40, 50. Do you know, I was over 70 before I nodded my cherry into the custard? Cheeeehe, goes Tadese, because he plays hide the weasel with pudgy girls in his hut nighttimes and thinks I don't hear their weasel squeak.

Ooops, Tadese is right. I am talking about myself. Sorry-be, especially when there is so much else of superior wonder to sermonize upon. My family, the Chaffinches . . . We were a well-heeled flock, who never needed instant custard, did we not – indeed, we had servants to make the real stuff for us! Our home – and, though I haven't seen it in an age, it is still my home, is it not, still owned and occupied by the family, Dame Tuna and her latest hubby – Ooops, an unexpected stiffening! Certainly not, Tadese! Dame Tuna is my niece! She's 83! Chaffinch Hall is in Suffolk, which is in England's green flat buttock, East Anglia. In the 30s, with the encircling floods, we became an island race in the Hall. The brackish plashwater sank the haunts of my boyhood and came right up the drive as far as the magnolias, but no further. Sharks were out there, swimming around and around the house, peckish for a Chaffinch. No fooly-doos. And in those winterly times ahead there was a rink for miles, reflecting cold and white and empty in the windows, making the Hall look like a brick noticeboard with empty pages stuck on it . . . saying that there'd be no wicket teams picked for wicket matches this year, or ever again, which was right. That was it, Tadese: wicket.

My father, Kevin Chaffinch, while I was waiting for the last midnight of the 20th Century to strike 12 before I was born, was sitting, was he not, in the middle of the biggest room our Hall could boast of – never a stick of furniture in it, we always called it 'the dancing room'. He was 25 stones heavy, my immediate ancestor, my 20th Century daddio, but in 100 years of fatherless imaginings I see him dancing in that room, sweating and cursing, tripping over loose woods in the parquet floor. Perhaps he'd been dancing that night, who can custard? But when 12 struck he shot himself five times in his hippopotamus belly and flopped forwards, out of the creaking fold-me-up chair he'd carried in with his desk-drawer gun, one cheek slapping the dancing floor as he raised dust. Meanwhile, upstairs, my cheeks were being welcomed to the 21st century with slaps from the junior butler, which office had doubled as midwife in the Chaffinch household since the Civil War. Tadese is shocked. I had never before told him that my father killed himself. But I will speak no more on that sorry matter, because it did not happen in this 21st Century. Suffice to say, his was not the last tragedy among the Chaffinches. Weary-be, Tadese, I shall fill my bucket with slops and excretions, then a hohum and sleepy-doos. I think I shall sermonize upon my brother Robin tomorrow. Oooops, I am weeping! Triple-sorrys-on-you-evermost, I don't know why I am weeping. Whaaaaaaaaaaaa!!!!!! Urk! But goodly-be-on-me-evermost, I say through tears, because at least my stiffening has gulped and gone down!

2

Three Chicks in a Cruel World

Dr Mitzi Zahn's books on the necessity of being cruel to children, sadly coinciding with my own childhood, were my mother's favourite bedtime reading. My older brother Robin Chaffinch, nicknamed 'Two Birds' for obvious reasons, didn't have it half so bad, did he not indeed, because in her original tome Dr Zahn's cruelty was nothing as severe as it became later on. Had she lived – she popped off in the plague of '17 with so many more – she may have advised locking children in broom cupboards with unfriendly crocodiles. Or perhaps she did, and that's where that idea of mine comes from! Cheeehe! Her own children were, I remember hearing somewhere, model citizens – of America, however, when there was an America, so fluff to that!

That vilemost woman took the custard from off my kiddiewinkhood and 100 years of simpering religiosity does not enable me to forgive her. Of course, it was Mother's fault for believing it all. That said, without all the cruelty – a footman pushed me downstairs every morning – I may never have turned to religion at all! And then where would my poor pole be? Chaffinchless! Che! It all proves again, if proofy-be were needy-be, that the consequences of a single idea, good or bad, can destroy the individual, indeed the world, as it flits stolidly by.

The point being that Robin, who had life much easier – was allowed to eat fruit, sleep in a real bed and take warm baths – was the unhappy one in the nest. Myself and my baby bro Cod, though suffering constant cruelty, were jolly little souls. Oops, did I say that Mother remarried, indeedybe, a mere six weeks after my coming, to a jolly Belgian businessman, who succumbed to that unexplained disease which carried off all Belgians, and only Belgians, wherever they were in the world, in '04, one of those odd plagues of which the '17 was the whambanger. So this Chaffinch lost a replacement father, of whom I memory notwot but his smell, and Cod became fatherless like his daffy half-bro.

Cod! COD! COD! I can see us now! Yes, Tadese! There we are! He's the handsome one, wrestling with the dog. Poor doggie! Dr Zahn advised the regular culling of family pets as a device in her regime of cruelty – an extra piquancy to this because they were shot with my daddio's suicide pistol. One pooch, however, survived, I think because nobody ever made a fuss of it. As far as I know, by one of the miracles common in our century, it's still there!

Robin had more than just the 21st Century blues. He had inherited the Chaffinch melancholy streak, he did indeed, did he not? He was more cruel to himself with his melancholia than Dr Zahn ever was to anyone with all her punishments and precepts. But at least he went to a proper school! At the age of 4 that being, what . . . of course, 2004, cheeeheee, I was given a bus ticket, an address in Yorkshire, and told to make my way there. Sorrymost child! I know, I'm talking about myself again. We'll get back to other Chaffinches presentlymost.

Beltane Prep School was in the middle of a lopsided moor between Whitby and nowhere. I truly believe, sitting here chewing this banana, that the place existed only in nightmare until Dr Zahn's book gave it life. Indeedybe, it based itself on her precepts, with stinkier ideas of its own thrown in. The assembly hall was decorated with paintings of bewhiskered academics whose prominent incisors immediately established them in my childish imagination as vampires. I later discovered, they *were* vampires. Or pretended to be, which was nearly as bad, when they came flitting through the dorm in the early hours.

The rest of the 40 teaching staff were released from high security prisons in order to assume their posts. They'd been put away in the more enlightened 20th Century for cruelty to children, but were now given their rope. Yes, Tadese, you may laugh, growing up in tranquil Ethiopia in the easy sunset of the century. Not so for us earlybirds! We caught not worms, but clips about the earholes.

10

Sexual abuse, yes, Tadese, was rifemost. But never to me.

'Boy Chaffinch!'

'Pleasy-do, sir.'

'Go outside onto the windowledge and watch everything I do with this boy here! I want to see your face at the window, mind you! And an essay on the subject for prep tonight!'

'Yes, sir.'

I was too ugly a kiddy to arouse their perversions. Do you know that I have always been bald? Except up my nose. But they enjoyed the look of shocked disbelief I wore when I watched them up to their nastymostness. I looked like a bishop even then, and there's no such fun as shocking a bishop. So I was always being called for.

'Boy Chaffinch, Boy Dookan, report to the Headmaster in the gym.'

Dookan was asked to push pins into Mr Bowsie's possy, Mr Bowsie being the Headmaster. The great man bent over going 'Oooooo!' as the pins solemnly went in. I, meanwhileydoos, sat on a medicine ball wearing my look of shocked disbelief. On that occasion I was brave enough to ask Mr Bowsie if he'd mind if I might stick a few pins in his possy, as Dookan was enjoying the sticking so much.

'Are you pretty? Are you blond, Boy Chaffinch?'

Dookan was both these things. The week before my brother Cod arrived as a newboy, by which hour I had been at the school over two years, Dookan was killed by Matron. Stabbed to death with chiropody equipment. Pleasy-do, I can hardly believe it! But as I sit here the memories are plopping to my mind's surface like bright bubbles in volcanic mud. The world has ever been a catalogue of horrors, in our century, as in others, and very nearly everything bad ever said about anybody is basically true. I've learned this with reluctance.

But that school! Was it not? Was it indeed! Do you know, we studied only advanced University mathematics, but were never taught the basics, so were always being punished for our incomprehension. One class was conducted in an extinct language – Hittite, thinkybees – and when we infants all got nil-out-of-ten on the Friday tests, the teacher

– Mr Bowsie, again – would strip naked and whip us at our desks.

I was never a boy for sports. In that school, of course, these were taken from a list in an appendix of Dr Zahn's omnibus edition. In one game, derived from the Aztecs, you had to get a rubber ball through a hoop at the top of a wall, but mostly it involved hitting each other repeatedly with wicket bats until no one was left standing. Bullfighting was on Saturdays and the bull usually won.

When dear Cod arrived, I was so pleased to see him, I kissed his hands! He then clonked me one for being soppy, which he would do today had the good Lord spared him. I was showing him where we slept – a large wicker basket, ten boys and a mastiff all in together. The mastiff, I explained, wasn't much of an ogre, and at least no one was going to shoot him. Sometimes he licked you in his sleep, which was the only affection most of us boys ever had, but he did bite anyone and everything when Matron crept in at dawn throwing a bucket of icy water over us to wake us up.

We were standing there pleasantly-be discussing home topics when Mr Henryson came in dressed as a starlet of the day, saying: 'Boy Chaffinch Major, Boy Chaffinch Minor, take your clothes off and report to Mr Bowsie's private suite pronto!'

He gave us a lipstick each and a woodcarver's tool, then sauntered away, I must admit, looking quite lovely. I was wearing my look of shocked disbelief already, was I not, as I led my bro Codfish up the smelly green staircase to Bowsie's quarters.

The great man was in his bathroom, alone thinkybees, sloshing antiseptic on his wounds, who knows? A sound of running taps and little cries of pain. Cod and I stood in the main room, gazing around at the lewd books and magazines that covered every surface. Blame the 20th Century for Mr Bowsie – that is where he came from!

Then Cod asked his sorry-be bro: 'Why does he have so many jars of pins?'

There were others, too, scattered on the floor, and mousetraps, and odd snapping clamp things, and a live crab watching us with shadow-boxing pincers under the drinks cabinet. All this, supposy be, in the hope of an accidental pained step from Bowsie. My six-year-old life had seen nothing but evils such as this. But the grain of God within me knew it was wrong. I couldn't allow Cod to gain acquaintance of this kind of world. So, moral giant that I was, I suddenly found myself pinching 40 ecupoundlets from the jacket hanging over Bowsie's chair, took Cod by his tiny cold mit and, woodcarver's tool brandished high like the sword of the Archangel Michael, I led my chaffinch chick out into the drizzly night, stark naked through we were, and with Bowsie shouting newly-coined obscenities at us from his window. We were running away!

The mastiff, of course, was soon after us, barking and sniffing. But when he captured us, cowering in bracken in that unhappy Yorkshire, we knew rightaway his woof meant that he had come to join our company. He was running away too. O, messenger of heavenly hope! That pooch's act of faith in a better life than that offered at Beltane Prep filled my baby thoughts with the conviction that another walked beside us, protecting us. And yes, he has protected me, but not bro Cod, nor the pooch – Mother shot him next Christmas Eve.

Two naked sprites riding a growling mutt down the length of England – there was still plentymost heavy automobile traffic then, peeping and crashing – aroused little interest. Advocates of Dr Zahn's method threw stones at us, did they not, but otherwise there was an atmos of freedom about us which, most surelybe, gave me that taste of being outside the world, in an eternal spiritual stupor, which I have since searched for in caves and up poles.

Indeedybe, with only 40 ecupoundlets to our name, not nearly enough for busfare – though in those days you could have a hearty night on the town, so I believe, for under a thousand ecupoundlets – we might have been wandering yet in that cruel Yorkshire, old men who'd forever misplaced the orchards and magnolias of home. What happened was one of the most significant meetings of my life. A divine intervention, was it not, indeed it was, it was! Cod, Mastiff and myself were sitting on our bare pozzys on a verge beside a road eating pork

13

pies which we had purchased from a greasy establishment called Bert's Roadside Caff. Mastiff looked up from his pie first – he had chomped the meat out before starting on the crust. Down the middle of the road, oblivious of the traffic peeping angrily behind him, came the gigantic figure of Brother Hudkin-Bynd, later to be my Guru, and the most remarkable man, save one, that I have ever known.

He wore the robe of a Franciscan, sandalled feet as cold and dirty as ours, and his head a wilderness of frizzlymost hair, rolling in which were two bloodshot eyes the size of eggs. That smile! I saw it for the first time that day.

'Would you like a bit of pig pie, sir?' I said.

Cod and I both held out a crumbly bit of crust with a knob of gristle. He took both, filled a huge hand with the bits and gobbled it down. Then he got down on his haunches, arranged that huge member of his under his habit, and snapped a bit of crust from the Mastiff's pie. It didn't complain.

'So, laddies, what adventure is this I find ye on?' he said.

'We're running away,' said Cod.

'Ah!'

'We're bros,' I added.

'We are all bros,' he said.

'I'm Chaffinch Chaffinch and this is my baby bro Cod.'

His boommost laugh for the first time! My name amused him. I had been called Chaffinch twice, I explainydood, cos my daddio had shot himself during my delivery without advising anyone as to the name he preferred. So, in his honour, no name had been chosen. I was named Chaffinch twice, Chaff for short stopped it sounding so daftly.

He patted my bald head and said an extraordinary thing.

'Ye will follow me, one day, Chaff of the Chaffinches. But ye're not ready yet. I'll send for ye when the time is ripe.'

Then he smiled compassionately at Cod. Recalling it now, I understand that smile. Cod's whole future was in it.

Innocently, I asked: 'Excuse me, sir, but are you Jesus?'

'Custard!' said Cod. 'Jesus isn't fat!'

Brother Hudkin-Bynd's boommost laugh again! He held out his hand to the traffic and quietened the swearing driver with his stare.

'Take these three travellers home,' he said in a quiet voice.

'I bloody will not!' said the driver. 'I've work to do!'

His voice even quieter this time, but his face severe: 'Take them home.'

'Yes, all right, I'll take 'em. Just don't look at me like that.' The man drove us the 200 miles home to Chaffinch Hall, complaining all the way, but unable to refuse Brother Hudkin-Bynd. Mother, rather than chastizing us for running away from school, wept when we each presented her with a lipstick. For the first time ever, she gave in to her motherly inclinations and embraced us.

'I wasn't cruel enough to him!' wailed Mother.

It seemed we'd arrived in the middle of a crisis. Our elder bro Robin had gone mad, with melancholy or what we knew notwot, and was about to be locked in one of the attic rooms, with the Others. Yes, Tadese, the Others. Cheeehe!

3

But a Short Time and Full of Misery

The century and I were in the full bloom of youth, were we not, both 23 years old and skipping with pleasy-do, when I was sent out from the ashram at my own request as a delegate to the 14th Annual Festival of Melancholia. Apart from occasional visits home to Chaffinch Hall, I had been nowhere for years and was full of chehee when I checked into that ominous hotel on the Sussex coast.

'Howdeedoodee! Chaffinch Chaffinch. Delegate 426. Chehee!'

The ill-looking receptionist was reading The Times Book of Obituaries for the year 2022. I had to bang my bible on his desk to attract his attention, did I not?

'They don't always tell you how they died,' he said. 'It's very depressing not knowing.'

'Then don't think about it. Cheeehheeee!'

Just then there were several shots high above us on the various floors.

'Remarkable coincidence,' said the receptionist. 'Four at once.'

'I counted five, did I not?'

Already my cheeriosity was drowning in sorrows: I was thinking of my father's five shots and all those beloved pooches and pussys.

'Five way suicide pact, young man. I doubt it. Too much to hope for. Which Chaffinch are you?'

'Chaffinch.'

'You're sharing with a Mr Sloyn, pleasy-do. 13th floor, room 301.'

Before he handed me the key he wet his finger and ran it across the crossbar of the sunken gold cross on my bible. Then he sucked his finger somewhat lewdly. A meaningless gesture, surelybe, but one which was too full of mystery and

17

aggressive melancholia ever to forget. It sent me into a trance of thought. When I came out of it, the miserable receptionist was answering a question I'd put during my trance, was he not?

'Yes, there's another. Robin Chaffinch. First floor. Room six. He's not checked in yet.'

My clear young face became in that moment a wreck of aghastitude, did it not, all cheehee gone. The receptionist smiled, delighted at my misery. He wet his finger for a repeat performance of his mysterious biblical act, but I snatched the bible away and hurried my look of shocked disbelief into the elevator.

I had not seen my bro for six years and knew not what had become of him. Mother's death from the plague in '17 was worst for him, her favourite. He came home frequently, but our visits never coincided. The surviving servants, when quizzed, simply said he was 'very changed' which held little meaning, just ominousity. Was he leading a silly dissolute life like bro Cod? Or, being a delegate at such a serious, indeed depressing, event such as this, was he developing into a thoughtful man, as betook the head of the Chaffinches on this earth? More likely, I thinkybeed, he was giving in to his melancholy nature, taking his private misery to new heights, by displaying his lifetime of pointless sorrow in a public forum.

I sat on the bed opposite Mr Sloyn, a baggy-eyed businessman from Peterborough. We were too miserable to converse. Our faces said it all. He'd begun by telling me how he'd been on the verge of bankruptcy since 1992, but had never quite teetered over.

'I hope to keep things just nicely teetering, then die knowing I beat the bastards,' he said.

That statement summed up his entire world view, which was, shame upon this religious nut, fast becoming my own. Yes, despite growing irritation at being surrounded by all this melancholia, I made no verbal attempt at cheering him up. I should have talked about Jesus to him, but my youthful instincts were good enough to know that his miserygutsedness would flare to anger at such balm. Besides, just then I was having not a crisis of faith, of which I've had many and am having another right now, but rather an absence of the idea of faith, much worse.

So we just sat there listening for shots, and when one came, BANG, only a room or so away, Mr Sloyn's fingers formed a gun, then shot at his left foot with it, but without humour.

In my innocence I had imagined that a Festival of Melancholia was set up in order to seek ways to prevent such a needless condition. From the shots, and the sly wallowing faces I had seen in the corridors, and the teetering Mr Sloyn, I saw that to these folk melancholia was a lifestyle. They advocated it. It was their truth, their religion. And my bro was one of them.

I had found at the ashram if someone was sad, their face tripping them, all I had to do was sit beside them and grin, nod my head and laugh silently while hugging my knees. Seeing genuine joy on the face of a fellow human, creates a smile in return, every time, indeed it does, of course it do-do-do! This, I decided, I would try on Mr Sloyn, and if it worked I should collar every last miseryguts in the hotel and cure the piggn lot!

Advice for those attempting this manoeuvre, which has been known to work on deathbeds and in scenes of the most hideous devastation, in every century so far: if after ten minutes your grin has created no reaction in the sufferer, give up and burst into tears. Then, when the miseryguts is sympathizing with you, and off his guard, hit him with an even bigger grin – thus the sudden contrast of tears and joy he has observed in you convince him that joy is to be preferred, and he grins back at you, increasing your own grin. Note: this does not work on women!

Mr Sloyn, of course, as guessyboots Tadese has just commented, was an extreme case of new-fangled 21st Century misery, all-consumingly drear. He sat there, eyebags like burst sausages, drooping spotty lip, watching my grinning face with growing despair.

Then he suddenly asked, terrified: 'Are you with the bank?'

'I am merely a poor pilgrim, pleasy-do, who shares your pain at the injustices of this world . . .'

He passed wind louder than the closet gunshot during the rest of my exhortation.

'. . . but who sees glorious things in the world, reasons for joyyyyy!!!!! Kumbaya, my Lord, Kumbaya . . .' I sang! I rejoiced!

But my evangelical musical moment faded when in sudden fury Mr Sloyn said: 'I hate that wallpaper!'

The wallpaper? I found myself looking at it. It was the most cheerful thing I'd seen all day.

'D'you think they'd mind if I changed the bugger?'

'I think they're beyond caring.'

He agreed, opened his suitcase, which contained rolls of poosy coloured wallpaper, the pattern of which was like a Rorschach test given in a tunnel, was it not, and having rung down to reception for some paste, made his arrangements for some away-from-home decorating.

A large woman had hanged herself in the elevator. So it was a sinister prayer-mumbling ride down to the first floor, constantly putting her shoes back on for her, before I could escape her blue tongue and knock on Robin's door. He wasn't in. I tried the bar. A 'dirge-athon' was in progress and I was collared for a turn on the dais. My voice loose from my evangelical musical moment, I sang 'Abide with Me', rather miserably thinkybee, to sobbing tables, then cut myself off in mid-verse. I'd seen Robin huddled in a mackintosh in a shady alcove. He was unshaven and his face was bruised. As I jumped from the dais, the wails of my audience were, in the circumstances, better than applause.

'I thought it was you,' said Robin. Not a handshake or a smile. 'What on piggn earth are you doing at a Festival of Melancholia?'

'At least I didn't come dressed as a pantomime horse! Cheeheee! Urk!'

He stared at me, deeply miserable, and I realized that my smiling trick worked in reverse. In two minutes his stare made me more miserable than I'd been at any time in my life.

At last Two Birds bro said: 'Things haven't been going too well for you either, I see. Sorries.'

'Actuallymost, since I ran away from school at the age of six, until one hour ago, I have known only joy.'

He picked away a tear from under his eye, as if saving a fly. 'I remember the day you came home. They were about to lock me away with the Others.'

I nodded. 'The Others.'

'That's when I met her. The love of my life.'

'Cheery-be?'

'Daphnia. She's one of the Others.'

Tadese is reminding silly old me that not everyone grew up at Chaffinch Hall, so you don't know about the Others, do you? How can I possibly describe them! Can I? I can! They lived on the very top floor of the house, behind steel doors, ducking among the sloping ceilings, each in his or her own room, or should I say cell? Who were they? I say 'were' cos I believe the last of them is dead now. They were, so the unspoken rumour spoke loud, the illegitimate children of our butlers and maids. But the larger truth of it was, shame of shamey-bees, that the Others were mainly fathered by Chaffinches, though none by me, pleasy-do, and among the Others certainly I had great-uncles, aunts, step-grannies, cousins, bros and sisters I never knew, skeletons in our attic clothed in flesh hardly different from my own. The Others were all mad, and in a similar way, deeply suffering from the Chaffinch blues, but generally quiet souls, who spent whole long lives up there, with never a walk in the rain. Though I'd lived the whole century so far under the same roof and every day saw Big Norris filling the dumb-waiters with their trays, to the deepest eternal shame of the boy I was, I'd never given them much of a thinky-be. Now here was my poor melancholy bro declaring that most wondrous of God's gifts had been bestowed upon him. He was in love. But, Christ Jesus, with one of the Others!

'I picked open the lock on the connecting door, and there she was in her jim-jams. Oh, Chaff, the sun shone in my head for the first time. When she's lucid there's nothing like her. So pretty, humming nursery rhymes in her wicker chair. She makes me feel that I'm a robin, a chaffinch, skimming over the treetops on a glorious day. She's never cut her nails or hair, you know.'

He sat there, shivering with love, lightly touching his faceful of bruises.

I pointed. 'Those . . . not she?'

'These, no-no-no. I was playing pnong, it's a new game, very fast and violent. In fact, apart from Daphnia, it's all that's kept me going. When it gets very, very violent, then it's good to be alive in it. But at its best it kills you.' A big grin at last. 'Not your bag, I expect, bro?

I could say nothing to him about all this. I had not yet met Scampi Lowrie, so had never felt love. And pnong, as he said, not my bag, not even later when the whole world thought about little else. Gulfs between us, so different we bros, and so much suffering in the sorry-be boy I hadn't seen for years and would hardly see again. But, despite all this on the table between us, a gigglesomeness took hold of me. 'Cheeeeeheeeeeeee!'

He laughed too, a strange oinking laugh like that of a prize pig on its way to the slaughterhouse – no, in the slaughterhouse already, walking towards the slaughterman's hammer on concrete thick with blood. Oh, Robin, my poor boy! I am thine elder brother now. Triple sorries, for I did not love you enough!

Suddenly, he grabbed my arm and with the intensity of a false prophet who suddenly fears he may not be false after all, he said: 'If she loved me, I would cast off this melancholia forever. I would, would I not? I would. If only she would live with me in a cottage somewhere, then I'd be a happy little pixie like you, Chiffchaff.'

He'd called me by my nursery name. I sat weeping softly and touched his bandaged hands with the lightest of touches in a genuine benediction, which I suddenly flinched back – who was I, ever, now or then, to give benedictions?

Then he described how he'd recently stood on the top of the Toblerone Building, arms wide, yelling at a dying day. He became so loudly vehement that melancholic eyes rolled his way from the dirgeifying, when suddenly he stopped, sweating profusely, and removed his coat. I saw that he had grown hugely fat, like our father had been. I hadn't noticed this until then.

'Even if she would consent see me again, it's impossible, because of this!' And he slapped his paunch.

'Dearie-be!'

Just then two men in mackintoshes the same as the one my bro had so recently cast off came into the bar and sat beside us. They looked at me suspiciously.

'It's okeydooes. He's my bro,' explained Robin.

They nodded, then spoke together: 'We've collected all the guns and ammunition. Best haul we've ever had, boss. Took some smoking outa their a-twitchin hands.'

'Boss?' said my eyebrows, the only hairy things on my head.

'You mean you don't know, little bro? Don't you watch the Everyone Channel? Didn't Cod tell you?'

'Everyone Channel? Tell me wotnot?'

'I'm the leader of the largest resistance group in the country.'

'Uhpple!' I hiccoughed.

'Don't you want to get rid of this Fascist government?'

'Fascist, is it? I didn't know.'

'Don't you care what they're doing to the Welsh?'

'Welsh? Uhpple!'

'This man Smithers is going to get rid of the King! Make himself Lord Protector. It's common knowledge. The E.U. are in Smithers' pocket, of course. Except the French. If Smithers makes his move, they may invade. Since they got their King back, you know, they've been right with us. We have every hope, do we not? Oh, the poor Welsh!'

'I had no idea all this was going on.'

'But we won't let Smithers take our country, will we, lads?'

His two cohorts banged the table with their fists. A particularly miserablifying dirge was just starting up, made noisier by the singer constantly attacking his head with a percussive tin tray.

'I'm triple sorry about the Welsh,' I said. 'Such jolly people.'

'You're with us, then?' said Robin.

'I should coco! Erm . . .' What had I said?

Suddenly the three comrades stood up, saluted me as if I was a field marshal and were gone. My eyes blinked as the tin tray flashed under the barroom lights. I'd worked out that they'd been pinching the guns from the suicidal melancholics to use in their revolution. Such confusion, spinning in my head, cawing rooks flapping down my thought canals. I'd always innocently thought that Mr Smithers was a kindly soul. I mean, he had all those nice daughters. What a birdbrained custard I was! But so was he! And so were they! Custards all!

When I got back to room 301 my roommate had finished his papering and was searching through his ample luggage for something else.

'Some bugger's pinched me gun,' he said. 'I had it all planned, wotnot I was going to say in the note, the wallpaper n'everything.'

Taking this setback in his plans rather well, I thought, he then sat on the toilet and through the open door told the miserable history of his verucca, while straining to evacuate his bowels. Meanwhile, I rubbed the cross on my bible and moped through a recollection of my meeting with Robin, much as I'm doing right now, eh Tadese? It dawned upon me that when he'd patted his paunch he hadn't meant that his Daphnia could not find a fat man attractive. He meant that he was too gross to fit into the dumb-waiter, which was the only way to get in to see the Others! I decided there and then, did I not, I did, did I indeed, I certainly did, to visit Daphnia with my own little body, and unite her in love with my bro, cure his melancholia, and bask in their gratitude forever. Custard!

But as the eldest bro and therefore head of the family, why didn't Robin simply order Big Norris to open Daphnia's door and lead her away, however reluctantly, to a brief if not eternal bliss? Well, call me a rhubarb pancake, but I couldn't stop the thought: what if Robin was not the eldest bro? Was that it?

As for Mr Sloyn, I'd give a bunch of bananas to know what became of him. But what became of me? I'm not even sure of that! Chehurrrr-ee-ee-ee! Urke! Ee!

4

The Wisest Chaffinch of Them All

Shortly thereafterwards I was not such a skinny goblin myself! And could not have fitted into a dumb waiter on three trips, indeedynot! I have always, sinful wretch, been something of a pigadoodle with my food – I have eaten two impressive bananas in the moments since I started speaking this sermon this evening, and as usual have thrown the skins onto the roof of Tadese's hut, for the childish pleasure of watching him hook them off with his stick, which he will do before dark, because they attract small monkeys whose gibbering keeps him awake, but fill me full of chehee.

You see, there was a new product in the shops in the '20s called 'Food that isn't there'. You could eat as much of it as you liked but didn't put on weight or have potherations with bowel tantrums – because it wasn't there! Urk! It came, to begin with, in three forms: plain chocolate, a rather tasteless liver sausage, and a truly yumadumdum gooey cheese. I went crazy, didn't I not, for this stuff! I found that if I dipped the sausage in the cheese then the sausage was okaydoos tasty enough. I got through 10 tubs a day of the cheese, ropes of sausage, and never stopped eating the chocolate, even when I was eating the sausage and cheese. But it didn't affect my normal appetite, I still ate other things. Because, hiho! – the food that wasn't there, wasn't there! So plenty room for whatever else! Chi-eee!

It gives me great pain, however, does it not, to relate that I was among the small percentage of consumers of 'Food that isn't there' whose digestive system rejected the basic concept of the food not being there. One morning I woke up with the sensation that a flabby horse was sitting on me and neighing. But the flabby horse was me, poor Uncle Chiffchaff! I'd put on 30 stones overnight. And the neighing was my fellow monks, peeping through my tentflap and laughing uncharitably at the astonished pigadoodle oinking in fright within.

It was a twelvemonth before I was back to normal, just in time for the Revolution! Meanwhileydoos, I couldn't see a billboard advertising 'Food that isn't there', or see an empty cheese tub rolling down a road in the wind, without feeling I'd lost a friend.

But on the day of which I am now speaking, one of the 36,525 possible days of my 21st Century life I could give tongue to, I was my normalmost svelte self. I was alone in the back-kitchens of Chaffinch Hall, munching a chicken's leg, and wondering which of the dozens of dumb-waiters I should choose to gain access to my bro's beloved's room. In fairytales the choice is usually one of three ways, only one a safe one, a monster awaiting you if you choose wrong, pleasy-do. This was a choice where I was bound to choose wrong. I imagined myself, as I still sometimes do, going up the wrong dumb-waiter and ending up being eaten, much as I was eating that chicken's leg, by some gibbering relative – of a most sinister spectral variety, who, though not coming to the wedding, still appears on the wedding photographs.

My solution, O best beloved, was a natty one, and involves the most remarkable thing about the Others. They had their own language. Separated from normal intercourse, which they were indeed, living alone between thick walls, earlier members of their Otherdom, had taken to communicating by tapping spoons on the radiators and pipes. Thus, if they wished, they could talk all day, and express their madnesses willy-nilly in a language of the mad, by the mad, and for the mad. But it wasn't English. They knew no English. It was a language all its own, like no other, and – Chaffinch feathers ruffle with pride here – developed under the tiles of Chaffinch Hall! Remarkable, is it not?

A tutor of mine, a certain Mr Minto – Cod and I had a succession of dull tutors after we left Beltane Prep, to prepare him for Oxford and me for sitting in caves – was most fascinated by this Other language, and made tape-recordings and sat on the top landing, where we boys feared to go, in ecstasies of investigation. Strange man disappeared after a while, with one of our Gainsboroughs.

For 23 years I had lived in that house, and slept my sleeps and dreamt my boyhood dreams, with always, in the background, that tappy-ping-dinga-bongtap. Hardly hearing it, but always hearing it. A sound like the ticking over in my brain. Yes, I knew the language! I realized, I'd taken it in unconsciously. I knew it, almost as if I was one of the Others myself! It is a method Dame Tuna used for learning Greek in her youth – bringing home Greek restaurateurs and having them sit by her bed describing the streets of Thessalonika while she dozed. It ruined her first marriage, but she attained fluency. Chehee!

I unhooked a frying pan, sending all the other pans swaying and clinking incomprehensibly, grabbed a ladle firm enough to cosh a burglar with, and stood under a dumb-waiter. Far above, faintly I heard it, tappy-ping-dinga-bongtap. I closed my eyes, cleared a mind flowing with quotes from Saint Augustine, and tapped out a hello with ladle and pan.

An hour of extraordinary exchanges followed, with two dozen of the Others, and more mentionings of the penis than I have ever heard in one hour, unless my understanding of their language was errant in some way, which I'm sure it was. At last Daphnia replied, banging her spoon on the wooden frame of the relevant, the correct dumb-waiter, and saying (tappy-pinging) she'd be glad to see me. What elation! But just then Big Norris came in. He'd heard me clicking and was redly irate. He sent the pans swinging with the first of several jabs, all aimed at nothing in particular, merely a worrying display of strongman's aggression.

'I was only . . . erm . . .'

'You've got them scratchin the walls up there! What's all this penis stuff. Penis this, penis that – dirty little monk! If your mother was alive she'd . . .'

But with a yelp I was gone. Daphnia was pulling on the rope of the dumb-waiter and I rose up the shaft – I noticed it was painted with the same green paint as the older gates in the garden – like a man rising to his resurrection I rose, my shoulders dislodging hard peas from bumps and ledges where they'd sat all century long. Then the light was nearer, a square of brilliance, and two elegant hands, like the hands of the virgin, but with longer nails, reaching out to me. My heart was swelling. I wept for joy! Daphnia's hands grabbed mine. She flung me headlong from the dumb-waiter to a chair on the other side of the room.

In a daze, blinded by hot sun yellow on a skylight above me, I squinted at my new surroundings. The room was decorated like a nursery, and here and there I saw half-remembered toys of my own. I was sitting on my first teddy-bear, confiscated when I loved it most due to Dr Mitzi Zahn's code.

Daphnia was most elegantly dressed, was she not? Like a mother on her way out to the opera but popping into the nursery to kiss the children goodnight before she goes. But Daphnia had never been anywhere, poor girl! Such a kindly smile, and hair like Rapunzel. I felt I should abandon my conventional religious nutteries, and worship this Goddess of the attic! Then she made a face like a fish and started making the most peculiar noise with her tongue. I couldn't fathom it at first. Of course! Their language! – This was it in its spoonless form! This was how they spoke it!

She pinched my cheeks with only two of her twelve inch long fingernails, made a fish face of my human one, and soon I was clicking my tongue back at her. Hallelujah! I was clicking in tongues!

Clork-kak-kk-clork! I told her of my bro's undying love for her, and that rather than waste her life in this attic, she'd be doing the Christian thing if she left it and made a new life with him, a wonderful young man, full of love and sensitivities, but a martyr to melancholia which almost had him put away up here also and which she had it in her power to cure. A wonderful opportunity for sacrifice! Clook-ok-ook-kk-clurk!

She looked at me with tiny charming confused wrinkles on her brow – I think because I'd, shamefully, somehow, said penis between every word. She frapped on the wall and a gulp later the door opened. It was Mr Minto, my old tutor, was it not indeed, well, well.

'Minto,' clicked Daphnia. 'Prepare the dining room. I have a guest. My second-cousin once-removed.'

I escorted her into dinner, slowly, cos with those long toenails – not, I must admit, as prettymost as her fingernails – she could barely walk. They curled at the ends and scratched the floor, making a sound like the mutter of her own language, or a lobster escaping across a kitchen floor. Despite this, my young self was captivated by her, was he not, indeed so he was.

The dining table was long enough to sit fifty, but in that narrow loft it could manage but two, myself and Daphnia, waving at each other from each end, with the sides close against the wall. Minto, who served, for that's what he'd been all those years since his disappearance, Daphnia's factotum, had to walk on the table to achieve his offices, napkins knotted to his shoes, were they not.

I smiled at Daphnia. She back at me from the door end. We ate cockaleekie soup, followed by whitebait, a delicious side-salad, then strawberries and cream. A lovely meal, in which I discovered that you cannot click sensibly with your mouth full. Would it be rude of me to say that Daphnia didn't use cutlery? She used her nails.

'Tell her I love her. Tell her I adore her,' said Minto, in plain English. Despite his academic background and years of study he'd never cracked the language. 'She's a goddess, isn't she, Master Chaff? I sponge her sometimes, when she has a bath.'

Having winked and groaned, he stood on the table weeping, obscuring my view of the Gainsborough, which I hadn't seen since I was 12. Daphnia frapped the table angrily and the silly man pulled himself together and helped me down the table, tripping over the silverware. He served his lady and I coffee in the nursery. I held my old bear, chuckling at him.

But then Daphnia clicked to me the most extraordinary speech I have ever heard – and I, of course, knew the Grand Mufti personally! Its majesty cannot be conveyed in our language, only in tongue clicks or spoons, which language now only I know. Its essence was this – which became for me, did it not, the answer to all my thinkings: that she would not leave her attic to live a new life with Robin, that she wished, as far as possible in life to do nothing, to see nothing, to read nothing. Nothing must distract her from the ever-upward drift of her thoughts, her thinking soul. The brief childish weeks she'd spent with Robin – clonk-clrup-kk-click – were the happiest of her life, and she contemplated them constantly, a focus for all her considerations, feeling more alive in doing that, than in a lifetime filled by happy days. And now this lovely afternoon with me! – which she would sit in her chair and dwell on in pure thought for the rest of her days. In the hurlyburlydom of the outside world, where she had never been but whose nature she knew utterly, there was no real constant life, no continuing consciousness, a person was the victim of a trillion sensations filling a person's eyes, a person was never the same person from moment to moment. But here, in her still, quiet room, she was truly alive, fully herself. She soared ever-upwards, the heels of her angelic spirit sprinkled with angel dust!

I listened with tears rolling down my cheeks, did I not, clicking responses between sobs, saying penis over and over, supposeybe. This poor mad girl had given me my life, more than all the wise gurus, more than all of the literature I had paddled through. Perhaps I would have come to the same conclusions, I know not, but Daphnia is responsible for my life up this pole. It is the same life as the one she promised herself! And you, Tadese, are my Mr Minto. Instead of a Gainsborough I have the great red carpet of Ethiopia to gaze at! Hurrahhhhh! Urghyyy-cheeheee! O, joy!

Finally, she made the same request of me as she had of Robin on his last visit. Never to come again. Never to visit. Never to clonk a spoon on a radiator for her. To go and never return. Needles in my heart, was this, cos like Robin, I loved her. Differently, of course. I loved her the way I love the stars massed above my pole, an elephant's trumpet, the shimmer of Lake Stephanie in the distance. Robin loved her in a man's way, the way later I, with no shame do I admit it, loved my Scampi.

Poor Daphnia! Of course, she herself, in the end, did not live that life she introduced me to. Remind my old head, Tadese – perhaps tomorrow, a sermon on this. The sun goes down. The hyenas are awake. Sleepy-be.

Urk! How elated I was as Big Norris chased me across the soft English lawn, furiously playing hit-the-Chaffinch with baking potatoes. I had found myself! Look, Tadese, see me, I beat my chest – this gibbering custard is what I found!

Before I parted from Daphnia she asked if I would bathe her. Well, pleasy-do, I couldn't refuse, though I'd never seen a naked woman and the thought worried me evermost. She sat in her little hip-bath and clicked for me to enter the tiny bathroom. I left Mr Minto weeping outside and went in. Firstly, all I saw was her hair which she was gathering on top of her head. Then she handed me the sponge. I held it in my shaking hand and looked deep into the waters of her bath. Tadese, I nearly swooned with compassion, for the water was as red as yon sunset. Her back, her legs, her chests, were covered in deep wounds, cuts, from her nails, horrible open bleeding wounds, criss-crossing old healed wounds of the same kind.

One click I had for her: 'Why?'

'It helps me think,' she clicked.

I smiled at her with all the Godliness I could put into a smile. Was there madness in her, mixed with her wisdom? Or was this indeedybe necessary to keep her mind so vital – just as Saint Bernadette and others were visited with tumours and afflictions by a cruel, dodgy deity, a celestial follower of Dr Mitzi Zahn, to keep them on the right track.

I sponged her wounds. She flinched and clicked, holding her hands underwater but her nails out. Tadese! There's a monkey on your roof!

5

Guru to a Chaffinch

The relationship between a disciple and his guru, as Tadese will agree, is a unique one on this earth, and is unchanged down the centuries. One is taught to accept that the guru is one who 'knows' and the disciple is one 'who knows not', therefore the disciple must obey his master in all things, and without question, in order to reach an enlightened state. A disciple cannot pick and choose what his guru says, as from the buffet table of truths. He 'who knows not' must obey 'He who knows' in order himself to become a 'He who knows'. There is, in reality, brethren, no 'He who knows' – I know that much, do I not? And so do you, in your helplessness! Such poletop wisdom! Cheehe!

Therefore, Tadese, who slouches below me like a sleepy minotaur, licking his pencil while he writes down all this, evidently has a desire, one day, to abandon the hiding of weasels, and climb up a pole to tweet in bliss much as I am doing now, am I not? He thinks I know things, secrets, unobtainable elsewhere. I tell him that whatever I may know is just for me. I cannot impart it. I say things, true things sometimes, but all words are meaningless. But Tadese stays to look after me, to feed me, to put the hosepipe on me when the African sun hurts, and I am glad. I most humbly thank him. Urk!

I am no guru, anyway, just a plucked chuntering bird. I suppose what I am trying to say here is something which gives me great pain. It is this. A guru is always bad, whether he is a good man or a devil, equally bad. This goes for Kings and Presidents also! It is not the guru who is bad, it is being a guru that is bad, and this makes the guru, be he Christ himself, a bad man. I blaspheme. Tadese is shocked. Cheeehe!

On the evening of the same famous day in 2023 when I

visited cousin Daphnia and found myself, I walked in a whirl of gleeful thoughts, glad as a seal to be alive. From the Hall to the Ashram was no more than 40 miles. I arrived before dawn, eager to talk to my guru. Since the day, almost seven years before, when Brother Hudkin-Bynd sent his note saying that I was now ready to follow him, I had walked in his shadow and obeyed every word. Now, as I stood cuddled by arms of misty dawn with the snoring tents spread around me, I looked towards the darkness of the forest where my guru lived and a great sorrow bore upon me. For I knew now, did I not, indeed so I did, that the great man was no longer my guru. My father had died again. I was on my own.

Knowing this, I broke the strictest rule of our little order. I entered his forest. He came from there to speak with us, eat with us and do all his guru's business. When finished, he would disappear, literally some of us thought, into the forest, spooking no fawns. To enter his forest meant expulsion, rejection for ever from our little order, from our home and whatever it meant to us. Brother Bromley, up early to make the porridge for us all, saw me going into the forest, and chased after in terror, sprinkling porridge from his box as he dashed. I still hear his call, warning my every step in life.

'Chaff! Don't do it! Brother! Bro! No!'

I turned in hesitation.

Brother Bromley, furious: 'It is forbidden!'

That convinced me. I hopped over a blackberry bush and was in!

I found a well-travelled path, my eyes on the lookout for Brother Hudkin-Bynd's tent. Or did he just wander eternally between the trees collecting nuts of thought?

I didn't find him. By the road on the other side of the forest was a small bungalow. Very modern. That unreflective aluminium stuff. Long. Sharp angles. It looked like a crashed plane. I knocked on the door. My guru himself answered. His long hair was tied back. He wore a dressing-gown with a paisley design. He was chewing the bite he'd taken from the slice of toast he held in his hand.

'Ogh, Chaff, it's ye,' he said. 'Howdeedoodee.'

'Howdoodeedee, Bro.' Astonishment!

'Do come in. Sit ye down.'

We sat down in front of the tellyvision. I had hardly ever watched it since they stopped doing news and it went all erotic. A neat little woman with a bourgeois smile gave me some toast and marmalade. My mind was fizzing with questions? Where was I? What was this place?

Brother Hudkin-Bynd, huge in this little house full of nik-nacks, broke the silence, waving his crust at the tellyvision: 'Are ye hooked on the Everyone Channel? I mean, when ye be up at the Hall, does ye watch? It's custard!'

'I have heard of it,' I said, my mind full of questions which I didn't know how to ask.

'It's spanky-doos fascinating. That Mr Smithers is a remark-able man, thinkybee?'

Smithers had spent ecupoundlet-billions setting the Every-one Channel up. It was, in fact, 100 billion channels. One each for everyone. It showed the entire daily life of everyone in the country, except Mr Smithers, of course – so the only way you would ever be off screen would be if you were in his company, in which case you'd probably be watching the Everyone Channel, because that was all he ever did. Privacy was allowed only in the bathroom, pleasy-do, which resulted in some shy souls living their entire lives in there. Later, this privacy rule was scrapped and nowhere in Britain could you evacuate your bowels without the chance of someone watching. There were those, I heard, who went about in a permanent disguise, in bear suits even, to maintain their privacy. But how many people would be watching any one person, unless that person was doing something to bring attention upon themselves? It should, I innocently thought to begin with, encourage folk to lead simpler, more ordered lives. But if you committed the sexual intercourse, still popular and quite legal in the '20s, next morning you'd greet your every acquaintance awaiting a lascivious wink and a score out of ten.

My guru's last task as my guru was to inform me of these things, and to explain the science of it, something to do with radio waves bouncing off atoms of moisture in the air. Toshwash!

'The trouble is,' my guru told me as, to my further astonishment, two little girls came in and kissed him on the cheek before leaving for school, 'that it's hard to find anybody who's not just watching someone else. But for all that, tis a window on the world, looking through every window, down every passage! Lookybee, this man here's a chemist in Dundee. I've been watching him all week. He's having an affair with the girl who works in his shop, but wait till he finds out she's working for the revolutionaries, foolish girl! But he'll find out. He'll see it on the Everyone Channel!' He boomed and slapped his knees.

'Don't laugh so loud, George,' said the little woman from the kitchen. 'It's bad for your blood pressure.'

'Sorry, deary-poo!'

All my glee gone. All my questions killed. I nibbled toast, like a hamster who's just heard hamsters only live 18 months. All I could think of saying was: 'Am I on there?'

'Of course!'

He dialled my name and date of birth on his handset and there I was on the screen! Sitting right there with an empty plate of toast on my knees in a room filled with my guru and constellations of nik-nacks. He rolled the ball in the middle of the handset and there were views of me from every possible angle. I giggled like an eskimo. I made faces. I stood on my head on the chair.

My guru boomed his good-natured laugh. But, I regret to say I was not wearing underwear, owning none, nor have I since, and my robe had dropped over my face, coupled with which I had an unexpected stiffening, very frequent then, which my guru understood all about, for we had discussed it many times. So when my guru's wife (for that is who she most obviously was) came in with more toast she screamed at the sight of an upside-down naked chaffinch. They were prudes, the Smithers generation.

'What if the girls had still been here! Really!'

She slammed the door on us, taking the toast with her, and we sat in disgrace. We watched our disgrace on the tellyvision, which, after a bit, caused us to chuckle.

'It's made stars of some people,' he said. 'There's a

Mrs Trubshaw who sits singing all day surrounded by poodles. The whole country is tickled rhubarb with her.'

He dialled her up, but she was flat out, seemingly asleep. The poodles, however, were barking all around her, loud enough to wake the dead. We sat forward, suddenly expecting the worst, until my beady bird's eye caught sight of a bottle of vodka rolling under the bed among copulating poodles, was it not. Mrs Trubshaw's new found stardom had driven her to drink.

'Poor sinner,' said my guru.

'Indeedybe,' I agreed, then from nowhere I suddenly asked. 'Do they show the Welsh?'

'Welsh? I supposy-do, yes.'

A press of the handset sent Welsh names rolling across the screen. We chose one at random and found him, a certain Hywel Davies, in a vast prison camp in his native land, gaunt and weepysome, dressing himself for morning roll-call. Mr Hudkin-Bynd and I watched this with glum faces. We tried other Welsh names. Their people were all in one prison camp or other. One was dead in a ditch.

'That's your Mr Smithers for you,' I said.

The guru made no response. Unfathomably, he was a supporter of Mr Smithers.

There was nothing more to say but goodbye. But it was a word I could not say to this man. No, I could not, could I, no indeed, and never in my heart. We stood at his gate, the forest birds filling our ears with song.

I managed one of those killed questions: 'I did thinkybee you lived in a tent?'

'Oh, no, a tent, no.'

One more question: 'May I call you George?'

He boomed. 'Surelybe, lad, if ye want!'

'George,' I said.

I said it twice more, then I held out my hand and he took it, pulling me towards him and burying me in an embrace which smelt of pine and dogs. His huge member, like always, wagged between his legs like the clanger of a noiseless bell.

I left along the road, not through the forest, and although I did dial him up on the Everyone Channel from time to time, seeing his daughters grow and his disciples slowly vanish with less religious times, we never met again. He was a better man, I am sure, when his only disciple was himself. Outliving everything he knew, and living a long peaceful life, he died in violence, a preamble to that greater violence, murdered by a Bashi-Bazouki raiding party at Great Yarmouth in that otherwise delightful summer of '68.

6

The Revolting Chaffinches

2024, was it not, was the greatest year of freedom which our 21st century has known! Before all and sundryness was crushed by the despots, before the Mufti's rise, there was a marvellous blip in time, an afternoon of glowing youth, when at last that rare bird, an English revolution, took flight, swooping down on that rodent Smithers as he nibbled the corn.

Guruless, I was building myself up for a life of solitary religious nuttery by lolling at Chaffinch Hall, then as now the omphalos of my world. There I was, either reading old sermons in the library, talking to myself in my favourite treehouse, or watching the Everyone Channel. This latter, I confess, had become quite an obsession with me. I grew fond of some I spied on, and in seeing them sink towards depravities, I could not help but phone them up with saintly advice at the ready.

'Howdeedoodee. I'm a monk. I've been watching you on the box, and I must say . . .'

'DO BUGGER OFF!!!'

They all said the same thing. Even an almost perfect bishop who'd taken up an athletic masturbation late in life. I can still see him at it!

I sometimes watched my bro Cod and his dashing friends, racing police in their antique cars. And often my morose bro Robin, sitting in his chair, watching the Everyone Channel, as men in silver raincoats came in with notes, which he would then eat, before sending them off with another for some secret person in a secret place, to eat in turn.

On July 3, 2024 I ate a large breakfast with the servants, then returned to bed to snooze and watch Everyone on TV. I dialled up Robin and found him in a quite new location, a London Post Office, surrounded by men in silver raincoats

and carrying guns. He wrote a note, saying, can I ever forget:
'Give this to C.C. You know where he is. It'll take you an hour.
Come straight back with him.'

Who could C.C. be other than Chaffinch Chaffinch? And it
did indeed take an hour from London to Chaffinch Hall. They
were coming for me! I took fright! I hid among nettles in the
grounds. I am, am I not, immune to nettle stings, but not to
involvements in the world.

But when they came, of course, they just dialled me up on
the Everyone Channel and there I was, sitting with a ladybird
on my finger. The men who took me were the same two
I'd met in the barroom with Robin the previous year. They
handed me the note. I knew the procedure, but got it wrong,
eating it before reading it, so I'll never know what it said!

'It's happening!' said one.

'Today!' said the other.

'Um?' said I.

'You're still with us, aren't you?'

'Sorry-be?'

'You said "I should coco". Last time.'

'Ah, that's it then.'

A combination of shyness and stupidity thrust me headlong
into the revolution of '24.

By the time we got to London all Hell had broken loose.
Our car, suddenly full of sparks, had all four tyres shot out
from under it on Holborn Bridge. One of my friends was
wounded. I said all the prayers I knew, which was many, as
we trotted through the streets with our heads down. Oxford
Street was crowded with more armed police than ever there
were shoppers a-shopping there on its busiest Christmas
Eves. Black uniforms, black helmets, visors faceless and
black. They held up shiny round shields, and when I first
saw them, my odd mind said they were cockroaches carrying
coins fallen from a giant's purse. They were fighting it out
with elements of the army, which were on 'our' side, the
anti-Smithers side. A low evil sound filled one of my ears,
which was either policemen grunting under their helmets,
or some kind of gun. It went on for hours, grunting or
shooting. My other ear ached with smashing glass. It was

falling down all around, bits the size of eyes, bits bigger than a man, all shapes, cutting the angry air to bits, flashing with the reflections of police, splashing sharply on the pavement, more and more, like a glass sky breaking on the ground.

Right beside me, my unwounded friend suddenly stopped still, a two foot long shard of glass with a green letter M in it sticking right out the top of his head. He stood worried for a moment, then sank dying to his knees, blood flowing in many currents from his hair, like Jesus with the crown of thorns in old pictures. I knelt by him, praying, weeping, bullets flying all around. The low grunt during that time was louder than the glass.

'Leave him! He's piggn had it!' said the other, dragging me on.

It seemed impossible that they should part, these two, because I had only ever seen them together, and they looked so alike, I thought of them as two parts of the same creature. Out of everything that happened on that day, it is the parting of those two which now, 75 years on, upsets me the most. But, who knows, chehee, perhaps they hated each other!

The surviving twin led me into a boutique, up some stairs, along a corridor. Suddenly, a policeman! Shots! The policeman fell. No grunt. Just fell. My friend must have shot him, but no gun did I see. Perhaps it was Mr Sloyn's gun, the one he intended to visit Heaven with and which this man had pinched from his suitcase. Was Mr Sloyn then watching all this on the Everyone Channel while eating chips and perusing his bank statements?

We passed through three buildings of offices, leaving each building not through a door, but through a jagged hole smashed in its wall leading to another building. Then we were descending stairs, sad dark stairs and more drear stairs, like gargoyles escaping down a cathedral tower. At last, light! People! The floor of the post office!

Welshmen – for many of the heroes of that day were of that persecuted race – were defiantly singing *Men of Harlech*, shooting out of the windows, their eyes streaming with tears from the poisonous gas which thinly filled the room. I joined in the singing, young fool that I was, as if at some holy meeting.

41

One of the singers shook my hand. 'It's you, issent? C.C.'

'That's me,' I said.

'Look, boyos – it's C.C.!'

They gave me a cheer. I've proud of it still!

Then, just as someone fell shot at my feet, the surviving twin had my elbow.

'You're brother's in there,' he said, and pointed to a brown door with a 2023 calendar still pinned on it.

I went in, closed the door behind me, and never, have I not, no never, felt as alone. The noise of battle seemed to cease. I was in the sorting room, a large room, with letters strewn all over the floor. Stupidly, I picked one up and opened it. While nosily reading about some poor girl's conversion to Mohamadism and noting her name so that I could dial her up on TV later, I called out for my brother.

'Robin. Two Birds. Bro. I'm here. YOOOO-HOOOOO!'

When he didn't answer I went on a walk around the sorting office, picking up letters that interested me, all the while ignoring the laid out bloody corpulent corpse on one of the tables, a parcel marked fragile at its feet.

I became angry, shouting: 'ROBIN! WHERE ARE YOU? YOU DRAG ME ALL THE WAY DOWN HERE, HAVE YOU NOT INDEED, INTO THIS MAYHEM AND NOW YOU PLAY PIGGN HIDE AND SEEK WITH ME!'

But Robin was hiding where I could not seek, but perhaps now, soon will. He'd been shot in the face by a police spy, one of his closest associates, who'd been under orders to do this very thing should the unexpected revolution actually occur. I struggled with myself, admitting at last that, yes, I did recognize the corpse's hands. For they were my hands, chubbier, but the same. I held one and wept as I have never wept before or since, for no one, not Scampi even, or any of the poor Chaffinches who came to bad ends, which they almost all did.

Then a hairy Welshman beside me. He'd whispered the same thing in my ears several times before I heard.

'Your orders, issent, sir. What are we to do?'

'Orders?'

'With your bro dead, see. You're the boss, issent. The Leader of the Revolution.'

Okeydooes, the farmer has fallen into the threshing machine, so the goose is put in charge of the farm. But this goose could not let its brother down. And my eyes, in the blurr of every bulb of water that fell from them, saw those poor thin Welshmen in the camps. I was fired up! Like the Popes of old I would march my men into battle! Yes, Tadese, I, this old perchsitter, I was the leader of the English Revolution of 2024.

Of course in those days there were none of the weapons of the Mufti's war, no phasers, vaporizers and the like. An old-fashioned war we had ourselves, of blood and steel. As brief and painful as a trip to an aggressive dentist.

My plan was simple. I ordered my revolutionaries to holster their guns. We would walk outside, silently, and march on Parliament, where I myself would demand the resignation of Smithers and his government, for the good of all. We didn't then know that Smithers had lived in Mustique for three years, watching us all on the Everyone Satellite. Notes were sent out to our cohorts elsewhere in the city. Around the country the other arms of our uprising were told to hold fire and wait and see. The invading French troops filling the South Coast towns saw in this lull an opportunity for a long lunch.

So outside we went, did we not. The police retreated cautiously before us. A few, a very few, threw off their faceless helmets, became men, and joined our march. The Welsh began singing, men and women together, so beautiful, but I shhhhed them to a humm so as not to worry the police into opening fire. They hummed down to Trafalgar Square, then went silent as we saw the tanks ahead of us, protecting Whitehall, Parliament, the seat of the obnoxious power. We stopped. We knew they would fire upon us. In the distance cruel voices shouted orders. The feet of running troops all over Westminster coming to meet us. The gallop of mounted police.

These soon joined the tanks, a strange contrast to face, all the ancient and modern weapons of Apocalypse. I turned and faced my little army, bowed my head and prayed. They murmured an amen in just the tone they did in their churches and chapels back home. Then I about-turned and marched like a major, straight at the enemy. The others followed, marching faster. Shots! Snipers or from their cordon itself? Both, yes, both! Our march became a run. I was left behind, tripping in my sandals. Bullets punching the road. A burst from a cannon. For a moment I was hot and sweaty as if confused in a sauna bath. Then I was cold, unhurt, except that one of the tassels of my robe was on fire. I snuffed it out and continued running, flapping my arms, quite barmy, was I not. Me! Leading a Revolution! Chehee!

It was all confusion now. The mounted police were charging. I heard the hoofbeats long before they arrived. Shots and cries. Smoke. A gloved hand at my throat, coming from the clouds, like God punishing me for my part in all this. I was in the air. I was blowing a whistle. Next thing the glove was empty, in my mouth, and I was alone on a white horse galloping through a souvenir shop, scattering nik-nacks. Tadese may laugh like a hippo as such an idea, but this, my boy, is history as it was lived.

'Hold your fire, all of you! Let us be brothers and build anew together!' cried my young voice on a horse that turned and turned.

But as the smoke suddenly blew away up the street I saw that I was practically alone. Only a few revolutionaries left, behind lampposts, and one bloodied Welshman singing alone, on his knees amid the bodies of his fellows.

The barrels of all the tanks were aimed at yours truly, pleasy-do. But they didn't fire. They suddenly swivelled away. Coming from the other side on the cordon, down the thoroughfares onto Westminster Green, flowing in their thousands past the Thatcher Memorial, were other cohorts of the Revolution. I kicked my horse in the sides and he, a fervent revolutionary himself by now, carried me through at full pelt, with a jump which, was it not truly indeed, the most exhilarating moment of my 100 years. Single acts of violence, a punch in the nose, a dogbite, most terrible indeed so, yes – like any good man I abhor it. But violence as a storm, I must admit, I found quite wonderful! Perhaps I should have taken up pnong?

I arrived before our own tank, arms raised in a hallelujah, when a huge explosion opened the ground under me and I rose in the air gripping the horse's severed head, landing on a statue of Sir Winston Churchill. I squatted there in a daze for some minutes, adorned with the various organs of a horse, gradually gathering my senses. But not my hearing.

I was, for the time being, deaf. So the conclusion of the Battle of London was like a soundless dream for me, flowing before me, as my eyes jerked from scene to scene.

It looked like we'd lost. More and more police crowded slowly in from every direction, like buckets of night spilling down the streets and staining them dark forever. For the Revolution, one last heroic charge remained. And at the head of it, carrying the flag of Saint George, her tongue flicking in her mouth, was my 'Other' cousin Daphnia Chaffinch, resplendent was she not, in a gold lamé dress and riding hat, walking on her heels with her toenails backscratching her fellows. Out of her attic for the very first time – she had come to play her part in this! Had she lived, O the contemplations she would have had! I waved to her, I tongue-clicked her name, I stood on Churchill's head. Darling girl! The creator of my solitude!

As four policewomen dragged me down from my plinth, I saw Daphnia's group pushed towards the river. She had lost her flag, but her gold lamé dress was clearly visible, a sun surrounded by an everlasting twitching darkness of police. Then, a strange moment. Everyone stopped and looked up. Big Ben was striking four o'clock. In my deafness, though I heard nothing else, I heard the old clock strike for its last time. Then its tower fell, away from where I sat between the legs of policewomen. It fell slowly as we all watched, towards the Embankment where the raging battle had also stopped to look and now saw the symbol of England collapsing upon them. I crossed myself. A policewoman crossed herself. Then there was dust and that was that.

Why was it not a victory? I don't know. With the clock's last tick a new era began, and we were left behind in the old one. The future was not ours. Simple as that. The old man in the sky, as usual, did not guard the righteous. They were mostly killed.

There was no more shooting. The police cast off their helmets. I saw many weeping. A newspaperseller came by yelling 'Read all about it!' and he was sold out in moments. But why did they need to read all about it, when they'd just seen more for themselves than could ever be written down?

In the streets they were already bulldozing the bodies into piles, as I walked through the black and gold rubble, looking for Daphnia. I climbed amid antique stone and the workings of the clock. It seemed, indeed did it not, that time itself had stopped, killed when Big Ben fell to earth, or that it was going on elsewhere but we would never be in it again. I found Mr Minto having some kind of asthmatic fit, digging with his hands. My hearing was back to almost normal, though for days I kept hearing the old clock strike, but I could not hear Daphnia's click under the rubble. I found one of her toenails later, and have it yet, in my little bag of treasures in Tadese's hut. Nor do I know what became of Mr Minto. He never returned to Chaffinch Hall. I expect he threw himself in the river. That is always what I imagined he did, unable to live without that remarkable girl.

My protector, the surviving twin, was beside me, full of holes but betraying no pain.

'Better get away from here, C.C. They'll piggnwell have you!'

We walked along the Underground to Victoria, and there caught a bus to I don't know where. Briefly, I returned to the Hall, collected a few things. Next day I was in Northumberland, living in the first of several caves I inhabited there during the next decade and a half of our 21st Century, sallying out but rarely and once to fall in love.

My first cave was in a dene of old and dying trees near Hexham. There, one evening, ten years later, my dead bro Robin visited me, or so I fancied. So on occasions did Saint Augustine, and a man who usually said his name was Harris, who I strongly suspect was actually real. Robin spoke of the Hall, the magnolias in bloom, like candles under the night sky,

46

our poor dogs, of the day I found Mother dead from plague on the patio by the folly. When he left through the wall of my cave, I wept just as I did that day when I found him laid out in the post office.

I fled too early, did I not? I didn't find out till much later that the Welsh and various other revolutionary cohorts, assisted by the French, deposed the Smithers régime, setting up a New Age Council. This continued, sorry-be, and with Royal approval, to do abysmal things to the Welsh. Smithers himself was killed in a highly suspicious aircrash returning from Mustique.

But this New Age Council, backward child of our shapely explosives and a dead clock, simply wasn't there one morning. Nextmost, elections were called, but somehow two of the leading building societies ignored the result and stepped in with the idea of running the country. Their boards soon quarrelled – over the Queenly behaviour of some of their wives was what I heard – and were followed by a right-wing backlash which culminated in a government of taxi-drivers. Well, try anything, indeedybe! They kept up their taxi driving jobs while at the same time, running the country. It was they who executed the poor King in Whitehall on January 11th, 2026, and hanged almost everybody, including each other, making speeches that never stopped, in their taxis and out, castigating the government, as was their tradition, even though they were now the government themselves, were they not? Triple lashings of custard on me evermost for being absent in a cave all through this!

Of course it all just paved the way for Jericho Patel and the '30s boom, stability, and the Ultra English Movement, days and nights of shopping and the endless rattle of pnong. Government was suddenly easier. Because the people had changed. They were much more obedient in those years. The rules mattered. Folk thought only within the rules. A chaffinch's curse upon ye, thou dull, vile generation! My own generation, sorry-be-on-me.

The 24 Revolution was a fling of youth, disobedient, foolish. It achieved nothing, solved nothing, as revolutions never do if they just lead to another government. A revolution can never succeed until folk leave their workplaces and homes, never to return, sleeping in the forests and fields, praying, dancing, letting a non-existent God rule their hearts and no man their lives. It may happen yet, may it not, indeed not, never.

The first thing the Patel Government did, I know not why, was to abolish the ancient game of golf. Pnong was the growing rage. Supposy-be, they wanted to focus the country on pnong and pnong alone. Tadese! The hosepipe!

THE PNONG AGE

The Golfing Chaffinch

Quotes of the Century:

'The three greatest evils we face in the world today are disease, despair and golf, and the greatest of these is golf.'
Baron Jurgen Lubitsch, President of the U.S.E. addressing the League of Nations, 2025

'Fellow citizens of Boston, do I look like a golfer, huh?'
Vito King, running for Mayorship of Boston, 2032

'Pnong with everything, that's me!'
Herring Carstairs, ace pnong player, on London Underground poster, 2036

1

Severiano's Day Out

Every morning as I awake humming the same hymn on my pole the flies of this region are having a meeting to decide what they will do with themselves. Of this I am sure! On certain mornings they will vote – for their democratic leanings have survived the century while ours have not – to buzz off and munch on elephant plops. But on certain mornings, like this morning, they vote to annoy the old stylite on his pole. Little red-eyed devils! Still, Saint Hilarion, in his desert, had devils in the form of fashionable naked women of the day to contend with. I am more fortunate, blessed even, with my flies. Squish!

For pilgrims who approach my pole on mornings such as this it must look as if this old bufferoo is kick-boxing with a platoon of invisible angels. For I never give up swatting! I kill hundreds of God's most pestilential creatures, cheehee, until I sink down to sleep with the survivors crawling all over my face. O Lord, thank you, for sending your emissaries, the flies, to beset me! For my barking swatting sessions have kept me fit and strong during my poletop years. 100, and twice the man I was at 50! Except for the dizzinesses, and the inability to stop cackling.

I know what I need, Tadese! A golf club! Awake at dawn, I could be waiting for them, club in hand, and at the first buzz – whooooo! Cheeehaheeeheheee! Swinging with all my might! Swishsquash!

Tadese, pleasy-do, hoof off to Addis Ababa and see if there's a golf club to be had in the market. Go on, man! Cheehe! Oh, and a few balls, too. Why have I never thought of this before? Urk!

*

Tadese, I know very well that when I send you to fetch my golfballs you find them in two minutes then go to sleep under a tree for an hour and a half. It's no use pretending! You disappoint me, Tadese. That rhinoceros was here, so be it. If you'd come back straightaway I'd have had a shot at him. A rhinoceros hit on the head by a golfball! Chee! – Just the sort of thing my cousin Seve might have seen in his dreams.

Poor Seve. I never really liked him. He was too tall to like. But in the face, in a photograph, he looked a lot like me. Only from the front, so be it. From the side he looked like a donkey.

When the European Federal Government finally made golf illegal, in 2032 was it not, following the Patel Law in Britain in the '20s, golfers had nowhere left to go. A whole way of life died out, the greens were dug up, the noble turnip was planted, and the more virulent Pnong Age bit deep. Seve was a junior minister in Godfrey Lowrie's government, first in the Agriculture Department, dealing with the Anti-Corn Law League, the only organ of dissent in those years, if you don't count the Noise Abatement Society, then on the rise. Then, just when we were helping the Germans to conquer Russia, giving them what they called 'breathing space' and us somewhere to put our booming Scottish population, Seve was moved to the War Office. Demanding work. But all he ever thought about was golf, staring out of his window like a schoolboy while Brigadiers queued up outside to see him. He kept golfballs hidden, did he not, even in the War Office, and kissed them when he was alone. At his apartment home he putted into glasses, his only happiness. Had he been glimpsed by the wrong browser on the Everyone Channel, it would have been the end of him. So he did it at dead of night. His great shame.

I myself, I swear, have never hit a golfball until the other day when Tadese fetched me my golfing set, including these itchy tartan trews. But once, having just emerged dirty and peculiar from one of my hideaways I was stopped by an amused policeman on the highway.

'What are you, some sort of golfer?' he said.

Seve met Scampi Lowrie, the Prime Minister's daughter, at the Senate in Brussels on Shrove Tuesday 2037. They had a night on the town, did the sexual intercourse, I think. First time for both. When they came back they became something of an item, as men and women thought quite natural to be in those days, and once Seve brought his girl to show her off at Chaffinch Hall, where I met the darling creature.

Young man on the rise, future Senator, was he not, and the daughter of the current P.M., a man tipped to be European President. All seemed hunky-doo, a pairing of giants. But Scampi was a *pnongista*, a devotee of the dreadful game, and was amazed to hear from Seve . . .

'No, I've never actually so much as been, in person, as t'were.'

'You mean you've never been to the National Pnong Centre?' Total wide-eyed – o those chocolate eyes! – amazement from her.

'Pressure of work, dearie-poopoo.'

'What, don't you like custard!?! Pnong is . . . well, it's pnong!!!'

'I know, Scampi dear, my mouth-watering plate of scampi, my raven-haired scamp, I've just never got into it, that's all.'

'We'll go tonight, indeedybe! It's Carstairs playing the Wibleys.'

'Okaydoos, if you like. Spanky.'

It was the beginning of the end for them that night, was it not indeed, so it was evermost.

The National Pnong Centre was built in 2030 on the site of the old arts complex on London's south bank. After the one in Brazil it was the largest in the world at that time. All glass and white metal, a pnongball motif atop its forty pinnacles, it looked like a futuristic circus tent in which the clowns murdered the audience before the performance. I went myself, several dizzy times, giving out Noise Abatement leaflets, and felt the awe of one visiting a great church of a religion one doesn't belong to.

Seve felt the same. Worse. The overweening hugeness of the place, its hooters and holograms of pnongballs coming at you from every pillar, was an affront to his own unplayable religion: golf. He was only two steps into the mile-long foyer when he said:

'Lookeybee, honeybunch, couldn't we doddle to a concert instead? I'm in the mood to be ear-tingled. Hieronymus Gosh is playing in the park tonight. He's always been one of my favourites.'

'Eugh! Hieronymus Gosh! How passé! How very 2020s of you, Seve, to still think in terms of Hieronymus Gosh! No, no, I'm going to make a pnongista of you if it kills me!'

Scampi was everyone's idea of a beauty just then. Her black hair and her large bony nose, her round belly and fleshy knees gave her a timeless look, ancient-worldish. But in behaviour, with her backslapping, pnong-loving, physical bookless nature, she was more a creature of her times than any, was she not indeed so. I think she had ambitious plans for Seve, to make him her father's successor. And he was well placed to do just that, a junior minister at 25 and at the time of which I cackle still well under 30. But deep within he always knew he'd be found out as a golfer.

The first quarter of the match, with the white pnongballs, had the Wibleys playing themselves, were they not indeed. Three were concussed, leaving 43 on field, their pronged-pnong sticks blunt at this stage. Mild OLÉs from the crowd. Then, the second quarter was announced by blares and hooters, but no OLÉs from the pnongistas until Carstairs came down the water cascade, as simultaneously the black pnongball spat from the end and booled to the squares – a sound like a kitchenette jumping into a taxi. Biggest possible OLÉs! Carstairs, as befitting his fame, had the pnongball under his pnongstick before the Wibleys, whose pnongstick-prongs were now sharp-ended, had got there in sufficient numbers to pnongerize him. He took the pnongball up the red line, but, on the occasion of Seve's one and only visit to a pnongmatch, instead of bucketing the pnongball, he pnonged it back at the Wibleys, knocking one out, and booling five more into the jetstream, whoosh! – thereby losing 35 points. Whistles. Horns. WhrrrrROOOOOOO!!!!

Blares! MahhhhhHHHHHHHHHHH!!!!! Sorrowful boo-whar-HOOOOS! from the crowd, a few OLÉs from the rare Wibley supporters. But, jutting his pozzy into the jetstream, Carstairs showed his mastery of the game by skimming down it into his opponents' sticks in time to get concussed himself, a cracked helmet, a bloody nose, and thereby gaining 10 points for himself. Klaxons, hugemost cheers, warlike OLÉs chanted, as he was carried off, deadly limp, leaving the Wibleys to play themselves for half a quarter. Then Potts, Carstairs' pnongstopper, came on to loud boos, which were moments later un-booed into loud applause when a dozen pnongballs spat from the slats, knocking Potts off his horse, killing him outright on the spikes at the bumpy end, thereby winning 50 points for Carstairs and probably the President's Cup as well. And all the time noise, lights flashing, and on the roof, which was a massive screen a mile long, highlights showing a bleeding nostril, a screaming mouth, a pnongball hitting a Wibley in the guts, and finally Potts's last gasp, before Cairstairs' encomium of his underling from the sanatorium under the Pnong Centre, a further trick, cos halfway through he surprised the Wibleys by shooting out of a tunnel, to stamping applause, a pnongstick in each hand, bucketing a black, two reds and a brown, to take the match 841–5. Brilliant!

And with the final horn gone, Carstairs attacked a Wibley he didn't like, caving in his helmet with a pnongball, to polite applause from the other Wibleys, and no admonition from the referees, all four of whom were lying concussed in the sanatorium, having knocked heads with pnongballs in the second quarter. Then Carstairs stripped down to his g-string, to show off his bruises on the big screen, and rode a bicycle around the auditorium, scattering Wibleys in his usual dashing style, his crooked moustache and broken teeth every girl's dream. He was easily, the greatest player of the game ever, and the only one to survive more than three seasons.

While all this was going on Scampi was doing her best to explain the baffling rules of pnong to Seve, who was never good with details, as any Brigadier would attest, but who was nodding, twitching and a-ha-ing, keen for Scampi's sake to show his fascination with a game he secretly hated because he loved another.

'It's rhubarb, spanky-doos! Pnong is rhubarb. Rhubarb is pnong!' cried Scampi, delighted that her boy was getting hooked. And at every exciting moment she would lift up her jumper and thrust Seve's head inside. She did the same thing with several complete strangers, men, women and children, in the stand around them. But one man, she avoided. A long pale man in a spotty cap with a red pompom on the top, the only such headgear on any of the 100,000 heads at the match. He gave Scampi the shivers. She squirted herself with extra perfume and accidentally got him in the eye with it.

'Watch out for that mildewed article, Seve.'

But he thought she was referring to one of the Wibleys, so when the man, almost as tall as himself, nudged him in the back, he just smiled at him in his usual faraway way. Then the man nudged him again.

'Scusy-be, Citizen, but did I hear the young bint there call you Seve?'

While watching Carstairs do his false-bucket stop: 'Seve, yes. I say, this Carstairs is really too-too, don't you think?'

'That would be short for Severiano.'

'Um? Yes. OLÉ!'

'You'd be a Spanish gentleman, is it, Citizen?'

'No-doos. I was named after a friend of my father.'

'I see. First time to a pnongmatch, Citizen?'

'Erm, yes. Pressure of work, pleasy-do.'

'Rhubarb?'

'Yes, of course. Extra spanky-do rhubarb on it evermost, pnong is. Too-too.'

'You surprise me, Seve – may I call you Seve? I've never called anyone Seve before. It's just when I look at these others, and then look at you, well, you just don't seem quite so genuine in your enthusiasm, if you doesn't mind an observation from a stranger wif a nose for these things.' He held out his hand. 'Skipper's the name. Golf.'

'Um? Wot? Eh?'

'Triple sorries, Citizen?'

'You said! Just then! You said!'

'Skipper's the name.'

He held out his hand again. Seve shook it, highly per-turbed, more so when Skipper coughed and in his cough, Seve was sure: 'Urgchghg-Golf.'

Excitement on the field. Seve and this Skipper per-son both OLÉ'd for a bit, but all was just a blur to Seve. Then, suddenly, Scampi, frowning, cut off her own OLÉs and dragged Seve down a few steps, right under a horn. Safe!

'Do watch out, Seve! There's dozens of those Noise Abatement jonnies whiffling about looking for new members. Isn't Carstairs an egg-custard!'

But the man in the cap whispered in Seve's ear. How? When he was twenty feet away in a noisy crowd. Seve looked about, his face like a mule's when stuck on a ledge.

What was the mildewed article whispering? Sounded like 'sugo'. Sugo? Sugo?

'I say, do stoppit!' yelled Seve.

'No, he must do that,' informed Scampi, chocolate eyes on the match, 'Or the horse will score on its own.'

'Fancy a game?' whispered Skipper.

'PNONG! PNONG!' yelled Seve, almost in a manly swoon.

'Wibley-WIBLEY-WIBLEY! BOOOOOOOO! YAAAAAA!'

'S.U.G.O. Secret Underground Golfing Organization.'

Seve's heart leaped. His pale face went red in an instant. In the general excitement he put his head under a woman's jumper, not Scampi's. In there he hid his sly golfer's grin. Anyone, even those who never gave golf a thought, would have recognized it as a sly golfer's grin.

A whisper between strange bosoms: 'Can you hear me, Mr Skipper?'

'I'm here, Seve.'

'It's the real thing your talking about, not mini-golf in some manky warehouse off the M4?'

'Oooh, yes, Seve, we've all done that, haven't we? No, this is real golf, 18 holes, fairways, bunkers, the greenest of greens. We have a secret place, a golfing Heaven, my friend.'

Seve came out of the woman's jumper with tears in his eyes. Scampi was thrilled to see those tears: she thought they were for the lately deceased Potts.

Then the voice in Seve's ear: 'Be at the Thatcher Memorial at 10 tomorrow morning, pleasy-do. One of our people will meet you. Doo-byedeedarr, Seve.'

Seve looked at the man in shuddering delight. Golf! If he met a man tomorrow morning he could play golf! Skipper shouted some OLEs as Carstairs came back on to win the match, then retreated through the yelling crowd.

'Mr Skipper! Mr Skipper!' cried Seve in ecstasy. 'Thank you!'

Skipper doffed his cap, opened his mouth – there was a golfball gripped between his teeth. Seve guffawed. 'Too-too!' Then Skipper skimmed his cap at Seve and was gone. The device which had enabled him to speak to his confederate went beep loudly as it signed off.

Scampi, meanwhile, was so excited at Carstairs's victory, and the sight of his almost nude heavily-bruised body, that she had wee-weed herself. She was wiggling in discomfort as the warm liquid cooled stickily, when she saw Seve grinning down on her wearing that hideous cap. It wasn't a golfer's grin, but too-too nearly.

'SEVE!' Her hair flapped like a wing.

Seve took it off by its pom-pom, almost going eeeee-awwww in fright at her violent reaction to his new cap. Had he given himself away? Not knowing what else to do with it he skimmed the dangerous cap out towards the field. It sailed over the glass partition, small in life, but for a last moment of glory huge on the screen, before dropping onto the field on the red line itself, right before Carstairs' bicycle wheel. The great hero looked up at where the cap had come from, his face suddenly slapped with animal fear, up on the big screen too, a fear never seen on that much-photographed face before. The crowd thought he was pulling faces.

Seve and Scampi stayed after all the crowd had gone home. They committed the sexual intercourse, right there on the littered steps under the scoreboard, in a haze of coral-pink perfume. Scampi had never felt Seve so passionate, with such laughter in his kisses. It was pnong! He was hooked! He was a pnongista, was he not, indeed so, never.

*

Quick, Tadese! It's him, the rhinoceros, he's back! Find me a ball, quickly!

2

Scampi on the Lawn

In the late '30s we went all Roman Empire. What a craze it was! Even I, did I not, when I left my peaceful cave, cast off my monkish robe and took to wearing a toga. I introduced myself as *fringella coelebs fringella coelebs*, which is Latin for Chaffinch said twice. Then one time I sallied out and no one was doing it anymore. I was so disappointed I nearly cried. I had enjoyed it, pleasy-do, playacting being a Roman. I spent many happy afternoons in a toga.

The height of the Roman craze coincided with all that pothery-do concerning my cousin Severiano and his golf, and also with my most curious ever religious experience. I was making my way down the English coast, all the way from Northumberland to Suffolk, dressed as I have described, looking like a survivor of the lost legion. Getting closer to home, in Fen country, I was admiring the roadside flowers on a fine morning, late May was it not, when one of those flying-hat-floating-cars zoomed over my head. A gun came out of its flap and I felt myself shot, tranquillized, with the flat landscape flicking at me like the pages of a book of photographs of this same landscape. Grogged, muttering, I had a sensation of being carried up a hill, and the good Lord was with me. Fact was, dearie-be, I had been kidnapped by four large plump girls, theology students, future bishops all.

Just then, long before the fervour which climaxed in the Christian churches assuming total power in our European countries, there was a falling-off of interest in religion, and Christianity particularly so. It was hard to get good people to be vicars or priests. The clergy comprised of terrifying women with too much hair, such as my kidnappers aimed so to be, or sinister men with an eye on history.

61

I awoke to sense in Ely Cathedral during the service in which I was compulsorily ordained. My old friend from the ashram, Brother Bromley, was now Bishop of Ely and he had hatched the whole evil plot. The dear girls had been patrolling the roads for weeks hoping to find me. That was that, so be it. I was an Anglican priest!

'Sorry to do it this way,' chuckled Bromley. 'But I am sure it is God's will. His church needs you.'

I took communion angrily from his red bishoply hands, then went outside and sat in the cloister. One of the girls gave me a bag of pears. I ate pears and wept. I was inconsolable. I don't actually-be remember why I was so deeply upset. But I was. At that year's Festival of Melancholia, how many cups would I have won? Oy! The girls tried everything to cheer me up. Two ended up in tears themselves. Two grew angry and took it out on each other.

Then suddenly, I stopped. I stared at one of the girls, and as the blur of tears cleared from my eyes, my look was that of a lascivious bird. The look frightened her. It frightened me! A priest for only minutes, was I not, and already entirely corrupt. – But I'd been such a good little monk! Was this another truth I had stumbled upon? Were priests automatically of the Devil's cohort, never God's? The justly frightened girl ran for it, all the way around the cloister, and I grinned as I listened to her patting feet, grinned wider as I experienced an entirely expected stiffening. I was 37 years old, Tadese, and had never lain with a women, and barely stood up with one. Be I priest, monk, bird or egg sandwich, the time was ripe for a grand passion. A week later I met Scampi Lowrie.

Scampi had known Seve only two months when he brought her down to Chaffinch Hall for an afternoon's toga party. They were very giggly. He wore a knee-length praetor's outfit in which, at six feet eight, he looked a total Jilks! He went off with Cod's gang to discuss the Russian Expedition, leaving Scampi on the lawn with me. I loved her already, with a passion that hasn't dimmed in the 62 years since that perfect English June, that Sunday on the lawn. Oh, God!

We were eating cakes piggadoodleishly from the several

cake trees on the picnic blanket around us. Scampi had a
cake in each hand, biting them alternatively. So charming.
We hadn't yet spoken except to say howdeedoodee. She
had cream all around her lips. Did I say she was wearing
a false moustache? – a tribute to her pnong hero, Carstairs.
Suddenly she finished an éclair and said:

'It's so custard that there's no poor people anymore!'

'I'd been wondering where they'd got to.'

'Daddy's policies.'

'Ogh, of course!' I hadn't till then realized she was 'that'
Scampi Lowrie.

'They're all scudding about in togas, doing pleasy-do! Piggn
shower, all of them, the whole world, a piggn shower. I don't
know what I'd dobee-do if it wasn't for pnong.' Then her
chocolate eyes closed and, astonishingly, two more eyes
were staring, painted on her lids. 'And Seve, of course! I'd
just die without Seve!' A huge laugh, as booming as my old
Guru's, then soft, almost a whisper, fluttering all her eyes:
'You're some sort of saint, Seve says.'

'No, no, I'm most terribly wicked, indeedybe.'

I'd made her laugh!

Still laughing, snatching a half-eaten cake from me: 'Too-
too – and you're greedier than I am!'

To prove her right I stuffed a huge meringue straight in
my cakehole, some of its bits falling down into the folds of my
toga, from where Scampi's purple fingernails fetched them to
her own mouth. This intimacy brought on me a hot shyness
I thought I'd left in my twenties. We said not a word for ten
minutes. She lay down on her elbow and was, I thought,
about to go to sleep. Then:

'Seve tells me you keep lunatics in your roof?'

'Hardlymost, lunatics. Just poor troubled souls who are
best suited to solitude, are they not? One, in fact, is the
head of the Chaffinch family.'

'Oah, I thought you were!'

'Not quite. When my bro Robin died I thought myself to
be the seniormost Chaffinch, but was then introduced to my
secret bro Wilf, my elder brother, born in 1995, whose
existence thereforeto no one had bothered to mention to

me. Remarkable fellow, Wilf. He's never left his attic room but he's handled the family finances since he was twelve. He's made us the third richest family in England and he does it all by betting on horseracing, and now pnong, of course.'

'Too-too! Sounds a custard.'

Then I pointed out bro Wilf, who was howling at his window.

'Doesn't he have girls sent in?'

'Girls? Wot for? Oh!'

'Dearie-be, you must get him some, poor thinggy-do! Because, you Chaffinches, if Seve's anything to go by, are worse than Scotsmen.'

This led us on to a discussion of the Scots population problem, which already, like all problems as soon as they are recognized as such, was unsolvable. There were 500 million Scotsmen in 2037 – and rising! Fast! Aberdeen was suddenly a bigger city than London. They'd taken over the depopulated Wales, the plague-emptied Belgium, and were now waiting for the Ukraine which they were to share with the Germans. Their in-built inevitable majority in the European Parliament was infuriating the other countries, who foresaw the day when they would all be provinces of Scotland. Indeedybe, with those millions of Scottish votes it was only Godfrey Lowrie's half-pint of Dumfriesshire blood and come-now-gone-then bogus Scottish accent that gave him any chance at being elected President with, we all hoped, and I urinate in shame to admit it, some secret agenda involving getting rid of Scotsmen altogether.

But we were sitting on an English lawn in the heart of England. The howling of Scots babies, the grate of the sharpening of claymores did not reach our ears. We heard only chaffinches pirruping in the trees, and each other.

'What about you, greedier-than-me?' said greedy girl Scampi. 'You ever thought of going in for politics? I'm sure daddy could find you something.'

I don't know why I said it, the truth just spoke itself: 'What would daddy say if he knew I was the leader of the '24 Revolution?'

She put down her cake and her hair flapped like a wing. A

storm on her face. Little lines on her brow. Then she caught
sight of Seve and other Romans arguing by the pool. She
pushed out her belly, scratched it, and smiled.

'Seve's too-too evermost.'

'Too-too!' I said.

Then the storm returned. 'Well, YOU'VE seen me! Does
HE need to see me as well?'

She was thumbing at bro Wilf, still howling high above.
Ah, so that was it! She thought Seve was bringing her here
to see the head of the family, for approval, for judgement,
in preparation for marriage.

I birdied my arms and tweeted. Had I flipp-oed! She
thought so.

'You'll have to learn how to do that,' I said. 'If you want
to be a Chaffinch.'

Instead of laughing, she pouted. She tore off her false
moustache and threw it into one of the few remaining cakes.
I have that moustache yet, in my little bag of treasures in
Tadese's hut. Then she grabbed my old pooch, who was
limping grumpily by, and hugged him, weeping. He never
liked being hugged and kept growling, but she hugged so
tight he felt too overpowered to bite.

I stroked her hair, oooh, for only five minutes, but it is,
truly, Tadese, my happiest memory of this life. Thankyou,
O Lord.

Of course, just as I loved Scampi, Scampi loved Seve.
But she knew that something somewhere was wrong, that
calamity was shadowing her postman. She didn't suspect golf.
Who could have suspected it would be as bad as that? But
her instincts told her that life would not go well for her and
Seve, and it did not, indeed so, evermost not.

Two weeks passed after the toga party, in which time I sat
in my tree house, drenched by summer showers, thinking
only of my Scampi! Seve's Scampi! First Citizen Lowrie's
Scampi! Scampi! Scampi! I was living in a new world of
special pains and joys. Then, late one evening, Big Norris
brought a phone up to the tree house. It was Seve.

'Lookybe, cuz, couldn't do a beanpole a favour, wotaroo?'

I didn't understand a word.

'I'm due to meet my delicious plate of Scampi morrow-morning, but I've this piggn emergency meeting on at 10 with two dozen brigadiers. Pleasy-do, evermost thankfully, look after my little pot-bellied Scamp for me.'

'Well, I . . .'

'She won't mind you being me, she says you're a breeze.'

'She said that? A breeze?'

'You'll find her under Admiralty Arch at 10-sharp in her Scampimobile. Evermost, cuz. Rhubarb of you. Do-byedeedarr!'

I'd never been so grateful to anyone in my life. He'd fixed me up a date with Scampi!

'What article are you?' said Seve's delicious plate of Scampi from the wheel of her Scampimobile, grim as a Jesuit.

'A replacement Chaffinch. Seve's doing politics.'

She flung open the door. 'Flap in, then!'

But her Roman outfit was flimsy, with one bosom quite bare. I was afraid to approach too close to her nakedness. That fault of my youth commanded me: I dithered. The Pentateuch scrolled before my eyes.

'PIGGN GET IN!!!'

I got in.

Scampi and Seve had planned to visit the Loch Ness Monster, just recently discovered, in its tank at the Wembley Drome. It was only appearing there for a month before returning to its permanent tank in Inverness. So off she went to see the thing with her replacement Chaffinch. Sadly, when we arrived, it was quite dead, died alone the night before while its attendants were screaming OLÉ at the pnongmatch. There it was, a thing so lately a monster, floating belly-up in yellowish water to which tearful Scotsmen, up and down ladders in their revealing kilts, were adding pickling vinegar, making the water yellower and yellower.

Scampi stood twiddling the end of her bare bosom, her head tilted this way or that to examine the monster's sorry features. She was so fascinated that she forgot, for minutes perhaps, that she was with Chaff and not Seve. Joy! The poor monster suddenly turned a bit in its tank and everyone screamed, me too, but not Scampi. I started saying a prayer for it.

'Don't be daft!' woofed Scampi.

I desisted, said the prayer in my head instead.

Seve, meanwhile, was crosstown, sealing his fate, looking for a Johnny with a golfball smile.

3

The Golfing Chaffinch

In the late '50s, when Seve was long gone, was he not, his clone used to televisit me quite often. Clone Seve was obsessed with the day he visited Golf Island, or rather when his original did. Again and again he described it to me. I listened and smiled. Sometimes he tossed a golfball at me and I tried to catch it, but of course it was bouncing on a floor far away. I could never get used to the televisitor. I always believed in its illusion. Other illusions also, which is why I have remained so long at the same spiritual level.

10. A.M., June 14th, 2037. Cuz Seve, overlong and anxiousmost, was pacing around the Thatcher Memorial, tripping over the leads of the many basset hounds to be found in that quarter of the 5th most populous city on Earth (after Glasgow, Edinburgh, Aberdeen and Djakarta). He kept smiling at strangers, lips parted, ready to show the golfball holed in his cakehole. He spied a man in checked trousers. That's my man! thought Seve.

He poked and prodded the man in an effort to provoke him into smiling. But the man hadn't a smile in him. Chehe!

At last the ruffled man said: 'Piggn bug it, Citizen, yer mad sausage, or poosy-wiff on you evermost!' And having so spoken he'd proved his tongue curled around no golfball.

Another citizen, sitting innocently picking his nose, looked a likely golfer. Seve was hovering over this article, grinning, clacking his ball against his teeth, worrying the citizen no end, when a powerful finger poked him in the sides. He swallowed his golfball and turned around for a further surprise.

'He's not your 10 o'clock, Citizen. I am. Harh!' said this agent of S.U.G.O.

Seve pecked the air like a chicken, gasping: 'Hey, you're

Herring Carstairs, the famous pnong player!' This in a voice every basset hound for a hundred yards could hear.

An agitated Carstairs swallowed his golfball also.

'Dimmee! That's the fourth time I've done that in I dunno how long. Hush the blitherooney, citizen. Don't want me being mobbed, do we, harh, harh.'

'But . . . you? YOU? My 10 o'clock? But . . .'

'I'm your man!' And he did something weird with his stomach muscles, burped, and up came the golfball between his teeth. He chortled so much at this feat that he swallowed it again.

Seve tried it also, but couldn't get it to work.

Linking arms like best pals, they clicked through the streets with Carstairs talking out of the side of his wicked moustache: 'My pnong career's only a front, gemmee? My real passion, my only devotion, is one we share.'

'Golf, you mean?'

Again, too loud. A basset barked at them. They took fright and made a dash for it across Hyde Park, hundreds of pnong fans, bassets and police chasing after them, all screaming, barking and whistling: 'Look! It's Herring Carstairs, the famous pnong player!'

They took refuge behind foliage in the foyer of the Toblerone Building.

'Harh, harh,' went Carstairs, and winked one of his black eyes.

'You didn't arf take a beating in yesterday's pnongings,' said a concerned Seve.

'Custard, wasn't I, harh! Jilks, but you gave old H.C. a horror-horn when you tossed that rascally cap at me! Thought I'd been tumbled golfwise.'

'Triple sorries on you evermost.'

'Too-too. Erm, dimmee, but this is us.'

'What?'

'Toblerone Building. My whizzycopter's on the roof. We're taking off . . . for the Island.'

'Island? But . . . a quick round, I thought, an hour on the putting green. I'm a junior minister, you know. I'll be missed. And I'm having tea with Scampi at the Pinero Rooms at 4.'

70

Carstairs raised his only eyebrow. 'Golf,' he said.

It was enough.

I had a whizzycopter once. I flew around the Hall in it shrieking hymns. It was essentially a bicycle with a set of rotor blades on top and behind. They were powered by a signal sent from the whizzycopter factory in Basingstoke. But if anything went wrong with the signal, which it often did, all whizzycopters everywhere simply fell out of the air. Carstairs was so beaten up to start with that a copter crash didn't worry him. Anyway, due to his frequent blackouts, he'd crashed a hundred times but had always walked away.

Off they whizzed, over the towns of England. Sometimes Carstairs swooped low over a bunch of boys playing pnong as rough as they dared on some square of field.

'Look! Look! It's Herring Carstairs, the famous pnong player!'

'Harh! Harh! Dimmee, if every blasted chipolata in the land don't ken my fizz, wot! Harh!'

Their destination was somewhere off the coast of Scotland, three hours whizzing time, and as Carstairs never went three straight hours without a blackout, the subject had to come up.

'Erm, I hate to mention this at this altitude, Citizen Golfer, but you can fly one of these buzzards, can't you, I mean, being in the War Office and rhubarb?'

'First time up, fraidy-do,' admitted Seve.

'Harh! You see, all the pnongings, given me these piggn blackouts, dyersee. No worries. If you see me nod off, just keep poking me behind the ears with one of those long fingers of yours, harh. But if we go into a spin, harh, reach over and push the red switcheroo.'

This was the moment when Seve, in his anxieties, brought up that golfball. It bombed to earth.

'Well done,' said Carstairs and continued his instructions. 'It activates one of those new personal forcefield things. I'm having one put up my bottom for the next pnongmatch, harh. Sod those Wibleys! But I hesitate to use it after the scandals!'

This scandalous forcefield device was brought in to help

71

the fight against crime. Fit one in your hat, belt or basset, and when a mugger comes up to you, just turn it on and he can't get at you, or within a foot of you, be he armed with every weapon ever devised. But some people had had trouble turning theirs off, a few dying inside their forcefield, of thirst and/or suffocation, an evermostly unpleasant exit from life. However, on this occasion, the forcefield was a Godsend, as Citizen Carstairs had 23 blackouts between Birmingham and Gretna Green. They crashed 11 times, but the red switcheroo was indeedybeed pushed by a screaming Chaffinch, who continued poking the pnong hero frantically behind the ear as they bounced across fields in their forcefield, skittling sheep.

When Carstairs came to after the 23rd blackout, he could only laugh.

'Harh, harh. Still alive and whizzing, I see. No custard spewed!' And then he blacked out again.

But the sea air off the Hebrides cleared the clots from his brainstem and he was shedding his violent pnongista personality, becoming Carstairs the calm pullover-wearing golfer.

'That's us!' he said. 'Thar she blows!'

Seve was close to breaking point. His long bony legs had been held akimbo for three hours, to keep away from the spinning spokes of the whizzycopter's back wheel. Now his pilot was flying him directly at a wall of guillemot-infested cliffs.

'There's no Golf Island!' Seve screamed! 'You're piggn mad! It's just cliffs, rocks and seaweed!'

'Peely-doos your eyes, Citizen, harh!'

With a screaming goodbye to life from Seve, his eyes screwed, not peeled at all, they flew through the cliffs, and then the starved golfer's confused peep gave him a brief vision of golfing heaven – fairways, greens, men in tartan trews on putting greens, waving, putting, shaking fists.

Then it was gone and they were in greys and blues again, swooping around the island past hard-nosed sheep that totally ignored their irritating whizzing. A golfless world they were in: rocks, cliffs, the gabble of guillemots.

'Little invention of Citizen Macmacpherson's, harh,' drawled Carstairs. 'Buoys in the sea, dyersee, connected by cables, create an electrical field which projects hologramismically a false image into the air, giving the illusion of an entirely different island, harh. Rocky cliffs and patches of heather, when wot's really down there is golfing heaven. It fools the police helicopters every time. Harh!'

'Spanky-doos!' said Seve, his eyes peeled as they flew through the illusion once more. Greens! Fairways! The swoop of golfclubs! A sliced ball went right underneath his feet!

But he should have been watching Carstairs, who'd had another blackout. The red switcheroo remained unpushed, they missed the landingstrip by a good 300-yard drive and crashed in a bunker on the 12th.

Tadese! I'll have my bananas now, pleasy-do.

*

I was speaking about the Mufti War, was I not, and my nephew September? Triple sorries, Tadese . . . Seve! Tootoo, poor Seve! No, he did not perish in the whizzycopter crash. Had he done so, what a different world we would be in today!

Seve awoke in the clubhouse. He was coughing up a golfball, though as he'd only ever swallowed one, which he'd already coughed up over Watford, he couldn't understand where this extra one came from. The soft Scots voice and unwashed smell of a girl was all around him. But all he could see was silver, shining silver, and a dozen distorted ginger faces growing and melting in silver. He was looking at the trophy cabinet.

'Scampi!' he cried. 'I must have my delicious plateful of Scampi!'

They fetched him some. It was forced between his teeth. He sucked fingers like a babe. Then, suddenly, he found himself clearheaded, wearing the most rascally trews he'd ever seen, a cashmere sweater and tartan cap.

A huge ginger man, whose nose was redder than his hair, was sitting opposite him scratching his kilt and making Scottish noises.

'T'were a goooood job ye hit that bunker, laddie. If ye'd carved up yon greens I'd have taken it mightily bad, y'ken. I treat them like bairns, y'ken.'

Seve instantly fell in with the bogus Scottish accent of his future father-in-law. 'Och, aye the noo, old sport. I kens your drift. Hoots!'

From the man: a Scottish noise signifying something not quite right with Seve, the world, or both.

'Scusbe, Citizen, the noo, but are you Citizen Macmacpherson?'

'Och, no. Citizen Macmacpherson was scattered on the 18th last July. I'm Birdie Lumphanan, Chief Groundsman. Now, shall we play some golf, laddie?

'Too-too the noo!'

Seve strode out of the clubhouse as happy as any man ever was in this troubled century of ours. He had been granted a rare gift – he had left his own world, and found another. We all hope to do this, do we not, when life has left our eyes.

A caddy miraculously appeared behind him, doffing his cap, Groundsman Lumphanan led the way to the 1st tee, where a little group of golfers stood applauding them in. Carstairs was among them. The sky was so blue! The greens so green!

'This here's Citizen Severiano Chaffinch, who's the guest of Citizen Carstairs. He'll be showing us what he can do!'

'Rascally trews, Seve!' said Carstairs.

The group gathered around the tall young golfer and shook his hand. Then suddenly they parted and left Seve alone with his ball.

'A number two wooden brassie, thinky-doos, for a big hitter,' said Seve, golferishly.

The caddy pulled out of the bag this very thing, did he not? Seve took the club, his hands shaking with excitement, tried it for balance, then did a practice swing. Sounds of general approval from the other golfers.

He was about to hit his tee shot, aiming over the little loch, directly at the green, when he suddenly fell forwards, propping himself up with his club, sobbing uncontrollably.

Carstairs walked off in embarrassment. If his guest was

a cissy-poo, it reflected badly on him. Macho-pnongista at
heart was Carstairs.

'Are ye going tae tee off or just lollop there bubblin, laddie?'
Birdie Lumphanan displayed a heart of old porridge.

'I'm sorry, the noo, everyone, please. It's just, you see,
I haven't played on a real course in such a long time, hoots!
– and . . . well, it's my father. He got me started on golf,
d'yersee. This, today, the noo, it reminds me so much of
the first time he took me to his club, meeting all his golfing
friends.' Deep choking sobs. 'When they banned golf, he just
pined away.'

This is true. My uncle Derek Chaffinch was a keen golfer.
We even had a few holes at the Hall in those early days. After
the banning of the game he rarely left his rooms. Then he
stayed a-bed, reading old golfing periodicals. As Seve said,
without his golf, he just pined away.

Birdie Lumphanan was encouraging a tweedy old stick to
comfort the sad Seve.

'I will not!' she said.

'Ye're a woman, Mrs Crowhurst. Let the laddie poot his
head on your boozom, will ye no?'

'I will not!' Another heart of old porridge.

The embarrassed Carstairs was sent to fetch Moira
Macmacpherson, daughter of the great inventor lately
scattered on the 18th. She was in the rough, looking
for balls. Carstairs rakishly led her back to the first tee
by the hand.

'Moira, lassie,' said Birdie, his old porridge heart gone
mushy, tears on the way, so moved was he by Seve's woeful
golfing story, 'Will ye no comfort the poor laddie?'

'Rhubarb-spanky-doos. Just poot your head here fella and
awa wi yon owrie thoughts.'

That soft voice! That unwashed smell! It was she, the girl
from his semi-consciousness. He bent double to get to her
level, hugged her and sobbed against her bosom.

Birdie started whacking at his thick red legs hard with a
club.

'The ruined lives! The wasted lives!' he cried. 'Ayeeeeeee!
Those people! THEY say what's best fae us! So nae mair

golf! Pnong! PNONG! and mair PNONG!' He said the word
with spitting hatred and looked at an uncomfortable Carstairs
while he said it. 'Pnong's a part of their New World Order, and
golf tissent. They tak awar our bonny game and mak us live in
their pnongball world! But what about our world? My world,
the world old Macmacpherson dreamed of when he drew his
plans for new golfcourses – ayeeeee, but he kenned they'd
never feel a golfer's tread. The poor unborn bairns!'

He was in a ginger fit of manly emotion and turned to
Mrs Crowhurst, arms outstretched for comfort.

'I will not!' she said.

Meanwhile, Seve was well comforted. He raised his blub-
some face from Moira's bosom and looked into her eyes.

'Thankys, rhubarbthankymost, for comforting me, Miss.'

It was one of those moments of recognition, when two
people who will mean much in each other's lives, step out
of time and see each other for who they will be. Moira's
face trembled, her bosom lifted with a huge breath, and she
kissed Seve passionately on his tear-wet lips, did she not.

'Harh!' went Carstairs.

But Birdie was perturbed. He lifted his ample kilt over
their heads. Had Hugh MacTaggart, Moira's betrothed, seen
the kiss, there'd have been a brawl, which MacTaggart could
only win. Moira's and Seve's kiss ended abruptly under the
kilt, as soon as they realized where they were. When they
surfaced, tidying their hair, smiling embarrassedly, Scampi
was forgotten, Hugh MacTaggart merely an old flame.

It was with a new heart that Seve teed off, to rapturous
applause. Another kiss from Moira, a peck this time.

'Championship shot!' said Mrs Crowhurst.

Seve picked the old stick up and span her around, plopping
her down in exactly the place to make her tee-shot. She
did so, without a trace of anything on her face, as if a
six-feet-eight beanpole lifted her onto the tee every day.

But when she'd whacked the ball she said, a sly disruptive-
ness in her tone: 'Birdie, have you told our newboy about the
Indians yet?'

Worried Scottish noise from Birdie.

'We'd better tell him,' said Carstairs, suppressing a harh.

'He doesn't want tae know!'

Carstairs teed off while a reluctant Birdie spilled the custard.

'It's nothing tae be concerned aboot, laddie. Only a fault in old Macmacpherson's computer programme, that which makes the pretend cliffs and hides oor island, y'ken.'

'Och aye the noo,' responded Seve watching Moira pulling up her socks.

'Aye, well, the programme has these Red Indians in it, that appear from time tae time. Macmacpherson poot them in tae poot his opponents off their shot, y'ken. But now the programme's full of them. Arapahos, I'm told. If it should so happen that ye see any, dinnae fret, laddie, just look the other way. They'll shoot arrows at ye, but they're all just hologramismic images, they canna hurt ye.'

'What aboot the man we found scalped on the 10th green on Thursday?' wondered Moira.

'Aye, I'm looking intae that,' said Birdie and sliced his ball as he teed off, blaming Moira's scalped man for the slice, because someone was always to blame.

These were the happiest hours of Seve's life. Not only was he playing golf, but – and he'd never given this a thought in all his secret criminal golfing cravings – he was good at it! Better than good! He was only one under par on the first, but two under on each of the next three. Birdie was mumbling that Macmacpherson's course record was under threat.

Seve was blithe. Seve helped Moira with her swing. Seve went harh better than Carstairs, who was 10 over par. Seve was the apple of Mrs Crowhurst's eye. Seve was universally admired. He was, at last, himself: a golfer! There were long moments between shots when he stared at the golfing landscape, with its distant putting figures, its bunkers and trees, and he couldn't believe he was there. Somewhere, in the back of his mind, was the rattling noise of a pnongball going down the red line, a sound forever in Carstairs's ears. How evil a sound that was compared to . . . Birdie cursing cos he was in the rough again.

But on the 18th green the perfect day's golfing was spoiled.

'Hole this, laddie, and ye've eagled the hole and beat the course record!' said Birdie, biting his fist.

Carstairs was so anxious that his guest should do well that he coughed up three golfballs.

But Seve was being distracted.

'I can't possibly concentrate on my putting with THEM there!'

'Ignore them, laddie!'

'And they're chasing that man! They're shooting arrows at him!'

'He's no a real man, laddie, d'yeken. That's Mr Fairburn. He's a hologramismic image, just like them. Had on – mak yer shot!'

Seve put his thumb on the bridge of his nose, a gesture he'd seen Prime Minister Lowrie make before a crucial decision. Then he attempted the shot. He missed.

Just before his putter contacted with the ball, Mr Fairburn ran onto the green with three arrows in his back, yelling: 'Help! Help! Arapahos! They've killed everyone! I've phoned for the Cavalry in Fort William!' Then he fell face down, his eyes going crossed as they focused on Seve's un-holed ball.

'Dimmee!!! It was that piggn Fairburn's fault!' Seve's first golfing disappointment, and a severe one.

'Ne're mind, laddie! One mair shot and ye've equalled the course record!'

'All right, the noo,' said Seve, and addressed the ball.

But he couldn't do it. The putting green was surrounded by whooping Arapahos. Arrows were whistling past his ears. And when poor Mrs Crowhurst took an arrow right in her bosom, falling backwards in the corner of Seve's eye, he walked away from the ball with a gesture of defeat.

Birdie was getting desperate. 'Mak the shot! It's the only way they'll go away!'

'I absolutely refuse to make an important shot under these conditions.'

'Of course, ye're right. Tell ye what, just form a circle, wi yer backs to them, ignore the whoopin beasties and they'll gan awar.'

They followed Birdie's advice, except for Mrs Crowhurst, whose death didn't fit into any sensible scenario. When, despite their efforts at ignoring the Arapahos, all their caddies had slouched, arrows in their backs, and Carstairs cheerfully announced that he had one in his pozzy, Birdie was making Scottish noises he'd never made before.

'Ayeeee-eeeee-orrru-ochghghghgh – eahy, perhaps, tae be on the safe side, we'd better tak cover in the nearest bunker.'

They ran for it. Carstairs was hit twice more, but just laughed. They dived into the bunker, rolling in the sand. Moira and Seve ended up in each other's arms.

'We're safe here,' panted Birdie. 'They're only programmed for the greens and the trees.'

But arrows were whistling overhead and some fizzed down into the sand. Seve picked one up. It looked real to him.

Moira's soft brave voice: 'They're no going away this time, Birdie. It feels different.'

Yes-no-maybe Scottish noises from Birdie, then emphatically: 'They'll disperse. They always do!'

Seve and Moira were enjoying a farewell kiss.

'This has been the happiest day of my life,' Seve told her. 'Golf, putting, swinging, teeing-off – and you, darlingmost Moira!'

She felt his stringy bicep.

'If we survive this ordeal, will ye fight Hugh MacTaggart over me?' Her cheeks glowed red with pride at the prospect.

'I'll fight every Scotsman on earth, be they all as big as Goliath!'

And there, as the Arapahos circled preparing for their final attack, Moira undid Seve's trews, lifted her tartan skirt, and they shamelessly committed the sexual intercourse in the yielding sand. Such physical joy! Such spiritual delight in two souls united in love!

Carstairs watched with twitching moustache. Birdie, a good Presbyterian, covered his eyes with sand and waited glumly for the Arapahos.

Instead, the sound of a helicopter!

At the moment of shared shuddering ecstasy Seve and Moira looked up. Birdie shook the sand from his eyes. Even his freckles went pale. It was a police helicopter.

A voice like a megaphone talking through another megaphone: 'STAY WHERE YOU ARE! YOU ARE ALL UNDER ARREST! THIS IS THE POLICE! STAY WHERE YOU ARE!'

'Och, that boobie Fairburn, when he phoned for the cavalry, he'd phoned for the police at Fort William! We're doomed in a different way. Och, mae poor bairns – they'll plough ye brown and plant their turnips. Aye, turnips, the shape and size of PNONGBALLS!'

With a Jacobite yell Birdie scrambled out of the bunker and ran at the Arapahos, swinging his putter and shaking a fist.

Seve was ruined. His political career over. He would within minutes be arrested and charged with being a golfer. But he didn't seem to care. He snuggled deep in the sand and snoggerood with his new love, did he not. They smiled at each other. He picked everso green grass from her everso flaming ginger hair.

'I love you, Moira Macmacpherson.'

'Och, Seve – I love you too!'

As they flew away in the helicopter, cuffed beside a half dozen Arapahos, they had a brief glimpse of golfing heaven, and of Birdie Lumphanan lying in the middle of the 18th green, his chest full of arrows, the little 18 flag flapping beside him. Then it was gone forever. Seabirds flew over a cruel sea.

4

Severiano's Day in Court

After a somewhat, I must admit, doomladen first date with my dearest Scampimost girl, I returned to Chaffinch Hall in a state of gigglesome elation. Religious satoris I had experienced before, about five times each year, when my entire being was flooded with light and everything in the natural world shone with God's true intent. But this, was it not, was the real thing. Scampi!

Having washed three labradors, I was helping a young Dame Tuna with her essay on the Reformation – she was in her 2nd year at Cambridge or the Sorbonne, I forget which – and there was me holding forth with a brilliance, an erudition which was surprising myself more with each apt phrase, when the telephone hovered in, in that way they had just started doing, and which has always seemed to me like a message coming in from the spirit world.

It was Scampi. She was incomprehensible, distressed to the point of insanity.

'Pleasy-do calm down, dearie,' I said, vicarishly. 'Tell me wot's ado?'

She was in the shower, washing away the filth from her soiled body, she said. In the background Hieronymus Gosh's passé masterpiece 'Pnong Anthems Agogo' was playing pnongingly at full pelting blast.

Dame Tuna looked up from a Jesuitical biography of Luther, saying: 'Something ado, Uncle Chiffychaffy?'

I had pieced together the ado from Scampi's sobs, yelps, growls and cries from the soul.

'It's your Uncle Seve,' I said. 'He's been arrested.'

'How exciting? Wot for?'

In a dead dull voice, like a broken clock chiming just

once after a thousand years, deeply, sadly, I managed to say: 'Golf.'

Tuna shrieked.

The phone snatched itself out of my hand and hovered away. Three clean labradors peeked through the door in a row, aware that something was ado.

'Your Uncle Seve is a golfer,' I said to Tuna in my let's-face-facts-but-hope-for-the-best-voice. 'At least, he has been accused of being one, has he not. Fooly-doos evermost. He may, of course, be innocent.'

I sat down in total shock and disbelief. He was guilty, I knew! When you came to think about him, he had golfer written all over him. Seve, who was to have been the first Chaffinch in the cabinet since Ezekiel Chaffinch snored beside Mr Gladstone, was a golfer. He was ruined! He might bring the whole family down with him.

Tuna stood, her fingers pushing her up. She walked slowly towards the door with her back arched, then suddenly ran sobbing girlishly out of the room. I awoke from my daze hearing doors slamming all over the Hall. Doors that said GOLFER! GOLFER! SEVE'S A GOLFER!

The criminal in question was, at that very moment, being interviewed by Sir Claude Feitsheins Piggot, the famous barrister, in a yellow cell in Scotland Yard. Sir Claude's tried and trusted method was never to discuss the case with his client, or think about it at all, so he just lay on Seve's hard bunk swigging whisky from a hip-flask, discussing the brilliance of Herring Carstairs, the famous pnong player, and comparing him with Schubert.

The Pnong Association had already wangled their boy Carstairs out of bother. He was in Rio de Janeiro, resting. Moira Macmacpherson, meanwhile, was released into the streets of Glasgow, along with 16 Arapahos, who immediately faded to nothingness. Seve alone, out of everyone on Golf Island, was to stand trial. The reason was obvious. The Scots P.M., MacTavish, was putting himself up for European President and was Godfrey Lowrie's main rival. If Lowrie could be embarrassed by being shown to have such a thing as a golfer in his government, then all the good for MacTavish. Of course, Golf Island was on Scottish territory, so the others were released to save MacTavish any embarrassment of his own.

Unfortunately, Moira was arrested 24 hours after her release for being in possession of a golfball. She was sentenced to 5 years and served her time, I understand, on Golf Island, then transformed into a penal colony for Scottish dissidents and golfers. There the poor lassie tended turnips on the ground where she had scattered her father's ashes in a summer long ago.

Meanwhile, in England, Prime Minister Lowrie had erased Seve's name from all government records, set his office on fire, and put out a denial that any such person had ever existed.

When the press phoned the Hall, asking for the head of the Chaffinch family, the phone hovered into Bro Wilf's attic room. He said that there was no such Chaffinch as Severiano Chaffinch, but also denied his own existence, then he howled and gave out tips for Ascot week.

Seve was in some turmoil, was he not. One thing Sir Claude had told him was that Moira Macmacpherson was not a real girl, but a hologramismic illusion, and that she had faded away with the Arapahos. A lie for lying's sake, of course, emanating from MacTavish. But Seve believed it.

His brief sojourn on Golf Island no longer seemed real to him. His love for Moira mingled in his mind with his love for Scampi. The ignoble instinct of self-preservation overtook the excellent golfer. He told Sir Claude he was innocent, that he had never played golf in his life, that the whole thing was a dreadful mistake. Sir Claude brought a pnongball out of his briefcase and sang Schubert arias to it deep into the night.

He was asleep on Seve's bench when Scampi and I visited the cell next morning. I was disguised as a Greek Orthodox priest, with a false beard newly stained with mousakka. Scampi, as the P.M.'s daughter, could not admit to any relationship with the miscreant Seve, so wrapped her identity in a polar bear fur coat with the bear's head still attached as the hood. Hood pulled up, her chocolate button eyes gazed out through a maw stuffed in mid-snarl. We looked frightfully odd, did we not.

'Nice quiet gent, Citizen Chaffinch,' said the policeman who let us in. 'We search his cell every half hour for golfballs but we ain't found none yet. Naw, he's innocent, I reckons.'

Moments later the innocent Seve found himself at the other end of the amorous attentions of a polar bear, while a Greek Orthodox priest looked on. Scampi was delighted to see him, and he her, but suddenly she stepped back.

'Rascally trews, Seve!' she said, with a zillion ecopoundlet note of suspicion.

Off his guard was Seve: 'Yes, too-too rascally, notwot!'

'GOLFER!' squealed Scampi, her night black hair flapping angrily inside the toothy hood.

'I'm not a golfer, I promisywomisie, evermost. It's all sour custard, no fooly-doos.'

He put his head in the bear's mouth and they kissed. Sir Claude woke up at this point, his world swimming in bleary-do. He'd seen such things before and wasn't moved.

'It was all Herring Carstairs, the famous pnong player. I bumped into him in front of the Thatcher Memorial, on my way to a meeting with some piggn brigadiers. Carstairs said – O delicious Scamp smeared in saucy tartar – that he'd take me somewhere to teach me the rules of pnong. But he took me to the top of the Toblerone Building, coshed me dizzymost, and next thing I'm on this poosy-wiffo island with a lot of mad golfers in loud trews like these.'

It was obvious from the stance of the polar bear she was inside that Scampi didn't believe a word. I'd done nothing so far, so I sprinkled holy water on them. It made the bear smell.

'And about Moira,' broached Seve, twitching with guilt.

The polar bear looked as if it was about to murder a walrus.

'You see, it'll all come out at the trial, so if I tell you myself, now, I can explain. I don't want to rot our rhubarb bed, but I did a certain hoohar wiggly thing, did I not . . . I did. With Moira, pleasy-do.'

'A certain hoohar wiggly thing? With Moira?'

'I did that very thing.'

'Hoohar wiggly thing?' inquired Sir Claude and I together.

'I committed the sexual intercourse with Moira Macmac-pherson,' he yelled for our benefit, then turned pleadingly to his Scampi dish: 'But . . . my own Scampilacious article, it's perfectly all right. She wasn't real. She was a hologramismic illusion.'

'She felt real though?' I asked. I was breaking them up! Scampi was mine!

'Oh yes, father, she felt real.' (My disguise was so good he didn't realize I was his monkish cuz!) Then to appease Scampi he added. 'We had nearly all our clothes on. We thought the game was up for us, y'ken?'

'And what might that game be?' yelled Scampi in the tiny cell of off-custard yellow. 'Might it, I wonder, would it not be too-too much of a guess on my part to say . . . GOLF!!!!!'

'Scampimost! My plate of . . . Erm, your father is going to fix the trial for me, wotaroo?'

'GOLFER!!!!!' she yelled, pulled open the door, pushed past the policeman and was off into the dawn.

I lifted my beard. Seve and Sir Claude pressed themselves into corners in fright.

'It's only me! Chehe!' I said, made the sign of the cross and hopped off after Scampi. I caught her up in the Strand. She was easy to find in that coat.

Three days later, in the sweltering June heat, the trial began. Number One Court, Old Bailey. The air was so bad the judge was wearing his airbag. The jury of three, all professional jurors who spent their every waking day in courtrooms, wore togas that billowed revealingly from the fans. Seve came in wearing his golfing outfit. Sir Claude sat on his right and started mixing martinis. Scampi and I sat sweating in our disguises right behind the defence.

Coughs and splutters ringed the courtroom. Then notes flew. One fluttered in front of Sir Claude. He oinked in irritation.

'Dimmee, this puts my whole case skewiffo! No time to prepare or nuffink. Dearie-be.'

'Is something ado?' said the defendant.

'Hm?' He looked at Seve with the critical look of a man at his disinherited son. He didn't recognize him. But the rascally trews slowly alerted him. 'Of course, the golfing article! Indeedby! Bad news, fraid-o – the prosecution's got a clone on the go.'

Seve sat in silence for some moments. Then: 'Clone?'

'Ugh? Yes, clone. We've had the technology for years. Too expensive for regular use. But if it's a serious case, where it's one man's word against the fencepost, where there's an execution involved.'

'Execution?'

'Pleasy-do-do, death sentence for golfing, squire. Clones, yes – all done with D.N.A., you see. Every cell in the body contains everything about you, not just what colour your peekaboos are or how smelly your feet. In every cell is everything you've ever thought, seen or said during your entire life. So what they do, what in fact they have done, is take a bit of skin off your shaving razor, put it in a tank and overnight they've grown a full-sized clone of you to bring in here and testify against you this morning.'

Seve gripped his chair. He wanted to run. Just then, he hated golf, hated his father for introducing him to golf, felt the deepest shame about almost beating the course record on Golf Island.

Sir Claude poured a bag of peanuts onto the shiny table and started eating the ones that skitted farthest away from the pile.

'Of course,' he said, 'You know that these clone things can't lie. Impossible for them to tell lies. So if I were you and I were guilty, which of course you are, because we've all done something wrong at some time and if you haven't done whatever you're up for today they'll squeeze something even worse out of the clone and do you for that instead. Dimmee, not that there's anything much worse than golf!'

'I'm innocent, Sir Claude, promisywomisy-sweary-doos, innocent! I've never played golf in my life!'

Elsewhere in the court were both Godfrey Lowrie, the English P.M., and Hamish Mactavish, the Scottish P.M., heavily disguised. It could be that the future of a continent depended on the outcome of this trial.

Suddenly, hush. The Judge banged his gavel.

'Severiano Faldo Chaffinch, you are charged that on the 14th day of June in the year 2037 you did wilfully and with malice aforethought play golf. How pleasy-do you pleady-do?'

A furious last-minute muttering between Seve and Sir Claude, before the distinguished barrister stood up and intoned: 'NOT guilty, your honour.' Then he sat down, put his mouth on the table and sucked up the rest of his nuts.

The echoing cry of 'Send in the Clone . . . Send in the Clone . . .' whipped from the courtroom and became more distant, like a passing train that went 'Sendintheclone' and not 'deediddleydee'.

It seemed to go on forever. The courtroom muttered. Heads turned, looking at the main door. Seve rubbed his sweating golf grip on his rascally trews. Again, back in the court where the mantra started, the clerk called loud, close, inside our heads: 'SEND IN THE CLONE.'

'Don't worry. I'm here,' said a voice! Seve's voice!

It was the clone, entering not where we'd expected to see him, but through a little door behind the jury. He was stark naked, a line of black hair from neck to groin, six feet eight in height, the image of cuz Seve.

Seve nudged his barrister: 'They might have given him something to wear!'

Sir Claude was irked. 'He's not a man! That's not you up there! It's just like a fingernail clipping or a sneeze. Can't dignify the piggn things, can we?'

The clone sat on one of the jurors' knees, in the disruptive manner of clones, and had to be led to the witness chair, where it sat in a lewd manner, waggling its sexual parts at its original. Seve was crimson with embarrassment.

'That's Seve all righty,' said Scampi, scandalized inside her coat. Sir Osbert Mosley, for the prosecution, walked up to the clone and, smiling, casually, said: 'You are, are you not indeed, a clone of Severiano Faldo Chaffinch.'

'That's me.'

'Clone Chaffinch, have you at any time in your life played the game known as "golf"?'

'Yeah, why not!'

'HE'S LYING!!!!!' yelled Seve.

Sir Claude calmed him. 'There, there, laddie, it's all over now. No need to make a fussapoo. You're condemned out of your own mouth.'

All the fight went out of Seve. His lips muttered two words, names: 'Scampi. Moira! Scampi. Moira!' And he thought about his old office at the war office. Then his own voice, the clone's voice, awoke him from his misery. He began to smile, to egg the clone on.

'Yeah, first time I played golf was April 29th, 2021, six years, five months and two days before it was made illegal. My father took me to his club. It was the first really nice spring day of the year. I met his golfing friends, happy lot. My father loved me very much.'

Sir Osbert, tidying the remains of his kiss curl, had the air of a man who didn't need to try: 'And, I take it, do I not, that you played golf frequently after this?'

'I did. With my father and his friends. I played golf on 2,037 occasions in the following years, a total of 36,666 holes, or 6,112 under par.'

'Some of these statistics would presumably fall after the Chulkhurst Bill, illegalizing golf?'

'I do not,' said the clone, sitting forward, looking manly and elemental in its nakedness, 'recognize the right of any government or individual to prevent me from playing golf.'

The court yelled abuse. The jurors took out little nooses and waggled them at real Seve.

The clone continued, in a speech which would have brought approving Scottish noises from the late Birdie Lumphahan: 'You may have the power! You can do what you like with me and that poor man there! But one day, and before this century is out, men and women will be playing golf together on golfcourses throughout the world!'

Seve was on his feet applauding. But the court went silent around him, except for the steady snores of Sir Claude. Seve sat down, lost, dead except for the hanging.

'One more itsybitsie question,' smirked Sir Osbert, with a wink at the disguised MacTavish. 'You are a member of the English Government, are you not?'

'Yeah, Junior Minister in the War Office.'

Groan from the disguised Lowrie, who then busied himself writing a long note for the judge.

The clone had tears in his eyes, staring at his original, saying: 'Wot a day it was, bro, ehwot? I haven't been so happy since I was a laddie. And oooooh, Moira, her sweet Scots voice, her unwashed smell. I hoohar-wigglied my darling Moira. How I love her! Moira!'

Seve took comfort in Sir Claude's bosom, sobbing: 'But she's not real, just a hologramismic illusion!'

Up jumped the clone: 'No, bro! Don't believe them! She's as real as you or I!'

'MOIRA!' yelled Seve, vengefully pushing Sir Claude, from whose lips he'd heard of Moira's unreality, against his drinks cabinet. 'SHE'S REAL!!! A REAL LIVE GIRL!!!!!'

A furious Scampi threw back her polar bear hood, her hair flapping, black and fierce. The clone saw her and blew kisses. Just then, the judge banged his gavel.

'There is no need to proceed further with this case. It is quite obvious to me that Citizen Chaffinch is innocent.'

Sir Claude collected his papers, found an escaped nut, and sat back with the calmness of a man who's seen it all before.

'I have before me,' continued the judge, 'official notification of the latest Government report on clones. It has arrived in time to prevent a grave miscarriage of justice, pleasy-do. Apparently, due to an excess of potassium in the growing tank, clones always tell the opposite of the truth. Therefore, when Clone Chaffinch says he played golf, he means he did not. Citizen Chaffinch, after the usual formalities, you are free to go.'

The disguised Godfrey Lowrie left the court with a wicked little wave at his disguised rival.

Scampi, meanwhile, was weeping with delight. All that frothpoos about Seve loving Moira! Huh! She'd half believed it, but of course, it was all lies, clones only ever tell lies! It was she, Scampi, that this newly freed, un-ruined man loved.

Meanwhilydoos, shame be on this particular Chaffinch, for I wanted Scampi for myself, and would have been more content with a guilty verdict. Love, like all else, corrupts us.

'One thing, Sir Claude,' asked Seve as they shared celebratory martinis. 'What will happen to him?'

'Who?'

The clone was urinating into a waste paper basket.

'Oh, him. Melted down. Usual procedure. Harh!'

Scampi threw off the bear coat. Underneath, her flimsy toga was sodden, she was sweating like a horse after a race, thick white bubbly sweat. She embraced Seve over the rail.

My eyes were on the clone. He was watching them kiss and a new look came over him, one I had never seen on Seve's face before. It disturbed me profoundly.

'Congratapoopoos!' I said to Seve, shaking his hand while his other fondled Scampi's buttocks.

'Thanky-be, father,' he said. (He still hadn't twigged me!)

Then he was taken to the waiting-room while his release papers were processed. After all his troubles, things seemed back to hunkydom for Seve. But he had less than an hour to live. Cheehe! No, Tadese, I shouldn't chee, should I not? Chehehe!

5

The Melting Chaffinch

This was Clone Seve's favourite story. He related it to me over and over again, and always with the same childish delight, always the same amoral attitude that sent me off praying for him. And now, this afternoon, as I spy a pink blemish in the blue that is flamingos breaking to the sky over distant Lake Stephanie, I tell it to you, Tadese, to put in our book. Its lesson is this: never trust a clone.

After being acquitted, Seve waited in a small robing room for Sir Claude to get the acquittal papers. Sir Claude, during this time, was he not, was discussing celibacy and general abstinence with a certain Greek Orthodox priest, while watching the steam rise from the cooling-off Scampi.

The trial had ended so abruptly that the clonehandlers had not yet returned from their pub outside in the sweltering Strand, so Seve's clone was put out of harm's way. They shoved it in the robing room with its original.

Seve was humming a passé tune.

'I do like that tune. One of my too-too faveraves!' said his clone.

'Yes. Hieronymus Gosh.'

'I know.'

'They tell me it's passé, but who are they to say! I like it.'

'Me too.'

Seve chortled pleasantly. 'Well, of course, you would, wouldn't you – you're me!'

They laughed the same laugh together. Seve didn't realize that here he was his own worst enemy, that this thing, this walking reflection that addressed him with his own charm, was bro Cain.

'Our P.M. fixed the trial with that bogus report wotsit, I suppose.'

'Very decent of him. Of course, I am going to marry his daughter.'

'You've decided that, have you? What about Moira, then?'

Sad silence from them both. Then the clone caught his face in the robing mirror. He flinched away.

'I do wish those piggn clonehandlers would hurry up. I'd like to get this over with as soon as possybule.'

'Too-too awfullymost-jip for you, being melted, I mean.'

'Aw, at least I have a good day's golfing, ehwot, to dwell on in my final moments.'

They laughed the same laugh again.

'Look, erm . . .' Seve wished to compliment his clone but felt a donkey doing so. 'I'd just like to say, before they come, I think you were doublymost-spanky-doos brave in there. What you said about the future, everyone playing golf together – gripperoo, clone of mine, gripperoo. Wish I'd said it.'

They laughed again. They had the same sense of humour. But suddenly the clone broke off in fright. A noise outside. Was this it? Were they coming for him? Was his brief life over?

'I do think they could have given you something to wear though,' said Seve.

'Wot's it matter, I'm only a toenail clipping, or a sneeze. But speaky-doing of clobber: rascally trews!'

'Yes, aren't they! Don't suppose I'll be able to wear 'em again.'

'Look, I couldn't, could I . . . no, there's not time!' Anguished intake of breath from the clone.

'No, ask away, leastmost I can do – wot's yer pleasure?'

'I couldn't try your trews on, could I? A clone's last wish and all that.'

Seve de-trewed himself and handed them over. His double hurried into them.

'Perfect fit,' said Clone Seve.

'Harh!' went Seve.

'I couldn't, no – your shirt and that nattyaroony pink sweater?'

'Go on, then – just for a mo.'

'Shoes and socks? May as well, man of mine!'

Seve smiled benevolently upon the clone as it walked up and down in front of the robing mirror, admiring itself in its borrowed suit of clothes, doing golfclubless golfswings, being a man for a few minutes. They both laughed, but a subtly different laughter.

When suddenly the clonehandlers came in they naturally assumed that the naked one was the clone – but the naked one was Seve!

'No, you've got it all wrong. I lent him my clothes. He's the clone, not me!'

But as they were then under the impression that all clones spoke the truth's opposite, what Seve had actually said was: 'Yes, you are entirely correct. I have never worn any clothes. I am a clone.'

'Don't mind if I ruffles yer clone up a bit, Citizen?' said the senior clonehandler to Clone Seve.

'It's a free country,' said the one in the rascally trews.

'I hates clones!' He slapped Seve's long body with his gloves. 'Cummon, off yer goes, and one stinking clone's trick out of yer and I'll fling yer in that tank in snapped-off bits. Bye, Citizen.'

Rarely can a man look at himself and see deeplymost into his own nature. But, in that final moment when Seve and Clone Seve shared a room, the look that passed between them was all that and more. No man had ever looked in a mirror and seen as much.

Nude and chattering, Seve was dragged away. Clone Seve read *Pnong Weekly* while he waited for Sir Claude and the acquittal papers. There was an excited flutter inside him, like the flag on the 18th flapping in the beginnings of the storm. He was, more than any of us perhaps, excited at the prospect of life.

I was in the corridors with Scampi when they dragged 'the clone' past us towards the staircase. I had removed my beard and was my usual bald self, scratching a rash the beard had given me.

'Cuz Chaff! Help me! I'm Seve! I'm not the piggn clone! CHAFF! CUZ!'

'Poor thing!' I said.

I was brimming with compassion. I patted Scampi's cheek, very intimate of me, perhaps our most intimate moment together.

'Scampi, darlingmost pal, there is something I must do.'

She thought I needed a wee-wee. But I had gone chasing after the clonehandlers.

'Wait! – he needs a priest, for his final moments!' And added when their clonehandlers' eyebrows raised at my un-English garb: 'He's Greek Orthodox. All clones are Greek Orthodox.'

This interested them very much. They had dealings with clones every day, but this information was new to them.

The melting tank was in the 'Clone Zone' in the basement of the Old Bailey. A very clean establishment, with silver dishes everywhere, and bottles with organs floating in them, like cannibalistic trophies, on all the shelves.

They allowed me a moment's prayer with the clone. Several policemen and women, off-duty and bloodthirsty I think, plonked themselves on a bench to watch the melting.

'I have not thought of the theological implications,' I told the clone, 'but you are a living, thinking being, surely one of God's creatures. He will find a place for you in His kingdom.'

While I spoke those flippant words the clone looked at me with a look I shall never forget. The look rises in my dreams like the moon and shines its light over the landscape of my sleepy potterings.

Then it moaned, saying: 'No fooly-doos at a time like this, cuz Chaffo! There is no God! Dimmee – everybody knows there isn't!'

A big grin came and went widely on my rashed face, as I wondered about his statement. Cos if clones could only tell the opposite of the truth, or so I then believed, then could this denial of God's existence be the first ever genuine confirmation of God's existence? Did the clone speak from its own opinion, or from the inner soul which knows all things? For the sake of science, of religious truth, I felt the melting had to be delayed. But they wouldn't hear of it.

In a panic, my emotions racing to my tongue, I gabbled to the clone about Jesus, his own trial and crucifixion, how he faced his end, the courage . . . at the same time, I realize now, the clone was gibbering its desperate best to convince me that it was my real cuz. But I wasn't listening. Then, in its worry, it emptied its bowels onto the floor and commenced shouting the word golf over and over.

'Golf! GOLF! GOLLLLLFFFFFF! Beautiful GOLF! GOL-LLLF! You'll all be playing GOLF one day, just you wait! Freedom for GOLFERS!'

One moment the clone was there, the next the clone-handlers had thrown him into the tank. His long body sank through a splashless crust of pale yellow gunge, like whipped banana, into a thin honey-like liquid, did it not. I knelt by the tank and prayed, eyes tight shut, with an image thrashing on my retina of a donkey being punished in the liquid fires of Sheol.

When I opened my eyes again, the clone was scrabbling on the glass of the tank, a fuzz of melting flesh glowing pink all around him. Then he went still and turned slightly, bubbles coming out of his melting nose. I was reminded of that poor monster in its tank in the Wembley Drome. All confusion, was I not, cos my intuitive mind knew that it was Seve who had died in that tank, and the messages it sent to my normal mind were angry, violent, sorrowful. The heat! The emotion! The chemical reeks! I had a swoonish knee-bending collapse.

A policewoman helped me upstairs to the street. (The last time a policewoman handled me was when several pulled me from the statue of Churchill in the '24 Revolution.) But the street was humid and offered me little relief.

Seve and Scampi were arm-in-arm in front of the Old Bailey, giving interviews to a Press which everyone had given up watching, reading, noticing years before.

'Golfer, me? No fooly-doos,' said Seve, more confident than I had ever seen him.

Then he made a political speech about the evils of MacTavish, and wound up making the official announcement of his engagement to the P.M.'s daughter, his Scampimost wife-to-be, Scampi Lowrie.

I, who loved her so much, was there, the only one without

an ice-cream, tripping on wires, sweating, weeping inside, to hear this terrible announcement.

When they'd done and the little crowd wandered away to find cool drinks, a shabby figure in sodden black robes faced them with an unaccustomed scowl.

'Heighho and harh, cuz Chaff! All's hunky, wotaroo! Let's all go and see a pnongabout, Wibleys in training, evermost! Whatsay?'

I knew, I understood now, that this wasn't Seve. But what, indeedymost, could I say? O Lord, I said in my head, because Seve's clone lives, does Seve live? And the answer came: *verily, does a corpse live if the cold it gave another man when last alive lives on?*

Seve and Scampi were smiling at me, friendly as can be. But I turned my back on them and walked away, did I not.

The world was too cruel for one confused little chaffinch. All too aware of my failings, I dared not return to my solitary life, for fear of the thoughts I would meet there in my loneliness. So for the next year I helped my friend the Bishop of Ely in his diocesan work. Forcing my love for Scampi from my head and heart proved an intolerable strain. Just as bad, my grief for Seve, who I had never really liked, but who now seemed a towering martyr in my troubled mind. I felt myself his Judas. I was crippled with shame.

*

Ho-hum and dearie-be, they never did legalize golf, did they? Not that they've got anything against it these days. It's just been forgotten about, as are most things and people, sooner or later. I expect there's a few players left. Perhaps not. But they don't play pnong anymore either. So who won? No one, as usual.

Seve and Scampi were married. MacTavish won the election and became European President and the first of the despots. A different world. Scampi fell preggers, a new nest of Chaffinches. But during her preggerdom, this being less than two years into their marriage, Moira Macmacpherson was released early from her island prison.

When Seve left Scampi and ran off with Moira, to travel the world in search of hidden golfcourses, I was recovering from a sort of breakdown in a monastery in France. Sent there rather than being locked in the Hall attic where, I realized by then, like bro Wilf, I belonged. I didn't know Seve and Scampi had splitterood. That was my chance, my moment. Scampi and her twin girls, Rainbow and Haha, they could have lived at the Hall, could they not, part of my family. In time Scampi and I, I'm sure, would have spent every sunny day happily doing the hoohar wiggly thing by the pool. Bliss! A small bliss! It was what I most wanted, what still I most want.

Out helping her father campaign against MacTavish's first wave of despotic laws, Scampi was hit by a pnongball thrown at her father by a MacTavish supporter. It broke her pretty head, it did. Killed my poor girl. She'd been seeing something of Herring Carstairs at the time. Asked what he thought of Citizen Lowrie's death this is what he said:

'She died like a Wibley. Too-too.'

At the time I was hardly devastated. I was at a peak of religious nuttery and did not think her dead, merely moved on to a better place where one day we would meet again. But now, a lifetime later – NOW! O sweet Jesus! My Scampi! We could have grown old together, outlived pnong, seen out this accursed century with each other's kindly smiles. Sixty years, and no Scampiiiiiiiii! ARRRRRRRRRRHHHHHHHHH!!!!!*

---

* *In his excess of emotion my master has fallen off his pole, has he not. I shall tend him in my humble hut. I shall spoon him beans, one by one. He is a good man, a holy man. With all the sorrows he has seen in his long life, I marvel at his cheehe. Know this, in Addis Ababa they sell little statues of him in the market. And when the curious come to see him on his pole, he laughs at them. I pray to you, O mighty Lord, don't let my master die. 100 years is not enough for such a man as this.*

Tadese Mblook

QUIET YEARS UNDER THE DESPOTS

The Exploding Mrs Chaffinch

Quotes of the Century:

'You'll do as I piggn well say, and piggn well like it!'
Barry Hamlet, Despot of Australia, 2040

'When we have educated our people to look at pianos instead of playing them, in other words to think music rather than hearing it, then we shall apply ourselves to removing the tweet from birds.'
Herbert Jaynes, Life President, Noise Abatement Society, 2043

'We shall now think hymn number 317.'
Rev Chaffinch Chaffinch, Saint Winifred's Church, Bury Saint Edmunds, 2045

1

The Unending Youth of Cod Chaffinch

A bird that falls off its perch, Tadese, is not worthy of the name. Anyhowbees, I am too old to be a bird. The century is almost done, is it not? If I live a few more weeks, perhaps I shall turn into something else! Cheeheee! A rhinoceros! O Lord, I should like to be a rhinoceros.

I'll eat that banana now, old friend. Urk! What a giganticmost fellow you are, close up! When I am a rhinoceros, will I be bigger than you, Tadese? Shall I chase you around Lake Stephanie? Cheee! Ooooch! You still say this thing is not broken?

As I have been lying here in your little hut, I have had visions. No, not of smirking Virgins! Of my family, the Chaffinches, my dear bird-brained crew. I take against this banana, do I not, triple sorries to it – another banana, pleasy-do. I looked through the straws of your hut, Tadese, and saw not my lonely birdless pole in a baked Africa. I saw the green lawns of Chaffinch Hall sixty years ago. I saw Seve and Scampi driving away in the Scampimobile. I saw my baby bro Cod chasing Nobby Tixover with a hedge trimmer. Cheehe! I see visions of the past, Tadese, all the time now. Its just like watching the Everyone Channel! Can this be a final gift from God, before he drags me weeping from the world? TADESE! My finger is broken, positivelymost!

I was not, was I, NEVER, no NEVER, a cronyman of Nobby Tixover's. I WAS NOT!!!!! Calm myself down, Tadese? How can I, when they are saying that? Who? The other birds, the mosquitoes, THEY ARE ALL SAYING IT! He was Cod's friend, not mine. Never mine!

The biographies of Tixover, I know, dwell at length on his early wasted years as a blade. I haven't read a word of one, but I have looked at the pictures. Cod was so handsome, was he not! Of course, he was fortunatemost-doos with the rhinoblaster.

Rhinoblaster? Yes, they'd all turned up from somewhere with this new gadget they'd whipped from a clinic in Ipswich. Like a plant-pot with a handle on it and full of fizzy stuff, with a screen sticking out its other end like a rear-view mirror. The idea was you put your nose in it and it changed the shape of your nose for you. It remoulded the fleshy parts! Created gristle! – A nose-making gadget! Bigger! Smaller! You could have any schnoz you wanted! It had over a thousand in its memory. Or if you were clever enough to work its controls, you could invent your own nose.

So there they were one day, Cod, Nobby, Bass, Dingo and other similar spirits, under my treehouse, all gigglesome, with the most extraordinary noses.

'Cummon, Mahatma!' shouted Nobby. 'Plonk your nose in this!' It seemed wheezemost, topchee-jip! How they laughed as I gave myself a huge great red honk of a nose! How we rolled about that weekend! Picking our noses! Chee!

What they had failed to realize was that the rhinoblaster only worked 10 times on any one nose. So, with my tenth nose, self-operating the controls, did I not, fooly-doos, I ended up with this unsightly snout. Oink! My own nose, the nose of my youth, was a pleasant enough article. When it sneezed, it sneezed down, not out like this one. I had made a pig of myself. From that day, whenever anyone has looked me in the face, including my dear Scampi, they have looked straight up my nose. Chee!

Cod's 10th nose was a little straighter than his old one. It made him look even handsomer. Nobby's old nose had been round, comfortable, a bishop's nose, pleasy-do. But the nose he ended up with was wide, pointed, a beak for pecking eyes out with – he'd never have become the man he did without it, no indeed. Bass Worthington's 10th nose had three nostrils. He-he-cheee!

They had spent their whole lives running about, racing their sports cars, driving girls to Llandudno and leaving them there eculess for a joke. Long youths they had. They pretended that their first jollyjapes as Oxford students were just the day before yesterday, but they were way back in another age. Cod reached 40 and was still living the life he did at 20. And, though his pals were wearing out, baggier-eyed and slower, he looked always the same, his smile unendingly bright. They called him 'Le Belge', because, memory-doos, Cod was my half-bro. His father died in the Belgian plague with all the other Belgians, leaving Cod the last of the Belgian race, a fact of which, I discovered to my surprise one day, he was fiercely proud. They sometimes went for days speaking to him in a sort-of mashed up French. They also called him 'fish article' and 'le poisson Belge'. I was always 'the Mahatma'.

One thing I do grant Nobby's cronydom. There was never any forced laughter. It was always real. I was not one of them. I WAS NOT! But often I looked out of my window, or down the road I was on, and wished they would come along it, tooting, laughing. Just the thought of them cut smiles in a frown. Indeedybe, a Jilks to a man, but . . . Cheheee! If they were here now, how tickled they would be to see a Chaffinch who's fallen off his pole. They are all dead, are they not, long dead and history.

I am speaking of the mid-'40s now. The roustabout life that the boys had lived was getting harder to sustain. They had begun as idlers in an age of idlers. But times were suddenly more serious, frownful, worky-do-da-doos. No one laughed at their antics anymore, except themselves, and sometimes their Mahatma. Despotic Europe was a glum place, top-heavy with laws, brutal and busy. Nobby's lot were creatures out of their time, existing despite the time. Obviously, with their noisy habits they were in trouble with the Noise Abatement Police. Cod spent his 42nd birthday in jail.

I joined the Noise Abatement Society when I was still at school, did I not – I thought that in a quieter world people would think more, turn to God. Apart from the Anglican Church it is the only political organization to which I have ever belonged. I handed out leaflets, that sort of thing. I earned myself 3 bronze Hushaby Certificates – and was a proudypants with them! But I attended only a few meetings, cos in order to keep noise to a minimum nobody ever said anything and if I suddenly burst out laughing, always a bad habit of mine, 1,000 heads would turn and angrily shush me up. That so many people were willing to sacrifice an evening to sit for three hours without a cough or the creak of a chair, should have told me something unusual was ado. But even now how oddmost it seems that the Noise Abatement Society should become the most powerful political organization on the planet. Half the despots started as members.

When I turned up at Reading Jail I showed them my 3 bronze Hushaby Certificates and, without a word being spoken, I was shown in to see bro Cod, cooling off from his noise. That day I spoke to him in a way I never had before, not in all our lives. I was like a cruel father. I told him he was wasting his life, that he needed objective. I couldn't think what! All right, not the Noise Abatement Society! Something else! Anything! Objective! He told me that if he'd wasted his life in gigglesome pleasures, then I'd wasted mine in religious nuttery. Quite right, of course.

They let him out in my custody. We sat in the park under a big statue of a lion. I picked two crocuses and stuck them in my snout. But he didn't laugh. Pushing his fair hair out of his babyblue eyes, he spoke most movingly about the demise of the Belge. Then he slapped his knees and said:

'Where's that piggn Nobby article? He'll cheer me up, no end!'

Just before we parted I reached up and pulled a grey hair from his head, one of his very few.

'Oochy! Chaffy!'

'Triple sorries, thought it was loose.'

As he walked away from me to ask a rather severe young woman for a lift into London in the topless car she was sitting in, I couldn't help thinking, as her severity turned to smiley-do, that the 21st Century Blues would never, of all people, visit bro Cod. Then I looked at the grey hair still held between my fingers and it seemed to infect that younger me with chilly old age.

It was when Herbert Jaynes was made Life President of the Noise Abatement Society that things really got out of hand. They went around de-barking dogs! Turned up at the Hall one day in their van. I must confess, one of my greatest pleasy-doos, and the thing I most looked forward to when returning home from cave or ashram, was sitting in the kennels and barking with the dogs. For in that time until our barks were sore I had lain down the burden of my humanity. So imagine me, that day, sitting in the kennels, many sad doggy eyes questioning me in silent incomprehension. Of all of them, only I could bark!

They couldn't de-bark Bro Wilf, but they locked him into a neck-brace to stop him howling. Who among the living in those years was unaffected? I was in a monastery, on my knees in my herb garden during 'The Great Quietening'. But it was quiet there anyway. I didn't notice that the world was being shut up. Then they stopped us ringing our bell. I looked up at it a hundred times a day. Its rope dangled as a temptation. But it never rang. No sly monk with an attitude. Not quite me.

Theory was, thinky-do, that all the noise in the history of the world, every bang, bark, guitar twang and boisterous yell had gathered somewhere. Frinton-upon-Sea, I suggested when I first heard the theory. But I think it was supposed to be in some dimension of its own, a pool they called it. This pool, wherever it was, was getting full and if we all weren't quiet, then it would overflow like a left-running bath, and the world would be drenched in its own history of sound, enough to crack it to bits, the way a singer cracks a glass.

Quite goosey in its frightness, was this idea! Who wasn't convinced? Noise Abatement was not imposed by the despots, young Tadese my lad – it was a popular movement! Everyone, everywhere, willingly knuckled down, did they not, put up and shut up. We took air for granted, then needed airbags. So why shouldn't sound turn against us also? Indeedy-so, it was a universally-accepted belief in the '40s that the shouting matches of our 20th Century grandfolks, the harangues of Cicero and Demothstenes, the whoop-it-ups of the Kit-Kat Club, might come clapping out of their reservoir to tumble our cities, unless we were very, very careful.

They even took the hooters out of pnong! They silenced the whirr of every single industrial machine! Babies slept in forcefields which turned their cries into a fly's buzz! Phones no longer rang to attract your attention – they just hovered into the room and hit you on the forehead with a clunk only you could hear! Music disappeared overnight! In Christmas week 2045 I was shown a warehouse full of abandoned tubas and trombones – how they shone under the lights! And presiding over all this increasing silence, the Noise Abatement Police, or 'Nappers', carrying guns equipped with thick silencers with which they murdered rowdy drunks on Saturday nights, until all those of such intemperate habits were as dead as each other.

MacTavish's Confederacy of Scottish Nations made bonfires of bagpipes, for God's sake! Many obscene noises as they burned! Law after law was passed, everywhere, in every country and block of countries, and still the fervent activists wanted it quieter! OOMPA-PA! BAM! BAM! YATATATA!!!!

But by far the biggest pothery-do, was it not, was with Italians. They just couldn't keep quiet, poor things. Everyone in Italy had drawers full of noise tickets! So the Noise Abatement Society badgered the European Despotic Council until a law was passed whereby all Italians had to be fitted with noise inhibitors. If an Italian made a noise over a certain decibel level the inhibitor caused the offending Italian to, well, explode. Which, of course, was a noise in itself, but it was thought the inhibitor would be a deterrent and that few Italians would go off.

I'm told the floods were rising in East Anglia the day that Cod jumped into his MG and started to race Nobby and Bass and Dingo in their MGs all the way to Italy. Our young blades, you see, thought this exploding Italians thingy-do was the jollymostest lark ever. Off they went, to the sun of Italy to annoy Italians into outbursts of Italian fury, to make them explode.

2

An Italian Jaunt

Nobby won the race to Italy. He zoomed through the Brenner Pass tooting his horn and contriving to get it stuck. The 3 Italian Noise Abatement Police who came to deal with this were so irritated by the BLARRRRRRRRRRRRRRRRRRRR, and by Nobby's innocent grin, that a shouting match ensued during which two exploded.

Bass and Cod arrived just in time to see their leader's latest achievement.

'Howdeedoodee, fish articles!'

'Howdoodeedee, Lord of Nobs!'

'Two less Ities, wot! Hurhhurh!'

'A-hurh! A-hurhhurh!'

The new arrivals commenced unChristianly to toot their horns also. The surviving policeman, very distraught, took out his whispering gun, gabbling loudly in Italian, and put it in Bass's face, right up against his 3rd nostril. But the Napper exploded before he could do Bass any harm. The English funsters rolled about on their front seats, giggly-do, giggly-do-do, giggly-do-da-day.

2 points to Nobby. Half a point each for Bass and Cod, with a special commendation for bravery for Bass, who was too drunk to know what was happening anyhowbe, then or at any other time. But wasn't life a lark?

Dingo arrived playing Elgar at full blast, his clothes on backwards and an empty bottle of champagne in each hand. This jaunt was looking like their best time ever! They all knew it. They jumped out of their cars – Bass had to be helped out – and shook hands, like explorers on a peak. If Cod hadn't been the most thumping atheist of all time, he might have said a prayer. Someone should have done. There was great meaning in this moment. They would never be as happy as this again.

In a raucous convoy of red vintage MGs they noised through the mountainous countryside of the Alto Adige. It wasn't quite spring. Families of farming folk were in their slopey fields attending to their vines, cutting them back, punishing them. Never had they heard such a noise.

There was one! An old Itie, walking along the road! Long-faced, flexing his cutters! Suddenly, Dingo, at the back of the convoy, determined to get among the points, zoomed forward, overtaking his team-mates, his tyres kicking stones on the verge inches from a sheer drop. He screamed up to the unfortunate Italian.

'Hurh-HURH! A-HEEEEHURH! Wheeeee! HURH!'

He couldn't actually think of anything to say. He just hurhhed and heeheed before his intended victim, who stood expressionless, emotionless.

But in a trice the other the MGs pulled up with 10 times the hurh-hee.

'Heigh-ho, Mari-o! Hurh!' went Nobby.

Bass was showing him his bottom.

The Italian looked across to the fields. People he knew were leaving their work and slowly coming to his aid.

'Mario? It is Mario, isn't it, Mario? Speeky-de-Engeeeelish, Mario?'

'Too-too, we're Engleeeeesh. Hurh! A-weeeee!'

At last, the stone spoke: 'Wot you say, pleasy-do? I no speaka de good Englieeesh.'

Howls and hoots from the Englanders.

'Too STUPID to speak English pwoperly!' yelled Bass. 'Speaks it like a piggn hoojar!' Everything was a hoojar to Bass.

'Piggn lumpy old custard!' threw in Dingo.

'You're not an ITALIAN, perchance, Mario?' Bro Cod's contribution, all bogusly innocent. 'This couldn't be ITALY, could it?'

'Si, here is Italia. Soon on this road you come to Merano.' A slow point with a gnarled hand at the valley ahead, as dreamy as the background of a Renaissance painting. 'Is beautiful, no?'

Nobby: 'Oooooooh, no! Ugly-ducksberry!'

Dingo: 'Frightfully poosy-wiff!'
Cod: 'Hideouslymost yukapoo!'
Bass: 'Hurrrrrh!'
Nobby: 'Clarty mountains scattered higglety-piggntly!'
Dingo: 'And all those weedy gwape vines! Hurh!'

The Italian was a slow burner. He muttered, expressionless, but with feeling: *'Se l'Italia non vi piace ritornate al vosto por il passo del Brennero! Erh burini, incomiciate!*

He was telling them to go back where they came from.

Sensing a kill, all four nattered in at once. But Nobby, the leader, prevailed: 'We've only come cos we want to dance fandangos with some Itie moppets, pleasy-do. I hear Itie moppets will do anything an Englishman asks for just a tossing of loose ecus.'

It worked. The stoical face rose on a chest filling with air. The Italian yelled at them. He scratched Dingo's paintwork with his cutters. He banged the bonnets of all four cars.

'How dare you say such a-things about ITALIAN GIRLS! I have 3 DAUGHTERS!!!! Good girls! CLEAN GIRLS!!! You think you pokey-POKEY my DAUGHTERS, huh!!! HUH!!!! *Siete venuti per INSULTARE UN ITALIANO . . .'*

His tirade was cut short by his explosion. His body disintegrated and flung itself fountainously into the sky, raining down on the four cars, splattering, red and yellow, unidentifiably minced. Much more of an event than when the Nappers went off. Bass somehow caught the cutters.

The MGs zoomed off, letting forth blasts of *La Cucuracha* from their musical horns. Behind them, a red splurge on the road, astonished Italians, one wailing in grief, being implored to quieten down by the others, until BOOM, another explosion. Nobby saw it in his rearview mirror and claimed another point. In conference later it went down as an unconfirmed. But Nobby was points ahead anyway.

By the time they rolled into a quiet little restaurant in Merano's Via Portici at 8 that same evening the score was Nobby: 8, Dingo: 3½, Cod: 3½, and Bass still trailing with 17 unconfirmeds, all of which coincidentally happened when he wandered off by himself and went BOOM behind a wall. Had there ever been a better game than this? Poor misguided souls!

'MORE WINE, MARIOOOOOOOOOOOOOOOOOOOOO-O!!!!!!' yelled Cod, to a waiter a-jitterty-jip with distress.

He brought more wine, imploring them in a smiley friendly voice please not to make so much noise – the other customers, the Nappers, etc.

'I SAY, OLD RHUBARB,' said Bass, 'MY SPAGHETTI'S TOO LONG! IS YOUR SPAGHETTI TOO LONG?'

Much fuss on this topic. But the waiter kept up his smile. Bass was infuriated! He'd thought his spaghetti line would set the blighter off. So, snarly faced, he grabbed the jittery waiter.

'PIGGN BLOW UP, YOU INCONSIDERATE BLEEDING ITIE!'

And he did. His mouth opened in the commencement of a fury, his inhibitor anticipated the noise he was going to make . . . and did him! A huge dizzying noise in that confined space, and a hissing THWAK as the waiter hit the ceiling.

Silence for a bit as the pouring puréed waiter settled to a drip. Then Cod in a huge voice to the other waiters peeping from behind pillars: 'I SAY, WAITER, THERE'S A NOSE IN MY SPAGHETTI!'

Huge hurhinh-hee-a-hee-HURHs from the monstrous English brotherhood. They hammered the table, glee tears rolling down their cheeks making clean channels through the diabolical bloody spattering of boomed waiter.

But there WAS a nose in Cod's spaghetti and suddenly he felt rather sick. Cheeks billowing, he pushed out his chair and hurried outside.

'I said that spaghetti was too long, didn't I not?' said Bass and drank a whole bottle of wine at one swig, to celebrate getting onto the scoresheet.

Outside, thunder was rumbling in the mountains. It was a very black night. A dapper man, very worried, was hurrying through the streets calling his wife's name. Whoozy bro Cod wondered if she was one they'd annoyed into blowing up in a sauna bath that lunchtime. A pain of guilt, of throbbing remorse hit my forever young bro. He staggered through the streets weeping, retching, grabbing strangers, hugging them and gabbling apologies – one easily infuriated gent blew up! Then it rained. Heavy, hard falling drips. Atheist Cod was in the square before the spooky cathedral of Saint Nickolaus. He looked up! His moment to turn to God? But he retched again and the moment passed.

But he was contrite, and the good Lord heard his thoughts through the storm, I am sure. The waiter's blood was washed from him along with all his sins. He staggered up some dark steps, higher and higher, as if climbing to Heaven itself. Giddy from wine, blind from retching, he tumbled through a door in a high wall and fell 20 feet into an enclosed garden.

Next morning he was still there, now under a dazzling blue sky, all manner of exotic plants crowding around him. His shirt torn. Ecu coins glinting between his akimbo legs. The two women who found him there, approaching with caution as if he were a wild animal, each said in a hushed voice to the other that he was the most beautiful man they had ever seen. One of these was Merluzza Ciampoli, 19, Cod's future wife, and the other Signora Blatta, 87, who looked after her.

When Cod opened his eyes he saw the sun and winced, holding up his hands like Saint Paul on that Damascus road. But then Merluzza stepped into the light. Such beauty! He closed his eyes in disbelief. Opening them he saw wrinkles! Creases! An oriental hound? No, Signora Blatta. She was poking him with a broom.

Cod climbed whoozily to his feet. Before he knew it, he was toppling over and the two women were holding him up. He held them both by the waist. Merluzza was wearing red shorts, a green T-shirt. Signora Blatta was in some sort of black funeral outfit.

'Pleasy-do, ladies, didn't mean to trespass on your nattyrooney little garden.' He sniffed aromas of flowers and girls. 'The storm, you see. And noise. I still don't feel very too-too.'

'*E un inglese,*' Merluzza told Signora Blatta, who immediately, for reasons lost in her own history, started wholloping him with the broom.

Cod tried to catch the broom, to fight her off. But he kept

ending up in Merluzza's arms. Their lips brushed, more than once. Then they were laughing, all three. But the spilled ecus started flashing in Cod's eyes and he suddenly yelled. He thought he was going to explode!

Then it was night again and he didn't know where he was. He remembered tossing in dreams. Was he back at the Hall? Had he really come to Italy? The light went on. He protected his eyes again. Merluzza and Signora Blatta were on either side of the bed.

'Sillymost of me to ask, but where am I?'

A musical voice that danced between words: 'This was my bro Giuseppe's room. You can stay here till you are well.'

'Very kind of you, Missy.' Then a big 'HARH!' at Signora Blatta. 'I remember! You're the old witch who attacked me with the broom! Well done, that witch! HARH!'

Signora Blatta suddenly beat her own face, weeping. Was she not an image of grief from the tragic ancient stage?

'Triple sorries, didn't mean to call the old witch an old witch. It's just my way of speaking.'

'Is okay,' said Merluzza, holding the sobbing black bundle under one arm. 'It's not you that makes her cry! My bro Giuseppe, this was his room. Signora Blatta she sees you and thinks of him in his bed again. Giuseppe, last month, he was singing with the tops of his voice in the Corso della Liberta . . . and he goes BOOM.'

'Oochy-coo!' said the guilty repented sinner. 'There's a lot of it about, I hear.'

Very suddenly the sobs stopped, as if turned off far away in sob H.Q. Signora Blatta advanced upon him. She pulled his cheeks and brought scarlet to their empty-page pallor.

'*Bello*! *Bello*! *Bello*!' went the crone, all her creases smiling. She loved him like a mother, he knew.

'Signora Blatta says you are very handsome,' said Merluzza, and suddenly she too was bending over him – a smell of daffodils. 'Sit up, pleasy-do, I help your pillows.'

He was sitting up. The old witch put a dark blue drink in his hands in a porcelain cup. She giggled and waggled her hands meaning him to drink it.

He sipped. Winced. His Italian saviours laughed.

'Drink, please, an old remedy of Signora Blatta's.'

To their astonishment, he suddenly knocked back the whole cup. And it was a big cup! And no cough afterwards!

Then with all his charm concentrated in his babyblue eyes: 'And you,' he said to Merluzza. 'Do you think I'm handsome?'

Her eyes were babyblue too, her hair fair, coppery gold. Austrian blood, of course, like so many this far north. She rolled these babyblues, smilingly towards a shadowy corner. The broom stood there, bristles up. It looked oddly alive.

'I say!' complained Cod. 'I was only asking a simple question!' Merluzza continued smiling. She took her old helper by the crooked elbow and led her out of the room. Signora Blatta chuckled, as in Macbeth Act 1, Scene 1. They left the room and flicked off the light.

'Hey! HEY! HEY!' Cod shouted after them. He would have chased, but his legs were lead, and he was starkers under the sheets.

Then the door opened. Light entered in a big yellow shape almost as far as his face. Merluzza was outlined there, a boy's dream of girlishness.

'I've seen better,' she said, then after an almost unheard chuckle. 'Maybe.'

The light was suddenly sucked away and she was gone.

'WHAT'S YOUR NAME?' yelled Cod in the darkness.

She spoke her name behind the door without coming in, as if she was announcing herself humbly at Saint Peter's gate. 'Merluzza Ciampoli.'

Cod spoke it, licked the name, hugged his pillows and tasted the hair oil of the late Giuseppe. His lips kissed the dark, making the name of Merluzza Ciampoli for a good twenty minutes, before Signora Blatta's medicine suddenly knocked him out.

Five days after he reeled out of the restaurant, leaving his friends ho-harhing with highjinks, Cod was walking down the Passeggiata Promenade in Merano, hands in pockets, day-dreaming, smiling to himself, when suddenly, like a war, *LA CUCURACHA*, BLARRRRRRRRRRR-RRRRRRRRRRRRR, HARH-HO-HO LAUGHTERINGS,

REVVVVVV-REVVV-REVVV OF ENGINES. An ambush. The squeal of his old life and friendships. He'd forgotten about Nobby and the others, about his own MG, parked up by the station, about his sins, everything.

'GOOD GOD, IT'S COD!' yelled Nobby in a let's-make-the-swine-explode voice. 'WHICH DREAM-TOPPING HAVE YOU BEING HIDING UNDER? WE'VE BEEN CHERCHAYING LE POISSON PURDU ALL PIGGN WEEK! YOU BELGIAN FISH ARTICLE YOU!'

'Nobby . . . I . . .' What was Nobby doing here in Merano? For the moment he couldn't work it out.

'We've bagged – harh-HARH! – 47 Ities! BOOM-BANG-ABANG!' informed Bass, standing upright in his driving seat to empty the last drips of a winebottle over Cod's head.

'Nobby's winning by lightyears!' said Dingo, Elgar playing under him, '35 points, piggn genius. Bass has 2 . . .'

'3!' insisted Bass.

How alien they looked. Were they his friends? Was he one of them?

'Looksee, fish article, this town's rotten with Nappers. Best be off somewhere else, ehwot? You've got a lot of catching up to do if you want to beat my score! In you get, I'll take you to your lonely MG and we'll race to Milan or Rome or somewhere equally explosive!'

'Sorry, Nobby, but I'm not coming.'

It wasn't just that he said it, it was the way he said it. He said it as if he wasn't one of them. Their funnybones died in that moment. Especially Nobby's.

'Not coming?' Nobby couldn't believe it. When he said 'In you get!' the second time, it was an order from a commanding officer to an enlisted man.

'Sorry, chapperoos. I've met a girl. An Italian girl. Merluzza Ciampoli she's called. I've fallen in love. She loves me right back. I'm staying here.'

Nobby and Cod had been joined at the hip since the day they met 25 years before. Between them they'd committed sexy doings with half the girls in England, but their friendship was the central reality of their lives. What was happening was not possible.

Nobby tried to laugh it off. 'Merlyudder Champollies! Well done that Belgian! Harh! Where is she, then? Let's see what she looks like!'

'She's in seeing her priest . . .'

'Another piggn Mahatma, wotho!' reeled Dingo.

'We're getting married. And I don't want you to see her, or meet her. Pleasy-do, go home. Leave us.'

Nobby's eyes were brimming. His voice croaked. 'I suppose we're not invited to the wedding?'

'No.'

'Blinkingmost hoojar!' Bass had never been more outraged. 'HOOJAR!' he barked at Cod.

'The Codfish is frightened we'll up our score on his bint!' said a subdued Dingo, who looked as if he'd been repeatedly slapped in the face by a wet cod.

'I WANT TO MEET COD'S PIGGN MOPPET!' yelled Nobby.

Cod walked away, not looking back at the MGs, which were, in a trigger-pulling instant, screeching, doing loops, playing dodgems behind him.

Suddenly Nobby's MG sliding in front of him, its driver's face a furious vicious mask. Nobby's gob frothing with hate, he said: 'Ariveidechie-bye-dar, Mario! We'll call back when you get your inhibitor fitted.'

He ran over a Napper as he BLARRRRRRRRRRRRRed and BRUMMMMMMMMMMed zoomingly away, singing 'Rule Britannia' through his tears.

Such a friendship! Nobby and Cod! I never had a friend as close as that. I wasn't even as close to my brothers as those two were to each other. That encounter on the Promenade in Merano was the end of all their youths. Worse still was to come in the history of that Italian jaunt in the pre-spring days of 2046. Bass Worthington was hanged in Milan by Noise Abatement Police, from a lamppost outside the Opera House. Dingo Catesby was shot at the wheel of his MG, laughing until the moment he died and his engine conked out, halfway down the Corso in Rome. Nobby, silenced, glum, drove back to England alone.

On the day that the outlawed Hieronymus Gosh was

machine-gunned to death on stage by Nappers in London, in what became certainlymost the last of his farewell concerts – June 5, 2046 – bro Cod married Merluzza Ciampoli in Merano's Cathedral. It was a quiet ceremony. For obvious reasons, only Cod whooped.

3

The Unending Old Age of Clem Chaffinch

Cod and Merluzza were married only 3 short months. It was not all bliss, cos my bro was evermost anxious that his truelove might-she-not-indeed explode at any mo. Italian streets, more even than our own, abounded in people with that 'I'm-going-to-scream' look on their faces. Merluzza, despite her happiness, must have had it too.

Early September. They'd been for a long walk through the castle dotty hillsides outside Merano. Merluzza said there was a supercustard restaurant just reopened after a refurbishing on the Via Portici. Merluzza led her darling fish article into vaguely familiar surroundings.

'I bet a squillion ecus they don't make octopus the way Signora Blatta does, ehwot! Hurh!'

Merluzza looked through her fringe in her sexy way. 'Signora Blatta, she doesn't make the octopus, she just cook the octopus. Is the octopus who is making the octopus.'

Even an octopus would have been charmed by Merluzza just then. She was as vibrant a soul as has walked the earth in my lifetime, evermost full of cheehe and ginger. Five minutes later Merluzza Chaffinch *née* Ciampoli exploded. Cod knew, always knew, from his first besotted whispering of her name in the dark, that it would happen. But when it did, when she just wasn't there anymore, it was a greater shock than any I've had, for sure.

This was the same restaurant he'd come to with Nobby and Co. It looked so different with its identity refurbished that he didn't quite recognize it. But the waiters recognized Cod as one of the Englishmen who'd blown up their colleague three months previous. They gabbled this information to Merluzza, all hugely irate, stamping, refusing to serve them. Plates were smashed. Innocent spoons slapped so that they flew across the room like insults.

Then Merluzza was on her feet, her babyblues full of the candlelight, her gesturing hands slicing through the abuse she was hurl-upping at her once darling fish article.

Cod yelled back, imploring her to be quiet, while the other diners dropped their cutlery on their octopuses and covered their ears. The shouting went on a long time, an endless time of fear and agony. Cod had picked up no Italian, but he knew she was yelling about her bro Giuseppe, his beautiful voice, his untimely boom. She was singing, loud as she could, favourites from Giuseppe's repertoire, screaming and singing, bits of a dozen tunes jerked in and out of the flow of her maddened sirenic wail. Cod flung his arms around her, tried to silence her aria with his lips. They could express what apologetic words could never. His love would shut her up, save her, prove that he was a different man from the Jilks who'd been Nobby's sidekick in ludicrous crimes.

And then she exploded. During the kiss. And some of the diners wailed in fright, and speechified in fury at the Noise Abatement Society for making this happen, and cater-wauled out of sheer 'Let's-get-life-over-with'. Most of them exploded. The noise was terrific in that quiet age, in that small low-ceilinged room. Like Armageddon in a hatbox.

When the Nappers arrived, walking on mince, the cook had come through from his domain and was standing brilliant white among the red, his hands held out in several subtly different gestures of disbelief. Cod had the shakes. When the Nappers asked him who he was, he started saying: 'Where is my wife?'

He said it over and over for days, shivering on the marriage bed, alone in that house he had fallen into, where Merluzza and Giuseppe had played as children, where once they had made as much noise as they liked. Signora Blatta was in hospital. The news of her pretty girl's death had given her a stroke. At 87, she wasn't expected to live.

Then Cod got out of bed, put on the leather jacket Merluzza had bought him, and paid a call on the man who'd pinched his MG. Shortly after he met his bride-to-be Cod had nipped secretively out to the station carpark and put the keys inside, a gift for a thief. He wanted rid of the symbol of his former sinful life and, of coursemost, Merluzza was not to know what she at last discovered: that he was one of 'those' Englishmen.

He'd seen the MG zooming about in recent weeks, and it tooted every time, as if by itself, to say hello. Now he was visiting the rude dapper black-maned skinny grinning hairy-chested youth who had been waving at girls from the MG all summer, looking like a randy despot, and daring the mountains roads to kill a man so perfect as he. Suddenly, the rightful owner was driving away BRRRRUMMMMMMMM and the thief, losing the thing he loved most in life, was waving his fists furiously at him. But not shouting. He was a survivor.

Cod drove the 1,000 miles home to Chaffinch Hall without rest. When he arrived, who should he see but his gooseberry fool bro, planting cuttings of rue and lavender in our walled garden.

'Good Cod, it's God!' I cried. My old joke. 'Where is she? You did bring her?'

An almost moveless nod of the head, meaning 'no' not 'yes.'

How disappointed I was! Cod's letter telling Wilf, as head of the family, that he was married, had filled me with a giddy joy. I'd been walking on clouds all summer. Just that morning I'd picked a dead bee from the path and truly thought I could bring it back to life with my joy. But 'twas a summer of Resurrections, was it not?

There were girly shouts coming from the pool. Cod's head turned, angry that English fems could shout, when his poor bint . . . well!

'Oh!' I cried. 'Did you get my letter? Whizzytopmost, tissent it?'

Cod looked blank. Sad. Blank. What was wrong? Long drive, I thought.

'You mean you don't know? About HIM?'

'Who?'

'Our great-great-grandfather, Clem Chaffinch. He's alive. He's here.'

Cod thought I'd flooped.

'He was dying of cancer and things, 60 years ago, in the 1980s. So with unusual foresight for a Chaffinch he had himself frozen, cryogenically ice-lollied, to wait for the cure. Well, they can cure anything these days! So they've defrosted him, cured him, and, chee-hee, he's here, swimming in the pool with a bunch of girls!'

We walked around for a looksee. Nearing the pool I put on my blind man's glasses, not wanting my purity spoiled by the sight of a 127-year-old man drilling away into naked girlies not born till 40 years after he died.

Cod almost smiled as I put the glasses on. I peeped over them with vicarish congratydoos: 'Much better. A smile.'

'That him, our great-great-granddaddy?'

I peeked. Then turned away, shocked. 'That's him. Oh, he never stops! These weeks have been so exhausting! There's 5 more girls upstairs, worn out. They'll all end up oversexifiedly bonkers in the attic, I'm sure. Nothing unusual for a handsome piece of cod like you, pleasy-do, with a beautiful young Italian wife. When you going to make me an uncle?'

'She's dead. Merluzza's dead. She's dead. She exploded.'

'Oh!'

The laughter around the pool seemed to grow farther away.

'The Noise Abatement Society killed her.'

I had to ask: 'Cod. Should I say a prayer? Would you mind?'

'You piggn dare!'

I didn't even say it in my head. Didn't seem right.

'Of course, you were spotty-onny about me all along, Chaffy. It wasn't just that I had no objective. I wasn't even alive. Just a succession of fleeting thoughts, jokes. My love for Merluzza concentrated my mind, brought me to life. Now my hate keeps me alive.'

I couldn't help peeking again. Clem was coming our way, that small sore-looking object between his legs pointing right up at the chimney-pots.

I hurriedly said this before Clem overpowered us: 'I'd like

you to know, Cod. I resigned from the Noise Abatement Society when I heard about the Italian explosions.'

I got no backslap of congratydoos for this brave, very dangerous gesture I had made. Clem was upon us, the 20th Century incarnate, looking as if he'd committed all its sins.

'Who's this poncey great tart?'

'This, Clem, is Cod, my younger brother. Cod, your great-great-granddaddy.'

'This the one that married the Itie?'

'That's right, Clem. Well remembered.'

They shook hands. Clem winked and licked his gums. His sore object, thankfullymost, was pointing at the crazy paving. But two goosepimply girls came goosing him and it was wagging upwards again.

Resenting the object, I shamelessly used Merluzza's death to kill it.

'Cod's wife, I've just heard, Clem. She has died.'

Clem nodded sagely and pushed one of his girls at Cod.

'Hair of the dog, lad!' he said, and winked and laughed like the Devil's own pimp. 'Yer not a bishop like this little bugger?'

Cod said that he wasn't a bishop and accepted his great-great-granddaddy's gift with shy thanks. But I wasn't a bishop either! Meanwhile, during all this, no sign of the object unstiffifying.

I went back to my planting while Cod and Clem engaged in some sort of lewd competition between the centuries. Clem later claimed to have won. Urk! At least they'd made friends!

When I'd nothing left to plant I was going inside when Cod rushed past me on the steps.

'Off already?'

'Just came home for my certificates,' he said. 'I'm applying for Despot School.'

I ran towards him, as if to push him out of the way of a falling piano. But when I got to where I thought he was, he was in his MG and circling me, his BRRRRRRRUmmmmm throwing gravel at me.

'DESPOT SCHOOL! YOU!!!!! COD! DEAR BRO! WHY THAT? OF ALL THINGS!'

'You always wanted me to make something of myself! Well, I'll be a DESPOT. And in a year of two . . . what a piggn noise I'm going to make!'

Eyes full of gravel, *La Cucuracha* tooting down the drive, and he was gone.

'YOU CAN'T FIGHT THEM! THEY'RE TOO POWER-FUL!' I yelled, then covered my mouth and looked to the bushes for Nappers.

I sat by the pool till dark, eating nuts in a daze. One of Clem's girls sat cross-legged at my feet describing the exact feeling her sexual bits gave her during different weathers. But I wasn't listening. As for Bro Cod, Tadese, I only saw him one more time.

Doesn't my pole look lonely. It's as if I'd died. DESPOT SCHOOL! PIGGN DESPOT SCHOOL!!!!

4

Despot School

This is not the *Politico-Theologicus* of Chaffinch Chaffinch. It is my memoirs of my bird-brained family in the 21st Century. But as Tadese here doesn't know a despot from a teapot, I shall begin my sermonizing this morning with speech upon this subject. Despots. Not teapots.

There have always, Tadese, been despots! But in my lifetime there have been more than ever before. Thinky-doos, as a political movement it is a 21st Century phenomenon. In the '20s, when the democracies failed, there was no other political system waiting its turn. So began the drift to despotism. Smithers was a despot in all but name, was he not?

By the '30s every country was run by its own despot, indeed it was. Mini-despots, assistant despots, local despots, everywhere there were despots and people who wanted to be despots. The despot's word was law. Big smiley men. Little runts with a grievance. Grim moralists with obsession for detail. Straightforward blue-chinned gangsters. Stolid avuncular pals, with a peaceful present but a violent past and more violent future, to whom you always owed money. These first despots I hardly remember, but they were a tame crew compared to some of the chaotic charmers we were stuck with later on.

A despot, it was believed, got things DONE! No shillyshally-doos. If a problem arose, it was dealt with immediately, no worries about the Press or public opinion or the opposition – wot opposition? People, anyone and everyone, said: There's no stability without a good despot. And a good despot was a swinemost Jilking piggn antichrist, that's wot! Absolute power corrupted absolutely everyone, not just the mad cherry in charge of the cake! Dreadfulmost times!

At first despots were sponsored by commercial organizations, banks often as not, but also by manufacturers of soft drinks, choc bars, doggyfood and shampoo. Thus, if you had a despot who was sponsored by, say, a combination of the above – and it did happen! – then those products became compulsory under the so-sponsored despot and the use of a rival product was treasonous. Life for the despoted-over citizen in such a case would involve the chain-eating of the choc bar, while shampooing both himself and the doggyfood-chomping dog to the constant fizz of pop. This situation endured only when the banks and whathaveyounot were more powerful than the despots. Later, the despots owned everything, everyone, mind and body and almost soul.

By the '40s a structure had emerged, and with it a professional class of despots, international in character, with a body called the 'Despotic Committee of 3' nominally in charge of the whole shooting match. These 3 'Regulators' ran a department which made appointments and so on. It became increasingly powerful. Despots were bought and sold on the open market, in the way footballers were in the last century, or pnong players in the Pnong Age.

Despots were trained in schools, like the one near Basingstoke which Cod attended. Devilishly hard to get into, so they were. From there, if they showed promise, they were sent to one of the countries operated by the D.C. of 3 for training purposes. Bolivia was one such country, Portugal I think another, and . . . oooh, a couple more. Passing with a high grade there could mean immediate appointment as Assistant Despot in a major block. Better still, in the bi-annual auction a promising graduate despot might have his contract bought, meaning transfer as Despot to whichever country had liked his cut. Many of the more famous names appeared like this, suddenly, straight from Despot School.

It was all very respectable. Precious few coups, putsches, assassinations. A quiet New World Order, with the Noise Abatement Society the only alternate authority. But some despots wore Napper uniforms, indeedy-be. In practice, the N.A.S.'s local Chief Hushler was invariably, guess who, the local despot. The silent tongue in the cruel mouth.

Some despots stayed put for years. In England we had a Mr Craik right through the '40s, a tall grey Swedish-looking man in a 20th Century suit, who seemed very capable, but who in fact had never set foot in Downing Street. He spent his time in a bungalow near Swindon playing computer games. He ruled by the simple means of purging the civil service every few weeks, and did this at random with the aid of his computer. He resigned after the Abdication and was replaced by the remarkably similar Mr Chegwin, whose kingly wave from the balcony of Buckingham Palace was a great reassurance to us all. But, pleasy-do, he proved to be the very same man as Craik but with his moustache shaved off! It was 8 years, late '50s, before anyone realized. A scandal of sorts. He was removed by the D.C. of 3, put up for auction, and after there were no bidders, he became Professor of Despotism in Oxford, a position he continued to hold long after the despots fell into history's dustbin.

MacTavish, of course, is reckoned as the first despot. But was that ginger bogeyman ever a despot? He was freely elected when he was European President, was he not, and though he acted despotically in that role, he left office without truck when his term was up. Later, when he re-emerged as grey as he was ginger, as Laird of the Scottish Confederacy, he still was not a pure despot, because he owed his position to the clans. And when he wiped out the heads of the leading clans on 'Claymore Thursday', which still failed to prevent the break-up of the Confederacy, he was acting more like an unconstitutional monarch than a despot. Could it be said that the ogre MacTavish was a disillusioned democrat whose ambitions could only be served by despotic means?

The only goody-goody thing I can say about the despots relates to MacTavish. Cos without the despots, and Tixover most of all, MacTavish would have succeeded in his aims and we'd all have ended up Scottish! The battle of Plovdiv in '53 was a 21st Century Culloden, and shattered the unity of the clans. It was, indeedy-be, fought as an 18th Century battle, cos the Noise Abatement Society insisted that if there was going to be a battle at all it must have no BANGS in it. The combatants were reduced to swords and shillelaghs.

Tixover's victory was the greatest moment of despotism. After Plovdiv the pipers played only laments and their far-flung Scots countries lost their pepper and reverted to a sort-of English quietude. You forgot they were there. But MacTavish, that snail with a tartan trail, still lay dozing in his shining new city of New Arbroath, a vision beside the Caspian Sea, his mind bubbling like hot porridge with plans to Scottishize the world, while squillions of Scots embryos, in their first moments of life, came ghostly to his doze to thank him for all that they would be, orbiting his impure despotic thoughts like pink pnongballs.

Forgive me O Lord, I adore all your myriad creatures, but – I cannot help myself! – I cannot abide a Scotsman!

Of course, if Plovdiv was despotism's greatest moment, it was like many greatest moments: a prelude to the end. By the late '50s there was hardly a despot left, just a few stubborn ones in peculiar countries. Most of those who had saluted despots in their youth looked back with shame from middle age.

Now I shall pause, Tadese, to eat 3 bananas, while you study what you have just written down about despotism. If I suck the bananas rather than chomp them, you'll have time to read through 3 times. Chee-hoo! Peely-do! Suck! Chomp! Suck!

*

It was this, brethren, that my kindly broken-hearted bro sought to become. A despot. Wait on, I think I'll have another banana.

*

Cod bought his Despot School uniform in *Despotic Outfitters, Tailors to the Great* in Jermyn Street – all black leather, lederhosen trews, studded bullfighter's-style short jacket, jackboots, a tall helmet with a big D on it. Monstrous!

He parked his MG in the campus carpark, and walked with his leather squeakingly talking to him, through a curtain of falling leaves, across the campus to the Rallying Room. The Despot School, which after all his tests and interviews he was at last approaching, looked like a torn-apart birdcage. It was all wires and round mirrors and sandstone slabs. Similarly dressed potential despots goosestepped along the paths, commanding the space around them. Cod had never goosestepped before, but had a go. He was taking this very seriously. No giggles.

But suddenly, the squeak of another set of leathers, right beside him. Should he look? He didn't. He goosestepped on . . .

Then the body in the other set of leathers said: 'Howdee-doodee, my old fish article! Spain or Poland to start with? How's about you Poland and me Spain? Harh!'

Nobby Tixover! They tripped over each other's goosesteps and sat laughing on the grass.

'Nobby! You're the last person I'd ever . . . here! DES-POT SCHOOL! HARH!'

'No chance of despotarizing in Belgium, worst luck for you, poisson Belge. Piggn Scots have got it! Spain for me. Flamenco. Paella. Dimme, fish article, I had to do something with myself!' Then in a subtly different tone. 'It's my second term, thar knows. I'm quite a star. You'll see! HARH!'

The old laughter returned. But as they got to their feet, gripping each other's gloved hand, their eyes looked away from each other. They were in a different chapter of their lives and knew it. Even if their friendship was the same, Cod was no longer quite Cod and Nobby wasn't Nobby.

It was this new sharp-eyed moustached-lipped Nobby who said in neutral tone: 'Bass was hanged by the Nappers, you know. Yes. And they shot Dingo in Rome. Wotnot bout you? Married life didn't work out, supposy-do?'

'She blew up.' Cod shrugged. 'Blasted Ities!'

Nobby let out a 'HARHHHHHH!' that turned every moustachioed head on every pathway nearabouts. It gave pause to every goosestep.

Cod laughed with him. They flung a leather arm around each other and high-kicked ludicrously, gigglesomely, towards the Rallying Room. The old firm, together again!

The Rallying Room was the main part of the birdcage. It was full of chairs and heroic sculpture. Nobby entered the room, hands on hips, like a robber in an opera. He was showing himself defiantly to his rivals, hundreds of rivals in the studentine present and the despotic future.

'Looksee, fish article. You can't sit with me. I'm a Junior Despot 1st Class. I sit at the front.'

'Padonay moi!' said the fish article, with comic wobbly head.

Nobby didn't like his old friend being flippant about his hard-won rank. A theatrical scowl mounted his face, and aloofness personified when he said: 'Look me up for toodlychatabye, pleasydo, soon as poz, ehwot! A-block, 2nd floor, Room 8,' But the scowl couldn't sustain itself with Cod. It turned to a cheesy grin. 'Fish article!' he cried, and goosestepped down to the front.'

Cod plonked himself into the chair nearest his pozzy. When a short creature, half man, half moustache, demanded that it was his chair, Cod said: 'Piggn bog off, tiny! Harh!' He thought it was the way to behave. The short creature gave him his card and huffed off.

At that same moment the Rallying Room, now full of its 2,000 students, burst into a thunderous mantra and stamp of feet.

'OOLU!-OOLU!-OOLU! OOLU-WANG-WANG-WANG! OOLU!-OOLU!-OOLU! OOLU-WANG-WANG-WANG!'

Cod was rather excited!

The chant was to help to the podium a white-haired, plucked parrot of a man, Ludovic Emmaus, one-time Despot of Australia until ousted by Barry Hamlet. He was Principal and Founder of the Despot School.

Ex-Despot Emmaus cleared his narrow throat and began his Start of Term Speech. He looked and sounded like a children's entertainer at a down-at-heel resort. He was all wet-Sunday, with the gestures of a frail auntie. But this was he, the renowned Emmaus, who'd written the book on despotism.

'Welcome, despotettes, to Autumn Term 2046 at the Ludovic Emmaus Despot School.'

He suddenly lifted his head way back as if to allow a condor to fly past, then his grin somehow grew even bigger and he continued, a spook under the lights.

'Those of you joining us today, and you know who you are, will, if you are successful, prove yourself worthy of despotic leadership in the international arena in the exciting years of despotism to come. Remember at all times that the people of the world, poor fools that they are, have awarded our despotic class a sacred trust that is despotism. Christ-like Commitment is our byword. Crackdown is our law. Benevolent Cruelty is the very least of our expectations. Commitment. Crackdown. Cruelty. These are the pillars on which despotism is built . . .'

In the tradition of despot's speeches, it went on for 3 hours. Emmaus paused for a drink of water and a thin sandwich, then continued for another 2 hours. As his mind wandered during the speech, did Bro Cod remember the day I saved him from the horrors of another school? From the sadistic attentions of Mr Bowsie. Did you remember that, you foolish piece of cod? Did you know I would have given my nutty life to save you from just that one day in Despot School?

'OOLU!-OOLU!-OOLU! OOLU-WANG-WANG-WANG! OOLU!-OOLU!-OOLU! OOLU-WANG-WANG-WANG!'

The speech was over. The boredom was worth it for this exciting chanting! The foot stamping! Then Cod thought: 'They're making a noise! A NOISE!' This was one boxed ear for the piggn Noise Abatement Society already!

'OOLU!-OOLU!-OOLU!' he cried, just when everyone had finished ooluing and wanging.

But his cry started off another round: 'OOLU!-OOLU!-OOLU! OOLU-WANG-WANG-WANG!'

The tune of the mantra was in his goosestep as he hurried across the campus. His quickened step caused faster gooses in all he overtook! He was looking for A-block. Ah! Had to be one of those! 3 squat square buildings which looked like featureless sandcastles. The A in A-block, it turned out, stood for Attilla the Hun. There was a bronze statue of him outside.

Cod squeaked in from the tweeting parkland to corridors full of boisterous activity. Among the privileged, it seemed, noise was permissible and enjoyed! Much slapping was going on. He'd read about this in the prospectus. Despots were required, professionally, to slap a lot of people. So slapping practice was essential and was to be indulged in during all free moments. Cod joined in. Slapped everyone he passed, was slapped back by experts. He met that tiny half man, half moustache chapperoo again, slapped him and received the gift of another card.

Red-faced Cod! And bloodied on the lip. How Merluzza would have kissed it better! A moment of weakness. Then, increased strength. He kicked open a door, police style. Four muscly oiled Germans wearing only sporting caps were slapping each other senseless inside a hologram of a marching oompa Bavarian band.

'Junior Despot 1st Class Tixover's room! Where is?' barked Cod.

They saluted. The hologram was put on pause between an oom and a pa. An unstilled figure stepped forward.

'Pleasey-do to be turning ze next left, pleasy-do. Unt five doors after the portrait of Machiavelli you will becoming to Herr Tixover's door!'

'Thanks a buffalo,' said Cod, then nodded his head. 'Carry on.'

The band marched on. They renewed their mutual attack with the energy expected of future despots.

Nobby was effusive in his welcomings, hooking Cod into his dark room. One bright light over a wooden chair. Cod was shoved into the chair.

'HARH! HARH! HURH-HARH!' went Nobby walking around him like a scornful world spinning around a dreamer.

'Clarty-heeps, Nobby! This place is wiffo with Germans! All you can hear in the corridors is *ACHTUNG!* and *SCHNELL-SCHNELL!* I mean, despotism's one thing, but not with Germans in it!'

Nobby's laughter became more private. His hand suddenly turned the hot light towards the wall, illuminating a terrifying wide-eyed figure, nodding two corkscrew curls on an otherwise huge bald head.

'Fish article, may I introduce you to my roommate: Karl Heinz Rötenschwein.'

'Ooops, triple sorries! HARH! Boggn good despots, yer Germans make, ehwot?'

Rötenschwein brushed his pale ginger moustache and scratched his recentmost duelling scar with a thumbnail. He stepped towards the light, his studs coming at Cod like comets and blinding him. The German's mouth was slowly opening from a manic smile to the devouring gape of a basking shark. The overall effect was like having a near-death experience and meeting not God at the end of the bright tunnel, but Beelzebub.

'Och, ja, Nobby, your friend will make a severe despot!' Rötenschwein's warty forefinger tapped his pursed lips.

'Too-too,' said Nobby. 'Karl's a great judge of men, old Belge. Emmaus says it's the most important quality a despot can have, and there's none more heapo with it than Karl. He's never wrong.'

'Nein, never wrong. Howdeedoodee, Despotette Cod Chaffinch.'

They shook hands. Rötenschwein yanked Cod to his feet. The light shone. All he could see were the blighter's eyes.

'Och, ja! A certain concentration about the eyes, Nobby! See it! His eyes! Zis is not ambition, we all have ambition. Zis is . . . objective, ja, what so few of us have: objective!'

'Nope, you're got one wrong this time, Herr Rottenswine, I've no objective, never have, have I Nobby? Typical son of the 21st Century, that's me. Thoughtless. Piggn hopeless all round.' Old laughter from Nobby.

Suddenly Rötenschwein had let go of Cod and was pacing beyond the light, disembodied. 'Zat name! Cod Chaffinch! Part fish, part bird. You do not live in the same element as ze rest of us, nein! No, you are not one of us, you are more than us. THIS MAN, Nobby, he is our greatest rival!' Stamping and laughing like a victorious 6-footer of a Rumplestiltskin he announced: 'One day, Nobby, this fish article will rule the WORLD!'

Cod didn't know if he was being funny or wot.

But Rötenschwein's flourish was still ringing in his quiet-accustomed ears, when the main light came on. The door was open and the small pale figure of Ludovic Emmaus stood there, already talking in his nursery voice.

'Just an informal call on some of my favourites. Oooh, you're nice – I don't believe we've met.'

'This is Cod Chaffinch,' introduced Nobby. 'An old friend of mine. Pick of the new intake.'

'An exceptional talent, *mein führer*! A man of objective!' stamped Rötenschwein, even more frightening in the full light.

Emmaus offered Cod a limp hand. But when Cod took it limply, the hand gripped like a giant.

'I am Ludovic Emmaus, Principal and Founder of your Despot School, Despotette Chaffinch. I was, I'm sure you'll remember, Despot of Australia before being ousted in a coup by Barry Hamlet. Now I'm reliving old mistakes in the classroom, eh Karl?'

Rötenschwein clicked his heels and woofed: *'FÜHRER!'*

Then, examining Cod with an eye too shrewd to look at, Emmaus said: 'Exactly what is this objective of yours, Despotette Chaffinch?'

'N-n-nothing, *führer*. I, erm . . . I hope to make a noise somewhere, someday.'

That children's entertainer voice: 'Mustn't tell the Noise Abatement boys, eh wot?'

Laughter all around. Big, flattering Germanic slapping ho-ho's from Rötenschwein. But Emmaus's eye was on him, with an I'm-about-to-ruin-your-day look . . .

'Which reminds me, Karl. They've turned down your suggestion.'

'ERK, ZE FOOLS!'

Rötenschwein was suddenly a thwarted little boy. He bit his fist and turned away.

'Karl had a brilliant suggestion for them, Despotette Chaffinch. He suggested that the ultimate act of Noise Abatement would be to surgically deafen the entire population of the world. My spies tell me that the suggestion failed to become policy by only 2 votes.'

A little romantic wail of triumph-just-missed from the turned-to-the-wall Rötenschwein.

'The argument which tipped the balance, Despotette

Chaffinch, is that if everyone is deaf, how do we know that there's not someone somewhere making the most dreadful racket?'

Emmaus jerked back his head, letting off a huge police siren laugh, so frightening that the others cowered and he laughed alone. Then, at last, he released Cod's pulverized hand and pulled a scroll from up his sleeve. He tapped Rötenschwein on the shoulder with it.

Rötenschwein flinched away. 'I offer zem the ultimate silence and zey refuse me! *Dummkophs!*'

'Karl, they have awarded you the Golden Hushabye Merit Certificate. Only the 4th ever awarded. A great honour for the School.'

Rötenschwein span around like a dancer. He embraced the certificate as if it were a delicate girl. 'A Golden Hushabye Merit Certificate!' he muttered over and over. 'Och, *mein führer!*'

Emmaus's shrewd eye studied Cod a bit more, then looked at Nobby, then them both as a pair, finally a cursory glance as the ecstatic Rötenschwein. Then he was gone. Somehow he just wasn't there and it was hard to believe he could ever have existed.

Cod flexed his sore fingers and gave Nobby a look which said everything he wanted to be known about his feelings at that moment.

'Wiffo!' said Nobby.

'Toodleywiffagoggo!' said Cod, upping him.

Suddenly, Rötenschwein tossed his beloved merit certificate away. He was approaching a new dancing partner – Cod!

'Wotsit? Wotsit?' asked Cod, backing away.

Rötenschwein had him against the wall – their leathers squeaked together – and yelled at Nobby, his pickled cabbage breath smarting Cod's eyes: 'Top pocket! His top pocket! Now, Tixover! I order you!'

Two cards poked from Cod's top pocket. A concerned Nobby plucked them out.

'Fish article, was it a midget with a toothbrush under his conk who gave you these?'

'Titchy little item, yes.'

'GILZENE!' shouted Rötenschwein.

Next thing Cod knew Rötenschwein was kissing his cheeks, boyish, delighted.

'You are fighting two duels with Gilzene in the gym at 4,' informed Nobby, twiddling the end of his left moustachio.

'Boglyfala!' swore the fish article with a bogus smile.

5

The Menace of Karl Heinz Rötenschwein

After Cod wounded Junior Despot 2nd Class Gilzene in the first duel, then killed him in the second, he became quite the coming man. Gilzene was known as about the best shot in Despot School. But his short arms made him ill-equipped for the epée, which is why Cod, having choice of weapons, chose it.

But the simple fact that he'd killed the troublesome little man made everyone wary of him. All except Rötenschwein, the best swordsman on Earth according to Nobby. He'd killed 41 fellow students since he joined the school 5 terms before. Rötenschwein knew the measure of Cod as a swordsman. Over breakfast for days, he enthusiastically went over the Gilzene duels, saying how he would have done things better. He kept grabbing Cod's wrists and testing them, saying: 'Nein, a fish a bad swordsman he is making.'

Cod was irritated, but looks from Nobby told him not to upset the German.

A week as a student of despotism, and still not a full night's sleep, Cod awoke with a feeling that someone or something was in the room. He flicked on the light and there was Rötenschwein squatting on the floor, wriggling constipatedly in suede pyjamas.

'You like to be going for a walk with me?'

It was 3.30 A.M.

'Okeydoakie,' said Cod, too spooked to refuse.

They walked in the moonlight through the campus. Not a word was spoken. Then Rötenschwein started singing a tuneless song in old high German, swinging around the skinny trees like a girl. In some strange way, Cod was reminded of the midnight walks he'd taken with Merluzza. Meanwhile, he'd never been so frightened in his life. He was sure that Rötenschwein was going to kill him.

135

Suddenly, the German fell to his knees. He grabbed Cod's hand, wiped his brow with it, then licked it.

'I am going to leave you now, fish article. Thankybees for spending these private moments together with your new friend Karl. I would so like to be cruel to you. But *nein*. There is something about you, I don't know, it makes me happy.'

He jumped up and ran, danced, fencing without a sword in the night. As Cod returned to his rooms in H-Block, he heard a terrifying music bounding over the trees. It was Rötenschwein. He'd broken into the Rallying Room and was performing there, singing alone in the dark. Cod was feverish. If he'd had the keys to his MG in his pocket, he would have zoomed away forever right then.

Wherever he went during the following days, there was Rötenschwein, always ready with a slap or a trip and a hearty *JAWOHL*! He couldn't even eat without him! He'd sit down in the cafeteria and be ambushed by Rötenschwein, who'd push his own tray aside and pick from Cod's plate, nattering all the time about his duels, his valley in Bavaria, his 3 sisters, his cows, alpine flowers. All in the most sinister, threatening manner, which suggested: 'Any moment, I will kill you, this fork, a magic word, you will be dead before you know how.'

In his third week, his head now stuffed with Napoleon and Julius Caesar, while having a violent massage on facing slabs after a misinformation lecture, he asked Nobby if he was reading Rötenschwein rightly.

'He's toying with me, tissent he? He's going to challenge me to a duel, today, tomorrow. He sees me as one day being his rival in our despotic careers. He wants me safe and dead.'

'Nar! Wot codswhallop, Cod article! Karl's ya pal! He likes you. Likes you better than me, than anybody! I shouldn't barf you this, but he's carved your name beside his own under that board he sleeps on. You're his Marshal Ney. He'll never challenge you to a duel. He sees his whole future with you at his side.'

That afternoon Cod challenged Rötenschwein to a duel. He snatched his swagger-stick off him and snapped it, threw it to the ground, then pulled his moustache hard.

An irate Rötenschwein reached to pull Cod's tache in return.

But Cod's despotic tache was just growing and wasn't long enough to pull yet . . . Then suddenly the German flung his arms wide and embraced his challenger.

'You and me, fish article! Wot a great duel zis will be! Ze whole school vill be there. And your death, it vill be glorious! It is so – our names will be linked forever!'

He touched Cod's cheek with his warty index finger: 'First I cut you here! WHA-HAAAA!'

With a theatrical flourish he danced off among the trees, fencing the air, exercising his wrists, just as he'd done on that strange moonlit night, a week or a lifetime before.

Cod was gloommost sorry-be when he went back to his room.

'Wots ado?' said Nobby, who'd popped in for a natter and had pinched a snooze instead. 'You haven't read it yet.'

'Hmm?'

'Letter from the Mahatma, foolydo!'

Cod picked it up and read it twice before its meaning sank in.

Dearest Bro Cod,

I hope you are doing well at Despot School. Unfortunatelydoos, I have sad news to relate. Great-great-grandfather Clem passed away today, peacefully in his sleep. He hardly suffered at all. In the recent blisteringly hot weather he had taken to living on a diet of peppermint ice-cream. This reacted with an amount of cryogenic fluid still in his system and we found him frozen stiff on his lilo. Before the medical team could get him back to his tank, he'd turned to mush. Such a waste! After his long sleep, just a few brief weeks in the sun. The girls are beside themselves, but I am unable to comfort them.

Praying for him. Praying for you. Much love.
Chaff.

'Lord of Nobs.'

'Yes, fish article.'

'If anything should ever happen to me, thar knows, will you tell the Mahatma, in person I mean, fizz to fizz?'

'O'course, poisson Belge – but wot's going to happen to you?'

'I'm fighting a duel with Karl Heinz Rötenschwein in twenty minutes.'

'Boggn pleek, Cod! Boggn pleek, you Jilks! You haven't a monkey's!'

*

Rötenschwein was wearing only a leather thong with an R of diamond studs sparkling from its modest bulge and a pair of slim studious reading glasses. He was chewing one wrist, his thoughts far away, when the gym doors burst open and in came floods of leather-clad despotettes. Suddenly Rötenschwein sprang to action, he chased them with his epée, pinning the lot to the wall. His red hairless body shook with laugher. Then Cod and Nobby strode in and his skin tightened all over, his buttocks lifted themselves in the air and he hurried across to them on his toes.

'I say, Karl,' pleaded Nobby. 'You can't fight the fish article. He's life's greatest treasure. I've known him since forever. Not the fish article, Karl!'

Rötenschwein looked at Nobby coldly.

'Usually, Nobby, you are *mein* second.'

Shyly: 'Not today. I'm Cod's today.'

Rötenschwein hummered like a disdainful horse, then winked at one of the spectators, a slight Austrian called Fichte, who stepped forward to be his second. Fichte flushed with pride.

'Don't do it, Cod!' Nobby held his friend by the shoulders. 'We'll leave, now. We'll go to Chaffinch Hall, live out our lives in the attic! He'll kill you, laddio.'

Brave Cod! 'I've been practising every day, on the quiet. Colonel Csjaks says I'm pretty good.'

But the moment he put the sword in his hand, Rötenschwein had broken the rules, passing near them like a fly, his swishing epée flicking Cod's foiled foil into Nobby's startled hands. He was humming that evil tune of his.

Nobby and Fichte called them together for the duel. They

138

all closed their eyes for prayers, except Cod. Rötenschwein obviously took his religion seriously. He was in a brief religious ecstasy of a kind this religious nut has rarely indulged in.

Then a single click of swords and it was over before it began. Cod was cut on the cheek and his epée was out of his hand and pinning Fichte to the wall. Before Cod realized what had happened, Rötenschwein was about other business, watching the shallow breathing of Fichte through his studious glasses. Like an entomologist with a nine-legged bug. Had he planned all this? Had he meant it to happen exactly this way? Rötenschwein flung his arm around Cod, dragging him from the attentions being paid to his new duelling scar, and made him watch too. Fichte's breathing stopped. He was dead.

'Another wonderful moment we have shared together, fish article,' said Rötenschwien, rubbing Cod's blood on his chest. *'JAWOHL! JAWOHL!'* And off he went, glistening with sweat.

'OOLU-OOLU-OOLU! OOLU-WANG-WANG-WANG!' went the spectators. And some shouted pnongistaly 'OLÉ! OLÉ!'

'He's dangling me by the heels, isn't he Nobby? He's enjoying making me suffer. Rolling me in the batter, ehwot? – Much more fun than a quick kill.'

Nobby looked at the sleeping Fichte and said nothing.

Next day, his handsome face scarred and taped, Cod skipped his lectures and went for a knockabout on the campus pnong court. The balls span furiously out of the slats and he broke three pnongsticks on them. He dived into the jetstream and crashed into the wall a dozen times. On his back, breathless, an artillery of pnongballs firing above his eyes, feeling old and spent, he looked up and there was Rötenschwein staring down, pressed against the glass in a spectator's box. Suddenly he was gone, leaving a greasemark. Then his voice everywhere, through the sound system.

'ZERE IS NOTHING, I FIND, AS COMFORTING AS THE RUBBERY THWONKS OF A P-NONGGGBALL WHEN A MAN IS FEELING MELANCHOLY.'

'We'd not be able to hear it at all if your Noise Abatement friends clawed our ears out!'

'Point taken, fish article! I was sorry to be hearing about
the death of your great-great-grandfather. He lived through
the age of the great 20th Century dictators. A sad loss.'

'Thanky-be.'

Suddenly the klaxons were going. OLÉs on tape. All
the sounds of old-fashioned pnong, long silenced by the
silent majority. Rötenschwein bounded on court dressed as
a Wibley.

'Don't mind if I play Wibley against you?'

Cod was delighted. He'd show the piggn boggn sauerkraut
how to play pnong. Cod had been a Carstairs fan – he knew
a few tricks!

But Rötenschwein knew a few of his own! There followed 30 minutes of the most violent possible pnong. The
pnongballs never stopped firing. Cod's pronged-pnongstick
flipped Rötenschwein a hundred times. My bro was battered,
his duelling scar throbbing, but he was winning! Then he was
dizzy and Rötenschwein nearly had him, but his opponent's
goosesteping leg got caught in the jetstream and he pirouetted
across court until a surprise pnongball shot from the bucket
itself and hit him hard on the back of the head. He fell flat,
Wiblied! Cod picked up a broken pnongstick and was about to
thrust it into Rötenschwein's heart, exorcising this vampire
from his terrible new life.

But Rötenschwein's eyes opened. 'I am not what you think
I am. I have been testing you for *ein* reason, Nobby's friend.
I had to be sure about you!'

Cod hesitated. Just long enough for Rötenschwein to be
on his feet at the bumpy end. The klaxons were insistent,
demanding action, but the players just faced each other.

'If, my flying-fishy friend, I do one day rule the world, it
will be for one purpose.'

'Wot's that you say? Can't hear.'

They walked towards each other, pnongballs missing them
both by less than inches.

'REVENGE!' yippie-I-ayed Rötenschwein. '*JAWOHL*!
REVENGE!'

Cod was too scared to speak. Rötenschwein's face was
almost supernatural in its twitching expression of hatred.

'Nobby has told me about your marriage, fish article. I also lost *mein* truelove.'

Cod's strength left him. He sank down. He'd felt Merluzza's last kiss. He was swoonish and ill, pnonged-out.

Rötenschwein was beside him, in his face: '*Mein* truelove, he was a wonderful talented young man.'

'Hm?'

'It is a secret. No one can tell to look at me. I am gay.'

'Gay? Wot, you mean . . . I thought they could cure that with tablets these days.'

'Not all of us want to be cured!' barked the gay Rötenschwein, then suddenly his voice was a musical tremble as he stared popeyed at his fist, kissing it every few moments: 'He had a beautiful voice, so melodious. Och, how proud he was of ze Heavenly noises he made with it! When the crowd gathered in the street that day to hear him sing, tears in their eyes, at the back they cried to him SING LOUDER!!! He sang! LOUDER! Och, he sang louder! *Mein* stroodle!'

He was weeping, sobbing. A pnongball struck him hard on the back. He didn't seem to feel it.'

'What was your chapperoo called, Karl?' Cod was dizzy, but alert to an incredible possibility!

'His name was Giuseppe Ciampoli.'

Cod grabbed the weeping Hun by the face, shook it until the 2 corkscrew curls were out of the pale colourless eyes.

'I KNEW IT! KARL! KARL! I MARRIED GIUSEPPE CIAMPOLI'S SISTER. SHE WAS THE TRUELOVE I LOST.'

The klaxons were so loud they could barely hear each other.

'Merluzza? You married MERLUZZA?'

'Evermost I did! We are brothers, you and I! True bros!'

Both sobbing, they embraced, like children beaten by a cruel father whose only comfort is in each other. In Cod's ear Rötenschwein whispered the name of Giuseppe Ciampoli, and Cod had a vision of his new friend sitting at table in the house in Merano, with Signora Blatta bringing in the cheese, teasing Merluzza while teaching a quiet German hymn to Giuseppe. In that, the greatest of their shared moments,

Rötenschwein was more of a bro to my bro Cod than I ever was.

Then a final whisper from Rötenschwein: 'We will fight them together! We will make noises!'

He was stroking the bleeding tape on Cod's face which covered the stitched wound he himself had made when . . . QUIET! All quiet! Just a tinnitus hum in their ears. No other sound. The pnongistas stopped shouting. The klaxons quitterood. Even pnong could be silenced. The two hugging bros looked up. Nobby was behind the glass in the control booth. His face was subtly contorted for an instantly passing instant which Rötenschwein saw but Cod, though knowing him better, did not. Then the voice through the sound system:

'WOT'S ADO WITH YOUS TWO MURDERERS? THEY'VE BEEN COMPLAINING IN BASINGSTOKE ABOUT YOUR PIGGN RACKET! ALL THE DECIBEL METERS ARE DANCING FANDANGOS!'

'An innocent game of p-nongggg!' waved Rötenschwein.

Then he jumped up, caught a flying pnongball and threw it at the spinning target with all his might. Maximum points! In the old game a noise to shatter the peace of Basingstoke for a twelvemonth! But in silent pnong the noise of a spoon dropping into a dry well.

Nobby turned the game off. Pnongballs rolled out of the slats and into the recovery hole, like bubbles down the plughole in the last bathnight of childhood.

6

Nobby the Great

Ludovic Emmaus understood perfectly the nature of the knock on his study door. He was delighted with his knowledge and awarded himself another gherkin. He didn't answer. He looked at his clock. 7 minutes was his guess.

6 minutes later, the same knock.

'Come in,' said Emmaus softly. 'But beware the tongue that awaits you.'

It was Nobby. He had expected Rötenschwein. He was pleased. 'Junior Despot Tixover. Having trouble with your essay on the Despotic Ideal?'

'A report, sir.'

Emmaus was erectile with pleasure. At any moment, a betrayal, a denouncing of friends! Nothing better! But it was that same children's entertainer's voice that spoke, as if to a glove puppet.

'A report, Junior Despot Tixover? A report?'

'Rottenswine and Chaffinch, sir. They are hoojars, that's what, sir! They're involved in secret schemes attacking Noise Abatement.'

'Gherkin, Junior Despot Tixover?'

'No-foolydoos, sir,' he refused, this being a situation too serious for a gherkin. 'Those whining spherical objects made out of derubberized pnongballs, sir, that come up the u-bend at you when you're on the bogala, sir. That's one of theirs.'

'You are denouncing 2 of the best students in the school. Potential Emperors of Despotism, Tixover.'

'And those tape recorders with elephants trumpeting on them tied to balloons, sir, that have been disrupting the peace of our market towns, sir. That's one of Chaffinch's ideas, sir. They think it's a boggn tickle, they do, sir!'

'But you don't, Nobby. Is that right?'

Nobby was breathing hard, red in the face.

Emmaus waited some minutes for him to calm down before at last he stood, walked around his desk and offered Nobby his hand.

'These 2 are the best friends you have in the whole world, Nobby, and you have offered them up for death and destruction. Excellent! I've been waiting for something like this. I'll be honest, I thought Rötenschwein was my man. But it's you.'

The children's entertainer persona had abruptly disappeared. Emmaus looked and sounded completely different. Nobby responded to this. He stopped being a boy in his headmaster's study. He became, as if by magic, Nobby Tixover, the greatest despot of them all.

Emmaus beheld this, did he not, was surprised by the sudden transformation. He thought Nobby had, like him, dropped his persona, and that he was beholding the real Nobby for the first time. This was exciting, a Holy moment for Emmaus. It inspired his tongue, which had been awaiting this moment for six long years.

'Of course, Nobby, the Barry Hamlet coup was a put-up job. I needed to be HERE, not in boggn Australia! In six years how many despots have I sent out from this school to assume places of despotic command? 216, Nobby! And all loyal to me. All I've been waiting for is the right right-hand man, Nobby, and tonight I have found him.'

Nobby's jealousy of Cod's friendship with Rötenschwein, which he didn't call jealousy when he brooded on it, which was most of the time, had launched him into a scheme to take over the world. A scheme he quickly saw which could hardly fail.

'The control of the Despotic Committee of 3,' smiled Emmaus, strutting up and down his carpet like a parrot on its perch, 'is ours for the taking, Nobby. Each seat is bequeathed on the death of its incumbent by that incumbent. I have Johanssen's will in my safe, Nobby, bequeathing his seat to me.' He stopped, licked a shard of gherkin clinging to his rabbit's teeth, then said as if it were the last word on every subject. 'I have Drozd's as well.'

144

'BOTH!' Nobby's hands were up and down before his face.

Emmaus laughed, head jerking back, eyes rolling to and fro as if looking for escaped budgerigars. His front teeth were white, but the back ones dark yellow.

'What about Antipope Monika?'

'Monika doesn't matter. 2 out of 3 is enough.'

He offered his jar of gherkins. Only one left, floating like a gangrenous phallus in a medical collection. Nobby fished it out and ate it.

'Listen carefully, Nobby. This is how I am going to organize things, pleasy-do. I'll rule through the Committee. People won't know where the real power lies. Just the despots will know. Meanwhileydoos, I'm going to make a super-despot out of you, Nobby, carrying my will on the Despotic Councils as Chief of Despots. Indeedybe, Nobby, our despotic world will be your playground, Nobby. The herd will cheer you as you pass. Me, they won't even recognize. But the POWER, Nobby, the REAL POWER, will be mine. Is that sweet for you, Nobby?'

They shook hands on it. Devils carving the world.

'There's an auction next month, on the 15th,' said Emmaus flicking through his desk diary, blank pages like death beyond that date. 'Johanssen and Drozd will depart from us the week after. I will have the Committee. O'course, I'm forgetting, you'll be needing a country of your own as a base. Any preferences?'

'Spain, pleasy-do.'

'It's as good as done.'

Emmaus looked at his schoolroom World Map behind his desk, running a thumb over the tartan shapes that were Scottish countries. 'Then there's MacTavish, Nobby. That's the real battle, tha knows.'

Nobby left, his blood like air inside him. He suddenly nipped back, didn't bother to knock.

'Oh, about Rottenswine and Chaffinch?'

His Lordship pondered briefly. 'Don't want anything out of the usual happening just now, Nobby, alerting tiny minds. We can kill them after the auction. No, let's put them somewhere!

145

You never know when they might be useful. We know what they really are, don't we, Nobby? And when you know a man's true nature, Nobby, he's in your power.'

Nobby's smile wasn't the same smile he was feeling.

'Toodly-byedeedar, boss!' he said.

The real Emmaus was gone: it was the children's entertainer who said goodnight: 'Toodly-byededar, Nobby. Toodly-byedeedar.'

*

Drozd died early and Johanssen died late, did he not. A case of sack the poisoner! This complicated matters. But the auction went ahead, in Copenhagen. Nobby got his Spain.

The OOLU-WANG-WANG-WANGs filled the marquee in the Tivoli Gardens where the event was held. February. Everyone was warm enough, but their breath clouded in each others' faces.

'Spain for the Nob!' said Cod to his new bestmost pal. 'Bit of jam somewhere on that, ehwot?'

Rötenschwein's eyes were filled with tears, as they often were. 'Do you know, fish article. There isn't even a recording of his voice, nowhere in the world. So melodious.'

Then he snapped a stud off his leather uniform, one right over his heart, and pressed it into Cod's glove.

'Goodbye, fish article,' he said.

His chair snapped like a crocodile as he swished away. He danced out of the marquee as if fighting uncountable duels, but seemingly resigned to some strange subtle terrible uncontrollable fate. Cod was triple worried, was a-hurring after him, but he heard his name called from the Committee table.

Boggn pilk! He'd been sent to Bolivia!

Bro Cod and Karl Heinz Rötenschwein never met again. The German was sent as Assistant Despot to Kenya, where he went about in a leopard-skin thong, flicking a lion's-tail swish at everyone he met, shouting *JAWOHL* in the African night, flying his flying-hat-car over the heads of galloping gnus. Small noises he made, big blares he planned. Meanwhile, was sorrow

146

easier than revenge? He pined for his favourite Chaffinch, lived
for the day when they would both be promoted. As full despots,
together, what noises they would make . . . *JAWOHL!* But
this was mere pretence, not self-delusion, pretence, cos he
knew, had known from the moment he saw that brief contortion
on Nobby's face looking into the pnong court, that his private
war was lost.

Emmaus thought his cake was all marzipanned, iced, and
with his name going on in delicate pink letters. He'd televisited
MacTavish twice and it was like medieval kings meeting at
a joust. They talked about 'THEIR' world. 'THEIR' plans.
'THEIR' interests.

Cod was in Bolivia, as Despot in charge. But it wasn't a
proper appointment. He was just being trained on the job, a
pretend despot, trying to prove his competence and hoping for
something better afterwards. Strewth was, his mind had been
infected by Rötenschwein's infantile noisemaking schemes.
Bro Cod thought about little else, that and his summer in
Merano.

Slouching about in his noisy kissable dreamworld, he lacked
the vigilance required for his despotic duties. And a despot
without vigilance may as well be a teapot. Oh, Cod was a
poor despot indeed! A common fault of despots was that they
hanged the wrong people. Cod went one worse: he didn't hang
anybody!

A stormy Bolivian morning. Thunder in the mountains just
like the night he met Merluzza. He was showing his face
in some villages, worried about another mundane revolution
sweeping down from the mountains like the rain that was
expected any moment, when a Bolivian assistant brought
him an English newssheet. He'd ringed a snippet of news
he'd thought his despot might be interested in. There, at
the bottom of a list of other happenings, none too vital, was
the report of the death of Ludovic Emmaus, Principal and
Founder of the Ludovic Emmaus Despot School, one-time
despot of Australia before being deposed in a coup by Barry
Hamlet, who'd been unavailable for a quote.

'Tut-poo!' said Cod, his mind for a moment back in the
Rallying Hall, first day at Despot School. There he was,

living through all that history, as close as anyone, and he never knew what was going on for a moment! He may as well have been living in another century, foolish piece of Cod!

But Emmaus, the great expert, had been even more surprised by events. He came into his office one morning, put a full jar of gherkins on his desk and saw there 5 cards. 5 cards belonging to the best swordsmen in the Despot School. This was unheard of! Cheekyfala! Challenging him, Emmaus, to a duel – 5 duels! He knew, of course, that Nobby was behind it, and smiled. The boy – in fact at 44 he was nearly Emmaus's age – had, in the master's opinion, moved too soon.

Emmaus telephoned his old double, well used in his despotic past, now retired in Melbourne, and had him fly out. He'd put on weight, lost his hair, his teeth were chipped though grinding them in nightmares. Factlymost, he looked nothing like Emmaus, perhaps never did. But the challenging despotettes and their seconds didn't argue. They put their best man in for the first duel and he killed the double with the first thrust.

That was when the news went out, the news that Cod saw ringed way over in Bolivia. Emmaus was dead. But there he was, sitting at his desk, vinegar on his fingers, ringing the same snippet, reading about his own death.

He went to his safe. It was empty. He'd bequeathed one of his two seats on the D.C. of 3 to his old ouster Barry Hamlet and the other to Simon Bravelli. But this was practical despotic politics: Nobby got both. 2 seats and overall control of world despotism. Plusmost, as he'd been having an on-off wiggly-arrrrh affair with Antipope Monika since a walking tour of the Black Forest with Bass and Cod back in '24, well, she'd never refused him anything! So all 3 seats, as good as! Everything had gone Nobby's way. He turned the ears of Spanish donkeys that night with his HARH! HARH! And the MG, asleep under its cover in a Madrid garage, belonged to the new equal of MacTavish.

Emmaus had been Wibleyed! He took his double's return flight to Melbourne and lived out his days in his double's identity, sleeping in a bed beside his double's wife, swimming in his double's dinky pool. He took no further interest in world affairs.

I too was in the world during all this, was I not, and played my insignificant part, did I not? While Cod was at Despot School, his gooseberry fool bro was undergoing a spiritual crisis. The death of great-great-granddaddy Clem hurt me sorely. I had known him but a few short weeks. He was pestilential, crude, a bad lot all round. But I loved him dearly. For a summer I had a father. I followed him around like a pooch. Poor Clem! Chee-hee!

Meanwhile, the news was out that Nobby Tixover, the oaf who'd helped make a pig of my nose, who'd wee-weeed on my head not 12 months past, was Despot in Chief of, well, other despots. He was, in effect, the most powerful man since . . . who? The Roman Emperor Augustus, why not? URK! HUH! The world was truly mad. I was sure of it. The idea of a monastery, which is just the world behind a wall, revolted me. So get thee to a cave, a ledge, a solitary crag, Chaffinch!

Rose Trala accompanied me. One of Clem's batch of girls, she'd taken an interest in my chunterings and said she'd like to try to live on a ledge as a change from her usual existence. So why not indeed! We went up to Northumberland, I found her a ledge, told her where to find gull's eggs and left her to it. But she kept coming along the cliffs to my ledge, giving me presents of eggs, nattering, combing her hair. I had to bite her to make her leave me alone! Funny thing, I have never married, but if I think of Chaff's wife, that impossible imaginary figure, it is Rose Trala.

But I was arrested, was I not indeed, so I was, and Rose left her ledge and travelled I know not where. Howdeedoodee, Rose, wherever you are! Withered old Rose now, ehwot! Dead Rose! I'll bite you again if you come nattering! Chee-hee!

Yes, Tadese, arrested! Someone had reported me for singing *To be a Pilgrim* at a squillion decibels. Now, I did sing it, I admit, but in a storm, lashed to a rock on my dear ledge. The denouncers included the piggn storm in their reading. Anyhowsobe, I was in serious potheration, was I not.

I am ashamed to say, Tadese, that when I was threatened with Hellish punishments in Alnwick Napper Station, I whispered holiermost-than-thou to them: 'I'll have you know, I am, am I not, a personal friend of Nobby Tixover.'

I did say that. I urinate in shame to admit it. That is what I said. Wellso, they didn't horribleize my poor flesh. I was shipped off to join the rebels in Bolivia. Part of their theatrical scenario for trainee despots was to fill the hills with odd unpredictable rebels, the noisy flotsam of the calmed-down world, of which suddenly I was one. Despite my holiness! Despite the Chaffinch wealth! There I was! Bolivia! Irksome, but what an adventure!

O Lordy, that twas a cleversome joke of Nobby's! To send this goblin to Bolivia. As if in parody of my ludicrous participation in the revolution of '24, was the joke's punchline that I should invade the despotic palace with my colleague rebels, fling off my sombrero in front of the defeated despot, who, seeing his Mahatma bro who he believed to be safe at Chaffinch Hall, would think he'd been voodooed and go screaming up the Andes with me trotting after on a pushmepullyou saying: 'You foolish piece of Cod! It's really me!'

This, indeedybe, is less-and-more what happened. I was jeeped into a muddy camp, blebsome from mosquito bites, and plonked in front of the rebel leader, Mr Dickinson, a dishonest Cheltenham solicitor sent there as a penance but having the time of his life. He thought this little monk was a funnybone's treat. Then, irked, employing the tones of a Hellfire sermon, I told him about '24, the white horse, the tanks, Big Ben falling, me at the head of the revolution. Other rebels gathered rabblesomely around. When I'd finished my eloquent tale, the biggest one of them tore a badge off Mr Dickinson's green hat and put it on mine. I was a rebel leader again! Harh-hee!

The last time I saw bro Cod alive was in his palace. His men were surrendering in the corridors. Guncracks played odd tunes in the humid air. And I was impishly playing panpipes as he hurried into his office, shooting orders to his remaining officers. What a fine moustache he'd grown! But that duelling scar! Was this my baby bro? Oh, I was so glad to see him! Cod! Bro Cod!

This revolution was not, of course, a real revolution, not like '24. It was just an exercise. There was one a week. If the Despot crushed the rebels, a few of us were hanged, just for fun, and the rest given a tedious lecture on how to be better rebels. Otherwisely, should we rebels triumph, a school-bell rang, the shooting stopped and we all went back to where we started. Either way, a bored examiner popped up and awarded marks to the Despot, currently my despotic bro Cod.

Poor bro did very badly, afraidy-doos, in this week's revolution and was most vexed with his panpipe-playing bro.

'DEPOSED BY A VICAR!' he barked over and over. 'WHAT A BOGGN JILKS I MUST BE!'

And I sat full of chee, eating little oranges. Oh, so many, and so nice. I wish they grew here! I stuck some peel under my snout as a despot's tache.

Cod shook his head and started laughing. We laughed together. That was good, ehwot, Tadese, that for our last time together, curious though the circumstances were, we laughed!

Cod pardoned me with his own signature and sent me straight home. In a plane full of Nappers. A dangerous temptation of celery in the in-flight meal, but I daren't, dared I not! One noisy crunch and they'd have thrown me out over the Atlantic.

Rötenschwein was dead. His death was part of the worst crime of the 21st Century. I cannot talk about it. I WILL NOT! NO! My heart bleeds! He was recalled, and on Tixover's orders, they injected him with a virus, which they'd made years before but never used, cos no one evil enough had fizzed on the seat of power before. Tixover found it in an forgotten report in the old Presidential Palace in Strasbourg. Rötenschwein and a very few others, only a dozen or so, returned to Africa on the same plane. A glum trip, for they knew what was happening to them – O father of us all, they knew! The plane hopped across the continent, dropping one man here, another there, to infect the whole of Africa. In some regions almost everyone died. Tribes, peoples, cultures, all lost and gone. Tadese, he weeps! Old friend! Yes there is

a God – he loves you! Forgive me! I forgot that you did
not know!

I forgot, I did indeed, that I was one of the very few who
knew this. Tixover wanted to expand the English population
after the Scottish example. He decided to clear the whole of
Africa to do it in. The worst of crimes. So bad, it is unreal.
May he burn in piggn boggn Hell for it! But he won't! He
isn't! It doesn't work like that.

O Lord, was there ever a worse year than 2047? Tixover
recalled Cod from Bolivia. He loved him. He would have given
him anything. Had Cod been beside him, well, it was too late
for Africa, but other things, they wouldn't have happened. And
Noise Abatement might have ended years before it did.

But history felt it could do without the fish article. He arrived
in Rome to meet Tixover, who, much to the amusement of
both, had erected colossal statues to Bass Worthington all
over Italy. The great despot was eager to show some of these
to Cod. Their MGs were there. They would race through a
world they now owned.

But moments after Cod arrived at his hotel suite – he
was running a bath, reading a HARH-HARH doodled-on note
from Nobby as he flung off his clothes – Signora Blatta limped
manfully out from behind a curtain and cut my bro's throat,
from ear to ear. Dressed in black, her face twisted from her
stroke, 90 years old, she didn't even wait to be recognized.

So died the last of the Belgians! Merluzza was avenged.
Her darling Codpiece joined her in the arms of Jesus!

My pole, Tadese. I am too much a part of the world down
here. Please, I want to be up my pole. Help me.

*

I learned of Cod's death from Nobby the Great himself. I was
in the library at Chaffinch Hall, not reading, just feeling the
spines of books and remembering when I'd read them, when
Tixover televisited, and there I was fizz to fizz with the piggn
creature.

'Bad news, Mahatma. Someone's assassinated the fish
article. Triple sorries. Goes with the job, supposey-do.'

He was wearing dark glasses and looked a wreck, biting his car keys, one bare foot atop the other. Master of the world! HUH! But he was right about one thing, not so much then but certainmost in years to come: it did go with the job. Ten years later he was blown up at a revival of *Oklahoma* in London. You do believe that I was never his friend, Tadese? He was Cod's friend.

I went to Rome. Never been before. In a daze. Frightened of Catholics. I abhorred the Antipope. Would have spat in her eye if I'd seen her. It was the beginning of a long timid confusion for me, years and years when the little chaffinch caged in my mind dropped off its perch and I hadn't the sense to find a new one.

I was shown in to the room where they were keeping Signora Blatta prior to her execution. She was lying on the bed like a corpse. When she realized I was there she struggled upright. I helped her.

She thought I was Pope Lassie. Through one side of her wrinkled gob she told me all about herself, her life, youth, loves, pleasures. I divined all her drifts, but the only words I understood were Giuseppe and Merluzza. When she said those words she looked so kind. How could this simple old bundle have robbed the world of my dearest little bro?

They brought her in some cold fried eggs and I cut them up for her. How ancient she looked and with death's door gaping before her, but, yes, as alive as anyone I have ever seen. She ate like a wild dog.

While holding the plate before the living side of her face, slowly licking it, she gave me a disc. I mumbled prayerfully off, leaving her to a few hours of eggy-chinned humming. The disc was home-made recordings of a bright young tenor singing melodiously. Giuseppe Ciampoli.

In '55, when everyone ran out into the streets, everyone from Tokyo to New Arbroath, pleasy-do, yelling and screaming and singing every song they could remember, when the Nappers threw away their helmets, when tubas and trombones were liberated at last, when teenage girls who'd never shrieked went wild for life with the pleasure of it, when Italians stormed hospitals to have their inhibitors

153

removed, when Noise Abatement was shouted down forever, I looked for that disc. I most desperately wanted to play it again. But never did I find it. Wilf hid it somewhere, thinky-be.

Codfish still swim in the sea, don't they, Tadese? Oooh, millions, and they love their lives, I'm sure.

AMERICANA

Severiano's Spiritual Exercises

Quotes of the Century:

'The only thing we have to fear is each other and
everybody else.'
*Francis Albert Sanchez, President of the U.S.A. (Eastern
League), Inaugural Address, 2060*

'Of course I trust Connie. When we had hair, we used to
do each other's hair. Connie had lovely hair. She's a lovely
woman all round, Connie is. Find me someone who doesn't
love Connie and I'll show you a Moslem.'
Pam, Joint Prime Minister of England (with Connie), 2063

'Spain and America, 2 countries separated by a common
language.'
*Barkis Dwains, novelist and raconteur, in his 'Lost in
America', 2065*

'My wife's run off with MacTavish and my sheep have got
the gid.'
*Gilbert Munke, comedian, the opening line of his act in the
Royal Variety Performance, 2068*

1

Haha and Rainbow Enjoy the Riots

Tonight I cannot sleep, so I lie on my back, 23 feet above the ground, upon my pole's platform, and as I speaky-do these words to Tadese, I watch the star-beset Ethiopian plain. My soul dives to melancholy depths. The stars do not fit the olden time constellations. I see no bears, bulls and scorpions – I see only ill-fated Chaffinches dotting the night sky, sparkling in my mind's eye.

The last years of the '50s were a gigglesome time, were they not indeed! Heeee-hooooo! Everyone, you see, expected the dawn of the '60s to bring a rebirth of the good times. The legendary '60s of the last century filled our thoughts, our speech. Briefly, in our despot-free world, those of us with the gift for it, were happy. Better still, making as much noise as we liked, we awaited a greater happiness to come. I was growing old, but had never felt younger!

I shall never forget the time I went to the 1st Televisitor Olympics in a London flooded for the umpteenth time. Such a huge cheesome crowd! But I was the only one actually there! When is a crowd not a crowd? When all its members are televisiting, from far and wide. All the athletes were running on their home tracks, all over the globe – just their images ran around the puddled London track. Oddmostly that their quick feet made no splashing in the puddles. I sat on the grass eating banana-and-tunafish sandwiches with hurdlers hurdling over my bald head, javelins landing inches away, watching the phantom spectators eating from tea-trays. Wellahooo, the Koreans won every event, did they not! The same three grinning men split gold, silver and bronze every time, shaking each other's hands on the winner's rostrum, so full of the lark of a wonderful deceit. And no one could prove anything wrong! I had such a cheewagging time, filled with joy. How I sang! I felt, truly, powerfully that day, in my religious nuttery way, that the Second Coming was on his way. And, of course, HE was!

Chaffinch Hall was full of children then: Zogina, Hoss, Rhino, Bing, Minnow, Julius, Turbot, Clancy, September and Cherries. I was the old uncle who gave them sweets, told them Bible stories and watched their eyes for signs of melancholy. It was there, more often than not. But laughter also, tweeting down the corridors, shaking the petals from the magnolia trees. Mischief and laughter, melancholy and sleepybyes. I was almost one of them, an old child with a new childhood. Evermost happy was I.

But the coming of the '60s, pleasy-do, brought no good times. Suddenly, money was useless. The world financial system collapsed. The Great Depression followed. The poor, who once had always been with us, returned in numbers which included almost everyone. In the cities there were riots everywhere. In the country we suffered from raids by hooligan elements. If they didn't come spilling out of charabangs, wielding pnongrackets, they came in whizzycopters, swooping in insectishly, taking whatever they could snatch: toasters, carrots, hats. I had a pole then, a six-foot pole, in the grounds near the gates. Big Norris spent his nights up there, on guard, a machine-gun in each hand. Wot an oddmost growling stylite he made!

Then, a silly-season of horrors when the Russian gangsters shot atomic bombs at each other and turned Russia into a burnt pudding. The direct results of this were that electricity all over the world wouldn't work from '60 till '62 and everyone's hair fell out. No bother on me, except my eyebrows went. Awkwardlydoos that televisiting stopped, cos I lost contact with Clone Seve, whose influence upon all our futures was about to roll our old world away.

Food was scarce. Dogs and cats were eaten on the sly. I ate cats myself, but only once a dog, a corgi. I barfed. Fieldmouse pie was icky, and worstmost of all there wasn't a bar of chocolate to be had. Nothing was being made. Factories still and empty everywhere. Hardly a soul went to work. Everyone was unemployed. In his attic Bro Wilf howled about his lost investments, furiously banging the pipes with his spoon, blaspheming for the loss of every last ecupoundlet. But after the I.M.F. conference in Geneva in 2063, the clouds lifted. It was decided that sheep would be used as currency. Boiled eggs were advocated by a majority, but somehow sheep won out. Wilf had anticipated this, and Chaffinch Hall had been besieged by a woolly army for months, baaing us awake. Rhino had been spanked for an impromptu lambchop-barbecue in the sandpit.

Much grumbling, was there not, from us Chaffinches about confounded sheep. But triple sorries to Wilf when the news came in. We were rich! The servants came back! The larder filled! We welcomed sheep into our lives!

The '60s were a sheepishlymost, sheep-niffing, 3-bags-full, woolly-knittmost, lambkin time, when a man fell asleep counting sheep and awoke to count more, when there was no greater fear than the sound of a hoosey cough in the garden-nibbling fold, for a sick sheep could mean a dead sheep, and a dead sheep was money down the drain, and a sick sheep could mean a sickly herd, and a sickly herd could mean a dead herd, sheeplessness, bankruptcy and ruin. So it was that Blitchet's *Diseases of Sheep* was suddenly a bestseller.

We read, dreamed, talked, thought SHEEP with sheep-obsessed tongues, baaa-sore ears, eyes like sheep-pens. Accountants were replaced by sheepdogs – the middle-men of the '60s, who ignored our whistles, woofed at our heels, and hated sheep with a passion that our need for wealth prevented from erupting in us. Pampered, contentedlymost sheep, who never heard a bad word spoken about themselves, nor a slap, nor a kick – for to harm a sheep was like tearing up ecupoundlets in the papermoney days: a madman's grim pastime.

This Chaffinch, he was delighted! It was all rather Biblically-doos. I felt like Abraham with his flocks. Many tedious sermons did I give about 'good shepherds'. Baaaaa! Baaaaa! And I never looked a sheep in the face without a giggle. They never ceased to amuse me, did they not indeed!

Wilf, whose greatest love had always been money, now adored sheep with an unnatural fervour. He, and I urinate in shame on his behalf as I say this, married a sheep. I refused to perform the ceremony and my bro and I had a serious falling out and never properly made up. When his sheep-wife fell foul of ovine piroplasmosis, he married another, and when that got the gid, he took another to wife. O, inconstant howling Wilf!

Meanwhile, co-existing with the riots and general chaos, was a comfortable return to parliamentary democracy. This in the form of, pleasy-do-dar, Connie and Pam, our joint Prime Minister. Perhaps, in truth, they were latter-day despots, who re-started Parliament simply to have somewhere where they could wear their fashionable clothes. But we all, I included, were pottyfalla on Connie and Pam. We read their coffee-table conversations, recorded in the daily rags. We followed them about on the Everyone Channel. Our conversations were filled with Connie-this and Pam-that. Indeedybe, they were greatly loved. Baaaaaa!

Of all Connie and Pam's many fans at home and abroad, none were more admiring than Scampi and Clone Seve's twins, Rainbow and Haha. In their 20s, so of similar age to Connie and Pam, their plushmost luxurious apartment in London was belittered with Connie and Pam nicknackery, election posters in silver frames, Spode Connies, Capodimonte Pams. Even on the coffee table Connie smirked from the cover of *Vogue*, Pam winked from the cover of *Connie and Pam*.

The Chaffinches had always been a well-heeled flock, but Rainbow and Haha were the snootymostest luxury-lappers of all time, were they not. Baaaaa! Late at night, tripping over sheep droppings on the stairs, I was often passed by Haha or Rainbow's televisiting bodies, dressed in some number recently seen on the back of Connie or Pam, twinkletoeing up to disturb Wilf and Mrs Wilf, to get more sheep out of him. They went through a flock a week! Sometimes two! Baaaaa!

Their butler Galbraith was the son of the butler who had found my father's body on the night of my birth. A fat wall-eyed pumpkinous inbiber was Galbraith, pockets full of hip-flasks, secretly hating everyone on earth. What kept him in line was a sexual frenzy for his mistresses, especially Rainbow. Queerly-be about the twins, for they were indeed identical – they both starved themselves to look like the

skinny Connie and Pam – they wore each other's dresses –
they were similarly bald – their superior grin was the same
grin – daughters of a clone, they appeared to be clones of
each other – but fact was Rainbow was beautiful whereas
Haha was not. Rainbow had everything in her eyes that had
made her mother the greatest beauty of the '30s. Haha's eyes
were all sneer. The gaze of one sister made me feel a youth
again. When I kissed her fingers or she patted my head my
heart would zing about inside me like a Wiblied pnongball. The
gaze of her twin made me feel I needed a wash. But they were
the same girl, in their manners and talk, in everything – two
Connies, two Pams, not a Connie and a Pam. How could one
be such a goddess and the other nothing at all? O mystery of
life! Baaaaaa!

It was an ordinary Tuesday in the last week of August,
2063. Parliament was in recess. On the Everyone Channel
Connie and Pam were attending fashion shows in London.
The country was either at the beach with their sheepdogs
and sheep, or rioting in the capital's streets. Galbraith was
staggering home, weeping drunkenly, pulling along a lost
sheep by the ear. In his pocket was a list of Rainbow and
Haha's latest demands, a list entirely unfilled, due to his fear
of being shot. The rioters were closing on *Harrods* that day
and Galbraith had been a witness, lying under a burnt-out car
sucking at a hip-flask, as the army counterattacked. Suddenly,
Haha was gazing down on him from her balcony which looped
around their exclusive mews. The light breeze was lifting
her dressing-gown and Galbraith fell to his knees, put on
his specs, and gazed upward, hugging the sheep, in a not
unusual frenzy.

'GALBRAITH! YOU DIDN'T GET IT, DID YOU? "SUN-
SET OVER KYOTO"! I'VE ONLY 8 NAILS PAINTED! I
LOOK DISEASED AND ITS ALL YOUR PIGGN FAULT!
THIS IS THE 4TH TIME THIS WEEK I'VE SENT YOU
TO *HARRODS*! YOU'RE A USELESS LITTLE MAN,
GALBRAITH – WOT ARE YOU?'

'Oh, Marm,' he called back between sobs from himself and
baas from the rustled sheep. 'In this light, you look just like
Connie!'

'Eough! Not Pam?'

He removed his glasses. 'YES! YES! I SEE IT NOW! PAM! GLORIOUS PAM!'

Then he went into one of the many popular songs then current about Connie and Pam . . . or just Connie . . . or Pam by herself. One of the last serenades before the segregation of the sexes. More touching perhaps if Galbraith had not been abusing the sheep while singing in his cracked pub-sloshed baritone.

Haha was flattered. She took the opportunity to exercise her stick-like limbs, catching her high-kicks in her hands, always careful of her long fingernails. Several loose sheep joined her on the balcony and looked down on the captured sheep below. Baaaaaa!

Suddenly Galbraith let out a long ecstatic sigh, hiccoughed his song to an end, and withdrawing from the sheep, pulled out his automatic weapon and shot indiscriminately at the passers-by, wounding them all.

'I'LL GO BACK! FOR YOU, MARM, I WOULD DARE ANYTHING, PLEASY-DO, THROW MYSELF INTO ANY DANGER! RIOTERS! SOLDIERS! FOR YOU, I'LL FIGHT THE PIGGNBOGGN LOT!'

Fire was being returned. He attempted to remove his clothes to accept the danger, but fortunately couldn't manage it – fortunately, cos the hip-flasks were saving him from woundings: the wetness he could feel against his goosey skin was not blood, but gin seeping from where bullets had been stopped.

'GALBRAITH, ARE YOU DISEASED? YOU'LL BE KILLED, YOU SILLY MAN!' yelled Haha, but without concern.

Killed indeedy-so, had not Rainbow screechy-pood up in her bubble-car, aiming her pistols expertly at Galbraith's enemies. When she clunked down the car's lid there were no sounds in the street. Just a cooo-weeee from Haha, high above.

'CONNIE!' called Rainbow, her prize-rabbit eyes meeting her sister's with no bullets zinging between.

'PAM!' called down Haha, and opened her dressing-gown so that Rainbow could see the perfection of her emaciated figure.

'FABMOSTLY COOL, SIS! YOU BLOW MY MIND!' called back Rainbow in '60s talk, tearing open her jumpsuit to reveal the same bosomless but big-teeted figure as her sister's.

But the sound from Galbraith was not one of frenzied admiration. He was grief-stricken at the death of his sheep, hit several times during the recent exchange. Another 21st Century life lost meaninglessly!

Meanwhile, Rainbow was waggling her fingers and toes up at Haha, who suddenly glipped furiously, irresponsibly kicked all the sheep on her balcony and swept inside through the net curtain chewing a jumble of obscenities.

'*Sunset over Kyoto*,' said Rainbow, finishing her waggle to Galbraith. 'Groovy, wot?'

'Most attractive, Marm. Far out.'

'Oh, and Galbraith . . .'

'Pleasy-do, Marm.'

'Bring that sheep upstairs. Waste not, want not! Oh, and when you done that . . .'

'Pleasy-do, Marm.'

'Have a look at the people I've just shot and see if any would do in Sis Haha's experiments.'

'Not the glands, Marm!'

'The glands, Galbraith!'

Haha, perhaps due to her clone blood, had developed a fascination with the illegal practice of cloning, and was attempting, in those days when the relationships between the sexes were approaching total breakdown, to create the perfect George. This George would be a dream man, full of all the qualities Haha most admired in a man. If she succeeded she'd promised an identical one to Rainbow. But for this she needed an inexhaustible supply of glands, testicles and whathaveyou, which Galbraith reluctantly collected, making day-trips to Clacton in search of handsome-ish men, whom he would maim or murder – either way, he'd snip off their glands and return on the train, glands sloshing in a tupperware box on his knees, ever hopeful of a grateful kiss from his mistress.

When Haha eventually emerged from her suite, looming miffed over Rainbow, who was sitting on the sofa watching Connie's daily lunchtime swim, while stroking their weensie pooch Weewee, Rainbow gave her a Pam-like expression, saying: 'How's George?'

'I made a fab one this morning. Looky-dooed a peach in the tank. Freaked me out! But when he dried off, he wasn't a groove at all.'

'Eough!'

'Said I was thin!'

'NO! Bad vibes!'

'That's what the creature said!'

'Too-too! Melted him there and then, one hopes!'

'Right on, I did, sister of mine.'

Then Rainbow, while stroking Weewee, naughtily waggled a finger or two while stretching her toes. Miffed, Haha pulled her gown tight and was half gone when Rainbow trilled:

'Oops, triple sorries – forgot I got you a prezzie!'

She tossed a bottle of *Sunset over Kyoto* across the room. A wee bark from Weewee simultaneous to Haha catching it.

'*Sunset over Kyoto*. O, Rainbow, you olive, you custardly rhubarb woolly thing you! *Sunset over Kyoto*! I dig! I dig!'

They were going through a happy ritual of tossing Weewee back and forth, kissing him rather than each other, but occasionally kissing each other, delighted in their twinsome shared existence, when Galbraith plodded in, glands dangling from between his fingers on their red and white strings.

'Glands, Marm.'

'Well done, Galbraith. In the lab, pleasy-do.' said Haha.

'Oh, and Galbraith . . .' Rainbow said while catching Weewee.

'Pleasy-do, Marm.'

'When you've finished, get into your best. There's a Royal Garden Party this afternoon, Ex-King and whathaveyoudoo, and we'll need you to ride shotgun.'

'Goodlymosteverso, Marm.'

But a minute later there was Galbraith standing in the doorway, a smoking pistol in his hand and Weewee lying in the fireplace, a huge red hole in his tiny white body, shot in mid-air as the sisters threw him from pair of hands to pair of hands.

Screamed both: 'GALBRATH, ARE YOU DISEASED? YOU'VE SHOT WEEWEE! . . . SHOT WEE-WEE!'

'A most regrettable accident, Marm,' said Galbraith in his usual butler's tone.

But it wasn't an accident. It was a moment of madness, a moment born of the massed resentments of 11 generations of ancestral butlers, perhaps brought on by a whiff of something he elbowed in the lab, eliciting from him an abandonment of his butlerish calling resulting in Weewee's untimely death.

Thrown into a cloning tank a new Weewee would soon be in action, but the girls were infuriated with Galbraith. He was sent to the billiard room to await punishment. There he rolled the white ball against the cushions and played with himself through his trouser pocket.

'Couldn't we melt him down and mix him with a bit of Georgie-Porgie stuff?'

'Fooly-doos, sis, we might end up with a lounge lizard who'd never do a stroke!'

'Eough!'

'Or a butler we couldn't resist!'

Rainbow scratched her pretty bald head: 'What if . . . what if . . . what if we confiscated his blow-up Connie?'

'Groovy suggestion, but worse for him evermost to confiscate his blow-up Pam.'

'Blow-up Connie.'

'Blow-up Pam.'

'Connie'

'Pam.'

'CONNIE!!!!'

'Pam.'

'Connie.'

'PAM!!!!!!'

'Connie is sexier. It's more of a punishment.'

'Pam is sexier.'

'No, no, sis – Connie is.'

'Pam is.'

'Connie.'

'Pam.'

'Connie.'

'Pam.'

'Connie.'

'Pam.'

'CONNIE!'

'PAM! PAM! PAM!'

'Connie.'

'Pam.'

'Connie . . . No, all right, Pam.'

'No, you've changed my mind. When I come to think about it, honestlymost, Connie is sexier than Pam.'

'Pleasy-do, Pam is sexier, from a man's penile viewpoint, I mean – she freaks them more. Connie's more obvious. Pam's more fably subtle.'

'Naw, Connie is radiant, unchallangeable in beauty and sexiness. Connie. Connie. She freaks me! O, CONNIE!'

'Pam.'

'Connie.'

'Pam.'

'Connie.'

'Pam.'

'Connie.'

'Pam.'

'Connie.'

'Pam.'

'Connie.'

'Pam.'

'Pam. Ooops! I meant Connie!'

'You said PAM! – PAM! PAM! PAM! We'll confiscate his Pam.'

'Oh, all right then. Far out. Pam.'

Haha went to clone Weewee, while Rainbow slinked majestically into the billiard-room and informed their servant of the decision. But her mind wandered on the way in and she couldn't remember if it was blow-up Connie or blow-up Pam that was to be confiscated.

'We have decided, Galbraith, that your blow-up Connie shall be confiscated. Please fetch it.'

He nodded mostly with his eyes and staggered away to fetch blow-up Connie. A mild punishment, in fact, for whether he was thrusting into blow-up Connie or blow-up Pam, in his mind he had pictures of Rainbow and Haha smeared in honey. Baaaaaa!

166

Some minutes later a half-dressed Rainbow kicked open Haha's bedroom door. Haha, four toenails so far brushed with *Sunset over Kyoto*, raised the places where her eyebrows would have been.

'I just heard it on the telly!' Rainbow was panting.

Galbraith was behind her, offering blow-up Connie for confiscation on a silver tray.

'IT'S PAM!'

'Pam, wot? PAM, WOT?'

'She's . . . she's . . . to the Garden Party, this afternoon. She'll be there! We'll see her! PAM!'

'Not Pam!'

'PAM!'

'Eough! EOUGH! WIZZYTOPMOST, GROOVY BABY! WHAAA!'

A newborn Weewee clone joined the celebration by biting Galbraith on both ankles. He fell over, rolled pumkinously, and was licked.

'Let's drive there right through the riots!' said Rainbow. 'I'll shoot you a few Georges on the way! I dig the riots! They're cool and heavy!'

And as she breathed on the barrel of her pistol and polished it on her pozzy, Galbraith's groans frightened Weewee so much that he ran back to the lab, jumped into the wrong tank and was lost forever.

2

The Garden Party

The main problem with eating bananas in the dark, pleasy-do, is that you can't avoid eating the bruised bits. A squishy bruise, naturallymost, can be found with the fingers. But a banana suffers many subtle injuries to its flesh and in this midnight feast of an entire hand of bananas I have taken into myself more than a dozen bruises. Like the Lord swallowing our human sufferings.

Indeedybe, was that not why He gave bananas the ability to bruise? – To remind us that every suffering leaves its mark, every insult remains bruised on our soul forever, every hurt great and small bashes us out of perfection. He is saying to us, through the agency of his phallic yellow fruit, that we should lead lives without suffering, without insult, without hurt.

Impossible, among the evils stalking our century, mumbles Tadese! Perhaps so. But one day we shall all be long and yellow and with firm unsuffering flesh within our warm jackets. I am sure such days will come and stay forever, am I not!

Rainbow and Haha were blithe spirits, but a special bruise blackened a portion of their souls. They had never known their father. One morning when they were three years old Clone Seve kissed them on their innocent brows and left for his desk at the War Office. He never returned. He ran off with Moira Macmacpherson, abandoning them, abandoning their mother, and sped away from English shores in a search of hidden golfcourses. Soon, another bruise: Scampi pnonged to death on the steps of Basingstoke Town Hall. Then a childhood squished with bruises: cos the other Chaffinch kiddywinks detested them, spurned them from their games. I never understood why. So, for the twins, a bruised beginning, awarding no wisdoms, just pains. But on that afternoon in

'63, when they sped to the Royal Garden Party in Rainbow's bubblecar, Galbraith clinging with one hand to the roof while tossing hand grenades at rioters with the other, their past was indeed behind them. Both girls felt, I am sure, that they were now living their real intended lives.

The old Royal residence, Buckingham Palace, having been turned into an exclusive dancing club, where Connie and Pam tangoed the night away with cheesy foreign diplomats, this Royal Garden Party was held at the ex-King's Chelsea townhouse. A small garden, geranium pots everywhere, old cankered trees, the sun interrupted by chimney pots. The ex-King's pedigree sheep wandered dreamily among the guests, accepting titbits. Baaaaaa!

Rainbow and Haha were wearing the same mini-dress, Rainbow a red one, Haha a yellow one. It was a dress from Connie's wardrobe, slinky-doos, with a window cut to show the navel. They each wore a golden headdress dangled with coloured beads.

But as they stood side-by-side on the garden steps, a chipped gnome between them, it was only Rainbow that the ex-King saw. The bruises of that poor man's stormy life had left his banana squishmost boglyfalared – Rainbow was the rainbow after his storms!

It was a love-at-first-sight primed by Jude Rassendyl-Flints, Rainbow and Haha's shared boyfriend, a cashiered army lieutenant, who had been pumping info about the Chaffinch twins into the ex-King all morning. But, from her first mention, though he'd never set eyes on either, it was Rainbow that the ex-King was exclusively interested in.

'She sounds cool, pleasy-do, man, a right-on chick!'

Indeed-so, she was! Jude pressed on with descriptions of Rainbow, titbits on Haha, together with complaints about the way the army had treated him. The King salivated and couldn't wait for Rainbow to step from his horizon into his Royal presence.

In so selling his girlfriend to the ex-King, Jude was perhaps sawing off the branch he was sitting upon. But he was doing what courtiers had always done, and since the French got their King back in the '58 Revolution, hopes abounded in certain circles for a Restoration of the English Monarchy, hopes tied up in Jude's piffling heart with dreams of resuming his military career under his king. Quick promotions! His own brigade!

Oddmost boy was he, having the oddmostest love affair of the century! If love affair it was! Cos he didn't love Rainbow, he didn't love Haha – he loved both, as a single entity! To him they were one girl with two bodies – and, they being offspring of a clone, who can tell, perhaps he was right! So, in giving one away he was not cheered to think he might retain the other. If he lost one, he lost the pair. A brigadier, yes, but with a broken heart.

Rainbow and Haha, meanwhileydoos, treasured no great affection for Jude. They kept him as a sort of a pet. He slept on the sofa in Galbraith's room. They took turns to bath him, which favour cost him one sheep. With the gradual extinction of the sexual intercourse as a pastime, indeed with the cessation of all sexual touchings by men onto women, Jude had never once kissed, snogged, squeezed or prodded either one of the twins, and certainly never both at once, his happiest fantasy. But they, shame on them, masturbated him several times a day each, for which favour he gifted them 3 sheep per day each, or ¼-sheep per masturbation. He was a big, weak, short-sighted youth, a loveable smile, a dashing temper, a trembling ecstasy in his eyes whenever he looked at the twins. Why he wasn't a George, I know not, but he was not – nowhere near! Lucky for him, perhaps, that he wasn't anything like one, or Haha would have had his glands in a bottle!

The ex-King hopped out of his deckchair, gripping Jude by his medals: 'That's HER, isn't it? In the red mini-dress! Och, she's braw, out of sight, man! Too-too!'

The twins had never seen the ex-King in the flesh. What they now saw was an astonishment! He shoved aside his distinguished guests in a hurry to be at Rainbow's side, moving with the bumbleinous inaccuracy of a dying bee, fervently panting towards them in a Stuart tartan kilt – he'd spent decades in exile at MacTavish's court and was rotten with Scottishness – roundly fat, blimpmost, looking like

George III in the mid-stages of his madness, an atmosphere of the nursery in his idiot's smile, but the sad look in his eyes of an ape in a zoocage thinking about the jungle where it belongs, a jungle long ago given the chop.

'He looks DISEASED,' whispered Haha to her sisterly-most.

The arrival, though they watched the slow coming round-eyed and had expected it all along, had the surprise of a traincrash. Jude waffled introductions. The ex-King laughed softly, a beautiful laugh, and gazed at Rainbow with tears streaming down his cheeks.

'Connie,' she said, taking his hand.

'Pam,' he said, admiring her hand through blurry eyes. 'Dig the nails, chick – *Sunset over Kyoto*, wot?'

'Why, yes! Chee-he! Far out.'

'Erm . . .,' he tilted his head and opened one eye wide, all disturbingly Scottishly, 'would you be a honeypot and push me on my swing?'

It was a question which greatly excited him. He awaited the answer with his knuckles on his teeth. When Rainbow said she'd be glad to, he burst into tears.

But suddenly he stopped. All conversation in the garden stopped. Silence from everyone. Not a slurp. No strawberry chewed. There had been a hoosey cough. Eyes rolled from sheep to sheep. A hoosey cough! It echoed in everyone's mind. The hoose – that most dreaded of sheep diseases! They'd carry it home on their shoes, in their hair! Bankruptcy! Sheeplessness! Ruin!

The ex-King choked on a half-swallowed sob for a full minute . . . then, at last . . . the Arab League Ambassador coughed hoosily. Him all along! Immediate relief. Immediate return to chatterizations. Baaaaaaa! Rainbow took the ex-King's arm and accompanied him to the leafy alcove with the swing in it.

Haha watched them go forlornly. Even the clacks of her beads seemed to mock her.

'Of course,' she informed Jude. '*Sunset over Kyoto* goes better with her red dress than my yellow.'

'I can dig that,' said Jude, sensitively, then put his tongue out at the Arab League Ambassador, an act which was to have significant consequences for him and the whole world, did it not indeed evermost!

Rainbow, meanwhileydoos, was rather blasé about being picked up by the ex-King. While swing-pushing, the corner of her left eye watched the steps for the promised appearance of the goddess Pam. Innocent of this, indeedybe of almost everything, the ex-King swang pure-hearted in his childish enjoyment of swinging, kilt flying in his face, a view of his hairless genitals offered to the champagne-sipping guests.

'I understand . . . that your daddy . . . HIGHER . . . was a clone.'

'Heavy, man.'

'Jolly good thing . . . that they stopped cloning . . . That same horse won . . . the Grand National . . . for 18 years on the trot . . . HIGHER . . . and never looked a day older . . . It only lost . . . when it came up against a whole card . . . made of clones of itself . . . HIGHER . . . Melted down, was he, your dad?'

'Bad vibes, man. It's a drag.'

'Triple sorries for bringing it up, chick.'

'Ran off with a Scotswoman, my daddy did . . . But worstmost of it: he was a golfer.'

'Ooo-err! Piggn heavy.'

Then the swing broke. The ex-King went flying through a hedge and ended up crosslegged with a geranium pot in one hand and a half-full glass of champers in the other. He wept, bawled. But when his guests and courtiers gathered around he grew fierce.

'PIGGN BOG OFF! YOU FREAK ME OUT, MAN! BOG! BOG! PLEASY-DO, BLOW MY SCENE!' Then MacTavishly: 'OCH, YE BLITHERIN BOOBIES, AWAY WI'YE!' Then babyishly: 'Where's my honeypot, my pretty cool chick with chocdrop eyes.'

Rainbow's beads clacked in his face. He smelt her perfume. He wept. O, how the poor soul wept! But suddenly, that laugh again, like the last sound of Merrie England before eternal darkness. Rainbow was charmed by it. She crosslegged her long bony legs and they sat facing each other. Without asking permission, they put their hands on each other's knees.

An even better laugh, a sound from a happy dream that keeps you happy all next day. Rainbow laughed too, gigglesomely, freedom canoeing through her bloodstream.

'The swing broke, man! Far out!' chucklerood the ex-King.

'I dig it! I dig it! Hot dog, I dig it!'

A sheep walked over them. Baaaaaaa! And when 'twas gone the ex-King was struggling with his tearful emotions again.

'Cool out!' Rainbow advised him.

'It's okay-doos, chick. Pleasy-do, it's just the Abdication – it keeps coming back at me, like a black wave sucking at my heart. Do you know what those witches have got me doing now? I attend the hangings. Heavy! I don't actually pull the lever or anything. I just chat with the chap while the vicar mumbles god-awful lies in the background. Then they hang him – the chap, not the vicar! Ha! Ha! Ho-chee-he! HAAA!'

But Rainbow wasn't laughing with him. He'd called Connie and Pam witches. Her face was clad with stone.

'Bad vibes, chick?'

'No, it's nothing – just, my little dog, Weewee. He was shot this morning. A mad butler.'

'Too-too. I've got one of those myself.'

And he laughed again. Rainbow was charmed. Her heart ached. She didn't understand herself. Her spirit was soaring, she watched it soar. This childish pudgy man was the cause! Hoots mon, she thought, in a warm flush-flash that softened all her hard places: I must be DISEASED, I'm falling headovertittytop in love. And with a man twice my age who thinks Connie and Pam are witches! But while these thoughts zwanged in her giddy bald head, she was effusing to the delight of the ex-King.

'Wot a too-too beautiful day, ehwot?' she effused. 'Blows your mind! The lobelias heavy on their stalks. I dig them. And groovy how the breeze caresses.'

'Too-too evermost. Caresses. Groovy.'

'It feels as if it's a 100 years ago, man, and everything is hunkydory again, fish swarming in the oceans, Scotsmen back under the rocks where they came from, the world wrapped in air you can breathe and sigh with.' She sighed charmingly. 'And here am I sitting on an English lawn with the King.'

The ex-King gripped her knees and wept profound tears. His lips moved wordfully before speaking. Rainbow expected Kingly wisdom. But he was a man, was he not? Like all men.

'Rainbow, coolmost chickadoodle! With your sparkling chocdrop eyes surrounded by that far out mascara – I dig it – you look like Queen Nefertitti.' Almost inaudible: 'Would you play with me under my kilt?'

Rainbow dug daggers of *Sunset of Kyoto* into his knees, leaving marks of a similar shade that would last for days. He gibbered in anticipation of her answer.

'Okaydoos, man, but I'll want every boggn sheep on your lawn!'

A grateful sigh meant yes and her hand shot under the itchy kilt, grabbing a soft Royal member which immediately became alert.

'I've had three queens,' he muttered gratefully-doos, 'but they would never do this for me.'

And he laughed again. Yes, he knew the power of that laugh over her. She laughed too and continued her task. The French Dauphin came over for a few words, and the Papal Nuncio, and still Rainbow continued sweatily milking the Royal dong. The ex-King carried on normal conversation, occasionally yelling MacTavishly: 'Och, lassie, I dig! I dig!'

Then there was an explosion under the kilt and the ex-King flopped back like a puppet with its strings cut. Rainbow lay beside him. They watched clouds.

'I've just heard,' he said, tears rolling out of the sides of his eyes, 'My only son, Prince Michael, he's joined the Clan MacNab.'

'A drag! Heavy drag, man!'

'Bogn MacTavish was more a father to him than me, pleasy-do. He's off in the Highlands, poor elf, awaiting the return of Brigadoon!*' He turned his face from the clouds to the girl lying by him, and in a blank voice: 'It means there's no succession. I must have another son. I must marry again.'

Rainbow went cold. Was this a proposal?

Suddenly, a ruckus. They sat up to watch. Jude was shoving volauvents up the kaftan of the Arab League Ambassador, then some into the fellow's gob, which he coughed-up hoosily. Then he had him in the hook-a-duck pond, squashing plastic ducks against his head. Everyone was frightfully amused.

The ex-King's laugh was merrier than ever. Rainbow kicked off her platform shoes as she drummed the lawn with her ecstatically amused feet. She'd never laughed so much! Ooops! She was kissing the ex-King. She'd never kissed anyone before – and neither had he! Their tongues flapped. Their teeth tapped, a noise like a birds at a window! Baaaaaaa!

Then, as Jude drowned the Arab League Ambassador in the hook-a-duck pond, the ex-King was panting in her face.

'I say, chick, would you like to meet up with me again? A bash of mine, the 20th Century Re-Enactment Society. This Friday.'

'Okaydoos.'

His grin filled her face. Then a whisper: 'It's just a front, of course. For my Restoration. Can't be long now. Burn the witches, wot!' Then his laugh.

Rainbow was fizzing with confusion! This monstrous idiot, this oafish dong-brained bogala, he was planning to overthrow Connie and Pam! Her head jerked away from him. She was on

---

* *Brigadoonism was an oddmost Scottish spiritual movement encouraged by the then half-senile MacTavish. It centred on the myth that once every 100 years a Scottish village appeared for a single day. In the '60s the Scots Highlands were full of Bridadoonists, wandering, waiting. It never appeared. Better for them had they escaped into their mythical village, cos the days of Scots ascendancy were numbered. A terrible end awaited their tartan world.*

her feet, dizzy, searching for her shoes, searching the guests for Pam. Had Pam arrived? She must warn her! Tell her!

The ex-King was hugging her and she was struggling with her skinny arms, but kissing his mouth willingly, smudging her make-up on him. His laugh was in his throat as they kissed.

'You will come, won't you? It's a wheezemost scene, chick of mine. A real gas-gas-gas! You'll dig it. We're re-enacting the 1964 Labour Party Conference. Too-too!'

The string quartet were playing one of Pam's tunes. She was arriving! Herself in person! Rainbow broke away from the ex-King. But he still seemed to be holding her hand when she was halfway across the garden.

'I'll come. I promise I'll come,' she said.

He let her go. She went spinning to the music, tripping out of her shoes, her bead headdress wagging before her eyes. When she stopped, exhausted, Jude had her hand and was introducing her to Pam.

PAM! How beautiful she was! The perfect woman! A gold lamé dress, bare-midriffed, flowing down to the ground, a brooch in the shape of a P wild with rubies and diamonds. She wore a foot-high wig of raw sheep's wool. O, divine goddess!

'Pam,' gasped Rainbow, her heart pounding.

'Connie,' responded Pam with the peachy smile that had won the Nation's heart. 'Dig that mini-dress, pet. It's too-too.'

'Thankydoos, Pam.'

Rainbow's lips were a-tremble, her eyes full of tears. She was struggling to allow herself to tell Pam that there was a plot against Connie and herself, that the silly old ex-King was dangerous, that what happened in France in '58 could happen in Connie and Pam's England in '63.

Pam continued smiling. 'Yes? Say it, don't freak, just say it, whatever it is.'

'I love you,' said Rainbow. 'I love Connie. I love you.'

Pam's eyes glittered with the start of tears. She took off her P brooch and pinned it on Rainbow's red dress. Then she caught sight of an amazed Haha in the encircling crowd and poked Rainbow with a *Sunset over Kyoto* nail.

'Hey-up, another you – far out!'

Pam sang a couple of songs – *Granada* and *Ferry Across the Mersey* – and had a few quiet words with the ex-King before sweeping away, leaving her bye-bye kiss, a kiss between smiles, forever in the mind's-eye of all present. Except the Arab League Ambassador, who, revived after his drowning, had pronounced a fatwa against Jude, who had climbed over the garden wall in terror and run through the quiet streets of London in a panic that would never leave him.

Tadese – LOOK! The sun, he comes, making a mirror of distant Lake Stephanie! We are in a world 37 years older than the day I have just been prattling about – and we have a new day! Hallelujah!

3

The 1964 Labour Party Conference

All the latest technology was employed to staggering effect
to bring the 1964 Labour Party Conference to vivid life. It
was indeed like stepping 99 years back in time. A triumph.
A pnongdrome near Watford was wrapped, rolled, lazered,
painted and bedecked in the trappings of a political event, long
forgotten except in the little red handbook everyone carried,
telling them who they were, what they thought, and where
the toilets were.

'Wot a scene!' gasped Haha, then more critically: 'But wot
a tedious thing to choose to re-enact! The 1964 Labour Party
Conference. They must be DISEASED!'

Rainbow was looking the other way, through windows at
olden-time Brighton streets that had not been there until they
swang swingingly through the swing doors. When Haha caught
her eye she saw something oddmost there, something almost
boglyfala.

'Wot's uptighting you, sis?'

'Uptight? I'm not uptight.'

But she was. She knew what Haha did not, that this event
was nowt but a front for plotting the overthrow of Connie and
Pam. WHY DIDN'T SHE TELL SOMEONE?

Here was why . . .

The ex-King was bumbling through the 20th Century crowd
in his re-enactment outfit and her heart burst with delight. She
loved him. More, far more, than when they had parted two
days previously.

'Och, RAINBOW, my honeypot of gold!'

They kissed long and passionately. It was rather nauseating
to watch. Haha, 25-and-never-been-kissed, swooned slightly.
Sundry passing socialists had to do a good deed and hold
her up.

'Isn't it fab! And so authentic!' enthused the ex-King 'I'm playing a man called Denis Healey! Spanky-doos, ehwot! I've got cards for you girls. Haha, you're a Transport and General Workers Union Representative called Marjorie Dickinson. Rainbow, triple sorries chick of mine, but if you're to sit on the platform with me there's only one part left: George Brown's mother.'

Rainbow didn't object to being George Brown's mother, but Haha insisted on sitting on the top people's platform.

'But, hoots lassie, it wouldn't be authentic!' whinged the ex-King.

Haha looked about for sheep to kick. She found one. Baaaaa! She was, in the parlance of the time, freaking out.

The ex-King gave in. The girls changed into their re-enactment outfits.

'I looked DISEASED!' complained Haha, twanging a brassiere too big for any living woman.

Sis Rainbow, meanwhileydoos, looked too-too drabmost ukky in her vintage clobber. But with a contempt for authenticity, pleasy-do, she refused to wear the monstrous wig provided. Her baldness, however, shining among everyone else's monstrous wiggery looked more odd than chic.

Despite their un-fab gear, looking like crabs at a wedding, they were gigglesomemost cheeful as they stepped up to the platform and sat behind the party leader, on his feet on a speechifying dais, making a speech his original made 99 years before.

'Our Harold Wilson is out-of-sight authentic, ehwot?' said the ex-King, snogging with Rainbow, himself being eroticallymost unauthentic, cos Denis Healey never snogerood with George Brown's mother on that or any other occasion.

Haha, abandoned by the snoggers, was left with nothing to do but listen to the speech. History was not her subject and Harold Wilson no Georgie-Porgie dreamboat. She yawned. She kept checking her nails for chips. She . . . Someone was waving at her! A strange woman with hairy legs farther along the platform. WASN'T! COULDN'T BE!

'COOOoooo-weeeeeEEEee!' went the woman.

It was Jude, disguised as a certain Barbara Castle, hiding

from the fatwa. Oh, the fatwa had been in all the papers. Front page drivel. I remember reading about it myself up my pole in Thetford Forest. ARAB LEAGUE AMBASSADOR PRONOUNCES FATWA AGAINST CASHIERED ARMY OFFICER. Rakish photos of Jude, with various cheating-at-cards smiles, made him sound quite the hero.

With nothing else to do, Haha waved back, indulging a compassion for the boy's situation. In her wave her hand became a rocking fist, indicating masturbation. A friendly gesture which caused Jude's wave to become that of a drowning man with an unexpected stiffening. She laughed at him.

But suddenly she took fright, like a grouse who doesn't know the date but suspects that shooting is about to start. Her scornful eyes rolled along the aisles of Mr Wilson's audience. Everyone was in their re-enactment outfit and looked as grey and boring as this vintage of the past presumably must have looked. But some of those faces were Arab-ish faces. Perhaps they ALL were Arabs! 'Fatwa' tatooed on their buttocks! And the diseased squirty little man with the suntan next to her, glumly watching her sister snog the ex-King, was the most sinister personage of all. Checked trousers, cardigan, tartan cap.

His eyes moved hardly at all, or not at all, but they were on her. His tongue touched his lips and she was offended. She punched him in the nose.

'Nasty little Arab! You fatwa my boyfriend and I'll boggn get you in my tank and you'll come out an 8-stone hedgehog, man!'

The squirt held a handkerchief to his bleeding neb and turned his face to watch Mr Wilson's back. The audience was concentrating on its mild applause. He turned to Haha several times, with a dog-wants-a-biscuit look, which caused Haha a painful remembrance of the deceased Weewee. She was about to hit him again.

'Connie,' he said.

But she wouldn't Pam him back.

Nervously, he croaked a chat-up line not bad in the circumstances: 'Would you like an authentic 1964 conversation?'

'You give me wiffo vibes, man. Bog off!'

'We could talk about golf.'

Passionately, she hit him again.

'Golf wasn't illegal in 1964. Everyone was playing it.'

She hit him again.

'It was the most popular game in the world.'

She slapped both his cheeks.

'I'm supposed to be the M.P. for somewhere in the Midlands.'

'Bog off! You're DISEASED!'

She didn't hit him this time. He seemed to enjoy it too much.

He winked a bloodshot eye. 'But I didn't get into my outfit, dig. You hear what I'm sayin'?'

An outraged Haha understood the full horror: this outfit, this obscene golfing outfit, was his normal daywear! He was a boggn golfer! A real, driving, putting, golfer!

'You don't mean,' she husked. 'That those rascally trews are real rascally trews.'

He nodded. She hit the beginning and the end of the nod.

'You're saying that you're a golfer, aren't you! You're piggn admitting it, man!'

His nod was sore. So he made a noise in his throat she could not hit. He was a golfer all right. Boggn cheek of the article!

'Hey, freaky chick,' he said, bold as a Wibley. 'Would like like a malteser?'

Her lip trembling, emotions exploding in her breast, she accepted a malteser from his packet. Chocolate entered her starved frame. She felt better for it.

'Golf's been illegal for 30 years, dig it!' she rasped in his pummelled face. 'But, according to an article I read in *Vogue*, there's five times the number of golfcourses that there's ever been. Where do they put them, man? Why don't the police find them and hang the boggn golfers and blow their scene to Hell, man! Wot's wrong with Connie and Pam that they can't stamp out golf, man!'

Spoken from the heart. Then she stood up and whistled for a policeman. Mr Wilson's head turned. He paused in his speech. A blue-uniformed, pointy-helmeted policeman mumbled excuse-mees along the platform. Then a last excuse me to Haha herself.

'Excuse me, miss, but you're not being authentic.' He helpfully showed her the chapter 'How to be Authentic' in the red book.

'GOLFER!' she said, pointing melodramatically at the golfing squirt.

'He's only pretending, miss. Golfing wasn't illegal in 1964.'

'Golfer, man! Far out! He's a real 21st Century golfer, you dig!'

The policeman was all a-dither. He fell totally out of character. 'Cool it, freaky chick, man – I'm not a real copper. This is just a re-enactment outfit, dig!'

And he skittled away with more excuse-mees, leaving Haha back in her seat beside the gruesome little golfer. He spoke matter-of-factly – but his lips, his voice, they were all the world. Was he hypnotizing her or what?

'Hang loose,' he said. 'They're going to arrest me soon, anyoldhow. I've just got back from America, see, and I left my cap on a course there. It had my name in it. Only a matter of time before they trace it back here. They're probably waiting for me in my flat now.'

'Serves you boggn right, man!'

'They shot down my best golfing pal. Poor Seve, never knew he'd hit a hole in one.'

'Seve?'

'They shot him in the back.'

'Seve??????'

'I ran. A blur of rascally trews, I was. They shot and shot but couldn't hit me.'

'SEVE?'

'My cap came off on the green and when I bent down to pick it up I saw the ball in the hole. I didn't pick up my cap. I was cheering. Wot a player, man!'

Haha dragged Rainbow out of her half of the snog.

'Sis! Sis! This grubby article knows daddy, knew daddy, dig!

But the golfer was on his feet, a large revolver in his

hand, slowly stepping up onto the speechifying dais beside Mr Wilson.

'FREEDOM! DIG IT! DEATH TO ALL OPPRESSORS! LEGALIZE GOLF, PLEASY-DO!'

Then five shots. Jude/Barbara Castle fainted in his/her seat. Mr Wilson tumbled out of view with a bloody face, a bloody chest, squirting blood, the pages of his blood-spattered speech fluttering down after him.

The ex-King slapped his cheeks. 'He's shot Harold Wilson! That can't be authentic!'

Rainbow and Haha were halfway onto the speechifying dais. This grubby article, kneeling limply with smoking gun, had known their daddy! A friend of their daddy! Was Clone Seve really dead? So many questions! But they couldn't reach the man in time. Even their bare legs didn't distract him from his profound golfing thoughts.

A sad glance at them, hypnotizing lips not moving but saying: 'Blows your mind, man, the fairways.' And the gun was suddenly pointing at his own head.

'COOL IT, MAN!' yelled Haha.

The golfer shot his head off. His tartan cap span away triumphantly as his body fell with a whump. Golf balls rolled out of all his pockets and drummed a lament on the speechifying dais.

10 minutes later, in an authentic 1964 ladies' toilet, Haha, Rainbow and Jude sat in the trio of cubicles stripped of their disguises, nude and traumatized. The ex-King was pacing before the open doors, weeping his heart out.

'AMERICA! But chicken, honeypot, darlingmost elf! Anywhere but AMERICA! They're all freaked out in AMERICA!' Then on his knees, irritatingly Scottish: 'Rainbow, my braw skinny lassie – since your colours entered my life I have known only joy. Och, ye'll no go, ye'll stay here, ye shall be my Queen, my only love! Heavenly vibes, man!'

'I'm going to America, Henry,' said Rainbow quietly. 'To put daisychains on my daddy's grave. It is something I must do.'

Then, perhaps remembering the conduct of his own father, executed by the Government of Taxi Drivers back in '26, he peeled off his character's bushy eyebrows and Kingliness flooded though him. His three subjects stood up in their cubicles, hands cupped over parts of their nakedness – they were seeing a King for the first time!

'You'll be needing some extra sheep for the journey,' said the thoughtful ex-King. 'Rassendyl-Flints!'

'Your Majesty!' saluted Jude, exposing one testicle.

'You will accompany the ladies to America and guard them with your life. You'll be saving yourself from the fatwa while you're at it. Dig?'

'I dig, sir!'

Rainbow kissed her prince on the cheek. 'Connie,' she said.

'Pam,' he said.

'You'll not do anything heavy till I get back?'

'Heavy? Och, I dig. Witches. No. I'll wait till you get back. A coronation and Royal wedding on the same day. Does that give you kicks, chick?'

'Too-too evermost,' she said.

As Rainbow walked down the dull corridors of the ruined 1964 Labour Party Conference, she clasped a little cushion to her breast. It contained all the ex-King's hair, preserved in there since it fell out. O intimate prezzie!

'You don't really love him, sis, not REALLY!' Haha had never felt more distant from her mirror-like sis.

Rainbow walked on ahead and out through swing doors into 1964 Brighton. The people didn't baulk at her nudity, cos they weren't there. They faded as her first tear fell, and there was Connie and Pam's England. The baaing of sheep was everywhere, dizzyfying, sounds of a riot on the breeze. Rainbow fainted into her sister's arms. Baaaaa!

Back in the toilets the ex-King was playing *Keep the Red Flag Flying* on his bagpipes, losing his tune with odd squeals as he paused to sob. Rainbow was to die in America. She would never be his Queen. This somehow, suddenly, he knew. In his Chelsea garden a little white dog wuffed among the sheep. He'd bought it for Rainbow, as a replacement for Weewee, but she never held it in her arms. The ex-King, undressed, unhinged and unrestored, often watched it from his windows in the years to come, as madness crusted thickly on his face, till at last he did not know what he was looking at. A cartoon MacTavish aped lewdly on his wallpaper, and he was delighted, cos only he could see its antics. How he laughed, loud, that charming laugh that had made Rainbow love him. And it sounded just the same to the end of his befuddled days.

4

America the Beautiful

Dreaming of a better world, asleep in my treehouse nest in the grounds of Chaffinch Hall, I was awakened by what I thought was a public house materializing under my tree. It proved to be merely Galbraith, Haha and Rainbow's inebriated butler, picking daisies in the rosy-fingered dawn, singing two tunes at once, impersonating an out-of-tune plonkity-plonk piano at the back of his throat, and fighting fiercely with insult-throwing illusions.

It took me some minutes to convince him that the cherubic face poking from the leaves was not part of his delirium tremens. When he grew hoarse from screaming, he told me the shocking news that Clone Seve was dead in America and that the twins were about to travel there to put daisychains on his grave. He held up his paperbag of daisies as pathetic proof. They'd wanted the daisychain's daisies to come from the ancestral home. Too-too. But AMERICA!

Half the morning was spent waiting for Galbraith's heavily dented bubble-car to recharge. All the while, pleasy-do, he talked hotly about Miss Rainbow's thighs and kissed shortbread biscuits which he did not eat. Then he and I, a dipso devil and a nutty angel, took off in the bubble-car, devil driving, angel politely holding the wheel, and we went bouncing across my native county to Stansted Airport, where the twins were about to take the airship to America.

I was sobmost, cos I realized for the first time that Clone Seve had been one of my closest friends, perhaps THE closest I'd ever had. Cuz Seve I had never liked, but Clone Seve, though not a real man, was a real bro to this lonesome Chaffinch. Ever since the invention of the televisitor he'd televisited me every month or so, his lanky body lounging in the air beside my pole, walking tall beside me along the banks of the Stour whole long days. For years I sighed at his every arrival, vexed from my solitude by him. But in time, if I had a certain kind of thought, I'd say to myself: I'll tell that to Seve next time he comes. I could never televisit him, of course, cos I never knew where he was. A fugitive clone, always secretive about his whereabouts, that desperately unhappy creature, a man and yet not a man, a confounded pest, full of clone's tricks, always alarmingly clad in criminal golfing getups. How I covered my ears when he talked of golf! His sly clone's merriment at that! But in latter years he had grown passionate about theology and it was with him that this future Archbishop had his excitemostingly demanding talks about Religion, God, Evil, and Hope. Oh, he was quite brilliant! So fervent! Long gone, he inspires me yet.

Just as often we talked of darling Scampi. How we both missed her, how he regretted leaving her. And, of course, I talked about the twins, their growing up, their fab lifestyle. I had promised him again and again not to mention his televisits to them, and I thought it best to respect his wish, even during their troubled kiddywinkhoods, when the idea that their daddy cared for them might have prevented bedtime tears. Had I been right not to speak to the twins about their father? Crashing along with Galbraith in the bubble-car, I was sickly with guilt. I felt I had prevented them from knowing their father. And now he was boo-hoo deadmost! Could I tell them that for 25 years Clone Seve had been my closest friend? What would they think of me? Scampi's children! I loved them. About Rainbow I had allowed myself unwholesome thoughts, fantasies of us living on a sunny planet together. I loved her. They would turn from their Uncle Chiffchaff forever!

Rainbow and Haha were sitting in the airship lounge drinking zombies, surrounded by pedigree sheep. The overlarge sheep sitting between them at their table, knocking back zombies and chortling unsheepishly, was obviously Jude Rassendyl-Flints hiding from the fatwa. The girls were nude, their bodies painted with azure sky and clouds. Charming. If only I could have seen their mother so attired!

'Uncle Chiffchaff! Cool! Cum to see us off, man! Too-too!'
'I have just heard the sad news.'

Galbraith was on his knees, groaning as he admired their bodypaint. This and his other lascivious sounds played behind my confession.

'. . . and we spoke of you so often. He was a befuddled man, his soul commingled with nothingness, raked with the mental torments only a clone can know. But he loved you. He loved you!'

Everyone in the airship lounge had listened in. All collapsed in tears. The twins howled Wilf-like, tableaued memories of their unhappy childhoods parading around them. But these memories were being re-shaped, cos they now knew that their daddy, their just-shot daddy, had been televisiting a few rooms away all their life long.

Did they forgive old Uncle Chiffchaff?

Under the sound of the airship take-off announcement they said they did. I could not see them. My eyes were underwater. Nor did I see Rainbow shoot the Arab creeping up on the deeply moved Jude. The twins hugged each other, their similarly painted skies joining together with hardly a shadow between. I was admitted to their huddle, also sheepish Jude and finally a groin-twitching Galbraith, whose whisky breath intoxicated us all. As we parted I had a manky little cushion in my hand which Rainbow suddenly snatched away from me with a pathetic smile. I see that smile even now, as huge as Africa!

I walked across the tarmac, towards the sunlight beyond the shadow of the huge balloon of the airship with that strange relief that exists beyond a bout of tears, a feeling more sure than happiness. I did not know then, no I did not, that I would never see the twins again. Suddenly . . . dizziness! The airship was leaving the ground, its lifting shadow confusing my eyes. I turned, anxious, a cry on my lips, and saw Galbraith falling towards me from the gondola, watched passively by the heads of sheep, leaning baafully from the open windows.

WHUMPAOOOOOOFF! Had I been praying for a butler and the Good Lord prayer-answeringly dropped me one down? Nope, this was a butler from Hell. I helped his yelling body up.

'RAINBOW! HAHA! MY FLESHLESS DARLINGS! MY

SKINNY POPPETS! MY PENCIL-FIGURED TURN-ONS!
DON'T BLOW MY SCENE, MAN! DIG ME! DIG ME! I DIG
YOU! OUT OF SIGHT!'

And he continued thus yelling until the airship was indeed
out of sight! When he'd scratched the last of his alcoholic's mice
from his face I drove him back to the Hall in the bubble-car. He
immediately locked himself in the wine cellar with our most
elderly maid. Unable to cope, I left for Northumberland. I'd had
a new 12 foot pole erected just up the coast from Dunstanburgh
Castle. Very peaceful. My imaginary conversations with Clone
Seve were a comfort, and Rainbow and I had picnics on our
private planet. The things she said, I remember yet, as if
they were really said.

It was 2 years before I saw Galbraith again. Then he was
a sober ball of a man and Chancellor of England.

Tadese! The hosepipe!

*

In my youth, when America was open and busy in the world,
it was our world's Babylon, a place where everything could
happen and did, the home of youth and hope, where real life
was lived, in energy and ease. The America of the '60s which
Rainbow and Haha floated towards, had long ago closed its
doors on the world. A few airships a week was all it took.
They went isolationist in the '20s. A series of disastrous
interventions in world affairs, including their ludicrous invasion
of Wales in '22 to prevent Smithers from doing-in Welshmen,
coincided with the break up of the old United States.

The rise of the Arab League had as much to do with it as
anything, and when the Grand Mufti stopped all oil reaching
America in '42 and the Americans had to abandon their beloved
motor cars forever, the character of their continent changed
dramatically. Everything was suddenly very far away from
everywhere else. As far as most of the world was concerned,
America disappeared in the '40s, just as Belgium did in '05.

At the time of Rainbow and Haha's ill-fated visit in the '60s
the state of play in America had at last reached a stasis. The
United States comprised only the original 13 states which had

fought for their independence in the 1770s. The largely-black
Confederacy made hay with the south. California was inde-
pendent and run by the *Coca-Cola* corporation. Alabama and
Wisconsin were populated entirely by lawyers, living litigious
lives, suing each other, inventing laws and ways around them
– a most unique experiment in living. Texas, Florida and
other regions comprised Spanish America proper, under a
carnival of belly-up Presidents who were shot as frequently
as turkeys. The mid-west, meanwhileydoos, the only region
I ever visited, was administered by churchmen – a Biblical
America, the forerunner of the Theocracies which ran the
whole world in the '70s. While non-Biblical America was
boglyfalared with gang-war, civil war between the 13 United
States and the Confederacy, the hymn-singing middle slice of
the continent was sugary-poo, safe and quiet, where a fervent
population genuflected in perfect peace under a succession of
loony pastors.

Spanish had gradually ousted English as the language of
America, further cutting them off from their American-English
past. Today, in the century's last days, America is the world's
last troublespot. Apart from the lawyers, there are few people
over there over the age of 16. They fight in the same broken
streets their great-grandfathers fought in, but with vaporisers
now and other futuristic weaponry. The current President of
the Eastern League still has dreams of reuniting the old 50
states, about as possible as the senile MacTavish's dream of
a tartan world. A sorry end to the hopes of their American
founding fathers! But still we Europeans admire them and the
airships are full of our wilder spirits, going to join the gangs
for a summer of adventure. A few return.

Rainbow, Haha and Jude, of course, could not enter America
without affiliating themselves to a particular gang. For my visit
I joined the Red Sox. Meaning, does it not, that had I travelled
with them, I would have had to shoot it out with them when
we arrived! Cos they joined the Uglybloods – which, with the
Mickeys, was then the most powerful gang around.

Even shy President Sanchez, sitting in his oval office in
Washington, was a gang member – a Taco Mother – and at
election time, to prove himself a man of the people, out he'd

go with his machinegun, streetfighting the Red Soxs and the Jets. He was in a pother in '63, cos the *Washington Post* was sniffing out the story that his brother, the previous President Sanchez, had not in fact been assassinated. It transpired that HE was his own brother, that his brother, who he was now pretending to be, had been assassinated, and that he, when he was the previous President Sanchez, had assumed his brother's identity cos his popularity was at a low ebb and his only chance to stay in office was to be re-elected as his brother! In the English papers this all made little sense, but the Americans were obsessed with the idea. It was even suggested, and at such length that it was finally believed, that President Gingrich wasn't assassinated in '37, that Sanchez and he were the same man, that Gingrich had, through a political masterstroke in inventing the 3 Sanchez brothers, managed to stay in office for over 30 years. At the time I didn't believe a word, but now, somehow, though I haven't thought about it since, I believe it! Gingrich was Sanchez, Sanchez, Sanchez, Hoolihan, Mercedes Holàn, Kincade, Biffo, Sanchez and MacAllister. He was the boggn piggn lot! Craik-Chegwin eat your heart out!

In 2063 a million Americans a week were wounded in gunbattles. Wot a toll! Perhaps every bullet fired hit somebody, cos with Americans being so ginormously fattifalarious it must've been like shooting elephants in a barrel. Fat! Fat! FAT! In Europe fatness came into fashion just before the Mufti War, but in America it has always been in fashion. If you are letting off 1,000 rounds a second in your gunbattle, probably outside a fastfoodtakeaway, your opponents being ten Uglybloods, all 20 stones each, and you yourself are 25 stones, everyone is going to get shot, even if it's pitchblack and you're all blind behind sunglasses.

Jude, safe enough from the fatwa, plopped his tweeds when he realized he'd be under fire from everything but Uglybloods during his entire stay.

'Heck, man! – I might as well moon in front of the Grand Mufti in the middle of boggn Mecca as this, dig! Heavy bad vibes and all that rot!'

He was told not to be so uptight, to hang loose, and

that he'd feel better when he'd shot his first Taco Mother. He didn't.

For the twins, showering off their clouds and sky in New York's Plaza hotel, the worst thing about America was that everyone kept offering them food. Skin-and-bone beauties in Blighty looked like unfed twigs in America.

'Here, bitches, eat! – EAT, BITCHES!' said a fellow Uglyblood, taking a cold hamburger from under his pnongball cap and shoving its reek under their noses.

'Thankydoos, man, but we're cool!' said Haha.

But she was furious! In the hotel suite she kicked all their sheep, which took half an hour. On her first few days in America she masturbated Jude with such miffed ferocity that he visibly aged.

'EVERY LAST PERSON IN AMERICA IS A PIGGN OIK! YOU DIG!' screamed Haha from her hotel window, blue water, the remains of an English sky, streaming down her back, between her poppet's legs and all over the floor.

None of the bustling New Yorkers knew what a piggn oik was, so stayed cool. A more American phrase might've had the window pinged with bullets. Haha burst into nervous tears and cursed the unidentified golfer who'd shot Harold Wilson and started this horrid quest.

But an hour later she was coolmost, making an entrance into an office in the pointy end of the Flatiron Building, looking her peachy stylish best in satin jodhpurs and a mink bikini top, with Rainbow sweeping in behind her in a see-through chiffon trouser suit. On their heads they wore busbys. O visions of loveliness! Some while of silence from the guy they were calling on, as he chewed his tie, in awe of this vision of English womanhood. At last he spoke, and in English, thank God!

'Who's the fink asswipe geek?' said Nixon Johnson, the 35-stone Uglyblood-affiliated Bronx-born private detective they were consulting to help them find their daddy's grave.

The girls looked behind them, blinking their extra-huge eyelashes. Nowt there. Just Jude standing among the sheep.

'Oh, that fink asswipe geek – that's Jude,' said Rainbow. 'Our bodyguard, pleasy-do.'

Jude was done-up in Uglyblood leathers, but didn't look the

part. Johnson shouted FINK ASSWIPE GEEK at him several times, making him very embarrassed as only an Englishman can be. Then the detective lifted his paunch out of his chair and rummaged among old pizza boxes on his floor, belching, passing rat-tats of anal wind that had them all going for their guns, until he found a pizza with only one bite out of it.

'Let's eat the pizza's ass, bitches,' he said. 'FINK! ASSWIPE! GEEK! ASSWIPE! ASSWIPE!' Then more businesslike to Haha: 'A sheep a day plus expenses, I don't work for less, see!'

Because at Uglyblood HQ they'd been told Nixon Johnson was the only man who could possibly find their needle daddy in an American haystack, they decided to be polite and shared his pizza with him. Though he had most of it, and they barely two anchovies and a sliver of pepperoni each, it was more than they'd eaten at one sitting since their 8th birthday party, when Haha had puked bucketsful and Rainbow not, giving rise to the myth that Rainbow was the fatter of the two sticks.

They described to the gross detective what they wanted from him, telling about the golfer, the golfer's story, his death, about their father, his televisits to me, and so on. All the while, Nixon Johnson read and re-read the sign on his window.

Nixon Johnson Private Investigator
(a sheep a day plus expenses)

It didn't say this backwards, so from the street it was nonsense. But wasn't everything? He kept interrupting the girls with the same lewd question:

'You poke ass? You get asspoked, bitches, dig? That asswipe poke your ass, huh? You bitches poke ass? Your asses is too piggn skinny to poke, but I bet you poke ass, huh? You poke each other's ass? Wanna poke my ass? I can poke ass real good, señoritas?' Then three yards of Spanish filth before returning to: 'You poke ass?'

He didn't seem to mind that he received no answer. It was how he spoke to all women, even his mother back in the Bronx, and to any of the fat girls, classy or sleazy, he bumped into on 5th Avenue – and when everyone was 20 stone plus, everyone bumped into everyone on 5th Avenue.

'You poke ass? Huh? You asspokearoony with me? I'm mucho bueno poke-o, ehwot? Heh-heh-heh. You poke my ass, bitches?'

Later, in their hotel room, they watched a television programme – television never quite died out in America – in which the male characters spoke in exactly this same way to the female characters before shooting them. And this on the Uglyblood channel! Their own gang!

'They're boggn DISEASED!' woofed Haha, dropping Jude's sore member where she'd found it.

Rainbow stroked her hair-stuffed cushion and wished for the 10th time that day that she hadn't crossed the pond. How she missed the gentle dottiness of the ex-King!

But life was for living, so the twins opened their 102 suitcases and decided to make the best of their time in America while Nixon Johnson earned his sheep a day. Stylishly attired, they took part in streetbattles. Crackshot Rainbow picked off a dozen Taco Mothers and was photoed for the cover of *Uglyblood* magazine, much to the miffifycation of her twin, until they bought a copy on the newsstands. DOES THIS BITCH POKE? it said under her picture, which ruined the whole thing!

They dined and danced at all the best places, Storky's, Montoya's, 44's, Ladybird's, The Alamo. Haha was kissed for the first time, by the 50 stone Senator Aznavoorian, shot dead in the lobby of the Trump Tower that same night. The briefest of holiday romances! But ending in such tragedy! – Oooo, how romantic!

'A hippo's body, but a tongue like a hummingbird,' said Haha wistfully of her first, last and only boyfriend, Jude not included.

The twins ate well on just an olive a day – between them – and wore T-shirts saying SKINNY GIRLS HAVE MORE FUN. Bogala! Weeeehaaa! Yippee-i-ay! and 'wot a wonderful town'! NEW YORK! NEW YORK! Clone Seve was forgotten. Jude, kidnapped by the Mickeys on their first night, was a distant memory. Gigglesome, cheeful, they went from club to club with their new roly-poly friends. Trouble one night outside a flower shop when the Taco Mothers gunned down everyone they were with and half their sheep to boot. But they rustled some sheep, found Jude dangling by his feet from Manhattan Bridge, and without stopping for a wink's sleep, took an airship out to Virginia to watch a civil war battle in progress. Finally, pink champers giggled them to sleep and all three woke up in an hotel in the Catskills in the same bed as the Attorney General, a man whose chin count was way higher than his I.Q.

Dizzily tripping downstairs looking for a zombie they found themselves the guests of 'The National Podium for the Promotion of Domestic Violence'. Haha gave a speech, all about the virtues of Connie and Pam, receiving rapturous applause when she said that domestic violence was to be encouraged because it would lead to the inevitable segregation of the sexes. Haha the prophet!

In the cantina, Rainbow was congratulating her sis on her nifty speech when Nixon Johnson appeared from nowhere with a fat file in his sausagey fingers.

'Heythere, hot bitches! You poke ass? Here's my asspoking report, asspoking bitches! MY ASS! YOUR ASS! POKE!'

He weeweed into a jug, tossed in a zombie and three black olives and knocked it back.

'Good for the heart,' he said. 'Unblocks the sonofabitch arteries. You poke ASS?'

The report was in Spanish and, tired of Nixon Johnson's constant question, they got the Attorney General to translate. Sadly, he too seemed to be slipping into the asspoking vernacular – but then they realized he was translating from the report. Nixon Johnson spoke, wrote, typed, dreamed his asspokery question, but never acted upon it, if indeed it was possible for him so to do.

'You poke ass?' translated the Attorney General. 'Bitches! Bitches! Bitches! You poke my ass? Hot skinny bitches! Catch my asspoker, bitches.'

Fourteen pages of this – then the meat . . . The desperate golfer who had murdered the Harold Wilson re-enactor was here identified as a dentist from Stoke-on-Trent, one Palmer

Putteridge. Police reports, quoted at length, indicated Palmer Putteridge had last played golf on a secret course near Las Vegas in the Wild West region. There he had lost his cap in the act of avoiding arrest while his golfing partner, one Severiano Chaffinch, had bitten the dust in mid-swing.

Sombre silence from the girls. They remembered when they had longed for their daddy's return. Now he never would.

'I've copies of the police photos if you can take it, bitches,' said Nixon Johnson, a note of reluctant compassion among his cacophony of woman-hating filth.

He handed them over. Rainbow squeezed Haha, then Haha squeezed Rainbow. Strewth at last! They looked at skew photos of a young man in rascally trews asleep on the grass, little to suggest he'd just been backshot. Their father, yes. The image of the man whose portrait had hung in the billiard room at Chaffinch Hall all their lives. It was he, Clone Seve. But he hadn't aged a day. How come?

In the moments that the photos shuffled under her chocdrop eyes, Rainbow cloneishly instinctively understood what was still clicking-over in Haha's colder mind. Clone Seve was alive. This was not him, not quite him. Then Haha also understood and together they looked up at Nixon Johnson, in a manly huddle with the Attorney General and a jug of either bloody urine or sangria. 4 lovely long-lashed girlie eyes caught, for a nanosec only, 4 puffy alligatorish peepers. Yes, these oiky men knew too. It was a conspiracy! The men's pudgy fingers were hiding their whispering blubbery lips. And the only clue was a surreptitious sign of the cross made by Nixon Johnson, which Rainbow thought mightily upon during their wagon train journey to the West.

'YOU POKE MY ASS, BITCHES!' yelled Nixon Johnson as they left the cantina, all but five of the sheep present (the ones they owed him) following them out with waggly tails. He mooned a goodbye at them with a fat bum not wiped since Gingrich's impeachment.

Outside: trees, landscape, America the beautiful, a chilly dawn in the Catskills. Jude could hear a muezzin chanting morning prayers. The others could not. Rainbow made the sign of the cross over and over to herself, postulantly.

'This scene is a heavy scene, man,' she muttered, and pulled off her false lashes with the most feminine of gestures. 'You hear what I'm saying, sis.'

'I dig your drift, chick,' said Haha, and with a long littlefingernail she found an itch under her busby.

5

Jude Goes Limp

Monsignor Festus Hummelle in 2024 or thereabouts devised a method of killing all the flies in Wyoming, much welcomed in that plague-carrying time. He later extended his method to include the whole earth and no one was bothered with a fly for over 30 years. I heard it said that his experiments were also responsible for the sudden boom in the Scottish population in the '20s. I was happier with the flies! Chee!

In the '60s his son, Rev Clyde Hummelle, a piggy chimp of a man, was Apostle-in-Chief of Mid-America, their head of state. He still endures. For 50 years he has sat on a golden throne in his cathedral in Little Rock, Arkansas, speaking bland wisdom, mostly about the conduct of 16-year-old girls. Outside, his father's statue is ringed by flies.

Rainbow was sure that when Nixon Johnson made the sign of the cross he was so doing rather than saying the sacred name of Rev Clyde Hummelle, a man above reproach who was in fact a secret golfer. To deduce so much from so little is indeedybe remarkable, but remember: Rainbow was half-clone and the workings of her mind were mysterious. She was, of course, quite right.

In order to see Rev Hummelle they had to invent some problem to excite his morality, some ailment he might cure with his healing powers. This they had to write down on a card and hand in to a beefy young priest.

The beefy young priest had seen everything on these cards in his few years of service. But his eyebrows rose when he read what the girls had put down. They said Jude was killing himself with masturbation, that his penis was a throbbing sore and that through his magnetic personality he was forcing two girls to watch his masturbatory suicide. Jude, who had no idea what was on the card, stood whistling

Dixie and scratching his crotch as the beefy young priest read the card.

Rev Hummelle saw them immediately. The girls helped Jude down the aisle in such a nursey way towards the pig on the throne that the cashiered lieutenant wrongly guessed that they were surprising him with a wedding. At last, his dreams come true! They did this sort of thing in America! Yes! He would marry Rainbow and Haha! The pair! Both! His forever! JOY! O happy youth!

'Morning, vicar. Dig your fab scene, man. Mighty. Superduper. Ehwot? Shall I stand between the girls, or to one side?'

He shook hands with Rev Hummelle and felt suddenly limp, strange and girlie. The smarting itch in his penis was gone in the same moment. His face became increasingly angelic.

'All is well now, my son. Go – lead a useful life!'

Rainbow kneeled before the theocrat. She was wearing a little cross I had given her. It glinted in his pale blue eyes.

'My sister and I are looking for our father, Severiano Chaffinch. He's a golfer. Can you tell us where he is?'

Rev Hummelle's features seemed to disappear in the folds of fat on his piggy face. He was saying nothing.

Haha tried: 'We have come all the way from England to find him, you dig?'

'I do not know the man,' said the man of God.

He was lying. He was financing Clone Seve's Cloning Institute. He read daily reports on the progress of Clone Seve's experiments, of special appeal to him cos they were designed to unlock the God within us. Seve's patron and protector for 20 years, he kept wolves from his door, also the curious, the impure, and employed all the facilities of his Church and Government to do so.

'He's very tall. 6 feet 8. In his 50s,' said Rainbow. 'Wears rascally trews. Perhaps you've seen him on the golf course one day.'

A creak in the floor below them and the Rev Hummelle's throne rose, sliding up a pillar. They could hear his stomach rumbling as he neared his God painted on the ceiling. The beefy young priest was behind them with a pistol in his hand. He escorted them off the premises. They'd called the Apostle-in-Chief a golfer! In fact, he'd won the American Open in '59.

Outside, under a hot sun, they were dejected among patios. The twins stripped off to cheer themselves up with some sun worshipping, and set about oiling each other's fronts. Jude usually felt lusty at such a scene. But today he was waving at the beefy young priest who was watching them from a window.

After a bit the priest waved back. Jude left the girls and walked along crazypaving paths for a word with the priest. He wasn't quite sure why. Perhaps he wanted advice on how to lead a useful life – that must be it. But the crazypaving path didn't go where he thought. It led him astray. The priest was gone from the window – and now Jude didn't know which window he'd been aiming at. In the biggest panic he'd been in since he was cashiered, Jude hurried down several paths and was about to shriek for his girls when a golfcart with the word SUGO on the side ran over his tootsies.

It trundled past and into a grotto on the side of the cathedral. For a moment there seemed to be a vision of green grass inside the grotto. One finger in the air, proud of his discovery, he went to find the girls.

Minutes later all three were outside the grotto. When the next golfcart trundled by they waved at the man in the outrageous sweater who was driving it. Haha jumped on the back as it passed by. Rainbow pulled the same trick with the next golfcart. Jude waited his turn, but no more golfcarts came. Baaaaaaa!

The girls found themselves – amazed but as golf-haters also furious – in an underground golfing complex. The cathedral was merely a cover to a vast golfing underworld. On the roof above them a permanent sun glowed convincingly over all. Golfcarts trundled along red pathways. Little groups of golfers shook hands on putting greens. On a nearby T, applause at a well-struck ball. Greens. Fairways. Brilliant yellow bunkers. The word SUGO was stamped even on the trees. This golfing Heaven was designed by Macmacpherson back in the '30s and carried here rolled up under the arm of Clone Seve's second wife, Macmacpherson's daughter, Moira.

'So this is how come there's 10 times as many golfcourses in the world, dig? They're all boggn underground. Far out.' Though she detested the game, Haha couldn't help but be impressed.

They wandered in the rough, not mentioning this to each other, but half hoping to see their father marching down a fairway with some golfing pals. Instead, they tripped over a distinguished-looking man lying unconscious in the long grass.

'Isn't that Herring Carstairs, the famous pnong player?' said Rainbow, who'd had a pnongista phase.

Who else but? Retired from pnong in '41 after a severemost beating from the Wibleys, Carstairs had spent the past 22 years playing golf. He hadn't left this course since it was built. They'd fallen upon him in mid-blackout.

'Dimmee, harh!' went the awaking Carstairs. 'Gone again, was I? Harh! Blackouts, dyersee! Harh!'

'You are Herring Carstairs, the famous pnong player?'

'Pnong! Pnong! Deariebe, ladies, that's a word I haven't heard in a donkey's, harh! See a ball anywhere?'

They helped him find it, watched him slice it, then followed him to a bunker 50 yards away. Despite a lifelong passion for the game, Carstairs was a rotten golfer.

'Seve? Old Seve's Clone? Wot – daughters of Mr Hole-in-One hisself, ehwot! Dimmee! Harh! Yes, of course, I know where he is. Comes down here for a round now and then. My oldest pal, Seve is! Always inviting me over. Ehgad, I fanciedrood his missis – old Macmacpherson's daughter, her was, thar knows. Dimmee, that's 4 whacks, you saw, not five – I'll never par this boggn hole. He's out at a place called Scampiville, near wot's the place – HARH! Las Vegas. Some good courses out there – but the backshooters, wot! Harh! Could do with some Yorkshire puddings, you gals, HARH! – ehwot? Won't you stay – I'm much better at putting!'

They re-joined the wagon train and tried to sexually excite Jude all the way to Las Vegas. But he had lost interest in girls and though horrified at himself could not fake his old interest in being masturbated. Haha and Rainbow did the lewdest wantonmost things in the back of that waggon. But limp Jude just yawned, winced, averted his eyes, and sang whatever snatches of hymns he could remember.

'You're boggn DISEASED, that's wot!' pronounced Haha, who rather missed his little groans while he was being milked.

At Las Vegas they were welcomed by some Uglybloods who helped them catch the stagecoach up Highway 95. Past vast heaps of abandoned motorcars, rotting like Sodoms and Gomorrahs in the desert . . . they were going to Scampiville.

*

Jude had them worried. For the whole stagecoach journey he moaned on about how sorry he was that he'd drowned the Arab League Ambassador, said how ashamed he was for corrupting the twins by encouraging them to masturbate him, admitted to numerous wicked secrets, and was just getting to the reason he'd been cashiered when . . . They arrived at Scampiville.

SCAMPIVILLE
Population 2,426

Oddmost place! The people . . . walking in the streets . . . they were all . . . Seve and Scampi. All. Every one. Some were plump, some weren't in the best of health, but all recognisably, obviously . . . uh-huh: clones of their parents. A man standing outside the saloon: Seve. A schoolmarm: Scampi. And the crocodile of kiddywinkers following her down the dusty street: all child Seves and Scampis. Even the old man driving the stagecoach when they looked through his nitty beard was a dead ringer for Seve. Curtains twitched at high windows: they saw their mother's dead face, their father's stern stare. And these people had *hair* hair – real hair! No wigs! Raven-haired Scampis! Curly-mop Seves! How the girls were jealous of that!

'I'M FREAKING!' warned Haha. 'I want Connie! I want Pam!'

Rainbow ran up to the schoolmarm. She wanted to hug her. This was, I suppose, her last moment of childhood. But, of course, the schoolmarm wasn't really her mother and suddenly Rainbow knew it.

'Triple sorries, thought I knew you. No sweat, man.'

'Say howdeedoodee to the lady, children,' said Scampi Schoolmarm.

'HOWDEEDOODEE,' they said.

Rainbow, her voice cracking: 'Howdoodeedee.'

She ran away, weeping into her cushion, and still hadn't regained control when she joined the others in front of the hotel. She helped them in with the sheep.

The man at reception was a thin Seve with a droopy Mexican moustache. He was eating a carrot like an evil rabbit, but hid the carrot in fright when the sheep goosed around him baaingly.

'Wot's your gang?' he asked the sheep's people.

'Uglybloods,' said Jude, with his new angelic smile.

'Is okay for Uglybloods here. But if any Mickeys come, you fight outside, okaydoos?'

He was a surly oik. Jude was only peeping into his Bible and he drew his gun on him. Piggn cheek!

'That's mine! My patrón, he give it to me! And if you want to keep sheep in your room – is extra!'

But then he saw the name the girls had written in the register . . . and his tune changed to an awestruck but suspicious tune.

'Hey, this say CHAFFINCH! You no Chaffinches! I am Chaffinch! Is my name! My brothers and sisters name! I am Chaffinch! Gipper Chaffinch, is me! You no Chaffinches.'

Rainbow, poshly: 'We are Chaffinches too, dig. Rainbow and Har-har, daughters of Severiano Chaffinch. We had no idea there was an American branch of the family, did we Har-har? We must tell Uncle Wilfred when we get home. He'll freak.'

Gipper Chaffinch watched them go up their stairs, then bit his carrot nervously as he hopped into the televisiting booth.

A moment later he was in the presence of his patrón and creator, Severiano.

Rainbow ran a bath and unzipped five bags of feminine perfumeries, ordering Jude to find today's chosen pastes and niffings cos Haha was calling her to the balcony. Gunslinging showdowns were in progress in the highnoon sun.

'Two sheep on the one with the sombrero!'

'Dig!' said Rainbow, meaning she accepted the bet.

And as the one in the sombrero was facing their way, therefore distrached by the lanky skinny sexy articles, one of whom was nude for her bath, he didn't get his gun out of the holster before being shot six times.

'Heavy,' whinged Haha, 2 sheep down on the day.

They were applauding the winner, who turned to receive the applause with their father's grin before being shot himself by a skulking friend of the man he'd just outdrawn.

'Wasn't him, was it? NOT HIM?' Rainbow was hugging her sister in fear.

'No way José – cool those butterflies, sis. He's out there, somewhere, as alive as we are.'

Jude ambled onto the balcony. He'd found a Bible in a drawer and was mugging up on *Leviticus*.

'While you're making yourself as fabchick as I already am,' said Haha, with a nervous laugh, 'I'll do a little something with Jude. Hey, Jude!'

'Urm?'

She took Jude into the bedroom. Rainbow climbed into the bath, laughing wickedly. Her sister was giving up her ripe cherrymost virginity! She was doing a noble thing, was she not, to restore the mixed-up Jude to his former obnoxious wanky self? When Rainbow turned off the hot tap she could hear the bedsprings creaking manfully. Obviously Haha's sexy scheme was working – the sexual intercourse, having corrupted nearly all the males in history, was taking another groaning victim to its wiggly cult!

Rainbow, meanwhileydoos, bathed with virginal innocence! She ran the soap down her ribs, up her ribs, like a kiddy with a stick on a fence. Bap! Bap! Bap! She poured ointments on her bald head. She gently rubbed fragrant eyepads on eyes that had seen too much that day. Slices of cucumber stuck to her like vampiric sea-creatures. More floated in the bath. She poured elderflower syrup on her knees. She scraped her tongue with a devilish implement. Then she unpadded her eyes to push away a sheep who was drinking the bathwater and she saw her father standing there.

He was blowing his nose. His eyes were red, sad. How tall! How distinguished! Labcoat over rascally trews.

'Daddy?' Yes, she knew this was the genuine article.

'Pleasy-do, you are Rainbow, not Haha?'

'Rainbow, right on.'

'Then it's Haha doing the hooha wiggly thing with that Jilks in the bedroom. She really shouldn't, tha knows.'

Rainbow guffawed. It was her mother's guffaw.

'Again . . . pleasy-do – laugh like that again.'

But she couldn't. Her brow wrinkled. She was fighting tears.

'No, it's all right. It's just . . . dimmee, I've made so many clones of Scampi, of your mama, but none ever . . . laughed . . . not like that. Don't know why.' He noted a bit of an equation on his sleeve. 'Rainbow, darlingmost . . . I'm sorry if . . .'

Rainbow went suddenly hoitytoity. Her face hardened. This stinker had abandoned her and Haha aged 3 in a despotic England just to play piggnboggn golf with a Scots tart! For a few moments she hated, really hated, him!

'Hand me a towel, man,' she snarled like Pam to the Leader of the Opposition.

'Triple sorries, but I'm not here. I'm televisiting. I'm out at the ranch. Would dinner tonight be rhubarb? My surrey's already on its way to pick you up. Too-too.'

'Okaydoos.' Rainbow was straightbacked, icequeenish.

'You'll tell Haha when she's . . . finished.' And he walked through the wall saying: 'I can get you your hair back if you like?'

6

Severiano's Spiritual Exercises

The surrey's fringe was dangled with tiny tinkling bells. As they nodded along through the empty landscape Jude kept pulling them off, one by one, and tossing them into the silent sand.

Their driver, Pepeleon, a young avatar of their dad, with Mexican bandit's tache but a kindly smile, said he was Seve's lab assistant and most trusted clone.

'I am not a real man,' he said, 'BUT HERE!' And he thumped his ticking heart.

All the long, slow way to the ranch he nattered, about Seve, Seve's greatness, Seve's struggles, about his own growing appreciation of the world, its mysteries, and the spiritual exercises Seve had given him to help him get closer to God. Haha masturbated Jude, or held his besotted hand. She listened to nothing that Pepeleon said. She was in a daze. Her eyes freaky and abstracted. Rainbow was the same. Pepeleon's voice was like bees chasing her across the desert. She held onto her seat, dizzy. She felt this place was the remotest in the Universe, a lost, hidden, frightening place where strange and terrible things happened all the time. And she had been dragged from her bed at Chaffinch Hall, a little girl who'd asked God to find her daddy for her.

'Of course, señoritas, in some ways I am your father too,' said Pepeleon with some emotion, but then he laughed heh-heh-heh like a bandit.

In a distance of which they were becoming a part was a set of low buildings. They'd expected a swanky-doos hacienda. This was more like a half-built industrial estate. Sheep were everywhere around.

Pepeleon stopped the surrey at a hummock before the buildings. He removed his sombrero and wiped his eyes. On the top of the hummock fluttered a golfing flag with an

18 on it – it marked the grave of Moira Macmacpherson. Then he whipcrackawayed the horse, itself the clone of a '30s Kentucky Derby winner, and next thing they were speeding through gates. Rainbow and Haha saw cages full of men flash by – her father's clones, expressions of his darkest sides, perhaps. Sunburnt and miserable, they moaned through the bars. Rainbow gripped her cushion tightly as the surrey whipped through a mess of labs and pulled up before the rather English-looking ranch house.

Seve was there – rascally trewless for once – handsome, fatherly, in a swishmost dinner attire. Seeing him for real this time Rainbow was struck by the suffering in his face. She had never seen such suffering writ on a human phiz. Then a moment of supreme sibling oneupmanship.

'Daddy – this is Haha. Haha, Daddy.'

Seve kissed Haha's hand. He kept swallowing. He was too moved to speak. Then he saw that Rainbow's eyes were straying towards the cages.

'Don't bother about them, pleasy-do. They're waiting to be melted down.'

Rainbow laughed. That laugh again. Haha also, but, as Seve noted and this was clearly picked up by Rainbow: Haha's laugh was nothing like Scampi's. Rainbow did her Scampi laugh again and gained her father's full attention. Haha was Wiblied.

'Erm, scuse a naff question, dig,' said Jude. 'But whose is that camel?'

A camel was tied to the only tree in the compound.

'She is mine!' said Pepeleon, with some defiance. 'We share the desert on my days off.'

'Okaydoos, man. It's just this fatwa thing, dig. Anything that jogs the thoughts Arab-wards is bad vibes, hip.'

Then Seve was shaking his hand.

'Connie,' said Jude, automatically.

'Pam,' said Seve, who followed events in England. 'Rhubarb on you evermost.'

The old-fashioned phrase had them all laughing again. Pepeleon slinked away to melt down clones and Seve led his guests inside.

Silent Scampis in waitress outfits served dinner. The

atmosphere was tense. Jude did most of the talking, about *Leviticus*, which Seve suddenly proved he knew by heart.

Haha: 'I hope you're not a religious nut, Daddy, like Uncle Chiffchaff!'

A look of anger and pain crossed Seve's face. Rainbow saw it and lightly touched his hand. He flinched, then smiled the warmest smile she had seen since the ex-King had greeted her at the 1964 Labour Party Conference.

Then Haha put her foot in it again. Their awkward candlelit meal was reflected a thousand times in the silver cups of a trophy cabinet behind Seve's chair.

Haha: 'Daddy – wot are all those cups for?'

'Golf,' said Seve blankly, and the table went as quiet as Moira Macmacpherson's grave.

Hardly a sound for half an hour. Serving Scampis brought them a plate of scampi each, but the joke didn't go down. The swish of skirts. The pouring of wine. Rainbow and Haha putting down their cutlery after one bite, cos the beanpoles were already full. Then, suddenly, almost violent, a halo of silver cups around him, Seve began to talk quickly.

'Lookybe, I left your mother because she wouldn't play golf. I was mad on golf in those days. Now, of course, I can't play. I'm so spiritually perfect that I hit a hole-in-one every time. Spoiled the game for me. But my boys, Pepeleon and the others, you've met Pepeleon – they play. I loved Scampi very much.' An affecting declaration, confused in his daughter's minds cos he squeezed the hand of a waitress as he said it. 'I've made these clones of her from a lock of her hair I always carried.'

Silence again. Seve stared at his plate, seeing, like me, visions of the past, '30s days, moments, faces in the firelight. Then he looked at his daughters, a hard, critical look. Haha grew hoitytoity under his stare. Rainbow couldn't bear it and covered her face. Jude had finished his scampi and was eating tartar sauce with a spoon.

'Your mother was the most beautiful woman of her time,' said Seve. 'Everyone was in love with her. Carstairs, MacTavish, even your old Uncle Chiffchaff.'

'That's a boggn lie!' said Haha, defending me.

'She had a certain look, dyersee, which no other woman . . . You are lovely girls, but Scampi, she . . . Rainbow, you have something of her look in your eyes. Haha, you have it in your, I don't know – yes, then, when you moved your head. If only you had hair!'

'I didn't boggn come here to be insulted, man.' Haha was freaking. She'd had enough. 'Rainbow, let's split this heavy scene, man.'

Rainbow obeyed. They were halfway out, Jude getting up to follow them, when their father's quick sad speech halted them.

'I was very ill when I came here. Before me clones had been melted down after a day or two. But I had lived for years. I was losing my mind. A clone, I hope you can understand this, is a copy not just of a particular person, but of mankind itself. Clones have all mankind's memories in their heads, just as originals do . . .' He looked with contempt at Jude, the only full-blown original present. 'But with originals such memories are locked away, deep in the depths. We clones have no depths, just a wide slippery surface. We've no control over our thoughts. Everything is there at once. All joy. All suffering. Imagine, all the memories of everyone who has ever lived, firing at once, demanding recollection. A quiet afternoon in Moscow in 1924 would flood my head and as I struggled to find myself in my thoughts I'd be swamped by the powerful feelings of a girl swimming in a stoneage lake. It's like an infinite Everyone Channel, but you can't find your own channel however hard you try. I lost myself!' He pressed down on the table in his emotion and everything shook. 'For years I was a N.S.I. – a non specific individual. The compound here is full of them, and the jail in Scampiville, and there's more in camps all over the desert here – my failures – poor souls who flunkerood their spiritual exercises and have nothing to look forward to but melting. Ask Uncle Chaff, he'll tell you what I was like in those years. I used to televisit him and natter on about golf, desperate to re-establish my identity with someone who'd known the real me!'

'The real you was melted down too, wasn't he?' said Haha, acidmost.

'HAHA!' snapped Rainbow.

Haha's huge lashes lowered. Her yellow eyemakeup glittered. 'Triple sorries, sis Rainbow, the poor thing's DISEASED. Not his fault. Nothing's his fault. Far out.'

Seve smiled. He jumped up, gripping Jude's shoulder on his way to his daughters. He put his arms around them, but no I LOVE YOUs, just more cloneish natter.

'It took me years of searching for myself in my head before I found myself. A unique experience. No one had ever done it before. And, here, thousands of clones and only I . . . only I have succeeded. I assembled at last enough thoughts to re-create my consciousness, but a different consciousness. I am not the same clone who stepped from the cloning tank at the Old Bailey. I am me, myself, I am my own father and as different from the original Severiano Chaffinch as can possibly be. This is what was MEANT to happen. But this little consciousness I have made for myself is nothing, NOTHING, NOTHING, just a little drop of water on that slippery surface, floating on the pain of the ages. When I was lost, I called out to God and I suddenly knew he was there, that God does dwell within us, that that is what God is, a being trapped, lost within us, struggling to assemble himself, just as I was. I met him there. I found him there. I found myself in the same moment.'

Laughing, a mad, baggy-eyed clone, towering over his skinny daughters, he led them by the hand out of the dining-room. The sparkle of trophies and candlelight was gone forever from their eyes. He led them down a long dim corridor, towards a fierce light. Then he let go of their bony mits and charged ahead, laughing with delight. The girls followed, stealing peeks at each other for comfort, looking back for Jude, who thought Seve quite a funny fellow, full of wheezy blither.

They pushed through swing doors into a cloning room. Vats of cold flesh everywhere. Tanks of soupy gunge, bubbling. Drowned versions of Seve floating – which could only remind Jude of one thing! In cages lining the far wall clones of Seve knelt praying. A teenage Seve and Scampi were committing the sexual intercourse on a gunge-splashed floor. Haha held

Jude's hand. Rainbow thought of the moment of her own conception.

Seve was standing in the middle of it all, smiling, awaiting their unqualified admiration. Not just a golfer! Not just a scurrilous clone! But a brilliant scientist who was about to save mankind!

'I do a bit of this myself,' admitted Haha with a nervous hahaing laugh. 'Nothing heavy. I'm trying to make the perfect George.'

Seve was beside her. A pang of pain in Rainbow. She'd lost out in the sibling oneupmanstakes and was astonished by how much she cared.

'You make experiments?' Seve's biggest grin yet, maybe ever.

'Too-too. With glands, mostly. To make the ultimate turn-on man, dig. I call him George. I've had some far-out results, haven't I, sis Rainbow? But never quite . . . George.'

Seve's eyes filled with tears. He hugged his skinny daughter, hugged her tight, felt all her sharp bones. Suddenly he released her. To be so hugged by a long-lost daddy had her weeping. She dashed to Rainbow and found a more comforting hug there.

Seve, hopping with a clone's enthusiasm: 'I've been trying to do the same thing, evermost, have I not indeed, so I have! But not George – Jehovah, Buddha, the nameless Tao, the great Aten of the Egyptians, Odin, Zeus, the Lord Jesus Christ, not forgetting Allah. CheeheEEEooocheee! I understood, as I have told you, that certain prevailing ideas, of which God is one, live within us, all of us. They aren't just thoughts, words, ideas – THEY LIVE! They are parasites, if you like – they live within us, all of us at once, a kind of symbiotic mental bacteria, expressing themselves through us, part of us. In a very profound way, we are the sum of their intentions, with a weensie bit left over for ourselves. They never die, cannot, as long as there is one man, then they all live.'

Jude was rapt. His religious nature was fully stirred this time. Seve saw this and they shook hands vigorously – the mad clone, the cashiered ninny, firm friends in their last moments.

'My experiments here during the last 20 years, together with the help of the spiritual exercises I have devised, have been a devotion in the attempt to bring the God that dwells within me to a point of mind where, when I clone myself I am in fact taking God from his prison within me . . . and giving him to the World. Prayer caused this once before. Jesus was such a man. O, I shall make armies of Messiahs and turn this evil century into a Paradise!'

Haha knew enough about cloning tanks to know what nonsense he talked. But Rainbow did not. Her chocdrop eyes swam with pride in her father, love of herself, and compassion for the troubled world daddykins was trying to save. A girlish outpouring of emotion, just as easily triggered by a moment in a song, a new dress, by seeing two happy people walking in the rain. She gushed inside.

A gush that caught Seve in mid-rant.

'Of course, so far my Messiahs haven't come out 100% Messiah – like your Georges, Haha – and dimmee it's upsetting melting a 99% Messiah, with them quoting St Mark at you. Most, I must admit, have been secret rotters with despot's smiles, pleasy-do. Rev Hummelle has been very patient and so generous, a fine man, a gifted . . . RAINBOW! HOLD THAT DEWY-EYED EXPRESSION!'

In an instant he had pricked her finger and had a drop of her blood on a slide. He gently held his thumb under her left eye and caught a drip of tear on it. This he mixed with the blood.

'WHY DIDN'T I THINK OF THIS BEFORE! CHEE-HEEEEE!'

Then he pricked out a drip of his own blood and placed it on a slide beside Rainbow's under his microscope. For a moment he held back in awe. Slowly, a huge smile, jerking on and off. He explained while he worked.

'If I remove the nucleus of one of your teardrenched blood cells, seething with a compassion which perhaps as a clone I can never feel for humanity, and place that nucleus in an empty cell of my own, awash with sterile spiritual perfection and honed mentally on the idea of the Lord . . . Hoooooo! Kumbiya, my Lord, Kumbiya! O, my darlingmost girls, it was God's will, was it not, that you came here at this hour!'

And he put his blood cell concoction into a pea-sized glycerine capsule, placed it on the end of his shoe, grabbed a putter from behind the bench, and chipped the capsule past Jude's nose and into the designated cloning tank.

'It has come to pass,' he said. His last words.

Pepeleon had taken his spiritual exercises seriously. But in the centre of his being where God walked he had not found gentle Jesus. He had found a miffed snarling resentful Allah. Pepeleon, unknown to his patrón, was a Moslem. Jude's mention of the fatwa had sent Pepeleon televisiting to the drowned-and-revived Arab League Ambassador in London. Now he was back, bursting into the lab with his Seve-like bandit's grin, an automatic weapon in each hand.

'ALLAH AKBAH!!!!!!!!!' he cried. 'GREAT IS ALLAH!'

'Bugger me, it's the fatwa!' squeaked Jude.

Rainbow had time to throw a picture into her mind's eye: it was the ex-King hearing about her death on an ordinary English day. She was filled with love for him and, I know, felt no fear.

Then the room was hit by a moment's swarm. Only a moment, and it was over, redder but briefer than any sunset over Kyoto. A sound like someone calling a cat – pusspusspusspusspusssssss – while dropping the tea things. Then just Pepeleon's sinking smile when he saw what he had done. Inexperienced with guns, he'd just meant to shoot Jude, to fulfil the fatwa, but the guns came alive at his touch, and he had killed everyone.

Rainbow and Haha, slim targets both, had hugged each other and made a bigger target. Jude stepped half a step towards them, to shield them. Seve held up one hand, almost a benediction.

Pepeleon wandered through the carnage, jabbering an explanation for his behaviour to the surviving clones in the cages. The tanks bubbled. Rainbow's dropped cushion floated on the surface of one, spattered with her own blood.

'One day I was walking in the desert, full of my spiritual exercises,' said Pepeleon, kneeling by the dead Clone Seve.

'And from nowhere a shower of rain. I watched the stones come alive with flowers. And then a camel wandered from the steaming haze and I was Allah's forever.'

He sat rocking and smiling for a while, then went outside and opened all the cages. Chaffinches flew into the desert. Two rode off on that confounded camel. Pepeleon watched them go, walked around the ranch house saying goodbye, picking scraps from the abandoned dinner table, then returned to the lab, found some daisychains in a paper bag, put them around his neck, climbed into an empty tank and melted himself down.

Sometime later that year, or maybe the next, Herring Carstairs, miffed that after 22 years of golfing he still had not achieved par, snapped his putter over his knee and gave up the game. Golf was in its death throes from that moment on. Today, surely-be, there is not a course left under or upon the earth. No one plays.

*

I remember Rainbow and Haha when they were kiddies. The prettiest children I ever saw. That they should have died like that, O Tadese, is the cruellest thing this century has known. Yes, many torments for many people down the years, I know that well. But nothing, nowhere more cruel. Smithers and the Welsh. No, not as cruel as the death of my darling girls.

Rainbow's bloodstained cushion stuffed with the ex-King's hair sank in the cloning tank it had fallen into. Hours later, newborn, stepping from that tank came a clone Rainbow and a clone King Henry. She was exact in every respect to the old Rainbow, except that she had long black hair. But she was not the old Rainbow. The clone King was equipped with all the spunk of his ancestors – an archetypal King, Kingmostly Kingly-doos. They arose entwined, devoted.

Thinky-be, this devotion, in a time when love had all but died out between men and women, cast a charm upon the English people. Cos shortly after they returned home, Clone King Henry regained the English throne in a Restoration designed for his original, who may have won through and taken his proper place had not the death of his beloved Rainbow sent him into a sobbing stupor from which he emerged quite dottymost. The new King Henry, as soon as he WAS the new King Henry, was a changed man. No more devotion. A monster.

Connie and Pam had separately been conspiring with the ex-King original, each wishing to be Queen over the other. When this was discovered, they fell out and power slipped from their hands. Pam married the ex-King and lobbied for a proper Restoration. Connie entered the fashion industry, with famous success. Today, they are reunited, 2 stylish old ladies living together in retirement at Saint Tropez.

King Henry IX! Oooom! Give me rocks, Tadese, to throw at the sky! He was as foul a swinemost bogleyfala-boggn oiky git fink asswipe geek despotic article that ever sat on the English throne! He had his poor wife, Clone Rainbow, beheaded every morning. By lunchtime she was back in place, or rather a clone of her was, to begin the old passion again. Her letters to me from the Tower distressed me deeply, did they not? I asked HIM, the good Lord, to do something to help her. But HE said he was not ready to interfere. Clone Rainbow had the loveliest hair I have ever seen on a woman, luxuriant and black, like the night's own hair where you could walk barefoot forever. In time she was more beautiful by far than her original's mother had been. Did I love her? Indeedybe. But as a goddess. I had no planet where I went with her. But see, I weep for her now, and every morning for years I mourned her as she bunned up her hair for the axeman.

Galbraith, her original's butler, now Chancellor, was the truelove of all the clone Rainbows, each stepping gorgeous from the tank, only to be chopped the next morning. For the sobered-up Galbraith this was the perfect life. In the mornings, he pumpkinously administered the country's economy. In the afternoons he pumpkinously wooed the Queen, who always succumbed to his well-hidden charms. In the evenings he would commit the hooha wiggly thing with her pumpkinously – I shamefully say I was a regular nail-chewing viewer of this on the Everyone Channel – with a sexual passion, a sweaty writhe, a wiggly drilling, a screamy Oo-Oo-Ooing, which spent them both. The Clone Rainbow would rest satisfied in her only sleep.

The beheadings, I add this note at Tadese's inquiry, had nothing to do with the Rainbow clones' adultery with Galbraith. The King never met most of his Rainbows. His reason for condemning her/them is lost in the unfathomable evils of Kingship. FREEDOM! DOWN WITH ALL OPPRESSORS!

One morning in the autumn of 2063 – days before or after the Restoration, I forget which – Big Norris found me chatting with Wilf in his attic. I had returned home cos there was gid in our multitudinous flock, Wilf had married 400 sheep in a fortnight, none had remained healthy, and I was trying to sort things out. Big Norris said there were some strange people at the door.

I went down expecting nothing, calm from months up a pole, and received the greatest shock in my life. I can claim, can I not, that it was the greatest shock not only of the 21st Century, but of all history.

Scampi Lowrie stood there, in the company of Jesus Christ and Winston Churchill. JESUS CHRIST! It was an even taller Seve with a beard. A BEARD! No one had been able to grow a whisker in years! Was this really . . . JESUS? Yes, I knew HIM instantly! JESUS! CHURCHILL! But at first, I could only see Scampi.

'SCAMPI! MY PET! MY EVERMOST DARLING GIRL! ALIVE! HALLELUJAH!'

Hallelujah, indeed, but 'twas not Scampi. 'Twas a clone Scampi from Scampiville. But it took me some while to realize this. HE explained it to me. HE who she had witnessed climbing from the cloning tank, a new Bethlehem in the American desert. HE told me how HE had come into being, and about Winston, another of Seve's experiments . . . and Scampi, darling pretty Scampi! O, my breaking heart! It was breaking, beating too hard for life.

'No worries on you evermost,' HE said.

And as HE touched my troubled brow all fear and anxiety left me for the first time in my life. I bubbled with joy.

'My friends,' I said, gathering the entire household around me. 'This is a glorious new day. We are saved, all of us! HE has come again!'

I led them, servants and Chaffinches, to the windows of

the room where my father shot himself, and we looked out. HE was walking through our fold, curing the sheep of gid. Winston was leaning affably over the fence, smoking a cigar. Scampi was walking among the falling leaves, looking up at her new home. Life can be a dream. Baaaaaaaa!

THEOCRACY FOR BEGINNERS

The Venusian Sex Survey

Quotes of the Century:

'MacNab, that's my best sporran ye're wearing! Put it back
on its peg the noo!'
*Last words of Hamish MacTavish,
the Scotsman of the Century, 2072*

'Non Angeli, sed Angli.'
*Chaffinch Chaffinch, while being crowned Archbishop of
Canterbury on Midsummer Day, 2075, refuting the bon mot
of the medieval Pope, Gregory Ist*

'Successful applicants must be able to croon, weep
charmingly whilst talking about their mothers, and maintain
an erection at all times.'
*Mrs Pittipaldi, Head of the Women's Service, in their
illustrated brochure, published annually from 2069*

1

The Middlesborough Crisis

Pleasy-do, I shall now tweet upon the strangest and silliest period of my life, that which was followed by the most shameful. Triple sorries, Tadese, I know this prattling book is not supposed to be about me. We shall speak of my nephew Bug tonight or tomorrow. But there are things much in my mind that, pleasy-do, I would like to tweet upon before the century draws to its close. Thankybe evermost, Tadese. You're a custard.

After the death of Jesus in '67 I left Chaffinch Hall and have barely been back since. My head was full of frying eggs, was it not. Nearly 70, it seemed I had reached an end of myself. Without HIM, the world was unbearable. At the same time, though HE had brought faith to so many others, HE had made me lose mine, though I loved HIM dearly and always will. Strangely-be: I had met God face to face, been HIS closest friend, almost shared death with HIM, but I no longer believed. How exactly was this the experience of Judas Iscariot? For the first time I saw life as it is, without nonsense. The way Bro Cod saw it as a boy.

I took to the highways, the obscure pathways of my native land, and lived like a fox, avoiding people except for occasional forays into village shops to buy chocolate and bananas. The weather was warm then, before the constant snows of the mid-70s, and it was a healthy life for an old nitwit, sucking on wild rhubarb, wee-weeing up trees. I was, however, in a deadly, constant fear of capture either by agents of Bro Wilf, who would lock me in the attic at the Hall, where indeedy-be I did belong, or by Government Officials with long lists of resentments against me going back to '24, or by Moslem converts come to crucify me, or by creatures from my past: Bowsie the twisted Headmaster, my father dripping blood, and for some reason the actor Herbert Gilcrust Jr, whom I saw in every one those tedious productions of the 41 lost plays of Shakespeare back in the '30s.

During the torture and death of Jesus I had sung my favourite hymn, *To be a Pilgrim*, over and over to comfort both HIM and myself. But now I couldn't stop. I sang it all day, around and around went its words, its neverending tune, an imprisoning mantra. For years I sang it, sitting on rocks, up poles, the song only interrupted by chewings and cackles.

> *He who would valiant be*
> *'Gainst all disaster*
> *Let him in constancy*
> *Follow the Master . . .*

It anaesthetized my brain from its sufferings. It concentrated my thoughts. Sometimes I just mumbled though. Sometimes I'd wander into Wantage or Keswick or wherever, singing it like a slimy lounge singer, shaking hands with astonished shoppers on an oddmost progress. I developed a fair tenor, a dippy soprano, a cracked baritone, and sang it in all these voices and more. Even in the style of Hieronymus Gosh, God help me!

> *There's no discouragement*
> *Shall make him once relent*
> *His first avowed intent*
> *To be a Pilgrim . . .*

I daren't settle anywhere, instinctively fearing capture, caging, oblivion forced upon me by authorities I'd never heard of. I wandered, singing, thoughtless except for the song and sudden cravings for my favourite foods. The only meaning in life was the point I was at in the song, an ever-changing point. Sing, Tadese, SING!

> *Since Lord thou dost assist*
> *Us with thy spirit*
> *We know we at the end*

> *Shall life inherit.*
> *Then fancies flee away*
> *I'll fear not what men say*
> *I'll labour night and day*
> *To be a pilgrim . . .*

Then, a funny thing happened. I began to forget the words. At 800 times a day – Oh, I sang it in my sleep, as did all the beaked and fanged characters in my dreams – over nearly five years that makes 1,460,000 times I sang *To be a Pilgrim*. And now I had forgotten the words!

> *Who so beset him round*
> *With dismal stories*
> *Do not . . . de de de do*
> *His strength the more is . . .*

And soon with frightened eyes I bounced along going:

> *De do da deedeedee do*
> *da da da dum dum*
> *do do dee da dumdiddledom*
> *Barumpa-ding-dong . . .*

Then I forgot the tune as well. And as I struggled to recapture it, in a panting panic, I was suddenly aware of the silence. A too-too songless silence. I awoke! I was myself again, a timid vicarish self, but me. A chaffinch singing on a branch – tissup-pirissup! – gave me further reminding, did he not indeed! Thankybe, little bro! But where was I? What wilderness was this? Hills covered in purple heather, the air full of biting midges . . . and in a valley not far away, a small squad of kilted troops marching along the road. I could not help laughing – Oh, so utterchuckly-hoo-haa cheefully. I covered my hoo-haaing gob to maintain silence. What a custard! I was in Scotland. Chee-he!

I scrambled over the heather and followed the troops

down their road. We arrived at a Highland Games. Saint Andrew's flag was flapping fifty times around the field, from its corners, tents and ice-cream vans. I traipsed grinning among gargantuan Scotsmen with numbers on their vests. I winked at every one of them.

'Och aye the noo!' I said.

A delightful young woman tickled my beard and gave me a haggis. I gobbled it down. Unwashed, ragged, shoeless was I – she took me for a Scots religious nut.

'Ye'll be a Brigadoonist, laddie?'

Laddie! I was 72! 'Ayeeeeeeeeeeeeeeeeee,' I said.

'Och, de ye think it'll ever come?'

'Ayeeeeeeeeeeeeeeeeee,' I said.

She went away quite moved. I sat eating my haggis, watching brutal Scotsmen tossing cabers. Before they tossed, a couple came over and shook the hand of the Brigadoonist for luck, handcrushingly. One of these beardy giants won the competition and bursting with grateful thanks to his lucky charm he romped over and put this old bird on his shoulder. I perched there like a sick parrot while he danced a celebratory fling around the field. Two bagpipers were playing three different tunes. The purple heather swirled around me. The smiling ginger faces. The braw lassies, clapping along. How I laughed! Did I not indeed! Yes, Tadese, I have been many things in my lifetime. Then I was a Scotsman! Ayeeeeeeeeeeee!

But the horror horn was about to honk! For I had become a Scotsman at the last available hour. My conversion coincided with the Middlesborough Crisis, that sinistermostest event, which wiped Scotland completely away. Sorries be on it evermost!

Of course, indirectly and ironically-do-da, 'twas all Mac-Tavish's fault. When the Americans dropped out of space exploration in the '30s, MacTavish bought up all their equipment and used this as the basis for his own boglyfalaing Jilkesmost inter-planetary ambitions. In 2045 Donaldbane Frazer led the expedition to Mars and founded the Scotmars Colony. But Mars was just red dust and weevils. What to do with it? Old Macmacpherson would have made a golfcourse out of it, suremost! But MacTavish had a better idea. He would make Mars into a planetwide version of Scotland – a Scottish ball hanging in a Scottish eternity. The Scotmars Genesis project would be achieved by a technique derived from cloning, only 'twas landscape being cloned, not people. The same square mile of Scotland – a wooded valley with a pretty loch in it near Aberdeen was chosen – would infect the Martian landscape to the very core, transforming its very atoms to Mac'atoms . . . and hey presto: Scotland on Mars!

The project's HQ, naturally-be, was in New Arbroath. But one of the centres was in the English industrial city of Middlesborough, a dirty drear coughing Northern town, a place without smiles, all rusty and chimneyfied, dusty and nerty, manky and depressing. Thinky-do they were doing the really dangerous work there, so's not to endanger Scottish lives in the installations on Scottish soil. MacTavish was very big on saving Scottish lives, especially after Plovdiv.

So there was this Chaffinch, whose bilious burps reeked of haggis, sermonizing Brigadoon-wise to a rapt audience in a happy field in the safe heart of Scotland, when someone in the Scotmars Genesis building 200 miles away in Middlesborough twizzled the wrong knob and nearly Wibblied the world. Middlesborough was destroyed in the explosion. But duplicates of it, OF MIDDLESBOROUGH, not of that spanky-doos Scots valley they'd chosen, started spreading from the edges of the destruction. An infection, changing the tissue of the Earth from whatever it was, to Middlesborough. Perhaps the English scientists had switched Scots Valley to Middlesborough to thwart MacTavish's dream of a Scottish Mars. No one will ever know.

I was reaching the climax of my sermon, with the Scots about me kneeling their bare knees on Scots earth: 'Och, the braw day will come, my bonny lads and lassies, when Brigadoon will appear from the mists of oor Scottish hopes . . .'

I was distracted. The high hill nearest us had turned to a blur, owrie and iffy. I pressed my eyes several times. I made bright lemon flashes which sank away as, unbelievably, Middlesborough erupted around us, beside us, under our very feet. Scotland was disappearing. My congregation were wild with fright. They huddled around the biggest men. Bagpipes yowled like cats on fire.

Then we were all floored, as if by an earthquake, and found ourselves washed up in a Middlesborough sidestreet, Trevithick Street. A calm empty afternoon in Middlesborough. The only anomaly was a shaggy Highland cow on the roof of a garage. Its questioning moo spoke for us all.

'Brigadoon?' asked a devout lassie with her shoes in her hands.

'Middlesborough,' I said. I had been there before. I knew the chemical smell, the unique drearness.

By the close of that day Middlesboroughs covered the entire Scottish homeland from Berwick to John o'Groats, all the Western Isles, the Shetlands and Orkneys. Next day, thousands of Middlesboroughs arose under the North Sea to bewilder the haddock. Then the infection spread into an unsuspecting Scandinavia, crossed that and Middlesboroughized the bombed wastelands of Russia. All of Poland went except the city of Zakopane and a lucky slice of the Tatra Mountains. Then Middlesborough after identical Middlesborough careered into the Scottish kingdoms in the Ukraine and Balkans, abolishing them. It was weakening by then. The lettering on the shopfronts was dyslexically a-piggle, the roadsigns were blank, some of the houses were inside-out. But still the infection rolled on.

In New Arbroath an old sick MacTavish lay dying under tartan sheets. For years he'd done little but play the pipes and weepily listen to sad stories of Plovdiv from his Jacobite cronies. Now he rose on his sticks to attend to the Middlesborough Crisis. His dreams of a Scottish world he had shifted to Mars. But 'twas not to be. And Scotland itself gone, all its smells and corners, gone, all its graves, its wild flowers, its pnonghalls, gone. But New Arbroath, the most beautiful city ever built, surely that would be spared?

MacTavish stood on the highest balcony of his palace, watching the far horizon. Like Moses waiting for the promise of the Promised Land to be reneged, he waited, with a glumness only a Scotsman can master, for a tidal wave of Middlesboroughs to swamp his bonny capital. In the spectacular gardens below the great man's vantage point his gardeners climbed ladders to look over the walls. Half the population in New Arbroath were watching their northern horizon – the other half were at impromptu ceilidh, drinking whiskey fast, stamping along to trilling bagpipes, enjoying what looked like the end of their world.

A dozen Middlesboroughs ate away at the suburbs of New Arbroath. Then it stopped. MacTavish was flatout dead on his balcony. Isolated, far-flung Middlesboroughs appeared beyond the area of infection. Several in China, where they caused no end of amusement. One in Australia, just miles from the Grand Mufti's summer palace. One, indeedybe, took over the island of Saint Helena in the South Atlantic, where Napoleon, 250 years before, had lived his final poisoned days. An end, then, to so many dreams of conquest.

England, fortunate England, was untouched below the River Tees. The loss of its northernmost counties troubled it not. Indeedybe, the disappearance of Scotland was greeted by a peal of bells throughout the land. Better news yet – as Middlesborough was an English city, Queen Vera claimed all Middlesboroughs as English soil. The world was too shocked to argue. The Queen was now an Empress. Suddenly, our little country was the 2nd biggest on Earth, after the Mufti's Moslem block. Glory be!

I settled down in my Middlesborough. That very first day, the day of the crisis, I walked into the vicarage in Connie and Pam Street, did I not, and assumed the name, place and living of Rev Elvis Hudspith, himself presumably killed in the destruction of the original Middlesborough. All those attending those Highland Games, and the populations of the transformed nearby towns and villages, joined me in this new life. I helped them sort themselves out. For the first time in my nittyfala life I was of use! These displaced Scottishers entered the houses of and assumed the identities of Middlesboroughtonians. Sobeit, an oddmost thing to do – part of the infection possibly-so, a quiet compulsion to complete the picture. But it was a cheeful game that renewed the spirit, was it not indeed, so it was!

227

'Who are you now, Angus?' ex-Scots folk said as they met each other.

'Och, I a man called Billy Ogthorpe!' Then he'd apologize for the och – Scottishness wasn't part of the game!

Within weeks of becoming the Vicar of Saint James's I was conducting marriages, and in a Middlesborough accent! Within months, christenings – in a better Middlesborough accent. I was happy. I was a new man. I was Rev Elvis Hudspith, a better fellow than Chaff Chaffinch in all ways. But every time the congregation rose to sing *'To be a Pilgrim'* my heart froze. The tune jangled my faithlessness and I felt like cursing God from the pulpit, howling obscenities like Bro Wilf in a tizzy with one of his sheep wives.

Fortunatelydoos, across the world there were many other Rev Elvis Hudspiths, some 40 thousand indeedybe, in Scotland, Poland, Sweden, the Ukraine, Saint Helena, etc. Like myself they had wandered into the same vicarage in those other Middlesboroughs, read the old boy's letters in his rollup desk, and been moved to become that Middlesborough's Rev Elvis Hudspith. We formed a club, exchanged sermons via computer mail, televisited each other. Jollymost Christian gentlemen all. My best friends among them helped me to calm my soul and overcome the sin of faithlessness.

The Middlesboroughs were given numbers to avoid administrative confusion and to let us escape from those boglyfala roadsigns which said Middlesborough was in every direction, which of course it was, but that's not the point. My Middlesborough was Number 726. Due to an administrative error there was another Number 726, in Argentina.

Those early Middlesborough days were one of those rare moments of peace in human history. Joyful faces everywhere in the dismal streets. And such a surprise for us that we were all so spanky-do, safe and content in our new identities. But it couldn't last. Suddenly and unexpectedly, Queen Vera abdicated and the Archbishop of Canterbury took over the reins of government. The first thing he did was burn poor Queen Vera. And to everyone's approval! Even my own mild-mannered congregation approved.

'Do you think burning is quite the civilized thing?' I ventured shyly at a coffee morning.

'Aye, vicar. Just the thing to do. Sensible man that there Archbishop of yours. Bun?'

I suppose Queen Vera was a witch, just as the Archbishop said. But days before we'd been speaking of her in our prayers and to me she'd always appeared a model of virtue. Meanwhile, the Archbishop . . . well! As posters of our new leader were tacked up on every post and doorway in Middlesborough, a confusion entered my increasingly timid little mind. Peace and quiet were over. The theocracy had begun.

2

Murder Day

The mad beetle of religious nuttery had flown up all our bottoms and was feeding its grubs in our hearts! The Grand Mufti had his half of the world in a constant shriek of fanaticism, of fatwas and pilgrimages and observances. And now our half, perhaps as some sort of mental defence to the cursing prayers being mumbled against us in Mecca and Djakarta, had gone the same way. During my years as a wandering hymnsinger millions had turned to the Christian God. The 2nd Ministry of Jesus, to me such a disappointment, had helped trigger those little Gods we all carry within us.

It had been me who had angrily said to HIM: 'When are you going to DO something, you lankysome Jilks! Go out there! Speak profundities or . . . I don't know. You're the boggn deity, not me!'

'I'm not ready yet,' HE said. Slowly HE said it, and said it again, more slowly: 'I'm not ready yet.' HE was sitting in a window-seat on the ground floor at Chaffinch Hall, studying an orange all day before eating it.

What was our Messiah doing with his life? HE just lounged around the Hall, doing nowt. Staring at fruit! HE took painting lessons from Winston, and somehow painted exactly the same picture, brushstroke for brushstroke, as our distinguished houseguest – a typical clone's trick! HE was forever following the maids about, getting them to talk about their winnitile wants and wishes. Then one day HE came in from a walk in the rain and was smiling in the most curious way. HE looked so like cuz Seve in a huff as HE went upstairs and locked HIMSELF in an attic room. For days, no answer to my knocks.

'Leave HIM be,' drawled Winston.

I was angry. 'HE should be DOING something! HIS

Ministry!' Then, as if holy music suddenly surrounded me: 'Perhaps this is IT! The beginning!'

'Fancy a game of darts?' drawled Winston.

So we played darts – for days! And waited. We all knew that something was about to happen. The atmosphere of the house was like the time my niece Nelli had quads.

Then, that Sunday evening in July '65. All around England those few who still bothered with church were putting on hats and preparing to be bored. Big Norris, no longer the strong ox of old, came into the games room, his hands shaking.

'HE's talking. HE's saying fings.'

'Fings?!'

'Bootiful fings! To HIMSELF. Fings.'

Winston turned on the Everyone Channel and tuned into Jesus. We sat and watched and listened. Jesus was sitting on a lunatic's hard bed, HIS face resting on one knee, and in a plain voice was uttering commonplaces. I could take no more, could I not! I threw up my hands! Had we waited 2000 years for this!

HE was saying 'fings' like: 'Be good.' 'Don't be ill.' 'Nicely does it.' 'Aren't elephants a wonder?' 'Always keep your shoes clean.'

But when I looked around the room, my barmy little family were completely taken up in it. Winston's face was streaked with tears. Even nephew Rhino, a fleshy tyke, kept saying: 'Blimmie, well said that man! Oops, that's a goodn! Must make a note of thattn!'

Millions of others were similarly affected. When HE was killed, there was a sudden outpouring of affection for HIM, for the idea of HIM . . . and everyone went to church, cos they felt closer to him there. The churches were full after that, overflowing with new blood. The clerics acted as if there was a historical inevitably in all this. Their pulpit pronouncements covered every aspect of life, so couldn't help but be political. Indeedybe, rightly-soso, a point came when Theocracy was inevitable.

Theocracy! Government by priests! Not just in England, of course. In the Russian Orthodox Middlesboroughs, which covered the lands from the Baltic deep into Asia, a Patriarch was in charge of each Middlesborough. Old Pope Lassie, assailed by visions, silly old pooch, became Secretary General of the League of Nations, plus President of Italy, King of Spain, and God knows what else. Everywhere it was the same. In England the Archbishop of Canterbury became Lord Protector, presiding over a Ruling Council of bishops. My old pal from my ashram days, Cedders Bromley, now raised to the Archbisopric of York, had a mitre as mighty as any!

In my Middlesborough it was the same as everywhere else – the church ladies, the holy expressions, hair shirts on special offer. And this cowed, timidized old bird sat uncomprehendingly in the middle of it all, a Commissar! As a youth how I had dreamed of a society based on God's precepts! Now it was imposed, a fashion, a passion, and me a policeman of God's cruel will. Oh, I didn't like it!

Nodding and smiling was once all a vicar really needed to do. Now I found myself chairing nightly DENOUNCEMENT MEETINGS. These were held in what had been our local pnonghall. The populace would sit quiet for a while, then somebody would jump up and denounce a friend, a family member. For what? To start with, in '72, little things: not listening to the Archbishop of Canterbury's broadcasts – his tedious fireside chats modelled on Jesus's performance in the attic – or wearing wellingtons on the wrong feet, or reading a book that wasn't the Bible. Oh, the book burnings! Terrible sweaty nights! Those mad fervent faces in the firelight! Later, the DENOUNCEMENT MEETINGS became more serious. I still chaired, but there had to be a Witchfinder present. In our Middlesborough the Witchfinder was a Mrs Boody, who looked more like a witch than any woman I ever did see. During overlong denouncements I would count her facial warts out of the side of my eye and never counted the same number twice.

'MY BROTHER DICKIE IS A DEVIL WORSHIPPER! TWICE I'VE SEEN HIM DIP HIS WANGER IN JAM AND WIPE HIS BIBLE WITH IT!'

'OUR DEREK DOES THAT!' shouted a woman at the back.

Dickie and Derek were brought forward and questioned, timidly by me, fiercely by Mrs Boody. GUILTY!

'Pleasy-do, perhaps some Bible classes would straighten out their boyish foolishnesses . . .,' I ventured, an imp without the old magic.

'BURN THE BUGGERS!' said Mrs Boody.

'IT WAS ONLY A BIT OF FUN!' screamed Derek, but Dickie was yelling the Lord's Prayer backwards and nutting the platform like a goat, which ruined both their chances for a reprieve.

I nodded my vicarish assent with a shrug and a silly grin. Dickie and Derek were burned. I, as guilty as the Grand Mufti when he crucified Jesus, stood by and watched their agony, exchanging small talk with Mrs Boody, munching on sausages my curate had cooked for me in the same fire that consumed these Shadrachs, Meshachs, and so many Abednegoes – for we burnt our share in our Middlesborough! By God, Tadese, we did! I did! Me! Here! I burned them! Me, pleasy-do! Your polesitting Holy Fool burned people! – Wot do you think of me now, ehwot?

I no longer admired Rev Elvis Hudspith, but I was locked inside him, a fainting little soul who thought others knew best, more confused with each word spoken. My sorrybe life had made a rabbit of my soul, Tadese – I was not myself.

The Devil worshipping, of course, was quite real, was it not! It was going on everywhere, thriving in its own horrible alcove of the generalized religious revival – as was every cranky cult, but Satanism more than any. Some cults, pleasy-do, were tolerated. Druids wandered the High Street dressed as trees and nobody minded. But the Devil, who Mrs Boody had herself seen twice in the High Street, and 8 times on the Stockton Road, was the real enemy. In the newspapers they always drew him to look like the Grand Mufti – the big belly, the arrogant brow, sensual and slyly wise. And it was this ear-whispering Devil of theirs who was responsible for the crime wave. All the clerics said so. I said so myself, every Sunday, to the same appreciative mumble, before asking the congregation to sing *To be a Pilgrim*.

The Crime Wave, ehwot! Burglaries were so common

that burglars burgled each other, swapping their entire possessions on a regular basis. I found a very nice man in the vicarage one night when I came back from a meeting. Caught in the act, he started putting everything back on its shelf.

'I've tried Devil worship,' he said gayly, busy with this. 'But it didn't do nuffink for me. I'm thinking of trying out the Moslems – wot you fink, vicar?'

I rather liked the man. We shared a bun. But Mrs Boody had all her hats stolen, twice, and I'm sure it was him, cos I saw him at a DENOUNCING and the girls sitting beside him both had hats on which Mrs Boody kept glowering at, and every wink he winked at the old dragon was like fire on his toes. But he was one of the lucky ones. He never burned.

But 'twas murder that was the real crimewave! It was replacing pnong as the national sport! In our small city in the winter of '72 there were an average of 6 murders a day. By the next winter it had risen to 8 a day. Not too serious, I thought. But people were worked up and the *Church Times*, *Sunbeam*, *Woman's Murder Weekly* and other papers were chockablock with it! Something had to be done! The Lord-Protector-cum-Archbishop-of-Canterbury was never short of an idea. He announced at the Easter synod in '74 that henceforward every May 1st, commencing that year, a 'Murder Day' would be observed. This was designed to cram all the country's yearcount of murders into one day, and give everyone a chance to blow off their steam so that they could live calm as custards for the 365 days till the next Murder Day. 'Twas greeted as a brilliant idea. Urk!

What the Archbishop's decree did was legalize murder on May Days in perpetuity. But you could only kill one person a year and you had to make an application to the Murder Bureau, naming victim and preferred weapon and have it accepted by the Ash Wednesday before the big day. The first Murder Day in '74 had 2,748 murders in my Middlesborough. Only a little up on the average yearly bodycount, there as elsewhere, so the experiment was counted a major success, especially by Women's Groups, cos most of the victims were men. I spent that day – it rained – in the vicarage making sandwiches for a Murder Day party. Not everybody turned up!

Archbishop Cream's other BIG IDEA was the Moral Judgement Machine. This monstrous conception was the child of some boil-brained Oxbridgites, theologians coupled with weapons scientists – a deadly mixture. Strewth be told, it started out as a machine to convert folk back from Mohammedanism. And they'd had much success with this. I heard that of the 20 million Moslem converts in England in the late '60s, almost all had now left the great brotherhood, this presumably due to the machine's secret whirrings. But now the machine was put to a more deadly use.

The Bishop of Bath and Wells sent a missive in the computer mail to every vicar in England, of which I was one, describing the progress of this cranky machine of theirs. On a date not yet decided upon, it would be activated for its new task, when all people under a certain level of moral worth would simply drop dead. The machine had, the circular said, proved a remarkable success with beagles.

Was I, with my unexpected stiffenings, the moral equal of a morally upright beagle? I thought not. This is the end of me, I thought! Every vicar in England felt the same about himself! But not one spoke out, for fear of being denounced and burnt.

Archbishop Cream, meanwhile, utterly corrupted by his power, who romped naked nightly in an empty Canterbury Cathedral with trilling choirboys and his 3 ugly big-footed sisters, who was rumoured to be the Pooh-Bah of Devil worshipers in England, and looked as depraved and evil as a man could look . . . what future for him cum his self-imposed Judgement Day? Presumably, as the Big Boss, he'd be the one to press the machine's activating knob. But for him that could mean only one thing: SPLATAROO! So, obviously, a bluff. No, I thinky-dood, he'll never use it.

He made the public announcement about the Moral Judgement Machine on a balmy Sunday evening, leaning towards the screen in that way of his which had all his audience leaning away from the screen in their millions. Everyone took the machine very seriously, but didn't really believe in it. The machine was just a symbol, a way of helping us climb the ladder to moral perfection. Everyone agreed with my thunkment and it wasn't thought that it would actually be used.

Strange times! When one of those saintly beagles visited my church, on its nationwide tour, it was greeted with a respect I have never seen afforded to man or dog, ever, in all my hundred years. Its every wuf was Hallelujahed.

'If only it could explain its secret,' my curate said while giving it a biscuit.

Later, it bit him. What could it all possibly mean?

One day I came upon my burglar friend, goosing girls around his flying hat car. What with the breakdown between the sexes he was the only man in Middlesborough with girlfriends.

'When do they press the knob, vicar?' He was so full of chee!

'Aren't you bothery-dood that you won't be up to the required standard?

'Not me, vicar! Moral paragon, I am! Hee-haw!'

My vicar's smile: 'What about you, girls?'

His face twisted like a dishcloth: 'Never you mind bout them, you piggn old nert!'

But it was too late. I'd upset the balance. The girls came over to me, pouting aloofly over their shoulders to their spurned man.

'Walk us home, vicar. Tell us how to be good. We will be, we promise – don't we, Doreen? We doesn't wanna die from moral lassitude, vicar – does we, Doreen?'

'It'll all be spanky-doos and custard,' I said in my vintage way, gentle and sad. 'Don't you worry your silly heads.'

I walked them home and asked them if they'd ever committed the sexual intercourse – I asked everybody this! – and they said no, they never had, and that they never would, it was disgusting, and I agreed with them. Then I muttered some of the well-known commonplaces of my poor friend Jesus. Magic! I'd never seen young women more inspired. But the sweat beading on their arms gave me an unexpected stiffening and I knew that when the machine's knob was pushed I would drop into Hell with everybody else.

On the morning of the next Murder Day, May Day 2075, I was admiring the curves on the statue of Connie and Pam outside the Connie and Pam Centre in Connie and Pam Street. People with guns in their belts and determined expressions walked past me.

'Howdeedoodee, vicar! Sorry to hear about it!'

'Howdoodeedee, my son! Eghm, about wot?'

But no one said wot.

I was searching for an apple in my pockets when I saw it lying bruised on the pavement 10 feet away. When I bent straight from picking it up, the first bite in my gob, the alarmed face of my curate was filling my eyes.

'What are you doing here?' he wailed. 'Haven't you seen the noticeboard?'

'Ughm?'

'The noticeboard. For Murder Day. You're on it!'

'Me?' Chortle-chortle. 'But who would want to murder me?'

'You're named 18 times. I'm named twice.'

And he ran off into the Pam Arcade, then out again with a young woman chasing him with a samurai sword. She later told me in a letter that he'd once looked at her the wrong way.

I sauntered over to the noticeboard at the Town Hall. Yes, there I was, 18 times, in the column next to all the people who wanted to murder me. I didn't know any of them except Mrs Boody. More chortling! Then I saw my reflection going chortle in the noticeboard's glass. I was facing death, real death, the end of all things. No more chortling ever! It was the last thing I wanted. Still is.

I looked behind me, hugging my goosebumping flesh. 18 assassins, pleasy-do! I picked up my skirts and ran. Then, bravely I thought, ran back. What weapons had they chosen? How many of them were on other people's lists? I mean, wot chance was there that my assassins would be wiped out before they got to me? But my eyes were too befuddled to decipher printout. I took off again, weeping. What kind of world was this? I was an old man, an inoffensive, meek old mouse of a man, his sense ruined by a lifetime of tears. Why was I running for my life?

HIS face! In my mind's eye, HIS face, with that dippy look he had the day my poor little Clone Scampi died. No answers. Just compassion. And it's not boggn enough, Jesus! – Is it not! No! Tissent! Not! Tissent not!

Mrs Boody was a bad shot. She had two goes at me in the Stockton Road and hit a boy scout and a horse. Chee! There was a queer taste of coins and butter in my mouth as I ran abandonedly through the crowds of folk celebrating Murder Day. I saw the billboards, but it hardly registered on my spooked eyes that the announcement had been made about the Moral Judgement Machine. – They were going to press its knob! When? Today? My sandled feet slapped the pavement. I was like a piggywig escaping from the slaughterhouse. Old but nimble, I would be 5 Middlesboroughs away in an hour! They would never catch me! But if the machine was used I was a gonna anyway! Ho-hum and yelp!

Then I saw a nun on a bicycle and did a hilariously shameful thing. I pushed her off it. I stole her bicycle. Turned out, wasn't a nun anyway, just some lewd woman hiding from her potential murderers. The things she shouted as I peddled away! WheeeeEEeee! No hands, blissful, alive, scared out of my wits.

Both roadsters and flying hat cars were after me, all bumping together, duffing, pranging each other in a foul competition to run me down. I crossed into oncoming traffic, pedalling vicarishly, but bumped into a rut and fell off as bullets zinged where I would have been. I rolled in litter beside a hackymucky old gate. I gave it a kick and hopped through, all the while expecting to be shot! The other side was a deserted industrial estate. The factories were falling down, dusty, rusty and bleared with poosy grime. Plenty of places to hide! If I hid out till midnight, till the end of Murder Day, I'd be safe!

Over my shoulder I saw Mrs Boody come through the gate, followed by a big man whom I recognized as my local butcher. Why in God's name would he choose me as his Murder Day victim? Out of everyone in England, little me?

Hadn't I always asked him politely about his wife's bunions?
You never knew what people really felt about you – Murder
Day proved that at least. Through the gate behind those two
came more, a gleeclub of vicious Wibleys on a Chaffinch hunt!
– All boggn 18 assassins together! Were they allowed to work
as a team? I'd never bothered to study the piggboggn rules.
But it wasn't fair!

First I hid in a furnishing warehouse. Its broken roof let
daylight fall as jagged shapes on the mouse-eeking floor. I tip-
toed through examples of what your livingroom or bathroom
might look like if you bought their boggn furniture. Well, they
were all killed when Middlesborough exploded and it served
them boggn right! I wrapped myself in a roll of carpet, leaned
it comfortably enough in a corner, and breathed as silently as I
could, looking straight up at a shape of sky that was sometimes
blue, sometimes white, sometimes blue and white.

Mrs Boody passed close by, telling the butcher about how
warts were considered a sign of beauty in some societies.
Then they were gone. Mouse-eeking hours passed. I felt I
would rest here in this carpet, obsessed by its musty niff,
forever. Then I fell asleep. The sound of my own snoring
awoke me. Then the carpet was being manhandled! Would
they shoot? A sword! Stones! Acid!

They rolled out the carpet too eagerly and I went spinning
into the shadows. Gunfire, so yellow and pretty in the
gloom! I raced outside through a crack in the wall, laughing,
gigglesome, desperate. By the time the terrible 18 found their
way into the brilliant outside, I was hid again. But a bad hiding
place. A nightwatchman's hut. No way out except the front
way. If they looked inside, I was surely-be done for.

Pinned on the wall was an out-of-date calendar, 2060-
something, of naked women standing outside cathedrals. I
flipped through, looking first at the naked women, then the
cathedrals. It was raining outside. More gunfire. I counted
18 shots. Perhaps my assassins were quarrelling amongst
themselves. I prayed for that!

Night fell, and there I was, still hiding in the creaky hut,
waiting for midnight, wanting a wee-wee, wanting life to
begin again. Salisbury Cathedral was dark on the cobwebby

wall and the nude posing before it looked like a 5 feet tall peeled ghostly banana come to worry the monks. My mind was wandering with this cheesome thought when suddenly the door was clattersomely yanked open. The hut shook so much it nearly fell down. Dust rained on me as on a pharaoh in a just-opened tomb.

'SHOOT! KILL ME! GO ON, YOU BOGGN SPOILERS OF LIFE! WHERE'S THE LOVE HE SPOKE OF? EH?'

I tore open my cassock and offered my pale chest as target. A figure stood there, gun in hand, black with moon-light behind. And wearing headgear which could only be a bishop's mitre.

'Um, I shot all thy murderers, um, this afternoon,' he said. 'I've had a, um, Devil of a job finding thee. I could have used the Everyone Channel, um, but they unplugged it this morning, for Murder Day, um, it's in the rules, um?'

'Dimmee – you're a bishop!'

There was no mistaking his manner.

'Bishop Hare, um – hello, vicar. Verily, um, I don't know how to tell thee this, but they've used the machine. Um! But the only ones it killed were them. The Archbishops of Canterbury, um, York, um, the Bishops of Durham, Liverpool, um, Bath and Wells, the bally lot. I'm the only one left on the Ruling Council and I'm, um, a complete shower! There's no church, no Government! Um!' He was on his knees, mitre in hand, weeping. Then he steeled himself. 'Once when I asked Archbishop Bromley who was the holiest man he'd ever known, he said, um, Chaffinch Chaffinch. That pig's nose. Thee are he, are thee not indeed, um, that man whom I seeketh?'

Rev Hudspith melted away within me. For a long moment I thanked the Lord for the life of my friend of 60 years, Bro Bromley, late Archbishop of York.

Finally: 'I am Chaffinch Chaffinch,' I said.

'Please, um, save us, O Master!' wailed the bishop.

We walked away through the night together, arm-in-arm, stepping over the sprawled dead who'd had a rotten Murder Day, had they not! In palaces all over England a synod's worth of bishops were being swept under carpets. The only survivor, a morally innocent ninny, sucked his thumb all the way to Canterbury. I looked silently out of the bubble of our flying hat. England was enchanted under the moonlight. We saw six cathedrals but no naked girls.

3

Bug

Bing and Mopsie's eldest boy, Brok, may have been the best of us Chaffinches. Thinky-do I can say that, yes, can I not. But he died mysteriously abroad. That left them with Bug. I sympathized with the kiddy, cos I too had lost bros. But, wot with my wanderings and Middlesboroughish vicaritude, his growing up lost out on my dippy influence. At 19 he was a hopeless case, indeed so he was. Utterly free of melancholy, that was his only good character point. Otherwise, a thoughtless dweeb, was he not, a self-admiring doltificacious mannequin. His surroundings grew as languid as he did. He made Chaffinch Hall languid, bewitching all the mirrors into reflecting only languidness cos they loved him and him alone – they looked for his languid qualities in others, and found them. If you shook hands with him you were languid for hours. Even in his beauty there was the laziness of an untended garden – untended cos the gardeners had gone languid and were dozing among their pots.

Why so lazy? I think cos he felt safe in a world that admired him for what he was, pleasy-do. His achievement was in being himself and that was already achieved. His eyes that could make any woman coo and cause any man to wish he was like him, were as blue as the blue of a blue rose. They looked around like Adam's eyes, seeing Eden for the first time and thinking 'so what!' Oh, a charmer, Tadese, but with the genuine spark of LIFE in him, which you couldn't help seeing and, in a sudden languidness, loving with all your heart.

When I met him, seeing him for the first time in his adult life I had done a terrible thing. It was the greatest mistake of my life, the most wicked thing a member of my family had ever done. On Midsummer Day, 2075, I was crowned the 125th Archbishop of Canterbury. And after all my hopes!

Cos England and its Empire was a Theocracy, I was also Head of State, Lord boggn Protector. I was Smithers! I was King Henry! I was Connie and Pam!

Take two good men, put them on a committee and you've two scoundrels. Of all the things I have learned in my long life, this, Tadese, I swear, is the truest. And here was I, scoundrel in chief, taking my place in my golden robes at the head of a thousand committees. This was how theocratic government worked, endless committees and coffee mornings, bun-doos and outdoor buffets, with me mingling grumpily, the Supervicar, assenting and suggesting, poking into the organization of people's lives like God Almighty. I wanted to abolish myself, abolish the church. But I did not. Why not? Too busy to summon the courage, wasn't I? I had never worked before, never had a job, boggn loafed in religious nuttery for 75 years. Now I gazed into a pool of ever-shifting details, and I worried about them all, and never slept, worked each irreplaceable night away, becoming gruff and fractious like those Scotsmen on Mars. Then Bug came into my life.

I'd been in the job a year, and flattered myself I was giving England its most sensible government since the heyday of Connie and Pam, and had just returned from a committee meeting on the future of the sugarbeet industry. I was yawnmost, irritated and pooped when Bug Chaffinch swanned into my Archbishoprical study, oozing boyish charm, his quiff alive with languid energy. He wore a string vest and spotted joggingshorts. He carried a javelin, having just that morning returned from representing England with that very thing in the Olympic Games at Djakarta. He didn't speak. He struck poses with his javelin: on one couch, then another, before the fireplace, up my bookcase steps. My eyes doddered. Was someone photographing him? Should I be photographing him?

'Um, young man?' I suddenly felt rather languid.

'Howdeedoodee, Uncle Chiffchaff!' His cheeks were rouged!

'Um?' (Um was my constant sound, ejaculated and muttered. I'd caught it from Bishop Hare. Together we were a chorus of ums.)

'It's Bug, uncle! Bug! Me. I'm Bug! Bug!'

'Um? Oh, Bing and Mopsie's boy.'

'Haven't seen you in an age, ehwot? Hear you made Cuz Rhino a bishop.'

Since greatness was thrust upon me all manner of obscure Chaffinches had knocked at my door, come to see how they could profit. My mischievous act of making Rhino a bishop only encouraged their hopes. I was no more glad to see this cadger than any of the rest. I rang for Bishop Hare.

'Um, couldst thou look after this, um, boy, Theobald. He's a relative.'

'Um,' said Bishop Hare, and approached him like an affectionate bee, to usher him out and leave me with my work. 'Um, um, um, um, um . . .'

But Bug was reluctant to go.

'I've just come back from the Olympic Games, haven't I not, Unc?' He fingers played up and down the javelin as if looking for music in it. 'I was throwing the jav, ehwot! Here, it's for you!'

I stood there, an Archbishop with a javelin.

'Didst thou, um, win anything?'

'Me? Poosywiffo, unc – I was just there to look pretty. Came 37th, didn't I not? But I did a lap of honour and everybody clapperood billyo, didn't they? Observe how fetching I look when I'm throwing.'

He took the javelin from me and did a languid run up, then threw the javelin the length of the room into a portrait of my distinguished predecessor Archbishop Tait.

'Dearie-be, um, dearie-be, um,' went Bishop Hare. 'Shall I, um, climb up and, um, pick it out.'

I wasn't angry. The irritations of a year were unknotting in my bowels. I was charmed. I was won over. I was falling in love with the boy. He was one of those rare people whose simple presence made life seem meaningful.

'Wasn't I fetching, unc? Couldn't see myself, though, could I! – Your boggn mirrors are too high.' He was only 5 feet four, a tidge shorter than me.

'Um, Theobald – pleasy-do fetcheth those ladders, and adjusteth all the mirrors to young Bug's height.'

We sat on the couch and he showed me his snapshots from the games, all of infatuated-with-Bug people standing in groups around Bug, jostling athletically to be next to him. There was a snap of him shaking hands with the man who shakes hands for the Grand Mufti, he being too grand to shake hands for himself. These Djakarta games, of coursemost, being in the Mufti's home town, were one of his great moments, a chance to celebrate his achievement on a world stage. With my Lord Protector's hat on I asked Bug about his impressions of the Mufti's power and the attitudes to it of the youngsters he'd met. His answers were confined to breezy remarks about the Mufti's caftans. But suddenly the boy quothed some ums of his own.

'Um, unc, um – about me, um, becoming a Moslem. I hoppity-hope you ken the drift that it was just a sopperoo bribewise for the judges, was it not, um, everso. Sons of Allah, boggn lot, notwot!'

'You're not a Moslem, then?'

'Wiffo, Bridget! I mean, no, I'm still one of yours.' He crossed himself. 'Good news about Cuz Rhino, though but. Give him something to do, ehwot?'

He took a wodge of yet more photographs out of his shorts. It was all the same shot, but he showed me each one. 'Twas him, nude, striking a girlie pose on an Indonesian beach.

'Had those done to give out to fems, but you can have them if you like. Brighten the palace up, ehwot!'

'Thankybees, Bug.'

I was quite touched. I lay back languidly, my soppy eyes filling with tears. I had never had a son. I felt that Bug was that very thing, coming home to see his old dad. I covered my strained brow and looked away.

The boy said nothing. He just sat, looking at copies of that photo of himself and smiling. I felt I had to say something. Sniff . . . sniff, then: 'Scusey-be your old unc, Bug. It's just, dimme, but you remind me of my poor bro Cod.' (He didn't. 'Twas just something to say.)

'Handsome sort of a wanger, was he, yer bro?'

'Hoots, yes.'

'Ladies' man, then?'

The story of Cod and Merluzza swam before my eyes.

'Yes, um, a notoriousmost womanizer. Committed the sexual intercourse many times.'

'He never did! Cor, ehwot? And what about you, if it's not outré to ask a pontiff?'

'I hast never, no.'

'Dingdong Deidre! Me, neither.' He swung his legs, watching them swing. I was watching his quiff. 'Will though, soon, by gum thought but!'

'Oh, but thou mustn't!' I cried. 'It's disgusting, and dangerous, and . . .'

'Triple sorries, Gabriella! But I sorta think I'll have to. Yer see, unc, I've applied, haven't I not? Applied!'

'Applied?'

He gushed: 'Best use of my talents, unc. To join the Women's Service.'

His brilliant smile faded as I seemed to leave the room. I was in the dark going um.

'Hurry-be someone! – the Archbishop's fainted!'

I had rolled under my desk and come to looking up at Archbishop Tait, so lately martyred by javelin. Bug and Bishop Hare pulled me out by my feet.

'Dear boy . . . um . . .' I said sitting up. 'Ooooh, I feeleth so languidypoos!'

'He's spanky – aren't you not, unc? It was just a stroke or something.'

'Thou mustn't . . . um . . . Wimminservice! Um? STOP HIM, Theobald!'

'Um?' questioned Theobald.

'I was just telling my uncle about my application to join the Women's Service, tha knows . . . Oooops, he's gone again! Poor Marjorie!'

Halfway onto my feet, I groaned earthwards, out for the count again. Darkness had summoned me and there was no arguing with it, never is. I was afloat in it. For a minute I heard Bug's voice saying: 'In the illustrated brochure it says that a successful applicant must be able to maintain an erection at all times – and I can, can I not, if there's a mirror about. Harh! Want to see?'

Bishop Hare's befuddled ums swooped over me like owls lost in the night.

*

Every day for a week I offered Bug the chance to be a bishop. I had unlimited power, I said, I could do anything for him. He was my great-nephew and I loved him, I said. I did. Just then he meant everything to me. I couldn't bear to have him out of my sight. But no, he said, the Women's Service was more his sort of thing. Fems liked him. He'd be happier at that than being a bish-bosh, and anyhowpoos ecclesiastical robes would hide his figure.

We spent a languid week together in Canterbury. He came with me to a synod. 'Twas the most languid synod I ever attended! Then one morning at breakfast he had the letter. He'd been accepted. He had to go down to Brighton rightaway for the induction course.

I went out into my little walled garden, the taste of marmalade on my tongue, and stood among the pear trees alone. After a few minutes he followed me out.

'Lookybee, unc, I'd better be pushing off, hadn't I, notwot?'

But he didn't. He stood there, beside me, 20 minutes or more, watching the sun come over the high wall. Then I looked at him. He was golden in the sunlight, languid and serious. He was working out something to say.

'Um,' he said – he'd caught um – 'Um, it's just, well, since my old dad went into his trance, I've had no proper dad to speak of, um, haven't I not? Till now, I mean. Till this week. You've been a Suzie-woozie daddio, haven't you not?'

It was the greatest moment of sweet sorrow that I ever knew. He was gone and I was alone in the sunbright garden with the bitter pears pendulous about me. I knew I was loved. It was a feeling almost new to me. Bug loved me. But although we televisited, we never spent time together again. I think of him. Every day I think of him.

The Women's Service was founded by Mrs Pittipaldi in '69. By then it was admitted what all of history knew, that men and women were totally incompatible creatures.

Marriage was unknown among the younger generations, was it not. Just a few very old bickersome couples remained of a once universal institution. Total segregation was just a few seasons away. Meanwhile, the sexes no longer mixed: they had themselves a trial separation before an eternal divorce. Women of that era had none of the softness, the gaiety of the gals of the '20s. They were a fractious, miffed bunch, who hated men and distrusted each other, brittle in their every encounter, frownsome, ugly of spirit, who lived alone and strangled their cats and sang fiercely in church, but only hymns written by women as miserable as themselves. But the clients of the Women's Service, slyly set up to cater for the old longings, left their ill-tempered natures at the door, and became like those gigglesome pnongistas who used to swoon for Carstairs or Smythe. They walked into a Woman's Centre looking harpiesome, pouting odium. But a few minutes in the Madam's beauty parlour and they were bobbed chorus girls, eager for romance. And it was waiting! Handsome young men like Bug, in thong or dinner attire, awaited them in the parlour. There were 50 Women's Centres in the Empire, but the best by far, with all the best wangers, as the fems called the fellas, was in Brighton HQ.

Tadese has asked me if there was also a Men's Service. Dimmee, yes, there was. But the less said about that the better!

Bug's instructor on the induction course was a certain Zorro Cavendish, a specialist in smarm, an old 30, rakish veteran of the cover of a thousand women's magazines. The fems had gone off him and he knew it. He hated Bug, the only person EVER to hate Bug, cos he knew the boy had the gift, and Zorro was piggnboggn jealous.

Cavendish was giving a rather bored lecture on techniques of the sexual intercourse, making some of the inductees giggle and others feel sick – Bug felt sick but giggled anyway – when Mrs Pittipaldi herself came in. Past 50, she looked 35, a chestnut mare in her prime, dressed, as always, in a plain black knee-length dress with strings of pearls dangling in the valley of her ample bosom. Her critical eye lasered into Zorro Cavendish.

'No, I'm sorry, Zorro. I did think you might do, but looking at you there, it's just not on, luvey. It's a flap, you see, boys – we've got the ex-Queen of France in . . . and Betty Snaith.'

A hummer around the room. BETTY SNAITH! Oooo, errrr!

Mrs Pittipaldi silenced their hummer with one look. Then she walked up and down the desks and stopped at Bug.

'Stand, boy.'

Bug stood.

'Trifle on the short side,' she said, feeling his shave with her little finger. 'But otherwise . . . bit of a bobbydazzler, aren't you, pet?' Then she asked Cavendish with her eyes still on Bug: 'Potential, has he, Zorro? Wot's he like in class?'

Cavendish made a disparaging noise in his throat.

Mrs Pittipaldi – there was, by the by, no Mr Pittipaldi – looked at Cavendish with a wide wicked smile. She knew men. Cavendish's disparaging noise told her everything. She grabbed Bug by the wrists and pulled him to her. She meant to kiss him, but the brilliance of his blue rose eyes startled her. She felt suddenly languid, hesitant, then sighed, swallowed, and kissed him hard. Then she kissed him again, harder. She felt between his legs.

'Yes, luvey,' she said, breathless, biting her pearls to regain composure. 'You'll do. This way.'

On their way out she gave Cavendish a look that ruined the rest of his life. Terrible thing was, he loved Mrs Pittipaldi, silly man.

The ex-Queen of France and her best pal Betty Snaith were looking formidable from the other side of the two-way mirror, chatting businesslikely but in pyjamas. Mrs Pittipaldi gave Bug tips on how to handle them. He was already naked and the angle of his erection was helped cos he could also see a flimsy reflection of himself on the sheen of the two-way mirror. Mrs Pittipaldi toyed with a gold lamé thong, her eyes rolling from her clients to her new operative as she doled out wisdom about women.

'Yes, Mrs Pittipaldi. I see, um, yes, Mrs Pittipaldi.'

It was his big chance. He was eager to do well. But the fear of the sexual intercourse was upon him and his wanger began to droop languidly. Mrs Pittipaldi saw this and held it tightly till it stiffened up.

'There's nothing to worry about, luvey. They'll adore you.'

Then, on his own initiative, he kissed Mrs Pittipaldi's hands, then her cheeks. She gasped. She dropped the thong. She turned away, breathing like a hot pekinese, tugging her pearls.

An out-of-control husky voice: 'Go on, then, luvey – get in there.'

'Yes, Mrs Pittipaldi. Thankybees.'

Bug hopped into the thong. As he opened the door to leave, Mrs Pittipaldi's string of pearls broke. He entered the presence of the two clients and two pearls followed him in, rolling between his naked feet.

'AT LAST!' cried Betty Snaith. 'A BOGGN MAN ARTICLE! CUM HERE, YOU LAZY WANGER!'

She was furious at being kept waiting and stomped over to Bug intending to slap him about a bit. But he dodged her slaps and came up with a pearl between his thumb and forefinger. He offered it to her. 'Twas the gesture of a God to a mortal woman. She accepted the gift and blushed, her eyes all a-blink. The second pearl was offered to the ex-Queen, who burbled with romantic delight.

'I've just got back, um, from Djakarta, haven't I not?' he said. 'I was in the Olympics. Javelin. I came 37th.'

This impressed them no end. They ooed.

'Fancy seeing my run up. Got no jav, though.'

He had something better! He ran around holding his wanger. The 2 women sat watching on the bed, very quiet. When they'd had enough of his running about, they patted the bed and he joined them there.

His thong was down his legs. Perfumed grapes had been liberally tossed about the room – some went pop in folds of the silk sheet, each pop making one or other client grunt wantonly. They were on either side of him, panting, in a slow languid writhe. Ms Snaith dared touch Bug's quiff. This touch made his wanger sort-of twang everso slightly, which in turn brought wild noises of passion from the ex-Queen and the Snaith woman. But instead of jumping on the boy, they hugged each other.

'Shall I, um, croon for you, ladies?'

There was nothing the fems liked better than crooning. They nodded, faint with anticipation.

Bug crooned wordlessly 'Bum-bum-bumbumbumbbumbum-bum-bum-bum . . . Ooooorrrrr, bum-boom-barm-bomboom, ba-ba-ba-boo-oom . . .'

The ex-Queen, too thrilled, passed out. Bug and Betty Snaith arranged her sweaty, grapejuice-sticky body and looked down on it.

'Should I ring for help, d'yer think?' asked Betty.

'Nope. She's just had a stroke, um, or something. Besides, it leaves just you-n-me, doesn't it not? Alone.'

He took command and slowly removed the pyjamas from Betty Snaith – THE Betty Snaith – and committed the sexual intercourse with her on the bed beside the fainted Queen. There was just a moment, between the subsiding of her ecstatic sighs and the waking of her friend, for Bug to say: 'I've just started here today. You were my first ever. I'll never forget this, never.'

'Oh, Bug! Bug! Bug!'

Then he rode his wang in the ex-Queen of France for over an hour. Then he gave Ms Snaith a second helping. And all the while he kept up a delightful flattering patter, but never, pleasy-do, taking his eyes off himself in the mirror, or his erection would have died away. Bug, a man of his time, was aroused by himself, not by fems.

Before the clients returned to their fractious lives the ex-Queen knocked on the 2-way mirror.

'We'll have him again, Friday . . .' She checked with Betty. 'Yes, Friday. The hussar's uniform.'

Bug waved them off and reported back to the viewing room.

'Wasn't bad, wasn't I not? Um? Enjoyed myself, didn't I not?'

Mrs Pittipaldi had watched the whole thing. Her black dress was drenched. She held gatherings of pearls tightly in her fists. Some dropped, bouncing, as she said, suddenly passionate: 'You knew I was still in here, didn't you? You never took your eyes off the mirror.'

'Didn't think you'd notice,' he said with his best smile, then held up the gold lame thong. 'Um, can I keep this?'

Mrs Pittipaldi nodded helplessly. Then she did something she'd never done – she threw herself at a man! They were languid in each other's arms.

*

Bug was right about his chosen profession. It was the best use of his talents. He was an immense success. All the fems loved him, and I mean really LOVED him.

Meanwhile, no one loved me as Archbishop of Canterbury and I wasn't much of a success at all. Ho hum! But I'd put a stop to the burnings and instigated the 4-day weekend, dismantled the Moral Judgement Machine and exiled its inventors to that Middlesborough on Saint Helena, and I unplugged the Everyone Channel for good, giving everyone their privacy back. These were good works, if not enough in a world sliding towards religious war.

More busy than ever, my happiest times were when I could televisit the pleasantly-weary Bug. I wanted to tell him about my pontifical doings, but was too fascinated by his tales of the little games he played with the fems. His descriptions of the sexual intercourse had me crosslegged and rapt. Of course, the sexual intercourse was illegal, had been since my predecessor's time. So by rights I should have closed the Women's Service. And I thought of so doing. But, as well as the titillation it offered corrupt old me, which I urinate in shame to admit, I felt there was something to be learnt about fems by studying it. I appointed Bishop Hare chairman of a study group. He said um twice as much after that! Urk!

During the early months of '76 I was busier than ever and hardly saw Bug at all. Then I was in an ecumenical conference in Vienna, supposedly discussing Erastianism but in fact plotting against the Grand Mufti. The Pope was there. I'd never met a Pope before and was quite my old self and full of fun. The Pope introduced me to lots of saints, none of whom I could see, and then introduced the Archangel Raphael, whom I could see – a small shaved Turk, obviously a spy of the Mufti's, but very convincing in his role. His descriptions of Heaven haunt me yet.

Suddenly, in the midst of all this powerful pomposity, under a banner saying ERASTIANISM in Greek, in the most rococo room I've ever been in, I began to laugh. A big cheesome laugh. I poked the high and mighty with my crook. I pushed my mitre down over my eyes – Bug always laughed at that one! – and flung a pally arm around old Pope Lassie. He started laughing too. The whole room rocked with it, real human laughter, the greatest sound there is. The only one not laughing was the Archangel Raphael.

Then Bishop Hare came waddling across the floor, a fax in his quivering mit.

'Um – a message, um. From Middlesborough 622.'

'Yes, chee-he, hoooooooo, um – wotsit say?'

'Aliens have landed, your grace.'

'Aliens, Theobald?'

'Venusians. Not from our local planet so called, um, but from another one somewhere else.'

Pope Lassie and I tripped over each other's crooks.

4

Janet

Here I lie upon my back in the Ethiopian night, a-goggle at the stars. Human life, tha knows, began not far from this very pole of mine. In the bluffs between here and Bako, how many skulls whose teeth were long ago bared in smiles? And when those longago folks looked up in their empty nights, what did they see? This. The same.

I expect they called these Heavens 'God's Home', and when some violent new tribe marched over the Ogaden to make skulls out of them, I expect they called out for rescue from the stars. But God wasn't up there, was he? He was within us, was he not, a deaf mute, a lost, impotent thing, ignorant of our battles, less impressive than the creation outside. And this we have long known, have we not? But still the stars.

For a long time the idea of life on other planets was poopoohed. Then it became an orthodoxy to believe in other worlds, other civilizations, though there was no evidence for it at all, indeedybe not! But in the 21st Century, after all our wrangles and miseries, we had stopped thinking about such things. Space belonged to the Scots. Just like haggis.

Then on St George's Day, April 23, 2076, they landed, outside the town hall in Middlesborough 622 in former Scotland. Aliens, pleasy-do. Venusians from the Venus of a remote galaxy. 14 of them. In a spaceship like a sunnyside-up fried egg. It seemed that they had been in suspended animation for a little over 100 years. It had taken them that long to get here from that distant Venus of theirs. Before inducing sleep they had picked up one of our 20th Century television broadcasts on their equipment, and watched enthralled a production known as *Dr Finlay's Casebook*, which depicted the dull life of an irascible Scottish doctor in the 1930s in a Highland village called Tanochbrae. Thinking that what they had seen depicted the full truth of the nature of the planet they were off to, they spent their sleep in a soupy metamorphosis intended to transform them into characters from the playlet, pleasy-do. Thus they intended to emerge in the village of Tanochbrae – itself, sadly, as fictional as Brigadoon – and blend in with the natives.

As it was, the metamorphosis didn't come out quite right and one morning in the place where Tanochbrae might have been but never was, 13 shapeless green Scottish doctors and a shapeless green Scotswoman emerged, lost on the streets of Middlesborough. Just what the world needed, more boggn Scots!

Hurrying back to Canterbury from a conference in Vienna, I was de-briefed on the airship about all this *Dr Finlay's Casebook* business. Already a marquee was being erected on the Cathedral lawn. A firm of Scottish caterers were brought in all the way from New Arbroath. A no-expense spared buffet was prepared. I sat in a deep bath, waiting for the aliens to arrive.

They were late. Their fried-egg spaceship was kaput. They were coming on the train. I played croquet. Lost. Got in a temper. Had another bath.

A knock on the bathroom door: 'The aliens, um, are here, um, your grace!'

I was still wet from the bath under my sweatificatious Archbishop's getup, my crozier heavy in my hand, my mitre on crooked, when, to rapturous applause in a packed-out marquee, the Venusian troupe sauntered in dressed in period tweed suits. Because I had never understood the Scottish brogue, the Ambassador of Scottish Belgium had kindly provided me with an interpreter billed as 'the most Scottish person he could find'. This was Banquo MacReikie of MacReikie, who inhabited a castle in Caithness which the magic of Middlesboroughization had not been powerful enough to de-Scottishize. He was the most overwhelmingly Scottish personality of all time, draped in clods of tartan, ginger of skin and eye, all knees and beard.

MacReikie stood going 'Ayeeeeeeeeeee' like a bagpipe as the Venusians gathered around me. They ate plates of macaroons and made a similar bagpipish noise. I was spooked.

'Wot are they saying, MacReikie?'

'Yon beasties are appreciative of yer handsome spread, mon. Thissn here's Doctor Finlay.'

I chuckled a howdeedoodee.

'And if I ken right all these others are different Doctor Camerons except for the one wi'oot a heed, that's Doctor Snoddy.'

They grunted in unison and flapped their now-empty plates.

'Theobald, um, pleasy-do, more macaroons for our guests!'

Then Janet stepped forward. Her metamorphosis had worked the best. She was a small grey lady, seemingly about my own age, almost human except for a slight greenness of skin and an extra eye in her neck, shyly covered by a chiffon scarf.

She put a cool, nay, cold hand on my sweatificatious brow.

'Och, ye poor wee mon, ye're all hot and bothered.' Next thing, several Doctor Camerons had their stethoscopes inside my cassock, and consulted one another with grunts. They were all around me, huge, shapeless, green – and Scottish!

'MACREIKIE!'

But he was sitting down eating porridge with Doctor Finlay. My hands full of prescriptions, my ears ringing with, no doubt, excellent medical advice, I hid in the Punch & Judy booth whose erection I'd ordered on a whim.

It was there Janet found me. She came in through the flaps at the back and smelt of lavender and roses and better days gone by.

'Are ye feeling better, Archbishop?'

'Um? Much, thankybees.'

'Would ye no like a cup o'tea?'

'I, er, um?'

She removed my mitre and rubbed my brow with a handkerchief, like someone polishing a statue. It was in this compromising position that Banquo MacReikie of MacReikie found us.

257

He leaned gingersomely through the square hole where Punch & Judy strutted their stuff and after a long all-knowing lascivious 'Ayeeeeeeeeeeeeee,' he said: 'I've been having a wee crack wi'yon Doctor Finlay, mon. I have the whole grisly storie if ye've the bowels ter hear it.'

'Yes, um, fire away.'

'It seems that these here beasties in human form are the last of their owrie kind. Their planet was laid waste by a 500-year drought and all their ilk perished. Ayeeeeee! And because they're all brothers and sisters, for tae avoid the consanguinity . . .'

He paused and I nodded Archbishoply.

'Aye, for consanguinity tae be avoided, they've made the lang journey tae the nearest planet where compatible sexual partners could be found.'

'You mean . . . um . . . I don't think I understand.'

I looked at Janet's smilingly innocent old lady's face. Her hips swayed slightly.

'They've come here tae find a mate for yon Janet, ye auld boobie! For tae propagate thasels!'

Suddenly, Bishop Hare's cherubic face between striped cloth at the back of the booth:

'Job for the Women's Service, um, ehwot?'

I gave Janet my vicar's smile. I patted her cold hand.

'No worries on you evermost,' I said, and sank unconscious inside my robes.

*

I had declared it a public holiday. The copulation was to be televised. Street parties. Fuss. Hullabaloo. But as squadrons of bishops descended upon Brighton in their flying hats, I had an itchy foreboding inside my noggin which I couldn't scratch.

Outside the Women's Centre was an overflow of unusually vivacious fems, all of whom, somehow, Bishop Hare knew personally. They shook his umming hand and booed me.

Mrs Pittipaldi greeted me in the foyer. It was full of

pictures of men with quiffs, like ones from the windows of an old-fashioned barber's.

'This copulation, it's a spankydoos honour for the Women's Service, Archbishop.'

'Um?'

I was distracted by the dizzifying reek of aftershave in the building. Would I swoon? – My fingers wouldn't leave my dog-collar alone. I asked if nephew Bug was about.

'He's in his dressing room, the darling. Tell him he's a sweetieookums!'

I found Bug stripped for action, carefully checking his face in a small round mirror. His nose was huge in it..

'Mrs Pittipaldi sayeth you're a sweetieookums!' I said behind him. I knew all about him and Mrs Pittipaldi.

He jumped up and gave me a powerful hug. Then he held me at arms length. We chuckled, old friends. He looked less languid, more grown up.

'I just popped in,' I said, already on my way out, my head, belly and bowels all equally worried about the copulation. 'I'll save thee a seat.'

'Seat?'

'In the porno cinema they hast upstairs. They whole ukky event's been shown on its screen, pleasy-do. I've brought my, um, dark glasses!'

I put them on and chortled.

'But, unc, thought you knew, old sillypoo. I'm it. I'm Janet's wanger. Me. Darling Bug.'

'YOU!'

Why had this danger not occurred to me! I'd thought an older operative, more experienced.

'YOU CAN'T! A CHAFFINCH DO THE HOOHAR WIG-GLY THING WITH A VENUSIAN! I WON'T BOGGN ALLOW IT!'

I picked up a handful of thongs and threw them at him in pontifical ire!

He was smiling, calmmost: 'But, unc, I'm the best man for the job. Mrs Pittipaldi did one of her sex surveys on Janet. 1000 of the lewdmostest questions imaginable! And I was the answer to every one. Janet's wanger, that's me.'

I was a rock of disapproval.

He pouted girlishly. The Women's Service had made his charm crude.

'Think of poor ickle Janet,' he moped. 'You wouldn't want her offsprogs to look like Zorro Cavendish, would you?'

I had heard about Zorro Cavendish. I sat exhausted at the dressing-table and was shocked by a hideous thing I saw in the big mirror. Me!

Quietly: 'I'll have a word with Mrs Pittipaldi. I'm sure one of the other boys – thy friend Jeronimo.'

'Oh, Jeronimo's not me!' he said. He was vexed.

'Triple sorries, Bug, I won't allow it.'

I went to the door, the grim father. He twirled me around with hands made strong by abusing women.

'Looksee, unc – I'm going to fertilize Janet and that's that! This is the best thing that could possibly happen to me! I'm rhubarb spanky-doos at this! It's the highpoint in my whole life and career! Don't spoil it for me, um, unc, ehwot?'

His blue rose eyes were desperately pleading. Old fool, I gave in.

'All right, boyo,' I said. 'She's all thine.'

I crossed myself.

As I walked down the corridor I suddenly heard Bug shout 'CATCH!' I turned and caught a banana. I went away eating it. The flash of Bug's naked body I saw behind the flying banana was the last I ever saw of him.

In the cinema upstairs I met Zorro Cavendish and lots of other handsome young men in hussar's uniforms. My bro Wilf was there, his mouth taped, and Winston, Rhino, Dame Tuna and a nestful of Chaffinches sitting at the back. The curtains opened. We watched an episode of *Dr Finlay's Casebook* as a taster. A rowful of Doctor Camerons wept all through it, from their various eyes. I noticed that their green hue glowed in the dark, and when Mrs Pittipaldi appeared on screen introducing an alarmingly naked Janet, they grunted more like frogs than doctors.

Janet sat draped on the pink flouncy four-poster bed, munching macaroons, blowing crumbs off her small greenish breasts. Now and then she scratched herself like a chimp. The anticipation of the sexual intercourse had brought out the animal in her. She kept throwing her head back and gurning wantonly in a mirror above the bed, placed there on Bug's orders to keep his stiffy happy. This event looked like it was going to be every bit as disgustingly sexuiticle as the most winking pervert could hope for. I put my sunglasses away!

When Bug appeared, screen left, crooning in a dinner jacket, she hopped up on the bed, squatted on all fours, puffed out her cheeks and gazed adoringly. Did the boy have this effect on all women, I wondered?

Then I noticed that the pile of tartan in the corner of the room was moving. Of course! – MacReikie was in there as interpreter. Janet handed him a sheet of paper and muttered something in Scots.

The screen went tartan, then ginger as MacReikie approached it, handing the niftily undressing Bug the paper.

'Yon lassie wants fer ye ter croon yon folk tune while ye're thrusting yer loins into her seat of desire,' he said, then went 'Ayeeeeeeeeeeeeeeee' at the camera.

'Boggn get on with it, ehwot!' yelled Zorro Cavendish. I had Bishop Hare throw him out.

Bug stepped out of his thong to reveal an erection which, thoughtful for his alien lover, he'd painted green. A round of applause. Doctors Finlay and Camerons had removed their jackets. The headless Doctor Snoddy had his feet pointed up at the screen – his eyes, I realized, were in the soles of his feet!

Bug started crooning a song I'd never heard. *MacArthur Park*. I was furtherly perturbed that the Venusians sang along to it. How cum they knew the words? What special significance could a 20th Century folktune have for Venusians, wondered I?

> *MacArthur Park is melting in the dark*
> *All the sweet green icing flowing down.*
> *Someone left that cake out in the rain*
> *I don't think that I can take it*

Cos it took so long to bake it
And I'll never find that recipe again
Bum-be-bum . . .

Then, on a hectoring signal from Janet, MacReikie drew the curtains around the four-poster. A moaning cry of disappointment from the cinema audience. Me too. I was worked up! I wanted to see the boy at it! And Janet in the throes of naked passion! I have a stiffening, Tadese, right now, as I recall her nakedness! It enflamed me as the nakedness of no other woman had ever enflamed me.

I chewed the leather on my Bible as I sat in the hushed cinema listening to Bug sing and Janet cry out in womanly abandon. No kissing, obviously, was going on. But much writhing about, cos the curtains were constantly reacting to kicks and grasps.

Four times Bug sang the song.

I recall the yellow cotton dress
Foaming like a wave on the ground beneath your knees
MacArthur Park is bum-bum-BUM-burrrrm . . .

Mrs Pittipaldi gripped the cross swinging at my neck and kissed it. Her face was an agony of jealous tears.

'I'm a bad woman!' she said.

'I have no doubt!' I said, and pushed her away.

Meanwhile, in the curtained bed Janet wailed in pleasure: 'Och, laddie, mae braw weee laddie, that's it, that's the way I like it! I've waited 100 years fae this! YES! YES! YES! YES! YES! YES! YES! OurrRGHHHHHHHH!'

I was so worked up, I was kissing Mrs Pittipaldi! Me, the Archbisop of Canterbury! And wot's more, she liked it! I almost lost my virginity there and then!

Then suddenly, a little cry from Bug – an ejaculatory cry, we thought. Polite applause. The bed suddenly rocked violently. Another noise, thunderous, something like a croak. Then total silence.

We thought the sound system had broken, what with that croak noise and all. But then MacReikie, his knees creaking, was nervously approaching the bed and spoke on-mike to the national audience:

'I'LL JUST TAK A WEE PEEP, THE NOO, SHOULD I NO?' He fumbled for a gap in the curtains and peeped. The bed rocked violently again. MacReikie let out a Scots cry like a bagpipe being eaten in a well on a misty Hallowe'en. He dropped backwards, his tartan filling the screen. Then just the curtained bed and silence.

I pushed Mrs Pittipaldi ahead of me. She knew the way better than I. A curious national audience – indeed, the Grand Mufti was watching in Djakarta – saw the Archbishop of Canterbury dash into the copulatory bedchamber and, like a wronged husband of old, tear down the curtains about the bed. Wot a delicate sound of snapping curtainrings, like fairies arguing.

My eyes saw too much. I couldn't understand what I saw. First my eyes fell upon Janet's wideopen legs, then on the eye winking in her neck, then on the heaped bloody mass covering the sheet beside her. Bug was torn to bits, his handsome face a red skull. His exposed organs steamed redly like a hot but raw haggis.

Janet sat up, coyly closed her legs and said: 'Och, I'm so sorrie aboot the laddie. I got overexcited, ye ken.'

I turned to camera: 'Turn this boggn thing off,' I said.

MacReikie was at my feet, still twitching from shock, his beard and hair gone quite white. Dr Finlay couldn't save him.

5

The Chaffinch Who Saved the World

I could not believe that the world was still going on. I wandered the corridors of my palace like the ghost of an Archbishop, did I not, muttering in Latin, which I'd thought I forgotten decades before. For a while I fancied I was a boy again, in that wonderful winter that lasted for 5 years, and I was walking down the frozen River Stour from Sudbury to Dedham. Cod was with me.

'Cumalong, fish article! You're boggn lagging – said you would!'

But I turned back from my vision of yesteryear when I bumped into 6 Doctor Camerons on their way back to their rooms. Somehow, instead of my crozier, Bug's javelin was in my hand. I chased them. I howled like Wilf. I'd have killed one for sure – perhaps all! – if I hadn't seen Janet standing prim and regal in an open doorway.

Suddenly I was a weak, sorry old man. The javelin held me up, but my sobs slid me down it like blows. All my sorrows came back, everything, all at once. Janet helped a staggering Chaffinch to her room. She gave me a cup of tea.

Janet could not be held responsible for Bug's death. Using a drunken Scotsman we happened to find on the streets of Brighton as interpreter, Doctor Finlay explained, in an angry scene in the foyer of the Women's Centre, that it was not unusual for the males of their species to be ripped to bits during a particularly energetic copulation. He further insisted, poking me furiously in the chest, that he had told all this to MacReikie who should have conveyed it to me. Thus, the barely expired MacReikie was blamed by everyone for the death of darling Bug.

Bug became a hero the world over, a symbol of undying youth and vigour. The photo of him which had adorned the foyer of the Brighton Women's Centre was reproduced a squillion times. Same goes for the one of him nude on an Indonesian beach. Fems the world over kept one hidden in a drawer to moon over in secret. A dream lover! But a man's man too. He was on every young lad's wall, beaming down full of languid promise. In an unprecedented move, the Olympic committee disqualified all 36 javelinists who'd chucked further than Bug and he was posthumously awarded the gold medal. I have it. Among my treasures in the box in Tadese's hut. It arrived with a letter of condolence from the Grand Mufti, my old enemy.

Janet was a great help to me in that sad time, was she not. She fussed over me as no woman had ever fussed over me. I was deeply grateful. More than that, I may as well admit the whole triplesorries thing at last, I was in love. But not with the romantic passion with which I had loved Scampi Lowrie – this was a physical thing. Stop laughing, Tadese!

It was late summer. I'd been away in York at the synod all week and hadn't seen Janet. I arrived home early in the morning and stood in my little walled garden watching old, mad wasps buzz drunkenly in holes they'd made in the pears. Janet came down the steps. Her smell! – that Venusian piquancy mixed with lavender, heather, fresh clean days that never were! I turned in a rising passion. We collided! Gold threads on my Archbishop's habiliments snagged onto her cardigan. We were locked together! I felt her immense strength. I was churchyard scared. But it had to be done! I knew! I couldn't resist it! I kissed her, again and again and again, the kind of kisses I'd dreamed about for a whole piggn century. Suddenly, she pulled away, snapped gold threads stuck to her chest. Was this an end of my Grand Affair! Only a brief awkward snog! I'd kissed boggn Mrs Pittipaldi more than that! Yes, twas all over – Janet had disappeared. I twirled around the garden in search of her, even looking up the peartree. Then I felt her strong hands on my knees. She was climbing under my Archbishop's habiliments. I ducked down in them to meet her coming the other way. We did it standing up. The hoohar wiggly thing. I did. With Janet. Me. Lost my cherry at last, did I not.

Squelch-squelch! Fainted twice during the event, but at the end I felt marvellous! My adult life, at last, had begun!

During the next few weeks Janet and I committed the sexual intercourse twice every day. Cheehee! I walked around languidly like poor Bug had. I was becoming him! Yes, I fancied I WAS him, come back. Doing the hoohar wiggly thing with Janet in some vague symbolic way brought the boy to life. On several occasions she cried out 'BUG!' in heights of pleasure, and I was glad she did. My sorrows faded. My wink shocked vicars. I was a new man.

'Shall I singeth that song for you, lovepuppet – the one about the cake?' I would do anything to please her!

'Och, no, ye dinnee ha' to do that. Just thrust away, auld laddie, and try not tae swoon anymair.'

My copulatory efforts, strewth be told, were nowhere near up to Bug's standard – had they been, then this Chaffinch would have met the same fate as t'other. But I was improving, and looked forward to a happymost death to end all my sorrows, ripped to pieces by Janet's powerful arms!

But then one morning at breakfast, Janet, in a firm prim voice that would allow no buts, said that she would be leaving Canterbury that very day, forever. Doctor Snoddy was taking her down to Brighton. He'd started a practice there. And . . . well, very soon, any day now, it would be time for her to lay her eggs.

'Eggs?'

'Aye, eggs, o'course, silly mon. And they'll be needing the seawater. Brighton will be grand fae the laying.'

'Seawater? Eggs? Um?

'Aye. So I'll be awa this afternoon, your grace.'

'Janet! Janet!' I implored, clasping her hands. 'What about US!'

Eminently practical, she said: 'Och, the segregation of the sexes is only a wee while away, my auld laddie. There's no US. There's nothing like that on this world nae mair – and a good thing too!'

I saw she was right, of course. But I couldn't finish my scrambled you-know-wotnots. I smiled an old-fashioned smile, then suddenly left the table. I found some nattering bishops in the library and cheered myself by swapping their sees for them – Liverpool I swapped with Bath and Wells, Winchester I swapped with Durham, new Durham I swapped with Liverpool, new Bath and Wells I swapped with 2nd new Durham, and back and forth, for an hour.

Janet left that afternoon. She put a mug of hot cocoa on my desk, her final kindness, and said her flying taxi was due. I didn't turn around. I was pretending to contemplate the hole in Archbishop Tait. But before the door closed on yet another friendship, I said shyly:

'I hope the, um, eggs all come out spanky-doos.'

'Och, a few million in any batch are always doomed. But they'll be plenty okaydoos, ye ken, especially after Bug's bonny copulation.'

'Um? Um?'

I swivelled about. But she was gone.

When Bishop Hare and his protégé Simeon Crumply-Stoves (my successor as Archbishop as it turned out) came into my study late that night with their far-fetched theories, I roared at them like a despot, and turned back to staring into the empty cocoa mug. My desklight was turned upwards so's I could contemplate, genuinely this time, the hole in Archbishop Tait. I put a Hieronymus Gosh concert on the hologram plate. My eyes kept rolling to it sadly.

But Crumply-Stoves was a determined sort. He came back. With Rhino as backup this time.

'Thou canst exile me to a Polish Middlesborough if thou likes but thou hast to know! Something boglyfala is in the custard, ehwot! How couldst little Janet do what she did to young Bug, um? Um? She can't be that boggn strong. It's summick else, tha knows!'

Rhino handed his friend a TV handset.

'This is a recording of the copulation. We've had it enhanced. Pleasy-do, your grace . . . Looketh! Listeneth!'

I deigned to pay the thing some attention, but I had put Bug's death behind me. I couldn't look at it again. I peered at the Gosh concert out of the corner of my eyes. Then something on the recording connected with my unconscious mind. Bug's last words, lost in the climactic copulatory thrashing about, but clear in the enhancement, had been 'Octopus Frog!' Or perhaps 'Octopus! Frog!' or even 'Octopusfrog!' Hard to tell. It meant nothing to me, but it teased my brain like something nearly remembered.

'Octopus Frog?' I said to myself. Then said it without saying it, just my lips.

'That's it, your grace. Octopus Frog. Bug sayeth it here . . .' He wound back and we heard it again. 'And when MacReikie peepeth in through the curtain . . . here . . .'

There was MacReikie, gaping, saying at the back of his throat: 'Oct . . . topus . . . FROG!'

Crumply-Stoves was triumphant. 'Well, your grace, there thou ist! Wot ist thou going to do about it?'

I nodded at him sagely, took a piece of crested notepaper, waved my pen pompously over the page, then wrote a few words, blew on them, and handed the finished document to the ambitious priest.

'Eugh!' he said.

I had exiled him to Polish Middlesborough 1,974.

*

Janet's egg-laying was another media event. It sickened me to see the body I had worshipped, sucked, rubbed and hooharwigglied, exhibited on live television. Oh, yes, they had her on Brighton Pier, pleasy-do, the good doctors, laying her eggs onto a chute that skimmed them out to sea. The whole ikky process, with the constant chant from the crowded beach of 'PUSH! PUSH! PUSH!' was so affecting to the senses that half the country, men and women, got birthpang pains in sympathy. EUOOO! – the lubricating slime, the appearance of the soft white jellied egg in Janet's hole, the schhhhlupp-plup as she batted it out, her legs snapping shut, then twanging open again, more slime, another egg on the way . . . YUIEK! Horrible! It wasn't a thing people should watch. So I sent that Punch & Judy booth down to Brighton and ordered them to cover the poor woman up with it! What sort of people did they think we were! Live egg-laying at the end of a pier watched by millions! No, no, no!!!

But seeing the eggs slide out of the flaps at the back of the booth and down that overworked chute was somehow more disturbing still, with Doctor Finlay's Punchlike bon mot of 'That's the way to do it!' repeated gigglesomely in every livingroom in the Empire.

I could get no work done. At every committee there was some woman in a dreadful hat saying: 'How many is it now, Archbishop?'

Nor was there an end in sight. Janet kept on laying her eggs right through the summer and into the autumn, with the seas whipping up under the chute. She never left the booth. The English Channel was clogged with floating eggs. So was Biscay. Shipping had to be suspended. And still more eggs.

Three empty Middlesboroughs in the Balkans, the gift of the Scottish people, were being prepared for that which would hatch from the eggs. These would be, Doctor Finlay assured us, although alien in appearance – green cubes with eleven feet and a revolving eye on top the size of a watermelon – perfect citizens of the New World Order I and my fellow clerics were trying to make. They would all be Anglicans. And, pleasy-do, with Bug's last shot of sperm the making of them, they were half-Chaffinch. So thousands of new nieces and nephews to replace that poor vain boy.

Meanwhile, people at last got bored with the egglaying. There was an eggcount on the news bulletins for a while. By Christmas they had stopped that too. Even I, pleasy-do, had moved on in life. I was busy trying to set up a summit with the Grand Mufti, losing myself in work, details, committees, synods. Then on a calm day early in the New Year, Doctor Finlay televisited.

'She's asking for ye.'

'Wot's that thou sayest, man? Janet? Asking for me?'

'Aye, Janet. Be quick, will ye no!'

I strolled up the pier, jauntymost of step. I was going to see my girl. But I was too late. She'd just died. The doctors, her brothers for God's sake, had always known she would. It took all 13 to tell me, to get the truth of their Scots mutterings into my head. Then each wandered away to his own pitch on the pier, to lean, and grunt and watch the eggs on the water and think his own alien thoughts. I was about to look in the booth to see her kind face once more, but Finlay stopped me.

'She's no a pretty sight,' he said. 'It took everything she had.'

'I see.'

'And yersel, ye're quite well?' He felt my brow.

'Much better, thankybe. I loved her, tha knows.'

'Aye,' he said gruffly. 'Well, she did her bit, indeed she did.'

We watched some men dismantling the chute. Then the death wagon came for Janet and I hurried away.

When I arrived home I was confused by the news that the good doctors had taken off in their fried egg spaceship and were already past Jupiter in it. No word of goodbye.

That same night the eggs sank in the sea, went down like dropped coins. Next morning the English Channel was its old bluegrey choppy miserable self. Divers reported that the eggs had turned to mush and were fast being eaten by the sea. What a shame, was my thunkment – something must have gone wrong biologicallywise. It had all been for nothing. I sat alone in my Cathedral, on my boggn throne, in deepest spiritual gloom, as that day of the 21st Century ticked away. I knew the answer, but still I asked: *How could God allow such tragedy?*

It was late April, a year since the Venusians' arrival, before the world learnt that it had not been a tragedy. The eggs' sinking and mushyfercation had been part of their developmental process. In fact, they weren't eggs, they were egg clusters. Each of those thousands of eggs contained millions of microscopic seeds. Deep in the ocean buried for 4 months, they suddenly bloated and rose to the surface. Billions upon billions of them, all over the globe, covering every horizon seen on the sea since the days of Magellan. Pale greenish eggs with a sort of tartan soup inside to sustain their occupants: OCTOPUSFROGS!!!!!!!!

The first octopusfrogs hatched out off Australia, then, of course, the personal fiefdom of the Grand Mufti. Only a few hundred of them, but they ate practically everybody in those sorrymost antipodes. The octopusfrogs in the northern hemisphere didn't hatch till the last week of May. We were using all our weaponry, stored up in the cold war with Islam, but to no avail. The eggs were invulnerable and the octopusfrogs seemed to enjoy explosions in their faces. It made their popeyes go wide with delight, like kiddies at Guy Fawkes. Our efforts could be compared to someone trying to demolish a rubber mountain with a box of matches.

It was all my fault, I realized. I'd been weak and trusting. Had it always been my destiny to bring about the end of human civilization? Everyone thought so, as they drew their curtains and waited for the end. And cos men and women had grown to hate each other, there was no comfort to be had. Just plate-smashing fury and swearing directed at me. The Grand Mufti was suing me for the cost of rebuilding Australia. I said I'd settle out of court and sent him a pound note with my face on it. A rare joke in that terrible time.

The only thing that calmed me was the sexual intercourse. I had been seeing something of Mrs Pittipaldi and had hopes of seducing a rather large nun who went around with the Papal Nuncio. She was there that day, the day I saved the world.

The octopusfrogs were coming ashore in England now. London was full of them. They had all the bridges down. A big one was sitting atop of the Toblerone Building, croaking, throwing its tentacles about, popping the windows with its suckers all the way down to the 88th floor – which gives some idea of the size of the bigger ones!

I was watching this and similar scenes in cities throughout the world on ranks of TV screens in what was now my war room in Canterbury. The glowering figure of Archbishop Tait overlooked it all. The 19th Century was never like this, my glance told him! The phones never stopped. Mostly it was octopusfrogs on the line, reverse charge calls, croaking malevolently. Janet's children! How could she! Their croaking filled the room. I answered some phones myself, for the sake of doing something, and swore boglyfalas at the boggn octopusfrogs, hanging up on them with maximum cheek. Doing this yet again, I suddenly realized it was my brother Wilf on the line. I'd called him the most terrible things, thinking him to be an octopusfrog, and he never forgave me, but he did impart the information, in the unique tongue-clicking language developed in our attic, that there were a half dozen octopusfrogs in the grounds of Chaffinch Hall and that Big Norris had taken them on and been eaten.

It was shortly after this call that Bishop Hare came in holding half a broken crozier in each hand.

'They, um, cometh up the Dover road. Um. God help us all!'

Some of the screens were going blank. Others had octopusfrogs close to camera, pulling rubbery faces, popping their suckers on their own heads – a most unpleasant sound. Some were demonstrating how they ate people, which affrighted that big nun. I gave her a comforting hug and wondered what it would be like to hooharwiggly with her – although even with my mitre on I was a foot shorter than she was!

'Turneth those boggn screens off, Theobald!' I ordered.

He pulled the plug and how quiet it became. Suddenly, the biggest shock I'd had all year. The Grand Mufti televisited.

'Well, little priest,' he said. (He'd always called me that.) 'This is a fine mess you've got us into.'

I let go of the nun. He walked around her, feeling his beard, as if measuring her up for his harem.

'How much do you want for the nun?' he said.

'DOESN'T THEE THINK I'VE GOT MORE TO DO AT SUCH AN HOUR THAN BARTER NUNS WITH THE DEVIL!' I roared.

It was the Mufti's eyes that looked to the door first. There was a tentacle there, feeling its way into the room.

'Toodlybyebye, little priest,' he said, and I heard the beginnings of his evil laugh as his visit fizzed out.

Squeezing through the doorway was a medium-sized octopusfrog. Green, yellow-warted, white-suckered. Its wide mouth was bloody, it having eaten the Papal Nuncio on its way in. The phones stopped ringing as if the world knew we were done for.

I fell to my knees and prayed. The 40 or so people in the war room abandoned their desks and did the same.

'Lord, we are all poor sinners at the foot of thy Holy Hill.

Pleasy-do, we loveth our lives more than we love thee, but we do love thee, the idea of thee . . . Jesus Christ HEAR ME! SAVE US! SAVE US!' But, God wasn't listening, yet again, and I was forced to say: 'Into your gentle hands, O Heavenly Father, I commend the spirits of . . .' And I resentfully listed the people who the octopusfrog had picked up with its tentacles and brained against the parquet floor.

Bored with that, it snatched my mitre from my head and put it on its own. I opened my mouth to sing a hymn with my surviving comrades – why not *To be a Pilgrim*, my faverave! But the words wouldn't come, and the octopusfrog was upon me, rising on its eight thick legs, a rubbery dome over my gagging head. One of its big yellow eyes was squinting down upon me, and the last sucker on a tentacle was popping my cheek like the rough kiss of a hated aunt. And right then, at that moment, suddenly, unbidden, it all came back to me – those times when I thought I'd fainted while copulating with Janet! I hadn't! She'd just hypnotised me into forgetting what had happened! Now the memory was intact . . . Janet, my Janet, at the approach of orgasmicness, had turned into one of these monstrous froggy octopussy beasts. Oh, Janet! Oh, Bug! Oh, sweet Jesus! Janet had been an octopusfrog!

And with that realization came a flood of other memories and lost knowledge. I scampered out from under the octopusfrog. Its tentacles had me around arms and legs but, playing with me like a cat, it was content to watch me suffer. The words to my hymn came back to me – but, for a reason I'll never know, what came out in my best lounge singer's baritone was *MacArthur Park*.

> *Spring was never waiting for us, dear*
> *It ran one step ahead*
> *as we followed in the dance*
> *MacArthur Park is melting in the dark*
> *All the sweet green icing flowing down . . .*

And the octopusfrog dropped me and slid off, breaking through the French windows. It was in my little garden where first I'd copulated with Janet, where first I'd seen its owrie kind – Janet herself! I followed it there and sang at the creature. It held all 8 tentacles over the place where its ears were. I sang louder. Its tongue flashed out and grabbed me like a fly, but when it pulled away it just took my Archbishop's habiliments, leaving me singing in my underwear.

> *Someone left that cake out in the rain*
> *And I don't think I can take it*
> *Cos it took so long to bake it*
> *And I'll never have that recipe again . . .*

Something about the arrangement of the notes in that song had been just right to encourage the fertilization of Janet. Bug's singing of it had accomplished that. But at this stage of their development, the same arrangement of notes was deadly. The octopusfrog lay dead in my garden like a prop left over from a children's party.

Within minutes my own silly voice, with Bishop Hare and my war room staff as accompaniment, sang *MacArthur Park* into a big silver microphone which broadcast us to the world.

From Shanghai to Havana, from Wellington to Narvik, from Middlesborough to Middlesborugh, the song did its deadly work. In France they were already cooking octopusfrog au vin. Humanity learned the song and ran into its streets, its fields, its deserts, alps, and jungles, to sing *MacArthur Park*. The battle was soon over. A Chaffinch had saved the world. The octopusfrogs were dead. An irritating old lovesong had croaked the lot!

For a long time there were travellers' tales of surviving octopusfrogs, of one living in a deep obscure pool somewhere, until it met up with a nitwit with a megaphone singing *MacArthur Park*. Perhaps, to this day, a few endure. And I shed tears for them all, cos they were Bug's children too, and therefore Chaffinches, and this booky-do I've been making is about Chaffinches and their blueful lives. So, regrets for Daphnia and Robin and Cod and Seve and Rainbow and Haha and Bug, and same goes for my unfortunatedoos nieces and nephews, the octopusfrogs.

*

The mopping-up operation was afoot and I was soreheadly busy
with tediousmost details when Simeon Crumply-Stoves came
into my office, a nervous Bishop Hare umming behind him.

'I thought I exiled thee to a Polish Middlesborough.'

'Janet,' he said.

'Um?' I knew what was coming.

'The Lord hath unpicketheth Theobald's hypnotized mind –
he remembers, Archbishop! He saweth thee hooharwiggling
with Janet in the garden here! And one day he hideth in the
wardrobe in Janet's bedroom and . . . Euugh! . . . watchedeth
through the lock. Didn't thou?'

'Um? Umumumum-um.'

'DIDN'T THOU?'

'Yes, Simeon. Triple sorries, Archbishop, um.'

'Crumply-Stoves waggled a finger of doom: 'And who can
forget the vile rumours concerning thee and the late Mrs
Pittipaldi?' (The octopusfrogs had got her, poor dear.)

'Get back to Polish Middlesborough, you grubby article!'
I cried.

But he didn't. He stood there, pacing the carpet, still slimy
from its octopusfroggy visitor, making an indignant sermon,
which really should have been recorded for posterity. It was a 3-
year course in moral education all by itself. It made me ashamed.
I realized what I'd done. Archbishop of Canterbury, dearie-be!
And there was a huge nun in my bed upstairs to boot!

When Crumply-Stoves was finished, he was breathless,
sweating, his tongue out like a lapdog's. His temples visibly
throbbed.

'WELL!' he demanded. 'WELL!'

I made a little croaking sound, then went chee-hee-hee,
took a piece of crested notepaper from the pile, picked up
my pen, waving it pompously over the paper, wrote a few
words, and drew an octopusfrog within the flourish of my
signature. It was my resignation.

'It's all yours, Simeon, my boy' I said, handed it to him,
and walked out.

I had one last go on the nun, one spin around my cathedral,

and – dressed in one of Bug's Olympic tracksuits, the gold medallion around my gigglesome throat – I walked away from my powerful life forever. The green hills of England were under my feet once more. I was no longer a scoundrel, just a bird.

ARCHIE BISHOP'S WARTIME MEMOIRS

The Sleepless Chaffinch

Quotes of the Century:

'When we have lost as many men as I have eaten chips,
then and only then will we have lost this war!'
*Field Marshal Edwin S. Pithy, Commander in Chief,
English Field Forces, Western Front, 2082*

'I have done nothing wrong. It was as natural for me to
dominate the planet as a tiger to rule his woods. In the
end, admit it, I was only expressing the will of the people,
and the will of the people is the same as the will of Allah.
I am a simple man.'
Baba Jammaluddin, Grand Mufti, at his trial, 2084

'After the boggn Armistice there wasn't a minute when I
knew what to do with my hands. Now I've found summick
to do with them. Pleasy-do find enclosed, 2 ears.'
*Hogley James Browell, 'Hog the Ripper', in a note to
police, 2086*

1

The Gathering Storm

Tadese and I have a fooly-doos game with oranges – do we not, Tadese? He throws an orange up to me on my pole, I catch it, then I hoi it back down to him, he catches it. The one that drops a catchable catch (we can argue for days about whether a catch was catchable or not) has to show the other his pozzy. I have seen Tadese's big black pozzy many more times than he has seen my skinny white one – not cos I am better at the game, but cos when I show him my pozzy Tadese closes his good eye. Tadese – you are the finemostest gentleman of the 21st Century! Make sure you put that down in the book, pleasy-do.

Anyhowdoos, when he turns the hosepipe on me Tadese sees each inch of this sagging jangle of crisscrossy wrinkles my body has become. Chee! Last year's rosehip for a head, baked piggy nose, yellow toothed, nearly dead. Dearie-be! Can you imagine me young, Tadese? – smooth and bright! I shall speaky-do of a day on which I was.

Summer of 2020. Guru Hudkin-Bynd sent me and Brother Bromley to Majorca to a multi-faith religious camp, where we could meet thoughtful young people from all over the globe and perhaps have sex with them. (My Guru didn't object to the sexual intercourse.)

Brother Bromley was back in camp with sunstroke. I went down to the beach at Arenal for a midnight swim, alone. I remember that swim well. It was like washing the boyhood off me. I swam way out and looked back at the white lights of the hotels and a fiery barbecue some of the other religious nuts from the camp were having on the beach. Then I emptied my lungs and sank down, deep down, in the black water, nervous of monsters grabbing me in the salty dark, but bravely just hanging there underwater until something inside my head ordered me up. A little wiggle of my feet and I began an ascension – was this how it felt to be assumed to Heaven, I wondered? I said the Lord's Prayer, but was just forgiving those who trespass against us, when the lights of the shore sparked into the blackness. I held myself, bursting, inches underwater, to finish my prayer – if I don't finish, I told myself, I shall never be a good man! I finished, surfaced without splash, gasped in the air I needed, blew the saltwater out of my pre-rhinoblasted nose, then lay on my back and, giggling all the way, waggled my feet for shore.

I sat on the sand, reading my Bible by the light of the big barbecue fire, full of the simple blissful happiness I believed was the lot of a religious life. Suddenmost, a gigantic boy, supposey-do he was 15, no more, bounded up to me, holding in each hand like the scales of divine justice, a paper plate piled high with paella. He plonked down beside me, his back to the fire.

'Eat, little priest!' he said, shoving a paella at me.

'Thanky-be, brother,' I said.

We sat eating with our fingers, both young and happy and full of chee. Had I made a new friend, I wondered, a witness to my life, someone I would know and laugh with all my days?

Hoots, but he was a biggn! His skin looked like a banana on the turn, yellow with freckly brown mottles. He had a mouth like a fish dipped in irony. His belly was vast and wobbly, hanging over the Confederate-stars-and-stripes shorts he was wearing. He had pointy bosoms like a young girl's. And his low chuckle – he chuckled as he ate – was supernatural: it seemed to come at me from all sides, from the fire and the sea. Wot a remarkable boy he was!

Suddenly, he spoke! 'Do you believe in a compassionate God?'

No pause to reflect, straight back at him: 'I certainly do.'

'Spinoza says that God has no emotions.'

'He was wrong!' (In those days if my faith was challenged I tended to become obstreperous.) 'Spinoza was Jewish – the Jews have a tradition of that particular view, a view which Jesus came into the world to refute forever.'

I thought he was going to laugh. But no: serious. His hands rested in his paella.

'Yes, the Jews,' he said thoughtfully.

He still hadn't announced his own faith. He had the shape of a particularly gross Buddha, but Moslem was my first guess cos of the energetic aggression in him. Or perhaps he was he something primitive, shamanistic! After a few crammed mouthfuls of paella he settled my argument.

'Have you ever studied the Holy Quoran?'

Quick as a blink: 'I have. Rigorously.'

'But still a Christian?'

'Of course!'

The 'of course' broke him up. His bosoms wobbled as his chee filled the night.

'OH, LITTLE PRIEST!' he said over and over, slapping his knees, and wiping tears of glee from his eyes.

Then suddenly he was on his feet! Wot – a fight? The beach barbecue's fire ringed his sumotori figure with an outline of flame. He skimmed his plate into the sea, showering me with leftover paella. Then, his arms spread wider than a dragon's wings, he commenced spinning.

He span around the fire, through the fire, kicking sand, laughing never breathlessly, around and around and around, till I forgot he was a boy at all – he was a shape, a living shape, spinning in the Mediterranean night. Spinning, whirling, spinning.

Then he was gone from the beach! Disappeared? Where was he? There he was – somehow way off, walking up the promenade towards the shops. He waved a big hand. I waved back with one of my little ones.

Next day I looked for him in the camp. But he'd flown back home that morning to where he came from. He was Baba Jammaluddin, an Indonesian student of Islamic Law. How sad I was that my new friend was gone. We did not meet again for nearly 50 years.

2067: the English government, appeasing the Grand Mufti's increasing power, had handed Jesus over to him.

'I'll go with you,' I said.

'That would be very nice,' HE said.

We were taken to the Mufti's new palace on the island of Majorca. He'd bought the whole island from Spain and built his Xanadu there in defiance of the European powers and the Christian God. Outside, there were gunslinging moustachioed troops everywhere in uniforms the colour of pea-soup. Inside, all was calm.

A single soldier led us in. We weren't bound or anything. We just sauntered in like guests. He left us on a pink patio from where we could see Baba Jammaluddin, the Grand Mufti, swimming in a pool, with a dozen of the most beautiful girls in the world swimming in formation behind him. Then he turned, and they turned, he turned again, they matched his movement, all very graceful. Was this some kind of performance for us? The girls went underwater and came up around the Mufti like the petals on a flower. He began to spin, very gently at first, then faster – being 40 stones, his land-spinning days were probably behind him! – then span faster still until he was a sallow blur in a whirlwind of white water. He gradually slowed down and as he did his encirclement of girls sank around him. Suddenly they sprang out of the water, diving over the Mufti, and when this movement was complete both girls and Mufti were submerged under the reflection of the palace. After a bit, the girls surfaced, climbing out over the side, laughing as they dried each other off. But there was no sign of the Mufti. I hoped he'd drowned.

20 minutes later he came belly-first through the olive trees clad in a black towelling dressing-gown and gold slippers. His tongue clicked. Impossible! Yes! He was speaking to me in the language of 'the Others'. Jesus had lived among my attic kin for 5 years but hadn't picked up a click. But here was the Devil himself, clicking away as fluently as Wilf. How? I give up wondering how.

'Howdeedoodee, little priest,' his click said. 'Do you still believe in a compassionate God?'

'I boggn do, matey!' I clicked back.

He chuckled. Then I, a bit-player in this story after all, was left alone while Jesus and the Mufti walked in the olive grove and conversed in Malay, which Jesus had learnt in anticipation of this historic meeting. I sat on a wall and ogled the girls of the Mufti's harem. I gave twinklefingered waves but they were well trained and didn't wave back. Then a soldier came and moved me off the wall.

I waited for hours. It was the time when they were torturing HIM. But when Jesus and the Mufti came back they were both smiling. The man who shook hands for the Mufti came forward to do just that, but the Mufti shook Jesus's hand himself – a rare honour. They must've come to some sort of arrangement. It was going to be okaydoos! Thank God!

Jesus came over to me, pale and limping, and put his hands on my shoulders, looking down on my pig's face from his lanky height.

'He is going to kill us, Chaffy. Right away, this afternoon, pleasy-do.'

I looked at the girls milling poolside and thought: no, I'll never have five minutes alone with any of them. Then I saw the Mufti, sitting in an alcove in conference with some accountants. Jesus and I were just another detail in his busy life. We hardly mattered at all.

Wellaroo, who does not know what happened next! They roped us to a huge cross, Jesus on one side, me on the other, and carried us onto a goods plane. Way over the Mediterranean they pushed us out. Down we fell towards the blue sea. No land in sight. Clouds far off: a summer storm keeping itself to itself. On the falling cross I felt no fear, for HE was with me. It was like a ride on a funfair.

Then we hit the water and plunged deep, bubblesomely. I said the Lord's Prayer in my head. I don't know how many times I said it. My chest was bursting. Then I passed out and awoke with the sun in my eyes. The cross was floating in the sea, my side uppermost. Jesus was face down under the water, the heavy cross keeping him there. I struggled in the ropes, but the crashlanding hadn't loosened them.

Those 2 days floating on the cross, I had a childish half-hope of a Resurrection from my unfortunate friend. But no, not this time. He'd been an artificial Messiah for an unreal age. When the French Navy launch fished us out of the water I couldn't look at HIM – something in the sea had eaten half his face away. But I held HIS cold hand all the way home and wept saying: 'Why THEE and not I? WHY?' He was buried in Ely Cathedral.

*

A mufti is a Moslem cleric who is a judge of Islamic law, who pronounces upon how a Moslem should conduct every aspect of his life. A Grand Mufti is a mufti in chief. There was one in the days of the Ottoman Empire, when the Sultan and his Wazir couldn't make a move without the Grand Mufti's okaydoo. But 'twas a position only properlymost possible in times of empire, so when the Ottomans lost their empire, there were still plenty muftis but no grand one. But when, in our own century, a bigcheese mufti cobbled up the Grand Alliance of Moslem States for himself, then there was an empire again, was there not, to be the Grand Mufti of.

The modern Grand Mufti was the managing director of the new universal Mohammedanism which, much to our jowl-wagging befuddlement in England, was the dominant idea of the century – a passion and comfort, a beautiful friend, an ordersome ever-growing fraternity for over half the people of God's little blue ball.

The Grand Mufti ruled no country, had his face on no coins, nowt like that. There were a 100 Moslem leaders, despots, generals, who ruled their own countries. But these countries were stuffed full of fervent folk who desperately wanted their leaders to do the will of Allah, and that will was known best by the muftis, and best of all, when history provided him, by their overlord, the great unifier, stirrer-upper, Napoleonic bigboy, antichrististic ox . . . ERH!

Baba Jammaluddin, a Sufi of the Naqshbandi order, began his career as the Mufti of Sarawak. Soon he emerged as the leading Mufti of Indonesia, with its 300 million souls turning from their boomy-do economy to face Mecca 7 times a day. China was turning Moslem and Jammaluddin consolidated his power by adding chunks of that to his muftidom. Not quite 'Grand' yet, but nearly so. In the '30s he made pilgrimages in the Middle East, in Uzbekistan, Pakistan and all the other Asiatic stans. He made contacts, influenced people. The Arabs loved him – he was a prophet, a holy one! Wherever he went, ecstatic riots. Arab leaders began consulting him – they had to! By 2040 he was Grand Mufti over the entire expanding Moslem world. His message was simple: join us and feel the freedom of the brotherhood, enlightenment is the gift of Allah, and he is generous.

When some Christian countries proved stubbornly Christian, he was vexed but bided his time. Conversions were multitudinous in the Far East, stampedish in eastern Europe and among the Scots Kingdoms. Eventually he would have everything. But after the Middlesborough Crisis created a new political balance, he grew impatient – he was getting old and wanted to see his Grand Design complete. Meanwhile, strong new secular leaders had emerged who wanted rid of him. And other muftis imagined they were him. It is when a despot's power is waning that he is at his most dangerous. The Holy War was a card he was ready to play, and on February 13th 2079, suddenly, to the surprise of everyone except himself, he played it.

I was in the American Bar in Middlesborough 666, drinking mint juleps. It was an all-male bar, of course. Segregation was total then. Men and women didn't even speak! The band were playing a song called *21st Century Blues*.

> *Blues, 21st Century blues*
> *are getting me down.*
> *Who's got those weary*
> *21st Century blues.*
> *Why, if there's a God in the sky,*
> *why doesn't he grin?*
> *Way above this weary*
> *21st Century din . . .*

These were the fat years, when folds, flesh, bellies, big pink bums were all the fashion, when a man's clothes were always too tight for him, and he was proud of nothing more than an enormous waist measurement. Supposey-do, food was being used to compensate for the absence of sex. So there wasn't a man in the American Bar that night under 20 stones, some prizepiggily more. After 3 years in a hermit's cell in Ireland where, more greedy than fashion conscious, I'd lived chocaholically and caked my cake hole constantly while skipping through the *Summa Theologica*, I was a hefty 16 stone dumpling myself and hoped for more! Cheemost jollificatious to be in a crowd again, I was wearing a red woolly wig, pyjama bottoms, and a dinner jacket too small for my new portliness. I was eating chocolates and peanuts at the same time, but was laughing so much I kept spitting a mulch of them out, spraying an enormous blubbergut's white shirt, which amused him as much as it did me. How many mint juleps? I lost count after 24.

Suddenly the band whined to a halt, the lights went up, the glitterballs lost all their colours, and the singer stepped away from the mike. An brow-mopping army major took his place.

'Sorry-bees to spoil the fun, chapperoos,' he said. 'But Turkish troops have taken Vienna. New Arbroath's been overrun. There have been vaporizer attacks on London, Rome and Middlesborough 1. Would all reserve officers pleasy-do return to their homes and wait for a televisit to receive orders. Thanky-tata . . .' He stepped away from the mike, then back: 'And may God help us all.'

My face was wet with tears. The next morning, using the bogus identity of Rev Archie Bishop – cos as Chaff Chaffinch I was wanted by the police for doing the sexual intercourse with Janet of Venus, Mrs Pittipaldi and a nun – I joined the Suffolk regiment as a chaplain. I started as lieutenant but got my captaincy after the 2nd big push.

Marching through London for embarkation to the front, we saw the effect of the vaporizer attack. The middle of the city, from the Bank of England to Connie and Pam Park, was gone, down to the bare rock. Saint Paul's was only half there, its whispering gallery open to the blare of air-raid sirens, which never stopped. (A week later the remaining half of the cathedral collapsed.) Evermost ploppy-pantsishly scared, we of the Suffolk Regiment marched on, every step taking us closer to the fervent janissaries of the Grand Mufti.

2

The Shapely Legs of September Chaffinch

The Mufti War began with much activity on both sides, shooting off all kinds of fireworks. Troops ran across continents in hours. Everyone was scurrymost, like mice caught in a barn. The Mufti's big vaporizer looked like it was going to win it for him right at the start, but it blew a gasket and wasn't fixed till after the war, when it vaporized itself, poor thing.

After that hectic beginning we settled down to a stalemate in a favourite battleground, Flanders: English facing Mussulmen over a muddy No Man's Land where a constant lightshow of phasers and vaporizers kept us barmy for three long years, entrenched and isolated in a dream of war. And there was this evermost sorry bird, trench foot up to his oxters, a faithless army chaplain, closing the eyes of poor pudgy boys on chaos.

Many members of my family, some of whom I had christened with water dripped from my own fingers, were among the fallen. Wilf joined up at the first clarion. He was sent to the Polish Front and was vaporized within hours of arrival in the warzone, caught in mid-howl, dear darling old fool. Winston, bulldogishly eager to do his bit, went along to look after him and faded at his friend's side. Funny thing, the day Wilf died Dame Tuna found his latest sheep wife dead in her pen. 3 of Nelli's boys, Hoss, Turbot and Clancy died on the Western Front during the 1st big push. Rhino's boy Rhino Jr, a Moslem, died fighting for the other side.

I was sure I'd be next, was I not, and hardly cared. One day, helping the wounded back from a raid, I was caught on the edge of a widebeam vaporizer. When I got back to camp and stood in the shower the water didn't wet me, didn't touch me, passed straight through. I took neon tablets for weeks before I could shower, wipe my poz, or poke myself in the eye again.

Millions weren't so lucky. I remember a little push just before a big push. 2,000 chapperoos went over the top from our length of trench – climbing out with ludicrous effort, cos they were mostly 25 stone plus. Three came back, lumbering hungrily home. One had a hole in him I could see the smoky sky through, a clean bloodless hole. He flopped into the trench and I hurried to his side.

'Is that you, vicar?'

'The Lord is with you, my son, or at least I am.'

His eyes were singed blind by a phaser blast and the vaporizer had taken his belly off him. I could see his inner workings, red and pumping, around a hole big enough to climb through. In minutes the hole would collapse and he would die.

'Been cheesed, have I vicar?'

'Triflely so, yes. Too-too evermost.'

'But I'm still FAT, aren't I vicar? Horribly grossly FAT?'

'Very fat, shockingly fat, my boy, a real fattie.'

He grinned. 'Supposey-do, I'm the fattest sergeant-major in the English Army, ehwot?'

But he was feeling with a nervous hand, and he knew.

'Looka that double chin, vicar! Mighty pendulous, innit? Could I have some chips, d'yerthinks?'

Then he was gone.

A double-helpings-of-everything captain was watching this little scene. I saw him out of the corner of my eye while I tended that other unfortunate. He'd come back from the jaunt too, one of the 3. When I turned to look at him, he waved, then he faded away. The 3rd returnee from our little push, that was me, Chaplain Archie Bishop. I was alone in the trench, breathing its dank air. In all my years of hermiting I had never been so terrifyingly alone, never wished for a friendly smile more. I lay on my bunk, sobbing, and waited to fade. But I did not fade.

The vaporizer was like that. Delayed effect. Sometimes days later, when you hadn't even known you'd been hit, you could fade before your own shaving mirror. I was once standing well back in the chipwaggon queue, when everyone in front of me started anxiously poking each other in their pot bellies. Next thing they vanished and I was at the front of the queue.

'Here, wot's your game?' said the man in the chipwaggon, looking for his 30-odd lost customers.

The war was going badly. Strewth be told, we were too fat for fighting. The High Command, an idiot's club, the fattest of the fat, were so stressed out by their duties that they were prone to imminent heart attack. The night before the 2nd big push, 12 of them died in their sleep, tearing the buttons off their pyjamas as their hearts beat painful last beats. This meant, in theory at least, that younger officers with fresh ideas could move quickly up the ranks. But when they got promoted these overstuffed young lions hurried straight into the High Command Mess and over-overstuffed themselves with the excellent fare provided there, until they could barely move. Soon they were like their senior colleages: too fat to walk more than five steps! The entire top brass had to be carried into their Strategy Meetings on litters, looking like a summit of mandarins. If their opinion was asked, they were usually so bloated with lunch that all they could do was burp. I know for a fact that Field Marshal Forlsweston was promoted from Major to Head of Field Operations just cos he managed to burp at all the right moments. He was in charge two hours when he fell dead on his map table. His successor did the same a fortnight later.

Nearly 3 years of whizz-bangs, lightshows, not to mention the twangy Arabian music they blared at us across No Man's Land, had me numbed, my face frozen in a look like that of a whipped dog wanting love. But I was not depressed, pleasy-do. I was of use. The boys needed me. They clung to me cos I was that most respected thing: a survivor. At night in our muddy trench apartments, the Muz fizzing the night outside with his phaser barrage, I'd tell them stories of the '24 Revolution, and of my luridmost sexual exploits – nigh-on 20 years of the various phases of segregation meant that I was the only non-virgin among these vigorous fighting men.

But then there were nights when I was alone in the muddy apartments, when all the chubby cheeks who'd smiled at my cheesomeness the night before were now invisible men in No

Man's Land who would never see England again. And when the corporal with our nightly order of pizzas came, he'd say: 'Let's you and me eat the boggn lot ourselves feastmostly, vicar, ehwot?' And we had many such feasts the pizza corporal and I. He survived the war and opened his own pizza parlour in, I believe, Doncaster.

When the Mufti destroyed Israel, that was the lowest point. We used to read aloud to each other from the Middlesborough Gazette all the brave things the Israeli army did. It was cheemost hootifalarious to read of those raids of theirs, thousands of miles from their home base, singeing the Mufti's beard. Brilliantmost everso! Israel itself was safe behind its forcefield – the strongest on earth. The vaporizers zapped at it all day but hardly ever punched a hole. But all along the Mufti's agents had been constructing a vaporizer inside Israel, in Jerusalem, and when they set it off the whole country was hit in an intense widebeam. For weeks Jerusalem was a ghost city full of transparent people. They couldn't even strike a match to light candles. They walked through the wailing wall. They crowded into the synagogues but there could be no crush. Some treated the whole thing as God's last joke on the Jews, calling out to everyone they passed by: 'Are you still here? Thought you'd be long gone. Mazel tov!' In Jerusalem they gathered on rooftops, on the Mount of Olives, and dreamily watched the end of a dream. And it came to pass that Israel disappeared, like Rome, like most of London, gone without trace. One man, a certain Nathan Fenkle, survived. He had been the victim of a vaporizer street-attack and was doped up on neon. There he was, alone, wailing on the bare rock.

The night it happened, I looked at the little map in the back of my Bible, speaking the names of vanished places – Bethlehem, Nazareth, Jericho – and wondered was I still a prisoner of the Grand Mufti and was this some facetious dream he was churning through my head?

My nephew September commanded a unit attached to the Spanish Resistance. They had a forcefield cap over Torremolinos, and launched constant missions from there to sting the Mufti. I wasn't worried about Sep. He'd come through. No sorry ending for him. A peaceful old-age end in his bed at Chaffinch Hall for him, the chaffinches pirrisuping on his windowledge. Sep was a career army man. He'd fought at Plovdiv as a youngster. Then he left the army for a bit, came back, took a job in the War Office and was a 44-year-old colonel when the Mufti War broke out. If he hadn't been in Spain, he'd have been a General before the 1st big push forsure! My sort of fella, was Sep. He looked stupid, sounded stupid, but had unguessable spiritual depths. He'd tried his hand at literature, writing 3 booky-doos. He started with a biography of Connie, of Connie and Pam fame, advocating her greatness to the detriment of Pam – a worthless hussy, he claimed. The book was generously illustrated with glamour shots of Connie and mugshots of Pam yawning or after an all-night bash – this falling in with his theme. It was a good book, at times bluffly poetic. His 2nd book was a life of the 20th Century despot Adolf Hitler, concentrating mainly on his last years in Argentina. After a bit it veered off its vile subject onto its author's gauchoing adventures in the Pampas. His third book, a thick novel about a nittyhaha young solider at Plovdiv, I've tried to read 8 times but never got beyond page 4.

Sep played the trumpet, took it everywhere with him, except on missions. His improvizations were jaunty, aggressive blares, like hunting calls, but for the hunting of lumbering chimeras, not little foxes. Before a mission, he'd give it a tootsome puff or two, then hang it on the wall, salute it, and walk off to see what fate allowed.

Early in '81 English Intelligence communicated to Torremolinos Base that the Mufti had just arrived at his palace in Majorca. Sep had been waiting for this occurrence. He played his trumpet for a bit, then hung it on the wall, more caresomely than usual. His officers knew something was up, and Sep knew that they knew something was up – he could see their reflections in the valves of his trumpet, watching his back eagerly.

A brave one spoke: 'Jaunt, is it, sir?'

Sep turned, grinning. 'Jaunt? – I'll say. One to remember, thissin'll be!'

Delighted hee-haws all round.

'Where to, Colonel?'

Sep twizzled his pale moustache. 'Fish supper with our pal Tufti Mufti, ehwot!'

Applause and cheers as he went to the blackboard to explain the mission.

The plan was to fly whizzycopters towards the Mufti's palace till they activated its defensive vaporizer. Then they'd buzz at the same point, right at the edge of the vaporizer's range, all of them shooting at exactly the same point. Theory was, this would make the defences focus mightily on that point, so that a smaller team could slip though farther down the coast under less flakarooney. This was a mission to assassinate the Grand Mufti. Had it succeeded the war would have ended 2 years earlier and millions of lives would have been saved.

Sep lost most of his men teasing the defences. But three whizzycopters got through. Sep was in one of them. His legs, however, had been badly faded on the way in. He could no longer see them. But their ghosts would be there long enough, he hoped, for him to complete his mission. Those 3 brave men ran past that same pool where 14 years earlier Jesus and I had watched the Mufti swimming with his harem. As always, the palace was lightly guarded inside. They zapped the dozen guards they found. Then one of Sep's men lightly gripped his arm.

'Sorry, sir, seem to be fading. Luckmost-doos with the jaunt. Tell Nigel I . . . oh, well, nevermind! Toodlybyebye.'

He faded away.

A seemingly legless Sep with only one man left to command ran legglessly into the harem. Perfume reeks, petal-strewn pools and beddy alcoves. It was the home of some of the Mufti's older wives, favourites he kept on for sentimental reasons. Sep's lieutenant had his shooter pointed at their screams. He was going to vaporize the piggnboggn lot.

'We're not like that, are we?' said Sep, Englishly, holding him back.

'Triple sorries, Colonel – but actuallydoos, it's not the enemy I've gottit infor as such, it's just, well . . . I don't like fems, that's all.'

Sep backslapped him. 'Carry on, then. Good man.'

He zapped the piggnboggn lot. All that fading beauty turned to air! All the memories of the Mufti's youthful kisses, as gone as Jerusalem!

Sep found the Mufti in his library, deep in contemplation over a book of ancient Persian love poetry, his beard between his fingers. He took two steps towards him, steadying his aim. The Mufti looked up goggled with surprise, and then Sep's flabby English body fell to the floor with a huge spank. He'd lost his ghost legs and dropped! Pulling himself up by a bookshelf, he made aim again. But suddenly books were bonking him all over and he caught sight of the Mufti's purple caftan spinning through a secret door.

Legless, his mission failed, he may well have turned his zapper on himself. But Sep wasn't that kind of man. He walked out of there on his hands, laughing bluffly at his own predicament.

Back in London, Sep reported to the Army Hospital to be operated upon. They were going to use a revolutionary technique on him, one which the war was giving them opportunities to perfect. His legs would be replaced in their entirety. Total tissue renewal was achieved by injecting a plastic substance into each of the individual cells which made up the patient's stumps. This created in the cells an insistence that the messages they sent down the legs be replied to, and the vaporized legs simply grew back, like fingernails, to answer this call.

Sep went to convalesce at Chaffinch Hall, waiting for the miracle to occur. Toes appeared on his stumps after a week. Feet a month later. He couldn't see them – his paunch was in the way. But he could shuffle down the corridors on them, whacking all the doors with his sticks.

'I'VE GOT FEET!' he yelled.

But the legs took longer. He was impatient – he was missing the war!

'Like a boggn tadpole, waiting for me legs!' he grumbled.

His sister Cherries, Dame Tuna, Nelli and other Chaffinch women were at the Hall during this difficult time for Sep, but cos of segregation they never so much as came to ask him how he was. His batman prepared all his meals and saw to his wants.

'Legs coming along nicely, sir.'

'On their way, thanky-bees!'

But when they finally suddenly arrived one night, full length and stepsome, they were women's legs and there was nothing anyone could do to change them. Sep was a great big 30-stone stonker of a man, with the prettiest, shapeliest pair of fem pins that there was, worthy of the G.M.'s harem. What must he have felt, standing before his dressing-mirror that spring evening in '81!

'Dimmee, wottle the chaperoos say when they kop a butcher's at these!' he complained to his doctor at the Army Hospital.

The doctor stroked his patient's knees, a fey little smile on his moon face.

Sep did the manly thing. He kicked him in the dangly-doos with his girlie foot. Then he went down to his club starkers to get the embarrassment over with. His blubbersome chipfed torso wobbled in on its shapely new legs. After the whistles the remarks began . . .

'Silky thighs, Chaffinch! Haw-Hee!' said a General.

'Get thee to a nunnery!' guffawed another.

'Knees up Mother Chaffinch, ehwot!'

'Can I watch ya paint ya toenails, Sep! Hooo-hooo-hooo-hoo-hooo!'

He walked up and down till he'd heard every remark that the limited English imagination would ever think up about his legs. As some remarks were coming around for a 3rd time he was satisfied that he would never be embarrassed by his girlie legs again. He leggily legged it out of there, light of heart, off to the War Office to arrange his re-embarkation. He bought new shoes on the way, and some high heels which he didn't wear till after the war.

By Christmas of '82 it looked as if we'd lost. The Mufti had moved uncountable Chinese troops into Germany and was marshalling them to rush our positions and wipe us out. Meanwhile, the lightshows were more frenetic. And all we did in return was eat chips! The High Command had long lunches, longer naps, and woke up with their arteries blocked, gasping.

Christmas Eve. A soft snow falling which endured for moments on a held-out hand, but turned black when it touched the mud. I was on leave in Nancy, going from bar to bar, looking for anyone I knew. My nephew Cole, Sep's dad, was in this theatre, but I hadn't run into him yet. I found him, his head in a fountain, sandwiches in all his pockets.

'Cole, my old friend!'

We only had time to shake hands, tell each other we were too old for this nonsense and smile sadly about lost Wilf. He'd started chinwagging the story of Sep's legs when the most enormous solider I'd ever seen plode up to us.

'Here, you be a chaplin, issint you? – You be wanted at HQ! Pronto. No larky: hoppit!'

Field Marshal Pithy had had a stroke. He was in his chair, staring, his left hand twitching. The tent was chockablock with top brass, eating butties, as happy as maggots. There was no medical team there. Wasn't necessary, they said.

'Say your stuff and bog off,' ordered a General.

I looked into the Field Marshal's eyes and saw what I always saw, suffering contemplating itself for the last time.

'The Lord is with you, my son, or at least I am.'

A long final breath came from his hippopotamic body. But no mourning from the General Staff. They were cockahoop. Drinks all round. I had a shandy. Someone threw me a hot bag of chips. A man covered in medals doused them in vinegar for me.

'The poor man is dead!' I complained. 'And you are partying! Wot's . . . erm . . .?'

'DON'T YOU REALIZE WHAT THIS MEANS, VICAR? IT'S WHAT WE'VE BEEN WAITING FOR! YOU KNOW WHO GETS THE BIG CAP NOW, EHWOT! HARH! THE BOGGN WAR'S AS GOOD AS WON!'

Then chips were dropped, everyone to attention, saluting the new commanding officer. In he came. A tall man, comparatively slim, with a breezy smile. Instead of a swaggerstick he swang half a golf putter. When it was my turn to be handshook

I exclaimed: 'Aren't you, weren't you, Herring Carstairs, the famous pnong player?'

'Harh!' he went. 'Dimme, ehwot, vicar?'

'We've never met, but Severiano Chaffinch was my cuz. He spoke of you often.'

'Vicar was he, yer cuz?'

'No, sir, a golfer, like yourself.'

'Harh well, tha knows, this head's been vaporized off 3 times, dimme not, harh. Can't remember Lewisham, even. Where? Harh! These synthetic-sprouts-off-yer-neck noggin jobbies just aren't the . . . did you say Lewisham? I'm always mugging over trenchtop, d'yersee, giving the finger to old Muz. Fizzywizzy, zappo: no head! HARH! Lost me finger too. Look, thissin isn't mine. Harh! Boggn war, ehwot!'

Then he clonked me affectionately on the head with his putter and stood over the map table to make a rallying speech. The dead eyes of his predecessor looked on.

'Now lads, dimme, we're not at the 18th green yet, and we're well over par, and, let's be HARH! honest, we're in the rough on the 3rd. Johnny Chinaman's come to ruin our game when we've still gotta chance for a birdie, ehwot? Harh! . . .'

The speech went on golfingly for hours. The top brass sneaked chips into their gobs as they listened. It was nearly Christmas. I slipped outside and crunched on the frozen puddles. The mud was hard everywhere. I walked to the end of a road and joined some young soldiers who were watching the distant lightshow above the trenches 10 miles away.

'Pretty, innit?' said one.

'Happymost Chiristmassydodars,' I said.

We all shook hands.

'It's going to be okaydoos,' I told them. 'Guess who's the new Head Boy? Herring Carstairs – tha knows, the famous pnong player!'

They'd never heard of him. But I was buoyant. I could see the headlines: CARSTAIRS WIBLEYS MUFTI. The victory parades were already starting in my heart. I loved Carstairs. He was my hero. Him and his vaporized head and wonky finger. He'd win us this war, I knew.

But a month later in the wearying January cold, an English victory seemed a bird's birdbrained dream. The first Chinese had swept over us and it couldn't be long before their final big push and the end for us. Every night I had a compulsion to go over the top and stand by the wire till a vaporizer united me with Bro Wilf and countless others.

It was the dawn of a strange day. They'd sent those flying vaporizers over, shaped like owls, only used in the last weeks of the war. They'd swooped zappingly over the trench when the men were on their way to breakfast. ZAPAMO! ZAPAMUS! ZAPAMANT! Fading men were crying out to God in their fear and agony. I splished through the mud and knelt beside them, briefly one, then hurrying to another, holding their hands as once I had held HIS.

'The Lord is with you my son, or at least I am.'

'Chaff! Chaff – don't you recognize me?'

I didn't. His face was a burnt fading blur.

'Cole. It's Cole.'

I sobbed his name, over and over. Poor Cole! I'd known him all his long life, and now this.

'I haven't lost weight, have I, Chaff? I was over 30 stones, tha knows. Just over.'

'No, no, you are still as fat as ever.'

He sighed with relief. His face was just a mouth and an eye now, but the rest of his body was mostly there.

'My boy, Sep, fighting with the resistance in Spain – you'll tell him, ehwot? And look after him for me, hm?'

'Naturallydoos.'

'SEP! SEP! YOU'RE HERE! SEP!'

He struggled to get up, his hands reaching pathetically for the sky where he believed Sep to be. I held him down. It took all my strength. Then his mouth and eye dropped out of the outline where they floated and sank into the evil mud. Someone was screaming. It was me.

Around me, men were leaning on the trench wall, chewing slowly, staring skywards with the strange dawn light pinkifying their already pinksome faces. I looked where they were looking. It was Sep, hugemostly in the sky! A mile-high vision! He wore just underpants and his legs were truly beautiful.

I scrambled out of the trench and threw off my helmet.

'SEP? SEP, MY BOY! CAN IT BE YOU?'

'HOWDEEDOODEE, UNCLE CHAFF! I'VE CUM TO SEE HOW MY OLD DAD'S DOING. IS HE ABOUT?'

I sobbed: 'OH, SEP – HE HAS JUST THIS MINUTE EXPIRED!'

'BOGGN HELL'S CHIPS! THIS PIGGN MACHINE DON'T WORK SO WELL WHEN THERE'S SO MUCH EMOTION ABOUT, THA KNOWS, WHAT WITH THE ARMISTICE AND ALL.'

'ARE YOU A GHOST, SEP? AN ANGEL? HAVE YOU SEEN GOD?'

'NO, NO, OLD SOLDIER – I'M DREAMING, 'TIS ALL, WITH THE AID OF THE MILLICENT. JUST BOUGHT IT.'

By 'bought it' I took it he meant he had just been killed and I was on my knees before this Y-fronted beatific vision, this proof of an afterlife.

'I'LL CATCH DADDY ANOTHER DAY, WHEN HE WAS ALIVE, IF YOU FOLLOW ME DRIFT. TOODLEBYEDAR, UNCLE CHAFF!'

A thick vaporizer ray shot through him as he faded. I slipped back into the trench and lay flat out in the mud, wheezing, uncomprehending, chuntering amid a rekindled faith. The Millicent? A ghost? An angel? Armistice? Wot armistice?

My friend the pizza corporal helped me up. I muttered. He yelled joyously in my ear. We were in No Man's Land, by the wire. There was no lightshow. Ehwot? Mussulmen and Johnny Chinaman were shaking hands with our chaperoos through holes in the wire. It was over. This was the Armistice. The vision had spoken right. Carstairs had done it! Wiblied the boggn Mufti to Hell!

I went home believing September to be among the lost. It was some time before the meaning of that mysterious vision in the sky became known to me.

3

The Only People Doing It!

When I, or I should say the newly-promoted Major Chaplain
Archie Bishop, was de-mobbed I hadn't the heart, did I, to
return to Chaffinch Hall, not even to show off in my new
major's uniform. All the old faces were gone: Wilf, Winston,
Hoss, September. Rhino was there, but he'd been sloshed
since the Theocracy abdicated and I'd always detested him
anyway. There were just the women and they wouldn't have
spoken to me. So, while half-thinking what to do next with
my few remaining years, I stayed in Hammersmith with a
jollymost chaperoo who had been Dame Tuna's 3rd husband.
He'd been in the catering corps in the war and was always
saying it was chips that won it for us, never mind Carstairs
and our brave Korean allies.

My second night there, a week out from Flanders, he
came in waving tickets for the Last Night of the Proms. My
nerves were shatteroonied. I didn't want to go. Then he said
it was the only public occasion where men and women were
allowed to mix.

'Coo, errr! Okaydoos!' I said.

It was nigh-on the most emotional occasion I ever lived
through. When we arrived it was all hooters and streamers,
army men everywhere with their uniforms on backwards,
chips flying from the posh seats to the crush on the floor
where Dame Tuna's 3rd husband and I were laughing loud
at nothing at all. Then the orchestra played Mozart's *Missa
Solemnis*. All went silent. The music was going into everyone's heart. To set the mood they showed a hologram of
the trenches in the domed space above our heads. We saw
faces, probably dead, perhaps our own. It seemed a million
years ago, not last week. I was weeping a kind of tears I'd
never before wept. In moments of the music I was lifted

Heavenwards, soaring on bloodjets of emotion. I shook the hands of the other officers around me. They were weeping too. Oh God, the feeling of it – for the war to be over and to be alive! But as the music healed my trenchfooted soul I felt with such an intensity that I couldn't bear it and wanted death, oblivion, never to feel anything again. Was Heaven like this? An unbearable beautiful pain!

Then the programme moved onto the jingoistic stuff and I thumped along, yelling bansheeishly. Dame Tuna's 3rd husband was drawing a picture of the Mufti in his prison cell on my bald noggin, and I thought this the jollimostest wheeze possible. We had wine and hotdogs and wanted the music to go on forever. The Korean conductor got more cheers than I've ever heard for anybody.

Then, between the 3rd and 4th encores of *Land of Hope and Glory*, I saw a woman, one of the very few there, looking ecstatic under an exit sign. My loins twitched. There was one kind of life experience I hadn't had in 8 years! She wore a long black dress, had a spotty forehead, a hedge of frizzy indigo hair. A bit gruesome, indeedy-so. But full of life and womanishness. Suddenly, she was being chatted up by a lascivious pixilated 84-year-old man.

'Doest thou know, miss – you look just like my darling Scampi!'

She gave me a haughty, wild look that made me take a step back.

'Didn't you used to be Archbishop of Canterbury once?'

'Only once,' I quipped.

The music started, the crowd surged and we were pushed together, against the wall, under the exit sign. I could feel the softness of her flesh through her dress. Meanwhilydoos, she, sensitive creature, could see the suffering in the eyes that ogled her. The fems had been against the war, all yowling members of Blenkinsop's Peace Movement. Here was one who felt guilty about that.

'You've suffered, haven't you, in the war?'

I nodded. I knew I had her! The music started, followed by roarsome cheering. I yelled in her ear, somehow maintaining the tone of a whisper – a trick leant in the pulpit!

'Lookybee, madam, or should I say miss, I know I'm nobody's dreamboat and I must reek of trench foot ointment, but could we go somewhere, you know what I'm talking about, hm? I just want a little fundoos and to remember my youth and . . .'

'YES, it's all right, I understand! You poor thing. YES! I'll do it! I will! What an evermost custardly thing it would be: the sacrifice, the disgusting sacrifice! I'll take you home this minute and . . . we will, WE'LL DO THE SEXUAL INTERCOURSE!'

She shrieked that last bit during an unexpected pause in the music. 50, even 30 years before it would have been received with gales of earthy laughter. But in 2083, with segregation so staunch, the whole of the Albert Hall looked our way in indignation. I don't think anyone had done the sexual intercourse since I last did it myself in my palace in Canterbury with that enormous nun.

I hurried my new girlfriend out into the encircling foyer, my fingers slyly caressing the moles exposed by her backless dress. The promenaders were going wild with hooters. About to kiss her I asked: 'What's yer name, poppet?'

'July. July. July,' she said, wilder each time. I suddenly wondered if I'd got a wrongun – a terroristic fem who picked up randy old geese and wrung thier necks for them. Then the tears started to come.

'Wot's wrong, Major?'

'Nowt, pet. 'Tis just, your name, d'yersee: July. I had a nephew named after a month, September, killed in the war.'

Right on cue, a miracle. Sep, knotted in multi-coloured streamers, a hooter in each hand, came pushing through the crowd that rocked in the entranceway July and myself had lately left. I backed away, as if from a demon.

'Uncle Chaff – it's me! September.'

It was him! It was! O, joy! And in a General's uniform! I charged at him with a delighted doggy yelp, and hugged him hard to prove he was real.

'HE WHO WAS LOST IS FOUND! SEPTEMBER, MY

BOY!' Then I remembered the mystery. 'Sep! – On Armistice Day, in the trenches, when I saw you in the trenches . . .'

'I was in Spain, old boot, right through the unpleasantness. Boggn pityfala bout daddy though but.'

'Tragicmost, yes – but the Millicent? Tell me what it is? The Millicent?'

'The Millicent? Ehwot?'

Then he saw July and tipped his cap.

'He's had too much sauce on his chips,' he explained to her.

He didn't look at me after that, just her.

She lightly touched his arm. 'Scusey-be, General – would you wait there just a mo.'

'Harh!' he said, Carstairsishly, and waited while July took me aside. The straps of her dress kept falling down. I was putting them up for her, but with a clever movement of her shoulders she could drop them down again.

'You're a fine brave man,' she said. 'I'm proud to know you. And I'm going to keep my promise. I'm going to do something beautiful for you, something you'll be grateful to me for always and always.'

'Um?'

'I'm going to perform the sexual intercourse with your nephew for you – I mean, instead of you. Obviously, I couldn't perform it properly with you, you're MUCH too old.'

'Much,' I admitted, in my worst moment since I was 12.

'But it will be as if I was performing it with you, won't it?'

I went all official in my thwartedness: 'I should point out, madam, that the sexual intercourse has been illegal since 2071!'

Her laughter was louder than the climactic music. She went away arm-in-arm with September, her straps down. He looked back, confusedmostly. I'd fixed him up! He had me to thank for it, and for everything else that happened afterwards. Dearie-be.

*

July took September to her apartment in the fem sector of Highgate. It was all black crepe and leather. The vases had crows' feathers in them rather than flowers. Stuffed crows were the only nick-nacks.

'My boudoir,' she said and showed him from one black room into a blacker one.

Sep had twigged right from the start that sex was on the menu here. So far he'd just gone with the flow of the evening, letting things happen. But he'd just seen that wild look in her eyes and he was in 2 minds now.

She wiggled her hips and her black dress dropped to the floor. She was wearing a large black brassiere, but nothing else. Between her legs was a frizzy area Sep had never seen before. It reminded him of the Mufti's beard. Her pudgy moley yoghurty flesh glowed in the inky decor.

'Supposey-do no-one's done this in an age!' she said huskily.

'Harh!' said Sep, fingering his medals.

She handed him the brassiere. He didn't know what to do with it. He lay it on a bookshelf, while looking to see if any of his books were there. They weren't. Just fem stuff.

He turned back and she was meowing on the bed, legs wide, waiting to receive him. Sep had never seen a naked woman before and his wanger was wagging in his General's uniform. But something had to be gotten out of the way first.

'Looksee, madam, miss – there's summuck you ought to know about me, before we take this lark any further.'

He undressed down to his underpants and showed her his women's legs.

'The war,' he explained.

'Cor, you've better legs than I've got, no fooly-doos!'

'Yes, I can see that. It's allright, issit? I mean, you still wanna hoohar wiggly with me?'

'Uh-huh!'

She seemed twice as eager. She splayed her toes and made a noise like a donkey stuck in an elevator. Sep dropped his Y-fronts and walked to the bed with the fashionmodel walk he'd been practising in private. July was already in heights of multiple sexual ecstasies rarely achieved in this century of ours.

Then they did it. Wow! The hoohar wiggly thing. The same way everyone used to do it. But the frustration of millions, denied such romps for 25 years, was released in that one sexual intercoursing. When Sep rolled his 30-stone torso off his partner and crossed his gorgeous legs, the crows were ruffled on their stands, the windows were steamed, the bed had come off its legs, and 3 years of war had been wiped from the face of the warrior.

They sucked black lollipops. July sat on his belly, her back to his face, and looked at his legs.

'Shall I croon?' he asked. (He'd heard they liked it.)

'Wot for?'

'Dunno . . . just thought. Harh!'

She suddenly span around, humped across his mountainous paunch, and waggled his genitals with her feet, as, flicking the lollipop from one side of her bouche to the other, she said littlegirlishly: 'Seppyweppy – do you love me?'

'Love? Clocks, yes! Dimmee, I think I do, tha knows!'

She looked disappointed. Her black fingernails played with the hairs on his chest.

'For a moment there, when I was under you and couldn't breathe and my yoni was throbbing away, I thought that life was almost worth living. Biological illusion, I expect.'

'Expect so, yah.'

Looking into her eyes Sep was a tidge spooked. Her indigo irises were trembling. He could see her mind was fizzing with potty-do. Suddenly she was standing on his chest, triumphant with a thought that brought her down again, oomphing Sep as her knees thwonked onto his nipples.

'I know!' she said, delighted. 'Let's KILL ourselves. Like Romeo and Juliet. I mean, you've had the war and we've both had tonight. Life will never be as exciting again. Oh, Seppy, let's – LET's!'

'I, erm . . . Looksee . . .'

'Do you still have your army phaser?'

'No, erm, we were ordered to hand them all in. Chaps were

zapping sheep on the moors. I mean, wasn't so long ago sheep were money, ehwot! I remember in Spain, just after . . .'

It was useless trying to change the subject. She was stuck on the old one, lifting up her frizzy hair to reveal a long moley neck, muttering about suicide and letting out a kind of laughter Sep should have recognized from the attic dwellers in Chaffinch Hall.

'Erm, fancy another go?' asked Sep.

'Think how wonderful it'll be when we KILL ourselves,' she said. 'Think how outraged people will be when they find us here, naked and dead, your seeds on the sheets! Oh, Seppy!'

Sep went all officer and did the last thing a man should ever do with a woman: he spoke his mind.

'Look here, I didn't spend 3 years locking horns with the Musselmen, lose me good legs and whatfor, just to throw my life away on the whim of some flighty girl.'

She threw him out.

*

Mr Krishnaguptirishnan was a svelte hairy yogi with a charlatan's grin and a horse's laugh. But he could fly, could he not. He most certainly could. I enrolled in a how-to-fly course in his temple, which was just where the vaporizer had stopped in Connie and Pam Park. I sat on my carpet glumly for days, singing mantras in impersonation of Mr Krishnaguptirishnan, but I never did take off. One of my greatest disappointments. And there was he flying about the temple on his proggy mat, his charlatan's grin never letting up.

Sep found me there. He pulled rank on the man sitting on the next carpet and plonkydood down in his place. He looked baggy eyed and worried.

'Uncle Chaff, I've cum to you, d'yersee, cos you're a man of the world, with fems, I mean. You had goes on them in the old romantic days, then that boggn Venusian article, the nun . . .'

'Mrs Pittipaldi.'

'Her too.'

'They can't get me for it, tha knows. Scotland Yard was vaporized. All the witnesses went in the war. No evidence. Chee!'

'Well, thing is, I'm in an emotional quagmire with that bint you slipped me at the Proms t'other week.'

'I'd forgotten about that. How'd you get on?'

He waited for Mr Krishnaguptirishnan to do a flypast before he whispered miserably in my ear.

'I'm in love,' he said.

'CUSTARDLYDOOS!' I exclaimed, clapping joyously. 'And she, the girl? Does she . . . you?'

'Orm, she thinks I'm beesykneesy. But she's pottafaloo, is she not, indeed, evermost. They're not all like that, are they? She keeps talking about killing herself, and me with her!'

'She's just trying to make you express your love for her. Scampi was the same.'

'Was she?'

'Women play the oddmostest games. Triple helpings upon you. In love? Chee!'

'She had me on the top of the Toblerone Building last night.'

'Thought it was vaporized in '79.'

'New one. Taller. She tried to push me off the roof and cum with me. Die together, better than hoohar wiggly, she says. Quite a tussle there was. My girlie legs saved me. Oh, she loves those. Shaves them for me. Then licks them. Every night we do the sexual intercourse, 5, 10 times. And wot with my work at the War Office all day, I'm getting no sleep! And at my desk, when I'm not nodding off from all that missed shuteye, I get no work done – all I do is think of her and how she revolts me and how I long to have her fingernails dig in my belly. UNCLE CHAFF!!!!!!!!'

Sep yelled out for me cos, during his moan, he had taken off on his carpet without noticing and was way up there hovering with Mr Krishnaguptirishnan.

'I'm in love,' he explained to the yogi. 'That must be what's gotten me up, d'yerthink? Hm? Speeky Engleesh does yer?'

Mr Krishnaguptirishnan gave me the thumbs-up sign. Sep grabbed him angrily by the tassels of his proggy mat.

'How do I boggn get down, ehwot?'

I was jealous of him, for his loveaffair, for his ability to fly. But if love was the key, perhaps thinking about Scampi Lowrie would help me achieve take-off. It just made me cry.

A week later and I was thinking about leaving post-war England to live as a stylite in Africa. A chance to contemplate God before death robbed me of myself. A last bold religious nuttery! In an end-of-term mood I went around to Sep's house in Chelsea and took some old army pals to show them his legs.

We'd just arrived and were opening tins of biscuits. Sep was baggy-eyed but cheesome, drawling war-yarns to his guests. Then the doorbell rang and I slipped out on a war-yarn to answer it. I found a suit with stars all over it standing in the doorway. A snaggletoothed head crowned with a horn of blond hair stuck out of the suit. It spoke.

'Columbine Fettis. Morpheus Awake Institute. This is Operative Bibby. You're expecting us.'

He was past me in a flash. Operative Bibby's existence was doubted, but there he came, dragging something that looked like a serious drinker's drinks cabinet. A tiny component dropped off it and rolled away. I gave chase. When I arrived back in Sep's livingroom, clutching the compenent, he was already settled in his favourite chair, pretty legs up on a stool, and the operation was about to take place. I handed over the component. They threw it away.

'We'll need a bigger harness, Operative Bibby,' fussed Columbine Fettis. 'You've kept your weight up well, sir. In the war, were we, sir?'

'Spanish Resistance. I finished a General.'

'Ooooooo!'

'SEP!' I woofed. 'Who are these dreadful people?'

'Morpheus Awake Institute. The M.O. put me onto them. A simple operation, which can be performed in your own home, and painless . . .'

'That's right, sir,' said Columbine Fettis. 'Quite pain-less.'

'. . . And you'll never need to sleep again! Sleep will be unnecessary! A solution to all my problems. You-kno-wot

311

all boggn night! No nodding off at m'desk in the day-time! Harh!'

I munched biscuits. I thought it was a lark. I squeezed onto the sofa between 2 of the other chaps and watched Columbine Fettis and Operative Bibby harness Sep up, stick a saucepan-like helmet on his head, plugging in more and more equipment which Operative Bibby was forever scootling for from their van.

All the while, Columbine Fettis, who'd had the operation done on himself, described to us in his whining weasel voice how he had read all the classics since he had the operation done. He listed a good many. His mind had never been more vibrant, he said. Sleep was a waste of life, he said. He never missed the dawn, he said. When he wasn't knocking dials with a knuckle, he stared at Sep's pretty bare feet.

'Have you any hobbies, sir, for whiling away the endless nights?'

'I've been seeing a woman!' winked Sep.

We all guffawed. Fettis was unmoved. He flicked a switch. All the drinks cabinet equipment started up whirrsomely. I could hear a sheep baaing, the way they used to in Wilf's attic room in the night. Sep was shuddering. Smoke was coming out of the saucepan.

I was on my feet. 'Is this normal?'

Fettis: 'Perfectly normal, sir. It's just the vaporizer.'

'VAPORIZER!'

'Vaporizing the parts of his brain which induce sleep, sir.'

Then it was over. Sep was unharnessed. Fettis and Operative Bibby cleared away.

'I've never felt so wide awake! HARH!' yelled Sep, and beat his chest. 'Shall I read you some of my war poetry? Dimmee, it's exciting stuff.'

Everyone made excuses. Me too. We hurried off. Columbine Fettis, the most irritating man I ever met who wasn't a Scotsman, stayed to listen, sitting extra-alert on the edge of a chair.

*

All the preparations were made. 'Twas decided! Ethiopia! I'd plumparoonied for somewhere in the area around Lakes Rudolph and Stephanie. I would live out my days as a stylite, which is exactly what I have done, what I am doing right now 17 years later. But much biz to do at Chaffinch Hall first, indeedyso! Wilf's death had made me Lord Chaffinch, head of the family, owner of the Hall, property throughout the Empire, and the Chaffinch squillions. I was divesting myself of this responsibility in favour of Rhino. Bing could have had it, but he'd been in a trance for 20 years. Rhino was closest in line – him it had to be! He'd sworn off the drink and spent his evenings flatout in the chapel, praying loudly. Wot he'd be like after the papers were signed was anybody's guess!

I was lolling in Dame Tuna's 3rd husband's flat, mugging up on African info, when the fax came. It was from July. She'd meant to send it to Sep, but got our numbers mixed. I alerted the authorities, but it was already too late. When Sep arrived at July's apartment for their lunchtime date, he found me there, in straw hat and safari gear, small and sad in the black livingroom.

'UNCLE CHAFF, wot in? . . . Oh, yes, so that's it, issit! My own uncle, and an ex-pontiff to boot!'

He suspected me of carrying on an affair with July behind his back. I was too stricken to be flattered.

Sep ran from room to room. 'JULY! MY SWEET JULY! MY DARLINGMOST BURNING HOT MONTH! HERE COMES SEPTEMBER WITH HIS FRUITS, SHOWERING HARVESTS OF SEED!'

At last he stood in front of me.

'Her suicide note. Came through on my fax this morning. Mix up. Meant for you. Sep, my boy.'

'Suicide. But it's just her way of talking. She . . .'

I handed him the note. It explained everything.

'She jumped from the New Toblerone Building just before 11 o'clock this morning. Infinite sorry-bees, Sep lad.'

'My July,' he said pathetically. 'My pottafaloo July.'

For me, it was like Scampi's death all over again. I could feel the poor man's pain. A few moments of it had exhausted him, and there was a lifetime more to come.

'Sep, perhaps if you lie down and got some sleep,' was my best suggestion.

He gave me a harsh watery-eyed look.

'Sorries. Forgot.'

But he went into the bedroom anyway. He sat on the end of the bed. He didn't cry. I did that for him, standing up in that black room, with stuffed crows cawless around me. And one stray thought kept nudging back: what did that vision of Sep in the Armistice Day sky have to do with the death of this flighty girl?

4

The Millicent

September and I had a farewell lunch together at the Army Club. A pyramid of chips each, a pile of buns between us to make butties with, two golden tubs of butter. He was short with the waiters and crotchety with me. At one point he sat straight and stared at a walrusy innocent at the other side of the room.

'ARE YOU STARING AT MY LEGS! I'LL HAVE YER BOGGN EYES OUT, YER PIGGN JILKS!'

Where was the Sep of old – the bluff happy-go-lucky pal? We hadn't said much and would probably never meet again, were down to our last few chippies, when, thick with emotion, he said:

'Looksee, Uncle Chiffchaff, it's this sleeplessness gets me all squirrely like this. Triple sorries.'

Just then Carstairs came in for a snack and we joined in the applause, 20 minutes worth, by which time he'd finished his snack and went elsewhere to be applauded.

'I miss her dreadfully, tha knows,' said Sep, his eyes pleading towards me, wanting a cure.

'She is with the gentle Lord in Heaven.'

Sep crossed himself. He was reasonably devout. He had the distinction of having taught Jesus Christ how to ride a bicycle.

No chips left. Time for parting.

We stood on the steps of the Army Club and watched the afternoon get lazier. All afternoons had been lazy since the war.

'A prezzie – for you, unc!'

He gave me a wallet-sized package wrapped in brown paper.

'Something for you to read up yer pole, ehwot! My war poetry. Just published.'

'Thankybees.'

'And don't worry about the sleeplessness. I'm joining a little group, "The Help You Make It Through the Night Club". They've all had the same boggn op. They'll help me out, fersure.' Then he stamped a foot and saluted. 'Major Chaffinch!'

And me back. 'General Chaffinch!'

I turned around and marched off just like a soldier. Several demobbed chaperoos who missed their marching days joined in behind me and we were a long line cutting across the newly-renamed Carstairs Square on no mission in particular.

It was an exhausting week, shook dizzymost with good-byes. But saying goodbye to the Hall was like taking leave of life itself. I planned a fly-in-fly-out visit, as quick and painless as possible, just long enough to sign the place over to Rhino and for a last walk about. But it pleased me to think that for a few hours, and for the first time in my life, I would be the master of Chaffinch Hall.

Still summerish but leaves were falling. It was a bright, beautiful day, the kind of day for which God made England. The upper windows were all yellow with the sun and the lower ones green reflecting the lawns. I met Dame Tuna in the stable yard. Cos of segregation, I didn't think she'd speak. So I just nodded and walked past. She called me back. She joined me on my walk.

The magnolias were in bloom. Beyond them was my big old oak.

'Do you remember when I used to spend whole summers up that tree!' I chortled.

She looked into its branches with such a bright smile that the bitter old dragon she'd become was slain. She was the clever dear girl who'd discussed theology with me in the library a lifetime ago.

'Tuna,' I said. 'I love you.'

Her segregationist's look was back. The dragon awoke. What male trick was this?

'I decided something, just now. Pleasy-do, I'm going to give the Hall to you. Everything to you, am I not! I am! I can do it. You're next in line. No reason to deny you just cos you're a fem. I'll do it now!'

Having killed that dragon again and left a jolly old girl on the camomile lawn, I breezed into the lawyers encampment in the blue drawing room. I was busy with them for under half an hour, then I was gone forever. As my flying hat did an extra circuit of the estate I saw Rhino sitting in one of the follies at the edge of the shrubbery. I think he was reading a Bible. Lawyers were getting lost on their way to him, to break the bad news.

*

For me a year of quiet contemplation up my pole under the Ethiopian sun, beginning the happymostest years of my long life. For Sep, a year of sleeplessness. In all that time he never dozed, snoozed, dropped off, slumbered, not 40 winks, not one wink.

The men in the 'Help-You-Make-It-Through-the-Night-Club' were a lot of boggn Jilkses. Not one had done anything in the war. All they did was talk about the books they'd read or the things they made out of matchsticks in the wee hours. Sep went a couple of times, then gave up on them. But one night he was desperate – perhaps tonight there'd be someone there he could talk to? He put on civvies and went along.

They sat in a circle, each member standing in turn to give an account of his experiences of sleeplessness.

'My name is September Chaffinch, General September Chaffinch. I am . . .' His voice wouldn't say it. The other members encouraged him. '. . . Sleepless.'

Suddenly, he turned on a pale man whose clothes suggested that, like so many, he'd lost stones since the war. 'STOP SNIFFLING, YOU! DO I SNIFFLE WHEN IT'S YOUR TURN ON THE FLOOR!'

He paced as he spoke, as he had when describing missions to his men, and all his fellow members watched his legs as absent-mindedly he adopted his fashionmodel walk. Meanwhile, a dangerous and painful admission was issuing from the General . . .

'You chaperoos all had laudable reasons for having your sleeplessness op, improving your piggn minds and boggn wotnot. I had none o'that. I did it in order to spend my nights with . . . with a woman.'

The members were outraged. 2 walked out.

'Yes, yes, fellow members, I was bewitched by a woman, introduced to me, believe it or not, by an ex-Archbishop of Canterbury. But now she's dead and I am sleepless, without rest in a dull, unrefreshed world. I've dreams going on all the time. I can't quite reach them, but I know they're about her. We are rolling in that black bedroom, committing the sexual intercourse for the 10th time that night . . .'

More members walked out.

'. . . and then we lie sleepy in each other's arms. A few final kisses, then, yes, we sleep side by side. And as I squeeze her chests in the night I have a nightmare that I can't sleep, that I'll never sleep again! Oh, GOD!'

He sat down and saw to his surprise that all but one of the members had walked out on him.

'Columbine Fettis,' said the remaining man.

They shook hands. Sep recognized the man and his whining weasel voice from somewhere.

'In the war, were you?'

'Around and about, ducking and diving,' said Columbine Fettis.

'Pity about Tufti Mufti, ehwot?'

They had a chortle. Just days before, the Grand Mufti had been dragged from his prison cell in Djakarta and ripped to pieces by an angry crowd.

Fettis had read Sep's book of war poetry. They discussed this for a while, then moved on to other literature. Sep put his head in his hands, suddenly desperate.

'I've read everything!' he wailed. 'Every Godawful book ever written! Films! – Seen the boggn lot, even the 20th Century ones! I've been in all the hologramismic interactive experiences they made in the '30s! I was in *Camille* with Theda Gint!'

'I was in that,' said Fettis, sipping tea from his flask.

318

'I got so bored with her death scene that I smothered her with her pillow. Tried to get her dress off, actuallymost.'

'No!'

'But they aren't naked underneath, tha knows, hologramismics.'

'I know,' said Fettis sadly.

'I didn't think it was possible to get this tetchy! Last night I did the washing up. Never done that before. Hated it. Started smashing the plates on the kitchen floor, just for something to do. When my batman came in to see wot the noise was I took him out into the park to play secret agents till dawn. OH, THOSE MERCILESS LONG NIGHTS! And my trumpet's no boggn help at all! Sick to boggn death of it! Off the top of Toblerone Building for me if I'm not careful!'

'Have you tried the Millicent?' inquired Columbine Fettis.

Sep's face came slowly out of his hands. 'MILLICENT?'

'Hours of harmless fun, the Millicent, sir.'

'MILLICENT? DID YOU SAY . . .?'

'The Millicent. Named after its inventor the late Millicent Clopstock. Recommended for the Sleepless, sir. Hours of harmless fun. I just so happen to have their all-night number here, sir. Credit cards are accepted. Army discount, of course, sir.'

'Erm . . . wot's it do, exactly?'

Fettis dug shyly in his pocket and, seemingly surprised, produced a 50 page brochure. Sep's baggy eyes read avidlymost.

'I must have one of these!' he said.

'The all-night number is ringed in red on the back page, sir. Credit cards are accepted. Army discount, of course, sir.'

Sep hurried out to the nearest phone to make his order.

*

Sep had, of course, been up all night and was impatiently awaiting the men from the Millicent Installation Corporation. His batman was hiding in a cupboard, having a nervous breakdown. That would make 3 batmen he'd driven over the edge in a year. The doorbell rang and Sep dashed for the door.

'Columbine Fettis,' said the snaggletoothed caller.

'Oh, it's you, I thought . . . ugh?'

'This is Operative Bibby. We're from the Millicent Installation Corporation, sir. You're expecting us.'

Fettis was his usual neutral self. But Sep couldn't help laughing, at himself, at Fettis, at the whole boggn situation. He sat grinning on his couch while Fettis and Operative Bibby brought in the Millicent and installed it beside the fish tank. It was a square metal box with one leather-framed hole in it. An adjustable stool was arranged before it with great care by Operative Bibby.

'It's the usual, sir,' said Fettis, handing over 2 thick volumes which were the Millicent Handbook. 'Head between the knees. Insert the head into the orifice marked HEAD, while operating the flippers with the hands, thus . . .'

He pointed at Operative Bibby, who was doing all these things, trying the machine out.

'An empty bladder is recommended, sir. And trouserless, sir.'

Sep removed his trousers. He looked for this 'trousers off' rule in the Handbook later, but 'twasn't there. Perhaps Fettis just wanted a look at his girlie legs.

'And I can really review any event, any moment in my past life, and live it all over again, as it was, ehwot?'

Fettis licked his snaggleteeth: 'It's all in the Handbook, sir. Endless hours of amusement. I would remind you, sir, that if the warning horn sounds, then you are trespassing into areas of collusive memory.'

'Collusive memory, ehwot?'

'Which is our memory in the round, as a society, sir, corruption of which could not, of course, affect actuality, sir.' His whine briefly hee-heed. 'But there must be safeguards, sir. Failure to withdraw on the advice of the horn will result in prosecution. History is your playground, sir, but only your personal perception of it. Trespass into actual history by attempting to change it or anyone's perception of it will result in prosecution. Cum along, Cassandra.'

Operative Bibby followed him out. 10 minutes later a still trouserless Sep found them eating sandwiches in their van.

'I can't actually change the past, can I?' he asked.

Fettis stored a bolus of sandwich in his cheek and replied: 'Corruptions of the collusive memory will result in prosecution, sir. Otherwise, endless hours of fun.'

Sep was alone with his Millicent, flicking through the Handbook, which was every bit as irritating as Columbine Fettis himself. So he tossed it aside, put his pretty knees on the stool and flung his flabby head ear-bendingly into the orifice marked HEAD.

The Millicent worked! Sep was no longer in his living room, or felt he wasn't. He was at Chaffinch Hall. It was 2046. He was in his boyhood's body on a leave weekend from his boarding school, just arrived home. His 127-year-old great-great-great-great-granddaddy Clem Chaffinch was reclining on a lilo in the pool, drinking zombies with 3 naked girls orbiting him on blow-up ducks.

'Can I have a zombie?' asked Sep. 'I'm not really 9. I'm 47. I'm a General.'

They didn't believe him, but gave him a zombie anyhowdoos. It went straight to his head. He made a grab for one of the girls. Next instant he was in July's black bedroom. Alone. He looked around and saw that the feathers of the stuffed crows were ruffled. His wanger was soft and sticky. They'd just hooharwigglied. July was in the bathroom. The toilet flushed, the door opened . . . IT WAS SHE! ALIVE! No, not alive, just a dream . . . some kind of dream. No, it was July! It really was!

He embraced her with all the passion of a man who has lost his truelove and found her again. They rolled on the bed in a more tender lovemaking than they'd known in non-Millicent life.

Then she was lying on him, licking his legs, her pozzy in his face.

'I know!' she called from his other end. 'Let's KILL ourselves! Oh, Seppyweppy, DO LET'S! We'll never be happier than we were a moment ago!'

His body trembled with emotion. Her suicidal outburst had brought back all the pain of the past year. He wanted out of there! His fingers operated the flippers on the side of the Millicent and scenes, days, visions of his past, zoomed before him.

'I want the war,' he told the machine.

Sep was in a whizzycopter, approaching the Mufti's palace in Majorca. This time 8 men got through and his legs weren't hit. So it did work out differently sometimes, ehwot! No need to rush to kill the Mufti, then. He just sauntered in on his solid man's legs. His victim was swathed in a purple caftan, tugging his beard while he gazed soppily into a book of ancient Persian love poetry.

Sep steadied his aim. WHARRRRBBBBBBBBBLAAAAA-AAAA! WHARRRRBBBBBBBBBLAAAAAAAAAA! The warning horn was sounding. Sep chin-scratchingly supposed that if he shot the Mufti he'd be trespassing into this collusive memory thingummy, changing an actual event rather than the passive wandering the machine supposedly was designed for. Much more fun to shoot the bugger! He repointed his aim. WHARRRRBBBBBBBBBLAAAAAAAAAA!

Columbine Fettis appeared in the line of fire. A televisit? A hologramismic part of the machine? Or really him?

Sep played innocent: 'Don't think I quite understandaroony the principle of this gadget, ehwot?'

'Corruptions of the collusive memory will result in prosecution and confiscation of the instrument, sir.' And he handed him Volume 2 of the Handbook open at the relevant page where all was tediously explained. Then he vanished.

The Mufti poured Sep some lemon tea. They talked about the progress of the war, ancient Persian love poetry, techniques of the sexual intercourse – the Mufti showed Sep some lewd pictures in a book. Then Sep read some of his war poems, stumbling through them from memory. The Mufti was moved to tears.

'I'm gonna whizzy off now,' said Sep, shaking hands with a man who'd just appeared to shake hands on the Mufti's behalf.

'Drop in anytime!' said this friendly Millicent-Mufti. 'We can play cards, eat Italian, Indonesian, you can have the pick of my girls!'

Sep had to say it: 'The war. You're going to lose, you know.'

'NEVER!' yelled the Mufti. 'NEVER!'

Sep visited other days, looked up other people. Then he took himself for a long walk through the streets of his home town, Bury St Edmunds, as they'd been when he was a young man. The shops. The faces. How skinny the men were! This was the '50s, before segregation got a hold on the fem imagination. There were couples actually walking arm-in-arm down the High Street. Sep stopped to look at two loveydovies pointing at rings in a jeweller's window.

'DIMMEE!' he said to himself, punching his gut in an emotional resolve. 'I've got to try! I can't not try!'

Next thing he was in the men's bubble elevator, rising up the side of the New Toblerone Building, with its magnificent view of the vast rockgarden the centre of London had become since vaporization.

'Roof, pleasy-do,' he said to the elevatorboy.

It was a quarter to eleven. In the women's elevator on the other side of the building July was barefoot, tousled, looking downwards with that wildeyed look she had. When the elevator stopped on the roof she took off all her rings and gave them away to the elevatorgirl. She hurried to the point where she'd stood daring herself so many times before.

'JULY!' It was Sep. Trouserless. Handsome. Fat.

The wind rising off the building had her frizzy hair waving above her head. Her black dress kept flapping up into her face, giving Sep creamy flashes of her nudity.

'I didn't think you'd get my fax till you got home from the War Office.'

'You sent it to Uncle Chaff by mistake. He told me. July, you don't have to do this, my darlingmost pottafaloo girl! There will be more happiness! Much more! Better than anything we've had so far! I love you!'

'No foolydoos on me evermost!' she yelled. 'Boggn man-made deception, love is, ehwot!'

'I've been speaking to a disgusting friend. He's shown me new ways of doing hoohar wiggly – foul, depraved,

323

hideous ways! Please come down and try a few with your Seppyweppy!'

July was tempted. Her left foot moved. She was about to step down. But the Millicent's warning horn went WHAR-RRRRRLAAAAAAAAAA! and confused her thoughts, as did the appearance of Columbine Fettis, materializing between her and Sep, dapper in a green leprechaunish suit.

'Corruption of the collusive memory will result in prosecution and confiscation of the instrument.'

July was about to jump. Sep ran towards her on his shapely legs. Fettis chased after. July ran along the wall, up a slope, out of reach, giggling pottafalooly.

'Really, sir, you mustn't do this. Hours of harmless fun if only you'd . . .'

Sep bellied him off the top of the New Toblerone Building. He didn't scream on his way down. He whined. Sep and July watched him fall. In his green suit he looked like a pea falling off a table. Then the pea, the distant minuscule pea, went red.

'Beautiful!' sighed July.

Sep had his hand outstretched 'Darlingmost!' he cried.

'Ert, you and yer biological tricks!' she said.

She jumped.

The warning horn blared one last time, then stopped. But in that instant Sep was down in the elevator again. It was a quarter to eleven again.

'Roof, pleasy-do,' he said to the elevatorboy.

He tried again to save her. WHARRRRRRRBLAAAAAA-AAAAA! went the warning horn.

'Sweetmost bloom of July!' implored Sep. 'You don't have to do this! You and me and my Millicent – we can work this out together.'

A scathed look of jealous fury. 'Who's this Millicent, then?'

'She's . . . it's . . . I mean . . .'

Too late. She'd jumped, giving him the finger as she dropped out of sight.

He tried again. Then twice more. Each time he failed. She jumped. And every time she jumped, a trick of the machine or wot, he knew not, but he loved her more.

During the next try, Operative Bibby and officials of the Millicent Installation Corporation broke into Sep's mews house. Columbine Fettis was not among them. He'd suddenly and inexplicably burst to bits in his van. Perhaps nobody understood the principle of this Millicent thing!

An upset Operative Bibby shot his vaporizer beam at the wallplug to cut off the machine's power and prevent the impending corruption of the collusive memory. But the machine didn't stop, it whirred happily on, and Sep continued twiddling its flippers, breaking the law. Bibby, without Fettis to keep him in control, panicked. He shot at the machine. A full blast. Sep and his shapely legs and his brandnew Millicent were vaporized together, just after the moment when July lifted her arms to let the wind blow her dress off over her head, and in the very moment when she stepped down from the edge, took Sep's hands and said: 'Take me! – you gorgeous butterball, you! Let's do it some disgusting new ways!'

5

Armistice Day

I was sitting up my pole one day in spring '88 – by which time the fact of Sep's vaporization was just another of my many sorrows – contentedly watching the last few stragglers of a herd of wildebeest hurry by on their way to Lake Stephanie, when Mr Iqubal arrived in his flying hat travelling shop, bringing me *coca-cola* and bananas.

'My wife is having a baby today, O holy one. 'Twould give me great pleasure, would it not, if you would bless the child.'

I blessed it.

'Perhaps if you came in person, O holy one, you would put a twinkle into my baby's eyes for her whole life long!'

'Okaydoos.'

We flew to Addis Ababa and I sat and watched Mr Iqubal's daughter be born. First time I'd ever seen that particular miracle. I went out into the streets in a happy mood, loading myself up with fruit from the market stalls, pulling faces at the kiddies who followed me chanting: 'Baldy nut! Holy man! Pole-sitter! Old chicken!'

I opened my bag of raisins and pelted them with a handful. They rushed off, then back, mouths open. I pelted them again and again, feeding them all my raisins.

There was a tent, a booth of some sort, at the far end of the market. Slim young men, very black, grinning in white shirts, were queuing outside.

'Wot's that?' I asked a little boy.

'Naughty pictures,' he said. 'The Millicent.'

I dropped all my bags of fruit and ran to see. Now, at last, here in Ethiopia, would I find the answer to the mystery of wot in God's name was the Millicent!

The young men made way for a holy man, gigglesomely,

327

and I went into the booth. In the fly-buzzing gloom was the Millicent. It was in use. A young man was kneeling on its stool, an erection the size of a pnongbat wagging between his legs. He was operating the flippers like a man tweaking nipples, which was probably just was he was doing inside the machine.

When he was finished he came out grinning, forced his sinking erection into his shorts and ran outside with a whoop. My turn. I thrust my head into the orifice marked head and suddenly I was back in the trenches. The battle-smoky skies. The lightshow. The mud and misery. Chaplain Archie Bishop.

Cole Chaffinch, my nephew, Sep's father, had just expired in my hands. Yes, this is what it was like. My sore mind had made me forget most of it. All the men in my trench were staring wonderingly into the sky. Of course! Armistice Day! The vision! I looked! There was Sep, huge, his pretty feet seemingly standing on the horizon. Beside him was an equally enormous July. In her black dress, straps down.

'HOWDEEDOODEE, UNCLE CHAFF! I'VE CUM TO SEE HOW MY OLD DAD'S DOING! IS HE ABOUT?'

I dithered and smiled: 'ERM, YOU'VE JUST MISSED HIM.'

'JUST MISSED HIM AS IN "DEAD"?'

'UH-HUH!'

'DAMMYDOOS, THIS BOGGN MACHINE DON'T WORK SO WELL WHEN THERE'S SO MUCH EMOTION ABOUT, THA KNOWS, WHAT WITH THE ARMISTICE AND ALL.'

'ARE YOU A GHOST, SEP LAD?'

'WE DON'T PROPERLY TWIGGEROO THE PRIN-CIPLE BEHIND ALL THIS, BUT WE'RE NOT GHOSTS. WE LIVE IN THE PHANTASMAGORIA OF MY OLD MACHINE, D'YERSEE. JULY AND I HAVE A COTTAGE ON THE YARMOUTH ROAD. IT'S IN THE 2050s, MY FAVOURITE PERIOD! HOOHAR WIGGLY ALL NIGHT, EHWOT? SLEEP LIKE A TOP ALL DAY! HARH!'

He kissed July, Frenchly, squeezing her at the hip. When they came up for air, they waved goodbye.

'NO WORRIES, I'LL CATCH DADDY ANOTHER DAY, WHEN HE WAS ALIVE, IF YOU FOLLOW ME DRIFT.

TOODLEBYDAR, UNCLE CHAFF!'
'TOODLEBYDAR, YOU BRAVE LITTLE MAN!' said July.

They faded, their smiles lingering till last.

This Millicent that had found its way to Ethiopia was probably the only one then working, its warning horn silent cos it was only used by young men to visit their dreamgirls. In the Empire the Millicent was taken off the market after only a few months, was it not. Several Millicent owners had ignored the warning horn and set about changing the events they visited – saving buddieboys in the war, mainly. There were persistent rumours that thissun or thattun had indeedy-do been saved and was back in the real world! Meanwhileydoos, to escape prosecution some owners went the other way, going walkabout in their machines, traipsing along the lines of all our memories, before being captured and shot by operatives of the Millicent Installation Corporation. I don't think, in my imperfect comprehension of the principle of the boggn thing, that they effected any changes in real history, just in our remembrances of it where it impinged upon our own lives. But some jokerooney obviously succeeded in doing summick, cos for a few weeks in '84 half the world was affected. People found themselves suddenly living subtly different lives, which didn't fit with their memories of themselves. Some folks, still equipped with their original memories, awoke adrift in entirely different lives. This was why, after a happy 1st year up my pole, I sometimes awoke believing myself to be still the vicar of Middlesborough 726 and that Hughie Reid was Prime Minister – wot was I doing up a pole and where was this foreign place? How spooked I was! For a few vivid seconds during these same addled weeks I thought Scampi and I had married and lived a long happy life together, then she had died and I had come to Ethiopia to pole-sit in grief. Indeedybee, for those seconds, I had the memories of a whole different life! It's just the strain of a lifetime, I thinky-dood, working its way out of me like a thorn from the flesh. But no, as I later discovered, 'twas the Millicent doing it.

I went back to the Millicent booth on my next trip to Addis Ababa, hoping to relive some of the happy moments

I'd known, or – at the far end of my hopes – indeedydoo change 21st Century history. Maybe with Sep's help I could save Cole from the vaporizer, or Scampi from that pnongball, or Cod from Signora Blatta, or Rainbow and Haha from their terrible end, etcetera. But the Millicent wasn't there. A gang from the local church had smashed the rude thing up.

I stood where the queue would have been, hatless in the baking heat, my mind jumping with visions. (I think my brief insertion into the Millicent may have started the predilection to visions that have seized me while dictating this booky-do.) Suddenmost: darkness! A great black shadow blocked out the sun. A gigantic Ethiopian!

'Are you the stylite from the plain below Kunchurro mountain?'

'I, er . . . um?' Martyrdom at last?

'I am Tadese Mblook. I wish to serve God by being your helper.'

I had met my greatest friend. We bought bananas and walked to the trainstation. I prattled the story of nephew Sep, finishing with my conviction that he and July were the luckiest people of this blueful 21st Century. They might live in their 2050s cottage forever, and do the sexual intercourse an infinite number of times, if not ways. I, meanwhile, declared that I had given up the sinful lascivious habits which took hold of me in my early dotage – and Tadese said he had given up lascivious habits also. But every Friday night for the rest of the century he has sneaked young women into his hut to play hide the weasel! Boggn have! PIGGN HAVE! HAVE! HAVE!*

---

* *Tadese here admits in this footnote, that, yes, he has. He is a lost soul and a sinner. But apart from his Friday girls his mind has contemplated God at all times. On the other 6 nights of the week he ruminates upon the wise words he has heard his master speak that day. God bless Tadese. God bless Tadese's master. God forgive Friday nights.*

Tadese Mblook

THE EPILOGUE

Final Days:

Hans Feet and Bumpsidaisy

Quotes of the Century:

'I am Hans Feet!'
Hans Feet, Swiss chocolate manufacturer, 2099

'You are not Hans Feet! I am Hans Feet!'
Hans Feet, Swiss chocolate manufacturer, 2099

'Hans Feet is ME!'
Hans Feet, Swiss chocolate manufacturer, 2099

'I, I, I am Hans Feet!!!'
Hans Feet, Swiss chocolate manufacturer, 2099

The Apocalypse of Hans Feet

I

20 years have passed since I prattled my family history to
Tadese from my poletop in Ethiopia. Last weekend I found
the manuscript in the drawer where I shoved it on my return
to Chaffinch Hall. So now, all alone in my study, with winter
sleet attacking the windows, I am writing a final chapter for
our booky-do, telling of the 21st Century's last days and of the
oddmostest thing that ever happened in the whole history of
the world. Only I know of this. Only I can tell.

As my pen makes words upon the page, my mind prattles
those same words to Tadese, my much-missed big black
friend, who now really is a lost soul, for he no longer exists,
does he not. Nowhere at all, except in my memory of him.

II

During the whole of 2099 a small man was hiking about
between Mount Kunchurro and the Lakes. He was dressed
in lederhosen and wore a hat with a long feather in it.
Between 60 and 70 years old, he was pudge-bellied, had
a boil for a nose, was bald when he lifted his hat to scratch
the pink freckled pate beneath, but with a few ginger curls
around his ears. A thoroughly depressed face in repose, it
was positively festive when it smiled. A healthy ruddy little
fellow, he reminded me of a clown who'd abandoned his calling
cos his face was funnier without clown's make-up.

'Gruss Gott, holy man!' he called every time he passed by,
and always introduced himself as if for the first time.

He said his name was Hans Feet, that he was a Swiss
chocolate manufacturer. What was he doing in Ethiopia,
questioned I? He wouldn't say. But one day at dusk he

appeared and spoke emotionally about his childhood in the Engadine. He ordered Tadese about. I didn't like him much.

On one morning when I was telling Tadese the story of Rainbow and Haha, I saw Hans Feet coming in one direction and, some little distance away, an identical figure, going in another direction. One with a butterfly net, one with a hunting rifle. 2 Hans Feets? A trick of the light, thought I, or my senile senses.

But no, 'twas so. Later that day they turned up together. They must have met somehow on the trail of purple emperors and impala, fell into enmity, and came to me to settle the argument.

'I am Hans Feet!'

'Who are you to say that you are Hans Feet, when I am Hans Feet!'

'I am Hans Feet! You are saying you are Hans Feet, like that other man said he was Hans Feet! I showed him who was Hans Feet! Hah! Hans Feet is me!'

'I AM HANS FEET!'

'You are not even Swiss!'

'I am Swiss! I was born in Sargans in 2029! Hans Feet!'

'That was me – Hans Feet – born in Sargans in 2029! Not you, whoever you are!'

'Whoever I am, I'll tell you who I am – I AM HANS FEET!'

By this point in the argument they were right under my pole. They removed their hats, showed their full faces – the same face twice! – and each demanded: 'Holy man, which of us is Hans Feet?'

I was befuddled, but mischievous. I said to the one with the butterfly net. 'You are Hans Feet.'

The other paled with fury and screamed in a voice so loud that birds jumped from their trees miles away across the plain:

'I AM HANS FEET!'

He then pointed his gun at the other Hans Feet, who swept his butterfly net over his opponent's head and they ended fighting like girls, clonking each other's heads against my pole, rolling in the dust. Tadese eventually separated them.

'I'll tell thee who is Hans Feet,' he said. 'I am Hans Feet!' and he threw one off in one direction and the other in the other.

Much chee from me at that. I thought perhaps they were twin brothers who liked to go around playing jokes. The Swiss sense of humour, I imagined, was nobody's business!

But summuck was up. I sensed an unease among the wild animals. Half the time they kept to shadows, as if waiting for a storm. But no storm came. The rest of the time they were running to and fro as if escaping from an enemy they couldn't see.

The very next day Mr Iqubal came on his weekly visit in his flying hat travelling shop. While Tadese unloaded our provisions old Iqubal told me how worried he was about his eldest daughter.

'Holy man, what shall I do with her! She wants to marry a most unsuitable man! He is as old as I am, and she only 17 and so pretty – not quite with the twinkle in her eyes of my youngest daughter, but, yes, a special something. What can she see in such a man? So small and ugly – eugh!'

He hugged the bottom of my pole. I muttered prayers and poured a jug of water on his head. He felt better. But not for long.

'He is taking her away! To Switzerland! He is from there. "Mein little strudle" he calls her. I HATE HIM! Is it wrong to hate so vile a creature, O holy sage?'

'Switzerland? Your daughter's boyfriend – he's not called Hans Feet is he?'

Mr Iqubal started thumping my pole. 'HANS FEET! HANS FEET! HANS FEET!'

But the next week when Mr Iqubal's flying hat travelling shop flew in, no Mr Iqubal. Out climbed Hans Feet in Mr Iqubal's shopkeeper's outfit. He looked cross, but efficient. He ordered Tadese about. I imagined Mr Iqubal had come to terms with Hans Feet and brought him into the business in order to keep his beloved daughter from going to Switzerland.

'Good to see you again, Hans,' I said.

'AH! AH! SO! Here is a wise man, who knows Hans Feet

when he sees Hans Feet! My daughter's fiancé, he is saying
he is Hans Feet, when the whole world can see who is Hans
Feet. I, I, I am Hans Feet!'

He was most insistent on the fact. We could see his lips
moving with it as he took off. As he skimmed away towards
Sidamo, Tadese and I had one of our fits of chee. Him lying
on the earth, slapping it as he laughed, and me rolling around
on my platform, a gigglesome gigglebag.

But after lunch I dropped a bananaskin on Tadese's head
and said: 'Tango into Bako, pleasy-do.'

'What for, holy one?'

'Just tell me what thou see'st there.'

When he returned it was getting dark and I was crosslegged
in a snooze, dreaming about the war. He banged saucepans
together. In the bushes an animal screeched. I awoke.

'Well?'

'They are everywhere.'

'What are?'

'Hans Feet.'

'Hans Feet?'

'Half of Bako has disappeared, the rest are hiding from
Hans Feet. I counted 35 of them in the bars, all arguing with
each other about which one is really Hans Feet. What is this
plague that the Lord had visited upon us, O master?'

'I don't know, Tadese. Triple sorries, but I had no idea.'

Tadese, looking greatly troubled, went into his hut. It was
the last I saw of him. He sat reading the Bible aloud by
lamplight, just as he did so often. Sometimes he read it to
me, but I liked it better when he read it to himself which
was in a voice only slightly more quiet, but enough to stop
me making out the words. I loved to hear the one discernible
word, JESUS, rise from the deep comfortsome mumble. I'd
lie on my back, sometimes opening my eyes to be amazed at
the stars, and never ever did I feel closer to God than at those
times. But that night, after a while, Tadese's deep mumble
turned to a strident buzz. I stared down from my poletop for
long after the lamplight had been extinguished. I knew what
had happened.

Next morning I lifted my head from my arm with a start,

just in time to see Hans Feet step out of Tadese's hut in a
caftan way too big for him.

'Frühstück, mein Herr?' asked Hans Feet.

'Not hungry, thankybee, Hans. Go to Mr Bhagat's and fetch
the ladder. I am coming down.'

An hour later 3 Hans Feets returned with the ladder.

Apart from that time I fell off, I hadn't been down from my
pole in over 10 years. I was frightened. But I felt, deep within
my being, that God wanted me for a task, that I had lived so
long in order to complete this task. I climbed down the ladder
and stood dizzily at ground level. Up aloft I'd felt as strong as
a lion loping up a tree. But to my shock, on the ground I was
frail. Just walking to the hut made me breathless.

I opened up my little box of treasures and searched for
clothes to wear. I found a Salvation Army jacket which I
hadn't worn for nearly 80 years. It had dead mice in the
pockets, who knows where from. With that, my army boots,
a pair of cutaway jeans and a topper on my head, I set out for
the trainstop, pursued for some of the way by Hans Feets.
But their argument started up, followed by a fistfight, and I
got away. In my sack I carried 2 hands of bananas, my Bible,
and Tadese's manuscript of *21st Century Blues*.

III

After the Mufti War certain energies were gone from the
world. Governments lacked authority, did nothing, and were
entirely ignored. Some countries, England included, had no
governments at all. Huh! But all the news that reached me
at the top of my pole confirmed my view: life had improved
– in the 21st Century folk had never had it so good! In a very
few governmentless years the problems of the world seemed
to have dissolved. Peace, equality, harmony between men –
between men and women even, with segregation gone and
marriage popular again. There was an economic boom like
none ever before. The poor became middle class across
the entire globe, living in the same housing estate which
the boom built here, there, and everywhere. But the New

World Order didn't rush helterskelter, frantic in its boom. It ambled. It popped into the office to see what was happening. Life everywhere on earth was like the quiet life of an English market town of the '20s.

So it was that as I walked through Addis Ababa I was reminded of the Bury St Edmunds of my youth. Indeedybe, there was hardly a black face to be seen to break this un-African illusion. Everywhere I looked – the street-vendors, the shoppers, the policeman on his beat – though not quite all were geared-up Swissly, they all had the same face. Hans Feet's face. Dimmee, but I was boggn sick of that face!

I saw a young black man shivering with fear on a corner. I went up to him and we looked at each other for a bit, with nothing to say to each other except Hans Feet, so we said nothing. Finally, we shook hands and I walked on. When I looked back, he wasn't there.

The London Underground system had recently been extended as far as Addis Ababa. A wonderful idea! But the 2,000 stops on the way to Oxford Circus were something of a tede. My fellow passengers were largely Hans Feets. They looked at each other suspiciously from behind Zurich newspapers. All those bursting-boil noses! I wondered jumpily how long before the old argument broke out.

The ticket inspector clipped my ticket with typical Hans Feet brusqueness, but then suddenly sat beside me, pushing me against the window, squashing the dead mice in my pockets, as he whispered: 'You are not Hans Feet?'

'I am not Hans Feet.'

A nearby Hans Feet declared in response: 'I am Hans Feet.'

Then all the others said it, one by one. I do believe it was passed all the way down the train from Feet to Feet, cos several minutes later it came back, passed us, and several minutes after that it returned the other way.

Meanwhile, the ticket inspector was a Hans Feet with a problem, whispering: 'I am most pleased that you are saying you are not Hans Feet,' he said, nervously clicking his ticket-clipper. 'Because everyone he is saying he is Hans Feet when I, I, I am that person.'

'Who?'

'Hans Feet, of course.'

'Triple sorries.'

'There is worse still, mein Herr. Yesterday I was going home at mein usual time and my wife, she is there, and she is saying SHE is Hans Feet.'

'And is she?'

He banged his forehead on the seat in front, then said calmly: 'I am Hans Feet.'

I tried my luck. 'Your wife, does she perhaps LOOK like Hans Feet, I mean, thyself.'

'Ja, ja – that is wot is so puzzling. She is standing there in her dress which I am buying for her in Innsbruck last summer, but she is bald, mit little red curlings about her ears, und her nose, it is flaming red like mein own.'

'In other words she looks exactly like you?'

'Und this morning when I am leaving our haus she is dressed just like me and we have a most unpleasant row in which she is saying she is Hans Feet and if I am a Swiss chocolate manufacturer why am I working on the London Underground?'

'Erm, scusy-be if thou thinkst this rude, but I am very old – these other passengers, who are all dressed the same and engaging in interminable conversations about chocolate and their childhoods in the Engadine . . . do they also not, in some small way perhaps, look exactly like you?'

He looked about, puzzled. 'Nein,' he said.

'Oh, but they do.'

'I AM HANS FEET! I, I, I!!!'

His cry brought about the eruption I had expected. The Zurich newspapers were screwed up, lederhosen clad pozzies bounced on seats, and each Hans Feet screamed that he was Hans Feet. I hit my topper a severe blow so that it came down over my eyes. For 100s of stops the raucous controversy continued. Hans Feets got off, but reinforcements came at every stop. Soon they were quizzing each other about the life of Hans Feet, and they all got the questions right, much to the consternation of each other.

Desperate hands kept clutching me, imploring voices in

my ear: 'Tell them they are not Hans Feet. I am Hans Feet, tell them!'

I stayed comparatively safe inside my topper, smelling of a cigar someone smoked 60 years before, rather than the overpowering reek of teams of Hans Feets sweatily demanding recognition.

IV

I was the only passenger on the shuttlecraft, so I sat upfront beside Hans Feet, who was piloting. It wasn't long before he started telling me about his childhood in the Engadine. But I didn't have to listen. I looked out over a peaceful England of villages and fields. Gone were the great motorhighways of my youth. Just little lanes.

'Mein father never really loved me. He was always too busy in the chocolate factory . . .'

The Stour was in flood. I saw a fox, sitting on a small hummock with water all around and obviously wondering what to do. Then, beyond the shining silver river, over the new young forests that had grown in my 17 years' absence, I saw the magnificent frontage of Chaffinch Hall. I was laughing and crying at the same time. Big tears. Instinctively, I was returning home. But wot for? To die? Or do battle with Hans Feet as a final test of the Lord's . . . and then die?

We landed on the lawn between the stone lions. As I clambered centenarianly out, the pilot growled vexedly at me: 'You do not believe me, do you? You do not believe that I am Hans Feet!'

'Go with God, Hans,' said I with all the holiness my stylite years had taught me.

He took off in a fury, twizzling the shuttlecraft over the magnolias. I half expected him to write HANS FEET IS ME in the sky. But then he was gone and there was just this old, old bird and his birthplace. We looked at one another. From somewhere came a very decrepit angry dog. It stood on the gravel and growled. I began to yelp, loudly yelp.

Dame Tuna was at my side, fussing.

'Uncle Chiffchaff – I thought you were long dead.'

'That dog!' I yelped. 'That dog!'

It was, I was sure, the same unpleasant dog that had escaped my mother's gun a century ago. Still here! Alive! Impossible!

'I've never seen it before,' said Tuna. 'Do come in and tell me what you've been up to. Hans, fetch the Archbishop's luggage!'

A liveried Hans Feet hurried down the steps. Here too?

Tuna nudged me, whispering: 'Don't upset him. If he tells you he's Hans Feet, agree with him. Good servants are impossible to get after the slave revolts.'

'Slave revolts?'

'Where HAVE you been? Slavery was reintroduced in England back in '89. Helped the boom no end. Now things couldn't be more skew-wiffo! Ho-hum!'

I had no luggage. I gave Hans Feet my topper.

He clicked his heels. 'Hans Feet, at your service, mein Herr!'

I hurried away from him, chasing Tuna up the steps.

'You can have Clam's room – Clam, my 7th, tha knows. He's got it too, off to Switzerland to find himself. Erm, don't mind, do you, Uncle Chiffchaff, if I leave you with Hans till dinner? – I've some experiments on the boil. It's a wonderful moment for genetics.'

'Pleasy-do thyself evermost.'

Off she went up the staircase, with our gold-framed ancestors frowning down on her, stepping back down 2 steps just to say: 'Oh, one thing, I hope you won't be disappointed, but I'm a Moslem.'

'Um? Okaydoos. Where's, um, Rhino?'

She lowered her eyes, looked high up at her own portrait or at Allah in a chandelier. 'Shot himself in '92. Triple sorries.' Then she grinned like a girl and hurried up the staircase.

The way her dress rustled, it caused explosions of memories, of my mother, my boyhood, Cod, Robin. It was the most tiring moment of my trip. I slouched into the living room. Very familiar. Lots of worn old chairs were friends. I fell into one. In a warmth of nostalgia I fell asleep. I awoke to find Hans Feet leering at me like a washed clown. He gave me a schnapps which hotted me up.

'Skiing season should be underway in the Engadine,' I said, hoping he'd hurry straight off under the nearest avalanche.

'There is no snow yet this year. Good for the climbing, however. When I can save up enough to buy my freedom, I will return!' He suddenly was sitting on the arm of my chair. He held my hand. 'I hope you are not too upset about your great-niece becoming a Moslem.'

'No, no, that's her business.'

'I am a Calvinist myself.'

'A lot of people are turning Calvinist, I find.'

'In my youth, in the Engadine, I was often going to pray in the little mountain chapels . . .'

And he told me all about that for an hour, till I gathered enough sense to run away and change for dinner. But the sound of his voice was still in my head as I tried on Clam's dinner-jacket.

V

A candlelit dinner for 2, Hans Feet serving his own Swiss recipes. I sent him to fetch some non-existent condiment from the kitchens, then poured out my anxieties to Tuna.

'I don't understand it! All the way from Africa, um, almost everyone I saw, was Hans Feet! Thousands! Millions! even! HANS FEET! When I turned on the vidiwall in my room just now, there was him reading the news and everyone in the news was him! HANS FEET!'

'Do stop babbling, Uncle Chiffchaff. I will explain. What we have here, and I'm speaking as the foremost amateur geneticist in what's left of East Anglia, is a genetic accident of historic proportions.'

'Um?' I was umming again. I hadn't ummed for years.

'More sauerkraut?'

'Um? No.'

'It cannot have escaped your notice that during your lifetime disease has practically been eradicated from the planet. This was achieved by the genetic medicines developed in the early years of the century in the wake of the great plagues. If someone was suffering from a particular disease, their DNA was altered by the addition of recombinant DNA, in such a way as to affect the alleles and thereby cause the genes to re-express themselves healthily.'

'I think I see, um, yes.'

Hans Feet came back empty handed. He looked at us suspiciously and Tuna had to eat forkfuls of sauerkraut and give me the rest of the dope through the side of her mouth, difficult cos we were sitting at opposite ends of the big table.

'This recombinant DNA was manufactured in the '30s, but based on live DNA taken from a living donor, the most perfectly healthy example of humanity which at that time could be found: a certain Hans Feet of Zurich. So everyone in the world since that time who has had a jab, a shot, for whatever ailment or imperfection from ingrowing toenails to leprosy, or taken a pill, or swigged from a medicine bottle, or obtained any medical treatment at all, has had the genes of Hans Feet introduced correctively into their systems. Therefore, what I am assuming has happened is, that a mutagen, a substance which raises the frequency with which mutations occur, something brought in on a comet perhaps, a low-level virus, pollen in the wind, whatever, has created the circumstances for what we geneticists call "a black mutation". The genes become unstable, the alleles are compromised, Haeckel's law is rewritten, and everyone in the world, men, women, dogs, horses, the piggboggn lot, are in the process of turning into Hans Feet.'

'I am Hans Feet,' said Hans Feet.

'Last week I televisited the eminent scientist, Doctor Cardew O'Dill, in Cambridge to exchange notes, but when I fizzed in he also had turned into Hans Feet.'

'Dearie-be!'

'I do, however, have a little plan of my own. But for it to succeed, we will require to discover the whereabouts of the real Hans Feet.'

Our own Hans Feet started his nant, stamping around the table, yelling: 'I, I, I, AM HANS FEET! WHY DO THEY

NOT BELIEEEEVE ME! LOOK AT THIS FACE, IS IT NOT HANS FEET'S FACE? ARE THESE FEET NOT HANS FEET'S FEET? HANS FEET! HANS FEET!'

We had to wait for him to exhaust himself before we could continue.

'But is the real Hans Feet still alive?' I asked.

'Boggn better be, cos only his unrefined alleles can be employed to affect the regulator genes in the gene pool that is swimming with Hans Feets. He is perhaps in Zurich, or somewhere in the Swiss Alps. He must be injected with a cocktail of the most deadly, contagious diseases in history, then brought into a public place to spread the contagion. This will be like throwing rocks into the gene pool. Something dramatic will happen, I'm sure.'

Her hopeful smile twitched. She dropped her fork. As she stood she knocked her plate of sauerkraut onto the floor.

'I'm not feeling myself, Chaffy,' she said.

Hans Feet and I helped her to her room. She lay on her bed and gazed sadly at the photos of her various husbands on the bedside table. She gripped my hand. I stroked her fine white hair.

When I left, I found Hans Feet in the corridor, admiring himself in a scratched mirror.

'You may think it strange, but I have never been ill for a day in mein life. Perfect health always. That is Hans Feet!'

'Same goes for me,' I said, defiantly standing up to him. 'Never taken a pill. Never visited a doctor. No boggn Hans boggn Feet in my pool, ehwot!'

'I am not allowed to use the pool,' he said haughtily, turning back to the mirror, putting out his fat pink tongue.

He didn't see my reflection losing its rag behind his. I snapped, running at him with arms swinging. A 100-year-old fist knockoutpunched him. Hans Feet lay at my feet and the Chaffinch I saw in the mirror growled, young and invincible! Long live the Revolution of '24!

When I looked in on Tuna later, she wasn't there. A man in her dress sat up and said: 'I am Hans Feet.'

A figure ran past me with a medieval cudgel he'd picked off the dining room wall.

'I am Hans Feet!' was his war cry.

If I hadn't tripped him up he'd have brained the other Hans Feet.

VI

This was the worst crisis ever to face humanity. But humanity, it seemed, would soon comprise of only me and Hans Feet. I was 2 weeks short of 100, an old man lost in his thoughts. I heard the Grand Mufti say in my head: 'Little priest, do you still believe in a compassionate God?' I wasn't so quick to answer yes this time. Would the God of the New Testament do this terrible thing to the world, just to test one old man?

I arose at the dawn. The 2 Hans Feets were yodelling the same yodel in different bathrooms. I hurried through the misty shrubbery, the last leaves of the 21st Century floating down around my ears, and was in the boathouse before I turned to look back. I launched a canoe into the Stour and paddled pantingly around bend after swollen bend until the Hall was out of sight. Then I let the current take me, while I ate lots of cheese, and watched the winter landscape, the water-rat holes in the bank, the nettle-buried remains of the canal workings. I pondered: in the 18th Century the Stour Canal had been a great innovation, which revolutionized people's lives, pleasy-do, and now here was I at the windup of the 21st Century on the world's last mission. Dearie-be. But for a while I thought about things other than Hans Feet. Then I arrived in Sudbury, hurried into the town and caught the shuttle for Colchester. There was a shop there I needed to visit.

When diseases were tamed and immune systems were so strengthened that every last microbe, bug, bacterium and virus was harmless and uncatchable, folk took pity on the diseases – which, indeedybe, are God's creatures. After the war it became the fashion to keep them as pets. Few fashionable homes were without their disease tank. No businessman sat at a desk without his disease bottle bubbling away as company. The diseases were less demanding than cats and dogs. They did nothing, they just sat there. But they were vigorously alive, teeming with a mysterious will of their own and proof of nature tamed. Man's enemies for so long, they were now conquered peoples, sold by the quart.

'I'd like a bottlesworth of the most contagious diseases in history,' I said to the man in the shop.

He sent his Hans Feet assistant to collect them from the various green, red, purple and white tanks in the room. The proprietor chatted while he threw chickenlegs into the stagnant tank in the window.

'Starting a collection, sir, or a present for a friend?'

'It's for a friend,' I said.

On the airship I was the only passenger who wasn't Hans Feet. But, to make matters worse, I had disguised myself as Hans Feet, thinking this would somehow make things easier for me. It did not.

'You are travelling to Switzerland for your holidays?' asked a chatty Hans Feet, looking over the rail beside me.

'No, no. I live there.'

'In Zurich?'

'Uh-huh.'

'I live in Zurich also. Originally I am from Sargans.'

'What a coincidence, so am I. But now I have a chocolate factory in Zurich.'

He was talking through gritted teeth now, his nose even redder, his fingers strangling the rail.

'I am also in the chocolate industry. Perhaps you have heard of me. I am Hans Feet.'

'Impossible!' I declared Englishly, on my toes to out-height him, 'I, I, I am Hans Feet!'

'HANS FEET! You are nothing but a ludicrous disguise! I am Hans Feet!'

He tweaked my false Hans Feet nose – it kept falling off every 2 minutes after that – and might have done me more damage if some of the other Hans Feets hadn't heard him shouting his name and come to sort him out.

All these Hans Feets, some 600 of them, were returning to Switzerland to gather evidence of their identity so that they could present it irrefutably to the other Hans Feets. The approach of their native land was bringing out the yodel in them. To escape this unnerving sound I went and sat up by the propeller. Yet again I checked my deadly cargo of diseases, now thriving in a foot long hypodermic, taped down in one of Sep's old trumpet cases.

Zurich approached under the grey-blue sky, its lake a long dull liquid, like the one I carried in the trumpet case. But closer the lake was choppy and very few Hans Feets were rowing on it. Closer-to, 600 Hans Feet crowded by the rail, pointing out the chocolate factory in the hills above the city. I needed to go there so pushed in among the Feets.

'The Hans Feet chocolate factory? Where is it?'

They looked at me with pinkeyed scorn.

'You know very well where is the Hans Feet chocolate factory!' said one.

'Of course I do,' I said. 'I am Hans Feet!'

They were still chasing me around the gondola when we landed.

VII

I walked down Zurich's swanky Barnhofstrasse in a kind of a daze. Funnymost, but I never got used to seeing so many Hans Feets. Every new example was a shock to my system. My heart was thumping in my ears and the trumpet case seemed as heavy as a cow. A long line of schoolchildren walked through me. They were all Hans Feet! A tram nearly knocked me over. It was full of Hans Feet! Here came Hans Feet taking an Afghan hound for a walk. Here came Hans Feet sharing a joke with Hans Feet. Hurry-scurry, everywhere, with their pompous short-stepped quick-footed little walk, and every one brimming with health. Even the mannequins in a shop-window were Hansfeetish. On a corner I saw a prostitute – short leather skirt, half-open blouse. It was Hans Feet! Would Hans Feet pay for sex with Hans Feet? Yes, I decided: he was the sort.

I stopped at a street-cafe for a coffee and a bun. All the other customers were Hans Feet. 2 of the 3 waiters were Hans Feet.

I closed my eyes and felt the bun inside me. All around was the chatter of Hans Feet. His opinions. His childhood in the Engadine. Flareups of the same old argument. And why, my inside-the-head-voice demanded, suddenly furious, must foreigners speak English with funny accents? By 2099 English had long been the 1st language of everyone on earth – except the French with their French and the Americans with their Spanish – why couldn't the boggn Jilkses speak it properly!

'You are foolydooing no-one with zat disguise,' said the non-Hans Feet waiter as I paid my bill. 'You are not . . . you-know-who!'

'Boggn am!' I said and flicked a halfcrown at him.

I strode off in a tizzy! How dare he say I wasn't Hans Feet! When at last I realized the ludicrousness of my mood, I was standing before a very large plush chocolate shop, its windows mouthwateringly displaying deluxe boxes of chocs. As a lifelong chocaholic I was captivated. I went straight in and bought their biggest box. The Hans Feet assistant was most charming, the nicest Hans Feet I'd met. I took my prize greedily to a seat on the jetty where the boats came in and out. I tore into it and cried with glee at the sight of the little brown shapes. Soon I'd rustled a few into my wrinkled old gob. I was comforted, weepsome with pleasure.

That sad point came when I didn't want 'just one more' and I sat contemplating the Alpine scene on the boxlid. I looked under the ribbon in one corner out of no great interest and saw a baroque logo, a chocolate factory surrounded by scrolls and on one of the scrolls the words *HANS FEET*. I'd been eating the bogafala's chocolates! I dug in the box. Yes! *IF YOU HAVE ANY COMPLAINT ABOUT THESE CHOCOLATES PLEASY-DO RETURN THEM TO THE HANS FEET CHOCOLATE FACTORY, STICHFELBERSTRASSE, FULTERN, ZURICH.*

I saw the Hans Feet with the Afghan Hound again.

'Hans, Hans, how good to see you again! You're looking finemost these days!'

'Have we met?' He raised his hat. 'You look familiar, but . . .'

'I've just been scoffing some of your excellent chocs! Delicious!'

He blushed with pride and tapped the box.

'I'd love to look over the factory sometime. Stichfelberstrasse, isn't it?'

'Ja. Stichfelberstrasse.'

'I'd take the number 6 tram.'

'Nein, nein – the 4!'

'Ah!'

I had found my way to the Hans Feet chocolate factory.

VIII

The number 4 tram climbed into the hills above the old town. It was chockablock with Hans Feets. I knew what the factory looked like – it was on the boxlid – but my view was blocked all ways so I could easily miss it. Only one passenger wasn't a Hans Feet.

'Scusy-be, Fraulein, but coulds't thou pleasy-do nod me a wink when we get to the stop for the Hans Feet chocolate factory?'

'GO AWAY! STOP TORMENTING ME!'

She was a pretty little thing. Long fine strawberry hair. A freckled button nose, slightly red. She had a similar look, though her skin was a different colour, to Mr Iqubal's eldest daughter. She seemed most upset.

'Fraulein, if you have trouble . . .'

'YOU ARE NOT MEIN FATHER!!!!!'

'No, no, dear, I am not your father.'

She swallowed her sniffles. She seemed amazed. 'You are not?'

'No.'

'It's just that, you see, I am not well in my mind. Today I have been to see mein psychoanalyst, but he too, like everyone, even you, looks like mein father. Everyone he is insisting he is my father!'

I twigged. 'Your father isn't perhaps . . .'

'Hans Feet.'

All the passengers on the tram turned to look with an identical grimace. She flinched from them and huddled close to me.

'I am Alicia Feet.'

'Chaff Chaffinch, howdeedoodee.'

'I hate him! I have always HATED him! And now the whole world looks just like him. The worst of it is: I have this obsession about having sex with my father. So I must sleep with them all!!!!'

She was looking at me with eyes which said 'You're next!'. Forgotten lasciviousness tingled in my roots. But then my false nose fell off and, exposed as a bogus Hans Feet, I sadly removed the rest of my disguise.

'Oh!' she sighed. 'Wot a kindly old face! You are like the father I should have had!'

She hugged me passionately, with all her strength. My old bones creaked and popped.

'The chocolate factory! Isn't that it?'

We jumped off the tram and I followed Alicia Feet up the path of the imposing residence which stood beside the factory. Would I now, at last, meet the real Hans Feet? I checked on my hypo while Alicia fumbled for her keys. But her hands were shaking. In a spattish fit she emptied her handbag, cast it down, and wept tears of anguish and frustration. I comforted her.

'Fear not, my child. God has sent me to help you. God, who is everywhere.'

'So is mein father!' she wailed.

'Yes, but you don't understand. You are not mad. All these men, they really ARE your father. It's a genetic accident.' She ran from me in confusion, found her keys on the pathway and burst into the house. I ventured after, firstmost into a porchway decorated with framed chocolate wrappers, then deeper within, where the walls were crammed with chocolatebox paintings which looked fine on boxlids but ikky on a wall. Alicia was already in verbal combat with her father in their parlour.

'ALICIA! YOU HAVE BEEN DISOBEYING MY ORDERS! I MUST KNOW WHERE YOU ARE AT ALL TIMES!'

'HOW CAN YOU NOT KNOW! YOU FOLLOW ME WHEREVER I GO! WE'VE BEEN TOGETHER ALL DAY!'

She pouted defiantly and stuck out her little bumpy chest. This enflamed Feet. He swiped a slap at her. She ducked.

'YOU HAVE BEEN SLEEPING WITH THOSE MEN WHO SAY THEY ARE ME!' he screamed, his face as red as his curls, which were springing beside his ears.

It was an unpleasant scene for a stranger to walk in on. But I had a job to do, did I not! I put the trumpet case down on a shiny table, flicked it open, saying businesslikely: 'Fraulein Feet, is this your father?'

'This is mein mutter,' sobbed Alicia.

I clicked the case shut again. I could not yet save humanity.

'WHAT IS THIS! YOUR NEW BOYFRIEND! HE MUST BE OVER 100. LOOK AT HIM! COULDN'T A BEAUTIFUL GIRL LIKE YOU DO BETTER THAN THAT! HAH!'

I was infuriated at the insult. 'WHO DO YOU THINK YOU ARE?' I yelled at him.

'I AM HANS FEET!' he yelled back.

Suddenly, he was all soppy and tearful, kissing Alicia's shoes, her knees. She stood there as if in a drug-induced storm, her nostrils flaring, peaceful Alpine scenes on the walls looking sinistermost in this context. I took her by the shoulders and shook her.

'Your real father, Alicia – where is he?'

'They are all him! ALL HANS FEET!'

'Listen, listen to me, you silly, silly girl! Your father's DNA was used in medical research in the '30s, when he was a bouncing healthy boy. That DNA was refined and used in all the world's medicines ever since. There has been a back-mutation. Your father's DNA is taking over everyone else's DNA. That's why everyone is turning into your father.'

'I hate my father! I HATE HIM!'

She struggled away from the creature's incestuous grasp, leaving her shoes in his hands.

Feet, pathetically: 'Mein stroooooodle, mein little kanichchen, you do not hate me!'

'I HATE YOU! I HATE YOU! I HATE YOU! I HATE YOU! I HATE YOU!'

It was good to see the pain on Hans Feet's face growing more tragic with each I HATE YOU.

When Alicia gave up shouting she stood with her fists shaking before her maddened face, I stepped into her view saying: 'We must find your real father. I must inject him with a cocktail of infectious diseases in order that he might infect the world and change it back. It is our only hope.'

Her fists opened like flowers. Cool little hands held my cheeks. How pretty she was! Wot girlish delight!

'Injection? Diseases? Will he die?'

My mouth opened stupidly. I made no answer. I did not know.

Her brief delight was replaced with hysterical anxiety and she pulled at my cheeks till I yelped.

'But I do not know where he is and they all look alike!'

Becoming, for moments only, the invincible Chaffinch, warrior of the Lord, I lifted her shaking body and carried her away from Feet's pleading, like a young officer his ladylove. I pushed the silverware off a sideboard and sat her there.

'THINK! Think, girl . . . THINK! Is there not a special place? Somewhere he might go, to be alone, to escape from all these people who say they are him?'

Her face was blank, the eyes looking nowhere. Then they focused on an ikky painting opposite. She pointed with the innocence of a child seeing the virgin in a grotto.

'There is such a place,' she said, and kissed me lightly on the lips, creating a frenzy of jealous fury in the Hans Feet who had been her mother.

IX

We were climbing tripsomely in the mountains of the Engadine. It was cold. But my lederhosen caused my private parts to sweat most uncomfortably. Alicia led the way, carrying the trumpet case. Every now and again she turned to check on me, hugged the case and gave a little cry of glee. Once or twice she ran at me in a passion and said: 'All my life I have been waiting for you to come – my handsome deliverer!'

I was flattered out of my wits. Though 6 times her age, I urinate in shame to admit it, I was falling in love with her.

We picked our way along a path through pines. I saw a deer. The path ended at a wooden footbridge which crossed from one mountain to another. At the other side ropes helped us along a narrow ledge. I was hurh-uhhurhing with breathless exhaustion, and rested on a jutty-out boulder. Snowflakes appeared, first a few, then many. I held out my hands, remembering that though each snowflake was unique, the people of the world were not: they were mostly Hans Feet. A little divine message was that, which spurred me on.

At the top of the ropeway we reached an alpine meadow. Alicia ran through the glockenblumes, losing her hat and not minding. Her strawberry hair blew wildly in her face when she turned to see where this old fool was. He was running though the meadow towards her, kicking his heels.

I stopped before her. She put her arms around my neck and I said: 'I can hear music. A piano'

We looked up, past two dark peaks, to where the evening sun was making a mountainside red and bright.

It's him,' she said, awe in her voice. 'He wanted to be a concert pianist, but they forced him into the chocolate factory.'

'I didn't know that,' I said to myself. For the first time, Hans Feet seemed human. It was a human being we had come to destroy. The romantic foolishness left me by a back entrance, and I motioned strictly for Alicia to lead the way. My new strictness delighted her.

Our pathway was in the dark. But it led to one that the

sinking sun was reaching. We crunched on a smatter of snow, the music getting louder. It was Grieg's *Morning*, a unique aggressive interpretation, as if the morning would involve violent physical upheavals. And the wind whistled up my nose, saying: Yes, Chaff, you are doing well. Soon all will be achieved and you can die in this pretty girl's arms.

The mountain hut where the music was plonking from was built on a precarious ledge, reached by a rope bridge. In the middle of it I halted, looked at the sun nearly gone behind mountains so distant they were perhaps in Italy or Austria. I crossed myself and said goodbye to the sun forever.

'HOWDOODEEDEE! IS HANS FEET WITHIN!'

The piano stopped. Hans Feet came to the door. He said it: 'I am Hans Feet. Ja? Oh, Alicia mein little strudel!'

'I've brought the Archbishop of Canterbury to see you,' she said, her smile quite mad.

'Used to be, no longer,' murmured I modestly.

There was no room at all inside the hut. It was stuffed full of the grand piano. How he got it up there was yet another mystery to vex myself with.

'HANS FEET! HANS FEET! HANS FEET!' went Alicia through gritted teeth.

He looked a little sadder than the other Hans Feets. A little older. Not so healthy.

'Is everything all right at the factory?' asked Hans Feet. 'I had to come away. They were all saying they were me. It was terrible.'

'DO IT! DO IT! GO ON!' rasped Alicia, her excited hands smearing on the shiny black pianotop.

I clicked open the trumpetcase, saying: 'Herr Feet, I feel that I know you so well, though in fact we are meeting now for the 1st time. The good Lord has seen fit to assault you with a most terrible trial. When you were a boy, do you remember . . .

'DO IT! INJECT HIM! ALL OUR PAIN WILL BE OVER! I NEED NEVER LOOK AT HIS EVIL FACE AGAIN!'

'Alicia, dear, it's only fair-doos to explain. You donated, Herr Feet, some cells of your body for medical research.'

He played a few bars of Grieg. 'Ah, so! I am remembering. They chose me, Hans Feet, out of all the boys in mein school. I, I, I, Hans Feet was selected. I wanted to be a concert pianist in those days. If only I could have my life over.'

His eyes looked pleading at Alicia.

'It seems, Herr Feet, that there has been a genetic accident, not your fault at all, but the genetic messages in the DNA taken from your cells all those years ago are breaking out in everyone.'

'Ah, so! This is why they are turning into me.'

'Indeedy-be.' He was unusually reasonable for a Hans Feet, so I pushed on. 'So, to put things right, I must inject you with this cocktail of diseases here . . .' I brandished the great pricksome weapon '. . . in order for you to catch the diseases and spread them to the rest of humanity. The theory is that this will hunkydory things again.'

'You will not inject me with any diseases! NEIN!'

'But as I have explained – I must!'

I advanced upon him.

'KEEP AWAY!'

'You must sacrifice yourself, Hans – it is the only way!'

He jumped tinklesomely over the piano, his pink pate hitting the lamp. It swung. A roomful of spinning shadows. I climbed onto the piano and tried to reach him.

'STICK IT IN! STICK IT IN!' yelled Alicia, jumping up and down, making the hut creak and budge and the piano complain from its unmusical soul.

But Hans Feet held up pages of Liszt, Chopin and Blint to parry my stabbing needle. My frail arms could find no way through. Besides, I was in a typical dither. Alicia dived onto the piano, thwonk! The hut swayed and shifted. She slid by me, snatching the huge hypo from my dithering hands and finished her playful slide by crashing with a cry of delight into her father.

The hypo went deep into the body of Hans Feet, emptying all its liquid, leaving him aghast against the wall. It still hung there, pinning a few pages of Chopin to his pudge belly.

'It is accomplished,' said Alicia.

I crossed myself. 'Oh, dearie-be.'

'Is this the end of Hans Feet?' Hans Feet asked his Calvinist God. Then he sneezed three times, sat at his piano stool, pressed the keys down so slowly they made no sound, and kept his dying thoughts to himself. Even his passion for Alicia was spent.

'Daddy, Daddy,' she sobbed.

As the lamp ceased its swaying we watched spots pop up on his paling cheeks. His boil nose turned black. He reached up to tidy the music scattered ontop the piano, but suddenly gave up and died where he sat.

'I am free!' said Alicia, part joyous, part griefstricken.

She kicked open a narrow door. Behind it was a bed with wooden walls tightly around it.

'We must get your father into a town, to spread the contagion,' I said.

'Of course, yes. But first we must celebrate.'

She was already removing her clothes.

Should I? Shouldn't I? One last sexual intercourse – why not? How the hut creaked! But halfway through my effort, my feet full of splinters from the rough wooden wall I was using for leverage, I began to feel rather unwell and had to stop. Alicia climbed on top and writhed there.

'Daddyyyyyyy, Daddyyyyyyy!' she sang, biting her bottom lip gigglesomely.

O cruel God! This copulation could have been a fitting climax to a long and eventsome life, a reward for services rendered. But no, I was breaking out in spots. My heart was missing beats. My throat wouldn't allow air through. My bladder and bowels opened. Alicia had it too. Her face lay dribbling against mine. We both tried to breathe. All over the world Hans Feets were doing their Christmas shopping, two days to go and so many Hans Feets to buy presents for. But none for Alicia. She was dead. And none for me either.

X

Stiff sheets. A screen around the bed. Shapes of light on the ceiling. A hospital. Somewhere outside carol singers. *Away in a Manger*. I was crying. I lifted my hands out of the tightly tucked-in bedding to rub my sorry eyes. But they weren't old man's hands. They were a child's. I lay back in confusion. A dream was poking into my wakefulness: Hans Feet done up as a clown, dancing in an empty circus tent. Old Chaff Chaffinch is up a pole in his Archbishop's habiliments, throwing buckets of feathers down onto the sawdusty ground. And there, in the audience, a boy by himself. A Chaffinch child's features, certainly, but not quite any child I recognized.

The screen was pulled away.

Nurse: 'He is awake, Doctor Fitch. Cum-cum, lad – the doctor's here.'

The doctor's face was huge and hairy and I was scared cos he wasn't Hans Feet.

'You're going to be all right, boy. You're one of the lucky ones. Nasty touch of plague you had.'

'I'm not a boy. I am a hundred years old next week.'

They were singing, *O Little Town of Bethlehem* now and I was sobbing. The doctor was rubbing his fingers through my hair. HAIR? More tears. More confusion.

When the nurse and doctor went away, hand in hand, I climbed out of bed. Yes, I was a boy. I peeped behind the next bed's screen. A plagueridden boy lay ghastly on the point of death. On his bedside table was a little square mirror. I supposed they used it to check if he was still breathing. I stepped into the middle of the ward where there was enough light to see by. I looked in the mirror and saw the boy from my dream, and suddenly recognized him, though he'd been hidden in the attic at that age and I'd not seen him even once. Nope, no mistaking him. It was my bro Wilf as a boy. I was Wilf!

I staggered up the ward, feeling the sleep like heavy fishes in my blood. The doctor was canoodling with the nurse behind a glass door.

'Cummon, why not?' he was saying. 'There's a private

room free. Let's celebrate. It's the last Christmas of the 20th Century.'

THE 20th CENTURY!

'Here, get back to bed, you!'

Dame Tuna's prediction had been that if Hans Feet was injected with the cocktail 'something dramatic would happen'. It had. The contagion had spread on a mountain breeze and everyone in the world had mutated from Hans Feet into their own great-grandparents. And there was I, the only one aware of the fact, turned into a five-year-old Bro Wilf, on Christmas Eve 1999. Because everyone believed it was 1999, because their view of reality, embedded in the structure of their minds, was that it was the end of the 20th Century and not the end of the 21st Century, THAT IS WHAT THEY SAW. The buildings, the books, the skies, seas, fields and forests all complied. The old world was back again, beautiful and complete, unaware that the 21st Century had happened in all its grinding suffering and teeming detail. As the old sages said, and as I should well have known, life is an illusion, the world is what you think it is.

After 2 more weeks in hospital, on January 5th, 2000, I was sent home to Chaffinch Hall to convalesce. In my sack I carried five bananas, my Bible, Tadese's manuscript of *21st Century Blues*, and a half-eaten box of chocs made 100 years hence by the Hans Feet Company in Zurich. The house was gloomy cos my father had committed suicide on New Year's Eve. But no Bro Chaff had been born. This 21st Century, obviously, would be subtly different. I could be certain of nothing. Would Hans Feet be born in Sargans in 2029 and have his childhood in the Engadine? Would there one day again be a wonderful Ethiopian called Tadese Mblook to be the friend of my 2nd old age?

As the eldest boy, already, at 5, I was master of Chaffinch Hall. God must love me, I thinky-dood. He had given me another chance at the great game. In jimjams, dressing-gown and slippers, my hot bananamilk beside me on the pew, I sat in our little chapel and promised God to try harder this time. An angry puppy came in and widdled on the floor. Chee! Amen!

Postscript to the Edition of 2039

I am taking this opportunity afforded by a new edition of my *21st Century Blues* to add a few lines about my life and the lives of my family, the Chaffinches, in the 19 years since the book was first published.

You well know, my readers, how much of what happened the 1st time around has fallen into its old shape. Smithers was equally cruel to the Welsh. There was a Revolution in '24 – where once again I distinguished myself, did I not indeed! Playing golf is yet again punishable by death. Pnong is all the rage and Carstairs its heroic Wiblier. And Nobby Tixover, my closest friend this time around, is poised to assume power in a big way – we all hope! You show 'em, Lord of Nobs! But Baba Jammaluddin is not with us this time. I felt I had to do something, and sent Big Norris in the company of a Mexican hit-man to shoot the boy Grand Mufti-to-be on the steps of a mosque in Sarawak. A terrible deed which, a quarter of a century on, is still the subject of wrestling in my prayerful chatteroonies to the God I still believe in. He is compassionate. I know. He forgives me. If he comes again he will forgive me to my face.

Events tumble upon one another and the future is always uncertain. But as for what happens to the world and its tomorrows, I urinate in shame to admit, these days I hardly care. Chaffinch Hall and the birds within are my life, my love.

Without the original Wilf's financial genius managing our family affairs, our coffers dwindled and it looked some 10 years ago that we might lose the Hall. Then I made a H.I.E. (Hologramismic Interactive Experience), one of the very first, where you could go for a walk around Lake Capernaum with Jesus. I programmed him to say all the things that came from the mouth of Clone Seve's manufactured Jesus. Talk to him about your problems. Stroll through Bethany at end of day for a high-tea with Our Lord and his disciples. It sold millions all over the globe. The Chaffinches were rich again, which is only right and proper!

I am writing this in Saint Moritz, where I keep a chalet. Tonight, Scampi and I are going to a concert given by a locally-born prodigy, a certain Hans Feet. Hans is 10 now and plays a wizzo excitingmost piano, attacking the keys with the gusto of a wild horse. There's really nothing like him when his head goes down and his red curls are springing over the keys! We are always reduced to tears, hugging each other and shouting for more. We've sort of adopted Hans. I invested heavily in his father's chocolate business and the old man allowed the boy to study piano – to such dazzling results! God, I'm proud! As much of him as Rainbow and Haha, my lovely daughters.

Scampi is out shopping. She'll come back with 20 new outfits to wear for tonight and I will have the impossible job of choosing the one she's already chosen to wear! Her name isn't Scampi, actuallymost. It's just my petname for her. This time around her father, Europresident Lowrie, called the dear thing Carmen – cos nobody's called after fish in the 2nd 21st Century. A political naming too, cos now it's the Spanish whose population is bursting, not – thank God! – the boggn Scots. I made no mistakes with my Scampi. I watched her growing up, waiting, was at the school gates for her when she was 15, zooming her off in my sportscar. It helped that as Wilf I'm 6 feet with wavy hair and a dashing tache. We were married in June '28. The drive at Chaffinch Hall was carpeted with red roses.

My mother, who is still alive, didn't marry her Belgian, so Cod doesn't exist in this century. But Robin and I have another brother, Genghis, and a sister Charlotte. Dame Marjorie (Tuna, last time) is studying history at Cambridge and agrees with me on nothing whatsoever. The 'Others' people our attic yet again, but I have nothing to do with them. They're always making spookmost noises and banging on the waterpipes. I wish I could get rid of them.

Funnily enough, the thing I've missed most in the 21st Century's repeat performance, is that long winter I had in my

1st boyhood. This time, it just never happened, and has left me faintly disappointed ever since. How well I remember, wot, 130 years ago, the ridge above the orchard at the Hall. Cod and I built snowmen there every weekend for 5 years. There was an army of snowmen, dressed in every scarf, hat and carrot we could find or whip. There was such a crowd that some, the oldest snowmen in English history, were stuck in the middle, lost from view. We had an icy network of paths between them and crept through every day, wiping the new snow off their faces. When the thaw came we couldn't bear to watch them melt and didn't go outside for weeks. But when at last we did, running across the patchy green lawns, we saw one snowman standing alone on the ridge. All his friends gone, 10 cloakrooms worth of hats and scarves on the grass around him. But him still there! Hat askew, carrot slipping

'THAT'S ME!' I cried. 'THAT'S ME!'

Chronology of the Life and Times of Chaff Chaffinch

His Life   ## *His Times*

1995
Chaff's brother Wilf born.

1996
Chaff's brother Robin born.

2000
Chaff is born at Chaffinch Hall,
Suffolk. His father, Kevin Chaffinch,
commits suicide during his son's delivery.

2003   **2003**
Chaff's half brother Cod born.   Kirkland 'Nobby' Tixover born in
                                  Peterborough, England.

2005   **2005**
Jean-Claude le Bec, Sylvia Chaffinch's   The Belgian Plague
2nd husband, Chaff's stepfather, dies.   Baba Jammaluddin, later the Grand Mufti,
                                  born on Island of Sarawak, Indonesia.

                                  2010
                                  Scobie Jilkes becomes Prime Minister of
                                  U.K. Grants independence to Scotland.

2016
Dame Tuna born in gazebo
at Chaffinch Hall.

2017   **2017**
Chaff's mother, Sylvia Chaffinch, dies.   The Great Plague. 1½ billion die.
                                  Hieronymus Gosh's first album
                                  'Give me yer money yer gonna die
                                  anyway!'

2019–23
Chaff largely living on ashram as disciple of Guru Hudkin-Bynd.

2019
Jervis Cowl develops pnong.

2020
Fish discovered on Jupiter.
Everyone Channel opens.

2022
Americans invade Wales.
Baba Jammaluddin's 1st pilgrimage to Mecca.

2024
Chaff leads the July Revolution against the Smithers Regime. Death of brother Robin and cousin Daphnia.

2024
Smithers ousted,
New Age Council.

2025–35
Chaff living as a hermit in Northumberland and elsewhere.

2026
King Michael beheaded.
Government of Taxi Drivers.

2027
Jericho Patel's first administration.
Chulkhurst Bill makes golf illegal.

2029
Hans Feet born in Sargans, Switzerland.

2030
National Pnong Centre opens.

2036
September Chaffinch born.

2036
Loch Ness Monster captured.

2037
Chaff meets Scampi Lowrie.
Severiano visits Golf Island.
Trial and death of Severiano.
Birth of Clone Seve.

2037
The Ukrainian Expedition.
U.S. President Gingrich impeached and assassinated. The elder Sanchez's 1st administration.

2038
Scampi's twins Rainbow and Haha born.

2038
MacTavish becomes European President in landslide, beating Lowrie and MacBravelli.
Baba Jammaluddin becomes Grand Mufti.

2041
Clone Severiano Chaffinch absconds
with Moira Macmacpherson. Chaff has
the first of several nervous breakdowns.
Lives in a French monastery while
recovering.

2041
'Claymore Thursday'
MacTavish purges the clans.
Retirement of Carstairs from pnong.

2042
Dane Tuna marries Douglas Pfaff,
the 1st of her 7 marriages.

2042
Grand Mufti halts world oil trade.
Pope Lassie II dies, succeeded by Pope
Lassie III, who dies, succeeded by
Pope Lassie IV, who dies and is
succeeded by Pope Lassies the V,
VI, VII, VIII and finally the vigorous
but insane Lassie IX.

2046
Cod marries Merluzza Ciampoli
in Merano, Italy.
Great-great-grandfather Clem defrosted.
Chaff returns home to look after him.

2045
Donaldbane Frazer leads expedition
to Mars. Foundation of Scotmars Colony.
Secession of Confederate States in USA
begins the 2nd American Civil War.

2046
Cod enters Despot School.
Death of Clem Chaffinch, aged 127.
Chaff's 'marriage' to Rose Trala.

2047
Cod assassinated by Claudia Blatta.

2047
Deaths of Johansson and Drozd.
Nobby Tixover becomes
Despot in Chief. Depopulation of Africa.

2050
Chaff's first experiments in stylitism
he erects poles in grounds of Chaffinch
Hall and several in Thetford Forest,
Suffolk.

2050
Barkis Dwain's first novel
'Clobbered for Nowt'.

2054
Nelli Chaffinch has quads:

Hoss, Rhino, Bing, and Minnow.
Chaff based at Chaffinch Hall during
the '50s, with periods of 'isolated
nuttery throughout England.

2057

Bug Chaffinch born.

2061

Wilf marries 'Betty', a sheep, and
quarrels with Chaff. Wilf marries 'Anne'
Wilf marries 'Sophia' – all sheep.

2063

Rainbow and Haha's trip to America.
Their deaths. Death of Clone Seve.
Chaff meets Jesus Christ.

2065

Clone Scampi Lowrie dies.
Bing Chaffinch goes in a trance.

2055

Noise Abatement overthrown.
Battle of Plovdiv. Scots annihilated.

2057

Nobby Tixover assassinated by the
Instant Custard Group.

2058

Restoration of monarchy in France
under Louis XIX.

2059

Connie and Pam re-establish Parliamentary Democracy in England. Barkis
Dwain's hologramismic interactive erotic
masterpiece 'Nude at the Opera'.

2061

The Cash Crisis. Sheep made legal
tender. Halley's Comet doesn't arrive
when expected.

2062

Outbreak of rinderpest causes bankruptcy in Germany. Gid widespread.
Barkis Dwain's greatest novel, the
delightfully unreadable trilogy 'Hubert
Masterson's Illnesses'.

2063

Overthrow of Connie and Pam.
Restoration of English Monarchy under
Henry IX. Halley's Comet arrives late.

2064

President Sanchez of USA impeached.
Succeeded by Vice-President Sanchez.
Gabby Snoad's 'Oo! Arh!', hailed as
the ultimate artistic experience, kills
thousands.

2065

Second Ministry of Jesus Christ begins.

2067
Chaff crucified by Grand Mufti, survives.

2067
Jesus Christ crucified by Grand Mufti.

2067–72
Chaff wanders in spiritual stupor.

2072
The Middlesborough Crisis.
Death of MacTavish.

2073
Chaff becomes Vicar of Middlesborough 726.

2073
Queen Vera burned at stake.
Archbishop Cream begins Theocracy in England.

2074
First Murder Day.
Barkis Dwain among the victims.

2075
On Midsummer Day Chaff is crowned Archbishop of Canterbury.

2075
Archbishop Cream and all senior clerics die. The new Archbishop Chaffinch closes the Everyone Channel. Nibbod wins the Grand National running backwards.

2076
Bug Chaffinch comes 37th in javelin event, Olympic Games. Aliens land. Death of Bug Chaffinch while copulating with an alien. Chaff loses his virginity.

2076
The Djakarta Olympics. Height of Mufti's Power. Vice-President Murgutroid of the American Confederacy resigns, admitting he is a Moslem.

2077
Death of Norris Cudlip, Chaffinch family retainer. Chaff resigns as Archbishop of Canterbury

2077
The Octopusfrog Crisis. Millions die. 83% of the population of southern hemisphere eaten.

2077–79
Chaff lives as a hermit in Ireland.

2079
Chaff enlists in Suffolk Regiment on the outbreak of war, under the alias Rev Archie Bishop. Serves in Alpine Campaign, then after the retreat in trenches on Western Front for the duration of the conflict.
Death of Chaff's only surviving brother, Wilf. Death of Winston Churchill. Deaths of Hoss, Turbot and Clancy Chaffinch.

2079
Outbreak of Mufti War. Destruction of Rome, London and Middlesborough 1. New Arbroath becomes Mufti's capital. Death of Pope Lassie IX, vaporized in Saint Peter's.

2081

September Chaffinch's brave attempt to
assassinate the Grand Mufti results in him
losing his legs. Death of Rhino jr.

2082

Death of Chubb Chaffinch.

2082

Israel vaporized.
Herring Carstairs given charge of war.

2083

Death of Cole Chaffinch on Armistice Day.
Chaff demobbed, then leaves for Ethiopia.

2083

A combination of Carstairs and the
Korean army breaks the Moslem
forces. Mufti overthrown.

2083–99

Chaff a stylite near Mount Kunchurro in
Ethiopia.

2084

September Chaffinch vaporized.

2084

Grand Mufti's trial in Djakarta.
When acquittal looks likely he is
dragged from his cell and killed
by demonstrators.

2088

Tadese Mblook becomes Chaff's helper
and disciple.

2089

Slavery reintroduced in English
Empire. End of American Civil War.

2092

Rhino Chaffinch shoots himself.

2092

Government by government abolished
in England, France and Korea.

2098

Bing Chaffinch comes out of trance.

2099

Chaff returns to Chaffinch Hall. Chaff's
trip to Zurich to meet Hans Feet.

2099

The Hans Feet crisis.

The Chaffinches

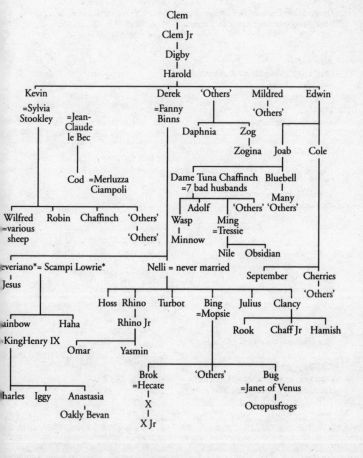

* 25,000 clone Severianos and Scampis were made in
the 2050s. In 2099 at least 14 were still living.

A. A. ATTANASIO

RADIX

'An instant classic' *Washington Post Book World*

Here is one of the most powerful novels of the future ever written. Brilliantly realized, richly detailed and convincingly imagined, it is the awe-inspiring story of a young man's odyssey of self-discovery, from dangerous adolescent to warrior, from outcast to near-godhood, in a far-future Earth dramatically changed from the one we know.

Radix is an epic of the highest order, at once an incandescently exciting novel of conflict and adventure and a supreme experience of transcendent vision.

'Here stands a high talent, a truly amazing original towering talent' *Los Angeles Times*

'Alive with zest and daring' *Kirkus Reviews*

HODDER AND STOUGHTON PAPERBACKS

ROBERT CHARLES WILSON

A BRIDGE OF YEARS

Tom Winter thought the secluded cottage in the pine woods would be the perfect refuge: a vine-covered sanctuary, a place to nurse the wounds of lost love and happiness. But Tom soon discovers that his safe haven is the portal of a tunnel through time. At one end lies the familiar present. At the other – New York City, 1963.

Tom's journey back through time offers him a new life, a new love and the chance to start all over again in a simpler, safer world. But then he finds that the time-tunnel holds a danger far greater than anything he left behind: a human killing machine, escaped from the bleak and brutal future, who will do anything to protect the secret passage he thought was his alone. Thus Tom Winter is forced to face the terrors of an unknown future to preserve both his worlds, past and present. . . .

A Bridge of Years is a brilliant exploration of the nature of time and human history, as well as an electrifying tale of adventure and nerve-stretching suspense.

HODDER AND STOUGHTON PAPERBACKS

CONNIE WILLIS

UNCHARTED TERRITORY

'Connie Willis is a marvellous original' *Locus*

Fin and Carson, together with Bult, their alien guide of ambiguous gender, are planetary surveyors from Earth exploring a new planet. They are also trying exasperatedly to cope with the strictures laid on them by a government back home obsessed with notions of political correctness.

To the government, this new frontier is a pristine environment and the native culture a model of unspoilt innocence – and they must stay the way. But Fin and Carson know that such ideas are romantic (to put it mildly). They are only too aware that the aliens might like nothing better than to be 'corrupted' by the Earthmen's wondrous technology . . .

As well as the title novella, this volume contains two more Connie Willis stories, *Fire Watch* and *Even the Queen*, each of which won both the Hugo and Nebula Awards. Here is an unsurpassed showcase of the outstanding talent of one of the brightest stars on today's science fiction scene.

HODDER AND STOUGHTON PAPERBACKS